The Upstart

*Also by Catherine Cookson
in Large Print:*

The Maltese Angel
The Rag Nymph
My Beloved Son
The Love Child
The Wingless Bird
The Bailey Chronicles
The Harrogate Secret
The Parson's Daughter
The Moth
The Golden Straw
The Obsession
The Unbaited Trap

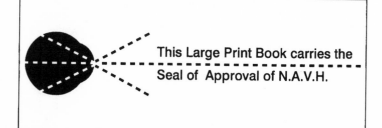

This Large Print Book carries the
Seal of Approval of N.A.V.H.

CATHERINE COOKSON

The Upstart

Thorndike Press • Thorndike, Maine

Published in 1998 by arrangement with Simon & Schuster, Inc.

Thorndike Large Print ® Basic Series.

The tree indicium is a trademark of Thorndike Press.

The text of this Large Print edition is unabridged.
Other aspects of the book may vary from the original edition.

Set in 16 pt. Plantin by Minnie B. Raven.

Printed in the United States on permanent paper.

Library of Congress Cataloging in Publication Data

Cookson, Catherine.
    The upstart / Catherine Cookson.
       p.   cm.
    ISBN 0-7862-1401-5 (lg. print : hc : alk. paper)
   1. Large type books.   I. Title.
[PR6053.O525U67   1998]
823'.914—dc21   98-9955

The Upstart

PART ONE

1898

Master and Man

1

After the cab emerged from the long dark tunnel of trees and on to the sunlit drive, it was but a few moments before it stopped and Samuel Fairbrother alighted. Looking back at the cabbie, he said abruptly, 'Wait there!'

'How long are you likely to be, sir?'

Samuel Fairbrother stared at the man before saying, 'I don't know. You can expect me when you see me. If you were my usual driver you wouldn't ask such a damn silly question.' And on this he turned away. Instead of walking straight to the door ahead, he first surveyed the front façade, and then told himself that Alice was right about one thing: it's got a front as plain as a pikestaff. He would have expected such a house to have steps leading up to it and on to a balcony stretching along its length, whereas all it had was a flagged terrace, which certainly didn't do much for it. Still, he hadn't bought it for the outside, had he? It was the inside he was taken with and, what was more, the fact that he had got it at a knock-down price.

That is what happened when you got in before the agents and you had the ready to cover it as it stood, lock, stock and barrel, except for a few pieces here and there that her ladyship had asked — aye, she had really asked him — if he would mind her not including in the sale. That had been another bit of luck in dealing with her, for she had wanted not only money to clear the debts but also, apparently, to get away from the place as quickly as possible, leaving the servants in place.

Well, now he had some sorting out to do with that lot in there before the family moved in tomorrow.

His hand gripped the big iron ring protruding from the black nail-studded door and as he went to push it open it didn't respond. His head jerked impatiently as he pulled on the bell attached to the wall.

It was perhaps thirty seconds before the door opened and the butler, Roger Maitland, stood to one side to allow the new master to enter. Neither man made any remark. It could have been that they had met so often over the past five weeks that there was no need for an exchange; but even so, the butler would surely have made some courteous comment, were it just about the weather, for was not this man now the owner of the house?

After closing the door, the butler stood with his back to it and watched the man, as he had done a number of times over the past weeks, walk straight towards the middle of the hall, there to stand and gaze up the stairs. He watched his head move as it followed the curve of the stairs to its head; from there, he knew that the eyes would take in the whole of the gallery that encompassed the hall on three sides.

The butler now waited for that man, as he thought of him, to turn about and deliver one of his trite remarks, such as 'How's everything going?' or 'Anything new to tell me?' But today was different: he did not turn round but walked to the far end of the hall, saying as he went, 'I want a word with you.'

The butler definitely paused before he moved in his stately step from the door and followed the man down a broad, carpeted passage to what had always been his lordship's study, and it more than irked him to see this man pulling out the round-backed, leather swivel chair and seating himself in it.

Taking his stand at least three feet away from the desk, he waited.

Samuel Fairbrother looked at him, and he

kept him waiting. He knew what the fellow thought about him and he knew what he thought about the fellow, but if things were going to run the way he had arranged them in his mind, then he would have need of this fellow. But not the whole crew of them. Oh no. How many were there anyway? Too many. He fancied he had seen about ten; but one thing was sure, he wasn't keeping the lot on.

'How many of you are there?' he asked now.

'Are you referring to my private family or to the staff, sir?'

Samuel felt the heat flooding his face and his jaws clamped together before he said, 'Don't you waste any of your cheap repartee on me; keep that for your associates in the kitchen. Understand?'

The butler understood, and he could not have been more insulted.

The hierarchy of the house as it had been, and his close association with his lordship, had assured him a position of deep respect from all the staff, as well as the confidence of his lordship who, at times, had acted more like a father towards him, for they had talked, really talked, man to man. And now this shoemaker, this cobbler, because that's all he and his people had been . . . to speak to him like that and associate him with the kitchen staff! and in such a derogatory way too! The man got under his skin. He was an upstart and he was known as an upstart; and tomorrow he would be bringing his wife and their squad into this house, this house that he loved and in a way had ruled. But the man was waiting for an answer.

'There are eleven indoor staff and five outdoor.'

'Sixteen servants? Aye, well, I won't be wanting that lot. Who are they?'

Roger Maitland swallowed before he began, 'There is the housekeeper, Mrs Bright. There is Mr Mather, who was his lordship's valet.'

'Is he still here?'

'Yes, sir. Lady Mary arranged that the staff be paid up to the end of the month.'

'That's over a week ahead. I thought they finished tomorrow.'

'No, sir; the arrangement was to the end of the month, so as to give them time to obtain fresh appointments. And this also applies to Miss Price, the lady's maid.'

'Didn't she want to go with her mistress?'

'Yes, indeed she did, but her ladyship and her daughter, Lady Irene Boulter, together with Lady Irene's child have gone abroad for a short time. And Miss Moore, the

13

child's nurse, is still here too. Then there is the cook, Mrs Wilding, and the two maids in the kitchen, Jane Cooksey and Bella Forbes. The parlourmaid is Miss Sarah Johnson and the chambermaid is Miss Florence Furness; and that leaves only the boot-boy inside and his name is Jackie Winter. I think you have met the outside staff.'

'I've seen the groom and one gardener, that's all.'

'Well, there are two gardeners, sir, and besides the groom there's the coachman and the stable lad.'

'Aye, well, there's one thing certain, I won't need all that lot, neither the valet nor the lady's maid, nor the nurse, so that's three fewer. And I don't see that we'll need a housekeeper if you're in charge and my wife is behind you.'

'I'm afraid I won't be in charge, sir, as I don't intend to stay.'

Samuel stared at the man, who stared straight back at him.

'You don't, eh?'

'No, sir.'

'Have you got a new situation?'

'Not yet, sir, but there's plenty of time.'

Samuel just prevented himself from saying, What are you going to live on? What you've feathered your nest with here? But

he had made up his mind that he was going
to need this fellow. He knew all the ropes.
He had heard from Willie Phillips, who had
been the old lord's solicitor and was his too
and who had, incidentally, been the means
of tipping him off about the house and the
need of her ladyship for ready cash, that the
butler fellow, here, was highly thought of,
and knew the ropes, and would be likely to
put him wise about lots of things. But here
he was saying he was not having any. Damn
cheek really! After all, what was he but a
servant?

'If you haven't got another situation why
won't you stay on here? Is it because I took
you for granted? Come on, spit it out.
You've made your feelings plain up till now;
or at least you've shown them in your expression. Why don't you give voice to
them?'

'Thank you, sir. I will gladly accept the
opportunity . . .' He paused for some seconds and stared at this common and bumptious individual; then he began, 'You see, I
have worked for his lordship for ten years
in this particular house, and for seven years
in his other establishment, in which I began
as cellar boy at the age of thirteen, rising to
footman by the time I was eighteen. From
then I was coached by a very fine man and

butler, but unfortunately he died suddenly when I was twenty, and although I was young for such a position, his lordship kindly gave me the chance to prove myself. And I confess I patterned myself on him because he was a gentleman of high degree, not only in his title but in all his ways and —'

'Oh, for God's sake shut up! I've gone along with you up till that last bit. A gentleman in all ways, you say. Some gentleman to leave his family in the state that he did, not only up to the eyes in debt but drowning in it. He had been living on tick for years. Of course, being a gentleman, he couldn't live like any ordinary fellow, could he? No, he'd have to have a houseful of servants, and his carriage and pair, and his shooting parties, and his other house in Dorset, until the bums went in there. Gentleman! A gentleman is, in my opinion, as a gentleman does, and that is he looks after his family and doesn't leave them in a position in which they're not only forced to sell the house, but every stick and stone inside it.' He now swept his arms wide across the desk as he went on, 'If you had said that his lady wife was a lady, I'd agree with you, because her aim was to pay every penny that he owed, but she could only

16

manage it by selling off the whole of her possessions. And not forgetting to see that you lot were paid to the end of the month. So, in my opinion, it was she who acted like a gentleman. And now, young man, you've had your say, and so I'll have mine. I'm a tradesman. I've got on, but only through bloody hard work and following in me father's footsteps, and his father's, an' all. And you know something? My mother wanted to make me into a gentleman, and she would have, only she died just as I was nearing thirteen, and she had me booked up to go to one of these public schools, where they're not above taking money if you haven't got rank. If she'd had her way I would have had some polish put on me, and would not have had to go into the rough and tumble of commerce where it's so often a bare-knuckle business. Your manner to me would have been quite different, wouldn't it, especially if I'd adopted the twang and taken a high hand: it would have been, "Yes, sir. No, sir. Certainly, sir." Wouldn't it, now?'

He half rose from the chair and, his fore-arms on the table, he leaned forward, saying, 'You know something? I've never regretted buying this place until this minute, but this has proved to me how wrong I've

17

been; because, you see, I was aiming to do what me mother did: give me family a different way of life. My wife has argued all along that they've got a good way of life already. It suited her, it's done her no harm to work hard, and therefore her family will be all the better if they follow her pattern. But no, I'm my mother's son. I've been smelling out public schools for my boys, and ladies' academies for my girls. And you know something else? I had thought if anyone can show me the ropes, it's that young stiff-faced bugger of a butler. But now you don't want to work for a common merchant-class individual, one who has shops all over the place that sell clogs. Perhaps you haven't heard of the few here and there that sell hand-made boots for the gentry, eh? Well, now let me tell you, you want none of me and that's reciprocated, I want none of you, or your kin. So get out of me sight.'

Over the years, Roger Maitland had acquired the habit of out-staring those whom he considered to be of no class. It had an intimidating effect, he had found; but now his lids were lowered and blinking rapidly, and he did not raise them before he had turned away and was walking slowly towards the door.

Samuel fell back into the seat.

Alice was right. He had done a damn silly thing. Just as she had said, what in the name of God! were they going to do with thirty-four rooms. All right, some of them were servants' quarters and there was the annexe; but it still left more than twenty, and they would have to be heated and cleaned. And even if she gave each of the children a room, that would take up only eight; theirs would make it nine. And think of the work! Yes, think of the work.

He had thought of the work, which is why he had talked to that stiff-necked bugger. Alice had said, 'Get it all straightened out before I arrive there tomorrow, because I want to know where I stand.'

Now he didn't know where he stood. But the one thing he was not going to do was enter that kitchen and find out who was going to stay and who was going to go . . . Oh! let him get home.

He rose from the chair; but then he stood looking around the panelled room, and asked himself, 'Will this ever become home?' But he could give himself no answer.

2

Alice said, 'What did I tell you? It was a mistake.'

'You liked the house.'

'Yes, the inside.'

'Well, you're going to live in the inside, woman, not on the outside. And I'll get that put right, gardens and things; I mean, flower beds, not just lawns.'

'But how are we going to run that place if they all walk out? Because Maggie, Annie, and Kate decided from the start they're going to stay here with Mother.'

'You could persuade her to come with us and bring them with her, if you went the right way about it.'

'Not a chance. She wants a bit of peace and quiet. She'll be glad to get rid of the lot of us . . . she's getting on.'

'Well, if that's the case you can put her in the annexe and see to her.'

'What are you talking about? You don't put my mother anywhere she doesn't want to go. She's not like her stupid daughter, talked into things. Oh!' — she now swung about and faced him — 'bullied into things.'

But then, in a lowered voice, and her expression changing she said, 'Why do you do it, Sam? What drives you? You see, let's face it, you're not cut out for the country gentleman, or the top drawer. It isn't as if you would consider altering yourself. No. No; people have got to take you as you are or it's their loss, you think. You're too pigheaded to copy the pattern you're cutting out for yourself.' She shook her head sadly as she added, 'I can't understand you at times, Sam. Your dad was never like this, nor yet your grandad, the bit I remember of him. You're a throwback.'

'Finished?'

'Yes, for the present, but I could go on, because there's lots of other things I want to say, and they concern your character an' all.'

'Oh, well, I might as well have the lot altogether. It's been that kind of a day; let's finish on the right note.'

Alice was about to continue when an altercation, seemingly just above her head, brought her eyes ceilingwards, and she exclaimed impatiently, 'Those two are at it again! Thank God! school starts on Monday.'

'Never mind about those two. Carry on. You were saying?'

'There'll be plenty of time for that later on.' And with this she marched from the room, shouting, 'Janet! And you, Eddie!'

She was mounting the stairs when her eldest son, ten-year-old Howard, called up to her from the hall, 'Mam, can I go out and see Barney?'

She paused for a moment and looked down on him, saying, 'No, you may not. It's close on tea-time and there's your packing to do. I bet you haven't touched it yet.'

The boy turned away and she went quickly up the remaining stairs, calling now, 'Janet! Eddie! Stop that row.'

On the broad landing she thrust open a door, there to see her eldest daughter, all of nine years, pinning down her second son by the throat with one hand, while the other was raised to strike, and she yelled at her, 'Good God! girl. What are you up to?'

The girl, releasing her hold on her brother, turned her face towards her mother, crying, 'He's torn pages out of my diary and scribbled over the rest. I'll kill him! I will.'

'Get out of the road!' She thrust the girl aside, then hauled her son on to his feet by gripping the front of his shirt and asking, 'Are you hurt?'

Master Edward Fairbrother may have felt

hurt but there was a grin on his round face as he said, 'I'm nearly dead, Mam. She tried to kill me.'

'And I will. I will one day,' cried his sister.

'Shut up! you. I'll deal with you later. As for you' — Alice now shook her son — 'something will happen to you one of these days. I'm warning you where your pranks will lead you. Why did you do it?'

The grin slipped from Edward's face now as he said bitterly, 'Because she thinks she knows everything, and she wrote in her book that she was going to work in a library. All because the teacher took us into that great musty place on the trip to Newcastle. She thinks she's clever because she knows the names of books. But she doesn't know what's inside them. She's a big-head.'

'That's enough of that! And if *you* read more books you might get something into that head of yours. It's big enough.'

She swung round now and, pointing to the door, she said to her daughter, 'Out!'

Janet walked out. Her dark head wagging, she walked across the landing and thrust open the door of the bedroom she shared with her younger sisters, five-year-old Alicia and Jessica, who was four. As her mother followed in behind her, the two children

23

turned as one and greeted her with, 'We're nearly finished packing, Mam,' and she answered them abruptly, saying, 'Leave it. Go downstairs; your dad's in. He wants to see you.'

As they scampered away, the door banging behind them, she turned to her daughter and stared down hard on her for a moment before she said, 'Don't look at me like that, girl! Or at anybody else for that matter. You're going to get yourself thoroughly disliked, not only by Eddie but by the rest of them. You understand me? . . . Oh yes, you understand me because you're older than your years, girl.' Her voice changing, she said, 'Why do you do it? Why must you fight and want to boss everybody?'

'Because I take after Dad.'

The words, loud and clear, startled Alice, as did their content. She hadn't imagined any of her children thinking about their father's character, and in this momentary heightened state of mind, the answer came: she hadn't given herself time to think about anything but their physical needs; keeping them well fed, well clothed and healthy, and seeing they got some schooling. But then, she wasn't so much concerned with their schooling as was Sam. It was becoming an obsession with him. Oh, life was difficult.

And now she'd have to face another period of it in that big house. Why couldn't he see that he was out of his depth there, and that he just wouldn't fit in? Did he expect to make friends among the county gentry? Surely not, with *his* manner and outlook; his outspokenness had lost friends even amongst his own set. Of course, there was no harm in being outspoken, but he was bumptious with it, and he was getting worse as he got older.

But, of course, she had experienced the side-shoots of his character before she married him, so she had taken him with her eyes open. And when all was said and done, he had been a good husband, and she could have done worse. Oh, yes, yes, much worse. And that is what she now tried to put over to her daughter by saying, 'You don't know how lucky you are, girl, in having such a dad. All he thinks about is working for you all, and your welfare, and setting you on the right road.'

'Yes, and buying more shops and expanding his boot, shoe and clog empire.'

'In the name of God! girl, where on earth did you hear that?'

'From him, Dad himself. I heard him say that to you: "One day I'll have a boot, shoe and clog empire." '

Alice bit on her lip, turned her head to the side and rapidly tried to think back. And yes, yes, those were his very words, that's what he had said to her. They had been arguing about his opening up a shop in Middlesbrough. A fresh avenue of trade, he had called it. And when she had said, 'When will you be satisfied? Aren't eleven shops enough?' he then came back at her, saying, 'I always liked even numbers in bairns and boots. I've got eight bairns and that's an even number. But I want two more,' he had added, laughing; 'but more so, I want twelve shops . . . fourteen, sixteen, eighteen, twenty.' It was then he had finished up with the remark about the empire.

There was a slight tremble in her voice as she said, 'Your dad was only funning.'

'He never funs, Mam . . . Dad never funs. Does he ever play with us? Not even with the lads . . . he never plays, does he?'

Alice's mouth fell into a gape now as she saw the moisture come into her daughter's eyes. This girl who never seemed to show emotion, this girl who, right since she was a baby, had always appeared older than her years. And she had never seen her cry, not even when she had had her hand smacked. She thrust out her arms and drew the stiff body tightly into her waist, and when she felt the hands clutching her sides, she said, 'There! there!' And she stroked the thick dark hair and adjusted the two plaits that fell way down below her child's shoulders.

It was wonderful hair; not black, yet not brown. There were reddy lights in it here and there. It was her one asset, because she was a plain child: her face was long; in fact, all her features tended towards length; her eyes were set in oval sockets, her nose was longish and thin; her mouth was wide and although it had shape to it, it didn't in any way tend towards beauty or even prettiness. The whole face contrasted strongly with those of the other three girls. Alicia, Jessie, and Fanny were all pretty, their faces tending to roundness, and their cheeks being dimpled. They would grow up into attractive girls, whereas this one, her dear Janet, and that was the first time she had thought of her as her dear Janet, would have two attractions only: her hair and her mind. Of course her figure might develop, that was yet to come.

She now held her daughter away from her and, taking the handkerchief from the cuff of her dress, she wiped Janet's face, saying softly, 'You and I must talk at times when we get a minute to ourselves. Eh?'

Janet nodded as she said, 'Yes, Mam; I'd like that.'

'Well, now.' Alice put her arm around her daughter's shoulders and led her towards the door, saying, 'Your dad's going out again, and once he's gone you come into my room and help me to finish getting me bits and pieces together. Will you do that?'

'Yes, Mam.'

'Now go and find the other two and tell them to come back and get on with their jobs. Then go into the kitchen and tell Maggie I could do with a cup of tea.'

She stood on the landing watching her daughter walking towards the stairhead, not running or calling out like the others would have done, but walking like someone deep in thought. And she was thinking, he never funs; he never plays with us. And on this she turned abruptly and walked up the corridor towards her own room.

It was just on eight o'clock. All the children were in bed, or at least in their rooms, with the exception of Howard and Janet. Howard was in the playroom packing up his train set, which up till now had covered a third of the floor space; Alice was with her mother in her room; it was Annie's night off and Maggie and Kate were in the

28

kitchen. When the doorbell rang Janet happened to be crossing the hall, so she went immediately to it and opened it, then stood looking at the man standing there. Recognition then parted her lips before she said, 'Please . . . please, come in.'

As Roger Maitland stepped into the hall, she said, 'I'll tell my mother. She's upstairs.' And she was about to move away when Maggie came hurrying from the kitchen and so she turned to her and said, 'Will you tell Mother there's . . . there's a gentleman here. She's with Gran.'

Then the gentleman spoke, saying, 'It is Mr Fairbrother I would like to see, please.'

'My . . . my father isn't in.'

'Oh.'

Janet turned again to Maggie, saying, 'Will you tell Mother, please?'

Maggie had not seen this man before but she saw he was some kind of a gentleman by his dress, his voice, and the way he stood; and so she left them to hurry up the stairs, leaving Janet to say, 'Would you like to come in here and wait, please?'

Roger Maitland followed the girl into what looked like a comfortable but much used sitting-room. It was a large room with good solid furniture, the sort and variety one would expect to find in this kind of

self-contained house situated on the out-
skirts of Fellburn and occupied by a middle-class family. But up to this morning he
would have definitely put a question mark
against the latter description.

'We'll be moving in tomorrow.'

'Yes,' he said, looking down on the sol-
emn-faced girl; then he added, 'Are you
looking forward to it?'

She glanced away as if considering the
question, before she said, 'I think I am. It's
a very nice house. It has what you call' —
she paused — 'atmosphere.'

Roger Maitland's eyebrows made just the
slightest upward movement, then he said,
'How old are you?'

'I am nine, nearly ten.'

Nine, nearly ten, and she was talking
about the house having atmosphere. Her father hadn't mentioned atmosphere and he
didn't think her mother, judging by the few
times he had met her, was the kind of
woman who would spend much of her time
questioning the impression the house had
made on her, except that it was giving her
plenty of room for her brood. He smiled at
the girl now, saying, 'I'm glad you think so.
I too think it's got atmosphere. It is over
two hundred years old, you know.'

'Yes, I know. I've read about it.'

Again his eyebrows moved; then he turned to look towards the door as Alice entered, saying, 'Oh, hello, Mr —' she paused before adding, 'Maitland.' She never knew how to address this man.

'Good evening, Mrs Fairbrother. I'm sorry to intrude, because I'm sure you are very busy, but I wished to have a word with your husband.'

'Well, he should be back at any minute; he's gone to a meeting. He said it would be over by half-past seven. And look' — she cast her gaze now towards the mantelpiece — 'it's turned eight . . . Won't you sit down while you're waiting?'

He did not sit down, but just continued to look towards her, and she got the message and sat down. Only then did he take a seat and in a conversational tone say, 'Your daughter tells me she is looking forward to taking up residence in the house.'

'Oh, yes, yes.' Alice looked at Janet, then added, 'We're all looking forward to it. I only hope' — she paused — 'well, I only hope everything will run smoothly. You know what I mean?'

He paused too before he replied, 'Yes. Yes, I think I know what you mean, Mrs Fairbrother.'

'Oh' — she looked towards the window

— 'I can hear the cab outside. That'll be him. Janet, go and tell your father there's a' — again she paused — 'a gentleman has called to see him.'

After Janet had left the room Roger Maitland turned to Alice and said quietly, 'Many would consider the term "gentleman" a misnomer in my case, as I'm always addressed as Maitland; but, believe me, Mrs Fairbrother, I'm most grateful to you for using it.'

Alice felt herself blushing, and he would have been surprised if he could have read her thoughts: poor soul. What a position to find yourself in. Neither fish, fowl, nor good red meat.

'Oh, there you are.' She rose quickly to her feet as Samuel entered the room. He came in slowly and, it could be said, almost aggressively, and when he reached the open fireplace and stood with his back to it, he addressed his visitor. 'Well? You want to speak to me? I suppose that's why you're here.'

'Yes, sir, I would like a few words with you.'

'Fire away . . . Oh, wait a minute.' He turned and, pointing his finger at Janet, who had followed him into the room, he said, 'Get about your business;' and he waited until she had left the room, closing the door none too gently after her. Only then, turning to Maitland, did he say, 'Fire ahead.'

Roger Maitland glanced at Alice, but when she made a move to leave the room, Samuel put out his hand, saying, 'Stay where you are, woman! What he's got to say to me is for your ears an' all, I should say.'

'Oh Sam!' It was a whispered protest. But his answer was in no way given in a whisper for he cried, 'Never mind "Oh Sam". This is the end of a day I'm not likely to forget, with one thing and another. So stay put. And you, go on,' — he pointed to the man he had hoped would guide him in his new enterprise — 'tell me why you've come. Have they all left before their time's up and the house is empty? Get on with it.'

Roger Maitland drew in a long breath before he said quietly, 'I've come to apologise, sir, for my manner of this afternoon. I went beyond myself. I forgot who I was, and who you were. And no matter what I thought, you were entitled to civility in what is now your own house. And I may add that I am more than willing to stay in my post if you will overlook my previous decision to vacate it.'

There was silence in the room, until the

fire spluttered and a piece of stone from the coal sparked on to the hearth. Samuel picked up the poker and rearranged the blazing coal, then replaced it in its stand before, turning to the young snot, as he thought of him, he said, 'Aye, well, I'll give you this much: it's taken some guts for you to come and lower your flag. But have you thought what it's going to be like with me as your master? Me, who's no gentleman in your eyes, someone who admitted he was so ignorant of the way of life in that house that he wanted you to show him the ropes? Have you thought of how you're going to work along of him?'

'I can only say, sir, I will give you my loyalty, as I gave it to his lordship. His lordship may not have been in need of so much help, but nevertheless —'

'There he goes again' — Samuel was looking at Alice as he thrust his finger towards him — 'pointing out my ignorance. And that's what it'll be like all the way.'

'Well —' a small, tight smile appeared on Alice's face as she looked from one to the other, saying now, 'I don't suppose that'll be a bad thing, after all. Now, now, Sam' — it was she who raised a hand — 'I think Mr Maitland —'

'You don't address him as mister; just

Maitland. Isn't that so?'

'Yes, sir, just Maitland.'

Samuel had turned to Alice again and she stared straight back at him and said, '*Mr Maitland*, as you say, has been very courageous by coming here and apologising to you. And I'm sure, as time goes on, you'll come to understand each other better, because, you know, in every war, there's faults on both sides. Now, if you'll excuse me, I must go and see if the girls have got your supper ready. Good night, Mr Maitland.'

'Good night, ma'am.' His words were soft, like a caress, and on them Alice walked out of the room as stately as any lady might have done and left them facing each other.

'You needn't think you're on a good thing there, 'cos I'm boss in me own house.'

'I have no doubt about that, sir.'

Again a silence fell on the room; then Samuel asked, 'What about the others?'

'Well, sir, they would all, with the exception of the housekeeper, like to stay on; and she is of an age now when she would like to retire.'

'I hope she's got enough to retire on.' There was sarcasm in the remark, but Maitland did not respond to it.

What he said was, 'She's going to live with her sister, so I think she will manage.

She has always been a saving woman.'

'Aye, well then, that's settled, is it?'

'As you say, sir, that's settled.'

Samuel twisted his neck up out of his high stiff collar, saying, 'If you were any other kind of a fellow I'd offer you a drink. But that wouldn't be right, would it, Maitland?'

Was there a smile on Maitland's face when he said, 'I never refused the offer from his lordship, sir. Although port was never my drink, I took it with him.'

'By God! you're a queer 'un, aren't you?' Samuel shook his head slowly now as he gazed at this man who had come into his life and who was, in a way, going to order it, but never reconstruct it. And he said, 'Well, what is your drink?'

'I enjoy a whisky, straight, sir.'

'Oh, well, that's a miracle; we've got something in common. Come on then, into the dining-room. There's no cellar here, just a cabinet. By the way, it's a pity the cellar there was empty, isn't it?'

'It wasn't quite empty, sir.'

At the door Samuel turned and looked at him, saying, 'No? Well, I didn't see any.'

'No, you wouldn't, sir, because there were only about thirty bottles left of any real quality; old vintages, you know, sir. When his lordship died, there were ten used and the rest her ladyship passed on to me for . . . services rendered; as she did with his lordship's gold watch and chain and cuff links. And in case of misunderstanding, and misunderstandings can take place at these times, I asked her ladyship to put it in writing. That apart, sir, as the wine is mostly claret, you'd be quite welcome to it.'

Samuel turned his face towards the stanchion of the door, put his arm on it, laid his head against it and laughed so loudly that it brought the two maids from the kitchen, Howard out of the playroom, Janet from the end of the long passage where she had been waiting to catch a glimpse of the gentleman when he should leave the house, and Alice almost racing down the stairs from attending her mother, who was in bed with a cold. And they all stood and looked from one man to the other, one straight-backed and straight-faced, the other as they had never seen him before, his face wet with tears of laughter. And one after the other they made their own sounds of disbelief before exchanging glances and joining in the laughter, not knowing why they were laughing, except that none of them had ever before witnessed this man in a state of merriment.

3

'You've got your way over Howard — he's going to a boarding school; but what good that'll do him, I don't know. I can't understand you, Samuel Fairbrother; you, who have always looked down your nose at the kind of young fellow such schools produce, now paying good money to make him like one of them. And let me tell you, it's only your money that's getting him in.'

'Tell me something I don't know, woman. But what d'you think I make money for?'

'So you can feel big.'

'Is that all you think I make it for?' Samuel's voice had dropped.

'Yes, at bottom.'

'Well, I can't alter your opinion. You've always told me you've known your own mind, and you'll know without me telling you that I know mine, because I know what I'm up to in everything I do. And Janet is going to that convent school, because she's the only one so far that I detect has anything up top; I mean, out of the ordinary.'

'My God! man, have you examined Alicia, Fanny, and Jessica? Alicia was six yesterday. Of course, she's grown up; she should be out there doing something big; perhaps yelling about women's causes and the vote. And the lads, of course, Eddie, James and Harry are all numskulls.'

'Aye' — he smiled wryly at her now — 'you might be right. You nearly always are about some things.'

Alice now slowly sat down on the side of the flounce-trimmed canopy bed, and she sighed deeply as she said, 'I used to say, Sam, you were made in a certain mould and it couldn't be changed, but somehow since you came into this house, or rather, since you first set eyes on it, something's happened to you.' She watched him standing before the mirror, pulling at both ends of his collar in an attempt to insert a stud, and his voice was a mutter as he said, 'Oh aye, have I become more refined?'

'Oh, that'll be the day. If anything, I think you've become more loud-mouthed than ever. No, the change is your attitude to the family. You know something? You've never bothered with them, not one of them. Some time ago, Janet said to me, with tears in her eyes, that you never played with them.'

He gave a sharp sound in his throat as his head jerked round and the stud went into place. And she said, 'You look surprised. Well, you shouldn't be, because, as you said yourself when we were having one of our . . . intellectual discussions, that you put them into me and it was up to me to deliver them and raise them. You provided the wherewithal and that was your part done. That was after Harry was born. I think it was then that I fell out of love with you.'

He was about to thrust his arm into his waistcoat when it became still and he stared at her for a moment before hitching the garment up on to his shoulder, and then he said, 'Did I hear aright?'

'Yes, Sam, you heard aright.'

He walked slowly towards her; then he stopped within an arm's length of her and in a low voice now, he said, 'Are you telling me you don't care for me any more?'

'No, I'm not telling you that, Sam. I do care for you, but I'd been in love with you up until then. I thought the sun shone out of you. I still saw you as a brash individual and somebody who was going places; but I realised on that day that the places and the opinion that Samuel Fairbrother had of himself and wanted others to have of him were much more important than me and my needs or those of the children I was rearing.'

'Lass, you've got it all twisted up.'

'No, Sam, no. I know you. You were thirty when you married me. And the shops you had then were bringing in a tidy sum, enough to keep us in comfort in a way of life beyond Sweetbanks Gardens. But as I once said to you before we were married, Mam was on her own and would be lonely, so would you mind living with her for a while? . . . no; you didn't mind, no rent or rates to pay, and three servants. No; you didn't mind. No; because it left you free to be on this and that committee. And you were a member of the Merchants' Club. But that wasn't enough. You must make money, and more money, and the way to do it was to open shops and more shops.'

'Aye' — he now thrust his face down to hers — 'and employ more men, so they could come off the streets and earn a livin', and feed their bairns. So I was out just to make money, was I? I wanted to be a bighead, did I? And while you are on, re-member I wasn't only offered, I was pressed to go on the council so I could run for mayor. That was the idea, and I turned it down, didn't I?'

'Yes, I know you turned it down. But the real reason was because you wouldn't have had enough time to expand the business.

You couldn't leave it in other people's hands. You never trusted anybody to manage, and you had to keep one eye on them. And it's got you running to this day; and it'll have you running till you die.'

She twisted herself along the edge of the bed away from him and she stood up as she said, 'But in the meantime you're going to educate your sons and daughters far above their station. And I'm telling you, Sam Fairbrother, that you're making a mistake. We've seen it before, haven't we? in this very town, and not by them that were sent to fancy schools either, but fellows who've just got on and forgot they were born here, especially in the Bog's End area. Now it's the best end of Newcastle for them, and they are too busy to visit their people or even recognise them again. And the same will happen to you.'

'My God!' He rubbed the sweat from his brow. 'Why does all this happen to me? Last week it was that you would have no more bairns, that eight was enough, and now I'm a thoughtless, big-headed nowt. And this has been revealed to note because I want to send me daughter to a convent school. And what's more, let me tell you, she's taken with the idea.'

'They're Catholics.'

'Of course they're Catholics. But there are Protestants there, too, and they are from the best families in the town. And why? because the education is better. And they learn something else there.'

'Yes, all about the Pope and Rosaries and Holy Marys, and God knows what.'

'They'll do nothing of the sort. I spoke to the Mother Superior and the priest and I told them I didn't want anything of that sort pumped into her. And you know what? the priest laughed. He bellowed like a bull.'

'Yes, he would, 'cos they're clever, clever enough to turn her into a nun.'

'Huh! Janet, with her mind, being turned into a nun? There's just as much chance of that as turning the Mother Superior into a stripper. Anyway' — he now pulled on his coat — 'I'm late for the meeting.'

'Oh, yes, the meeting!'

'Aye, the meeting that's going to bring me in another shop. Well, if I have no interest in me family I've got to have something to care about, haven't I? Good night to you, Mrs Fairbrother. And thank you very much for this conversation. I'll chew on it when I have time to think.'

He marched out of the room, the door clashing behind him.

Maitland was standing in the hall, an

43

overcoat on his arm. It was as if he had been waiting there for some time. 'It's bitterly cold, sir,' he said; 'I think you might need a scarf tonight.'

He helped Samuel on with his coat; then, taking the scarf that was hanging over the back of a hall chair, he handed it to his master; and lastly he proffered him his hard hat. Then, opening the door, he said, 'I hope you have an enjoyable evening, sir.'

Samuel paused on the step and, his voice a growl, he said, 'I might have it so good that you won't see me back.'

'Oh, you'll come back, sir. I have no fear of that.'

As Samuel walked across the drive to where the cab was waiting, he wondered why he felt closer to that fellow than to any member of his family and that definitely included his wife at this moment . . . fell out of love with him, had she? . . .

Maitland did not close the door until he saw his master had entered the cab.

As he crossed the hall towards the dining-room, Florence Furness was descending the stairs and when she reached the bottom, he said, 'Have you seen to the mistress's fire, Florence?'

'Well, I was going to,' she answered, 'but,' and she hesitated, 'they . . . they were

44

talking rather loudly, you know, and . . .
and so I left it for the time being and saw
to the children. Shall I go back and see to
it now?'

'No, no. Wait until the mistress comes
downstairs.'

'Yes, Mr Maitland.'

Florence carried on to the kitchen and
there, going straight up to Cook, who was
at the table arranging cold meats on a side
dish, she bent towards her, saying softly,
'Sparks were flying up there. I saw him
coming out of the bedroom. He slammed
the door after him. He looked like the
devil.'

'Did you hear anything?' Mrs Wilding
paused in her arranging.

'No; nothing except him shouting.'

The scullery maid, who was sitting at a
side table shelling peas, said on a giggle,
'He's always shouting. He's a funny man,'
only to be silenced by Cook, crying, 'You
speak when you're spoken to, Bella Forbes!
And when we want your opinion of the
master we'll ask for it.'

The menial, squashed as usual, bowed
her head and got on with her work, and
Cook turned back to Florence and said,
'Where is he?'

And in an equally low voice, Florence answered, 'Well he was making for the dining-room or the library. But I bet me life that the mistress will be down in a minute or so and collar him just to see what he thinks about the latest. I'm sure the row was about Miss Janet going to the convent. Well, I ask you, and them not even Church of England. They never go anywhere. But, of course, neither did his lordship. Still, his lordship was a different kettle of fish. It's a different house now, isn't it, Cook?'

Cook's small bosom rose and she let out a long breath before she said, 'Yes, I suppose it is, but it could be worse. She gives us a free hand, the missis, something I didn't expect, and she's not stingy. It's a good meat house, even better than in her ladyship's time, you must admit.'

'Yes, but she doesn't have the same kind of dishes. It's plainer food, isn't it?'

'Well, what's wrong with that?' Cook now pointed to the side dish covered with slices of beef, pork and ham, the variety separated by slivers of hard boiled eggs topped with parsley. 'Anyway, I hope it passes his lordship's scrutiny.' She pouted her lips and jerked her head towards the far door. 'He's as fussy about their meals, no matter what they are, as he was about his lordship's, even when it was on a tray.'

'You know, Cook, he seems lost these days somehow.'

'Well, he would be a bit. He misses Mrs Bright and Mr Mather, and of course Miss Moore. They were four of a kind, in a way, eating together, chatting together.'

'Aye, I suppose so. Anyway he seems to spend what spare time he has either in his room or in the library. I think he's feeling the change an' all . . .'

The subject of their conversation was in the library. He was standing before the fire, not with his back to it, as did his master, but looking down on to it, his forearm resting on the edge of the long marble mantelpiece and with one foot on the flat rim of the filigree brass fender that surrounded the hearth.

The stance of a butler was no longer apparent. He looked relaxed but thoughtful, and he had plenty to think about. The question large in his mind at this moment was whether he was to stay or to go. He'd received a letter from her ladyship's daughter, Lady Irene, that morning. It had come from America. In fact, he'd had two. The second was from her ladyship herself, but they were both asking him the same question: would he come to America and take up the position there? It should happen that Lady

47

Irene, who had been widowed now for more than two years, was about to marry a very wealthy American businessman. The wedding was to be quiet, out of respect for his lordship's recent demise. But Lady Irene's future husband was setting up a new establishment and both women had said they would be delighted if Maitland would come and take over the household. The remuneration offered was staggering, so tempting, almost four times what he was getting here. It was an offer that only a fool would refuse. And he considered himself no fool. Yet, and that was the big question in his mind . . . yet? What was keeping him here? Why was he hesitating? This was a very ordinary family, in some ways very, very ordinary, yet at the same time complex, especially the head of it, a man who seemed to be fighting himself all along the line; ambitious to rise, yet hanging on to his roots, and acclaiming this with his voice and his attitude, yet determining that his family were going to move up the scale, although at the moment this appeared to be against the principles of his wife. There she was, a comparatively young woman, just about his own age; perhaps he could give her a year. She had borne eight children, yet still remained very comely. She could be called pretty, yet she had no style. Whereas her ladyship and Lady Irene could wear hessian sacks and still appear attractive. Mrs Fairbrother's dress, although fashionable for the day, with its leg-of-mutton sleeves and tight waist, had a skirt almost trailing the dust — that was one thing he could never understand, women's apparel below the knees. Even since the mud fringe had gone out of fashion they were still far too long — had no distinguishable point; in fact, it seemed to emphasise her station in life. Yet she was a kind and thoughtful woman, although sharpish of tongue; but then she would have to be to combat her husband. Oh, yes, she needed that, because he was a force to be reckoned with. And then there were the children. Would he miss the children if he went? Yes. Yes, he would. He had never had much to do with Lady Irene's little daughter; she had been kept in the care of the nurse up on the nursery floor. She had been born into a house of sorrow, for her father had been killed in the hunting field only a week earlier. But the children of this house were of a different breed, naturally, and even if they had been born here they would not have been brought up mainly in the attics, not with the parents they had. Yet here was the father aiming to put them into the category in which they would be segregated until they were considered civilised enough to mix and eat with their parents, before being dispatched to a public school.

He straightened up as the door opened and the young girl, Janet, entered, only immediately to turn and speak to someone in the corridor; 'Come on! Come on!' And then, her hand going out, she pulled her brother into the room, saying, 'He wants to ask you something. Is it all right? Were you busy?'

'No, I wasn't busy, Miss Janet. I'm at your service.'

'It's about the school he's going to. He's worried.'

Maitland turned to the boy, who had reached his eleventh birthday three days ago, and he said, 'What are you worried about, Master Howard? Come; sit down.' He pointed to a chair. 'I always think you can chat better when you're sitting. Don't you?' He had addressed the last words to Janet, but she didn't answer him. She just sat down on one of the leather-topped stools and watched her brother pull a similar one from the side of the fireplace and slide on to it. But when he didn't attempt to speak, Maitland said, 'What is it you want to know?'

The boy blinked, then looked down at his hands where they were pressed tight between his knees and said, 'Just what it's going to be like. Do they knock you about? I mean, the other boys, the big ones? I read in a story —'

'Oh, a story. Stories!' Maitland flapped his hand at the boy. 'Don't take any notice of what you read about schools. Of course there'll be some rough and tumble. You have rough and tumble at the school you go to now, don't you? You've been in one or two battles. What about the cut on your chin and the scraped knees? But from what I heard of *that* story your opponent had a black eye.'

The boy grinned, but his face reassumed the worried expression when he said, 'Is it true they make you take ice-cold baths, and is the food awful?'

'With regard to ice-cold baths, that's ridiculous. But about the food; well, it certainly won't be like you eat here every day.'

As he smiled at the boy, he thought, a very good job, too, for the lad was flabby. He was tall for his age but, he guessed, much overweight for it, too.

Maitland turned to Janet as she said, 'Mam will send you boxes of food; tuck boxes every week.'

'Aha!' Maitland wagged his finger at her now. 'There are generally restrictions on how many tuck boxes a pupil may receive. It's more like one a month, but I'm sure he'll soon get used to the food and the routine of the school as a whole.'

He now turned his attention to the boy again, saying, 'I understand it's a very good school. It is highly thought of. And in a way, you know, you're very lucky to get a place there. I've known of boys who have had to wait for a vacancy.' He didn't know any such thing. He only knew that money talked and that money was getting this boy into a well-known establishment where his intelligence or brains would never have earned him an entry. Now, if it had been his sister . . .

The boy got to his feet as he said, 'Will you look after my trains, Mr Maitland, and not let our Eddie get at them? because he'll take them to school and swap them.'

'Oh, he wouldn't do that.'

'Oh, yes, he would. He said the other day he could get a model of a horseless carriage for three engines and a set of bogies.'

'Don't you worry, Master Howard; I'll see that they go under lock and key.'

Even as he made this promise he was asking himself, What am I saying? It would be touch and go if he'd be here another week or so. He'd have to give them notice; perhaps a month.

The boy smiled at him, then glanced at his sister before hurrying from the room.

Janet made no attempt to follow her brother; she remained seated on the stool, her attention concentrated on Maitland as she said, 'He really wants to go, you know. It's only last minute nerves.'

'You think he really wants to go to that school?'

'Oh yes . . . well, not that particular one, but any school. He'll be happier away. You see, he's afraid of Dad . . . Father.'

Maitland drew his brows together as he stared at the girl. Over the weeks since she had come into the house, he had become accustomed to her frankness. But even so, she startled him at times; as she had just done; so perceptive for one so young, and he now asked her: 'What makes you think he's afraid of his father? I mean —'

'Well, most people are, aren't they? because if he doesn't bellow or shout at you he just ignores you. It's as if you weren't there.'

'Oh, Miss Janet,' he said, and was about to say, I'm sure you've got the wrong idea of your father. But her description was so

53

accurate that all he could do was to smile as he said, 'Well, apparently, *you're* not afraid of him.'

'No. No, I'm not, although he's never acted like a father. Well, what I mean is, from what I see of other fathers. Mr Atkinson, for instance, he talks to Fred; that's his son, you know. Of course, he's sixteen, but still, Mr Atkinson has always talked to him as if he was . . . well' — her face puckered as if she were thinking — 'well, not an idiot. And they go to cricket matches together. Dad has never once taken Howard out. Mother has. But then it's not the same for a boy, and Howard has minded that. Now Eddie doesn't. Well, you know Eddie, he's a rip.' She smiled again. 'Nothing or no-one can upset Eddie. But Harry's different. I think Harry's like me, don't you?'

'No; I wouldn't say he's like you. He's quiet and of rather a shy nature, while you, Miss Janet, are neither quiet nor of a shy nature.' He was smiling widely at her and he watched her nip her bottom lip, droop her head, then wag it. It was the only childish act he had seen her perform.

Her head was still bowed as she said, 'You won't leave us, will you?'

He actually started. He did not say, What d'you mean? How do you know? Surely she couldn't have seen that letter. No. No. He dismissed the suggestion: he always locked his private possessions and correspondence in the top drawer of the chest, and the key to it was on his watch chain. He put his finger between the buttons of his coat and felt for the keys, and as he did so he told himself she would never go prowling around his room. That wouldn't be her style at all.

She was looking up at him now, saying, 'I dreamt about you last night,' but he didn't say, You did? He just waited, and she went on. 'It was a very odd dream, all mixed up. I was in my new uniform, my school uniform, you know, and I had that silly hat on, the one that's like the straw benga I told you I hate, and I came running into the hall and it was full of cases, travelling cases; and you were dressed very smartly; well' — she jerked her chin now — 'you're always smartly dressed, but you were dressed for going away. And the funny thing is that Father was standing at the drawing-room door. And you know the day he laughed loudly with his arm against the stanchion with his head buried in the crook of it? well, he was standing like that again. But he wasn't laughing. He was making no sound at all.' She stopped abruptly, her mouth half open: she couldn't go on and tell him the

rest of her dream, for that would be too . . .
too embarrassing, too frightening, for it
didn't concern her, was nothing to do with
her. Or was it? She was biting tight down
on her lip now and she stood up while continuing to stare at him.

'You're a very strange little girl, Janet,' he
said, without this time prefixing her name
with Miss.

'Why? Why am I strange? I don't want to
be strange.'

'I mean that it was strange that you
should dream that dream.'

'Was it? Was it foretelling what was going
to happen? Are you thinking of leaving?'
When he did not answer, she said in a whisper, 'Oh no, Maitland.' She too had dis-
pensed with Maitland's prefix of Mr. 'Don't
go! Please, don't go! Everything would be
spoiled. You've . . . you've made things so
different. Even Dad. He would never have
thought of sending me to that school, the
convent, if it hadn't been for you. I know
that.'

'Oh, I had nothing to do with your being
sent to the convent. Believe me.'

'Well, perhaps not going to the convent,
but going to a better school. And anyway'
— she now nodded forcibly at him — 'it
must have been you, because I remember

you telling Dad about Colonel Stacey, he who lives up in Rowan Manor on the hill yon side of the town. You said he had two daughters and they both went to the convent and from there one had gone on to a place called Garters in Cambridge.'

He laughed at this, saying, 'Garters is right or nearly so; it's a ladies' college, and it's correct name is Girton.'

'Well, there you are. He must have got the idea from you.'

'I don't think so, Miss Janet.' He was standing straight now — he was the butler once again — for it was the only defence he seemed to have at the moment against this unusual little girl.

As he looked into her plain face, he could see her, ten years ahead, as a formidable female, strong-minded, one of the new women that were already on the march. And she would likely be leading them. He knew a sense of relief when the door opened and her mother entered, saying, 'Oh, there you are, Janet. Your supper's ready.' And she held the door wide to allow her daughter to pass. However she didn't follow Janet but, pushing it closed, she walked up the room to where Maitland was now restoring the fire, and said, 'Has she been talking to you again about her uniform?'

As he dusted his hands he turned to her, saying, 'No, madam, except perhaps that she's not very fond of her hat; too much like a boater.'

'She's not very fond of any part of it. D'you know what she said about it?' She smiled widely now. 'It makes her look too young. Did you ever!'

He returned her smile, saying, 'In years to come she'll look back and long to be this age again.'

'Oh, I don't know so much. She's a very odd girl, you know, Maitland. Well, odd is perhaps not the right word. I used to think at one time she had no soft feelings; you know what I mean? But . . . but I've been proved wrong.'

'Oh yes, madam, she is capable of . . . very soft feelings, and they belie her penetrating mind.' He paused a moment, then added, 'I wonder how she will eventually use it.'

'Oh, she'll likely take up teaching of one thing or another. She's very good at arithmetic and she's always been top of the class for her spelling and composition.'

As he looked on his mistress, this youngish, comely woman, someone who possessed no outstanding qualities, not even of intelligence, he repeated to himself, She's very good at arithmetic and she's always top of the class for her spelling and composition. He wouldn't have been surprised if she had added, Well, I'm glad she's got something to make up for her plainness.

She said now, 'I'm going to miss my Howard. I can't see why Mr Fairbrother couldn't have let him go to a day school somewhere nearby; in Newcastle for instance, and so, like Janet, he could be at home every night. But that place is twenty miles yon side of Durham. It will take half a day to get there. D'you know anything about the school, Maitland?'

'Only that it has a very good reputation.'

She seemed about to turn away when she added, 'Did his lordship's son, the one that died youngish, go there?'

'No. I understood, madam, that he went to Marlborough. That was before he went on to university, but this school, you know, has a record of sending many young men up either to Oxford or Cambridge. And who knows, perhaps Master Howard might be one of those of the future.'

Why did he say such things? But why not? Money could get the boy into one or other of the universities. It was being done all the time . . . She was laughing and he looked at her enquiringly and she said, 'You know,

Maitland, in some quarters, you could be known as a kidder.'

'A kidder, madam?'

'Yes, you know, somebody who has somebody else on.'

'Oh no, madam. I'm not of that turn of mind. I wouldn't have anybody . . . on.'

'Well, you know yourself that Howard isn't all that bright. Now, if it had been Janet; well, she's a different kettle of fish. But not Howard . . . Getting to university? No!'

'Madam,' his voice was solemn for he knew he had been exaggerating somewhat, but he had to say, 'all the pupils in the public schools in this country are there simply because their parents have been able to buy them in.'

'Is that a fact?'

'That is a fact, madam.' And as he said this he told himself he wasn't so far out after all, because hadn't his lordship spoken often of the sons of his friends as being as dim as the fog over London?

She stared at him hard for a moment before she said, 'You know, you are a very comforting man to have in the house. And I can't imagine it without you.' And she gulped in her throat before continuing, 'I suppose her ladyship, and her daughter, felt much the same way. You oil the wheels, so to speak. It's what Mr Fairbrother would call being made for the job, if you know what I mean.'

He made no reply and, flustered, she hurriedly added, 'I haven't explained myself right. I never can . . .'

'Oh, it's quite all right, madam, I know what you mean, and, in a way, I consider it a compliment.'

Her head made a little movement by way of acknowledgement, before she turned and hurried from the room. And after a moment he resumed his previous position, with his forearm on the mantelshelf. Now the situation made it impossible for him to leave this house, and it had come about not through its mistress but through her small daughter. Yet at the same time there was an inner voice demanding, Why? Why was he throwing away the chance of a lifetime?

4

Samuel looked down on the card in his
hand and read, "Mr and Mrs Peter Hallberry, of Dale Cottage, Brandon Park, Fellburn." Then, looking up at Maitland, he
said, 'D'you know anything about this pair?'

'Only that they used to visit here at one
time.'

'Well, they've taken their time in intro-
ducing themselves, haven't they?'

Maitland did not answer immediately, for
he was thinking, they've likely run short of
money again, and so want to use the only
means they have for their livelihood. What
he said now was, 'They have very good con-
nections and their speciality is in opening
doors.'

'Opening doors? Making introductions,
you mean?'

'Yes. Yes, in the right quarters.'

'And I'll bet they don't do it for nothing.'

When Maitland remained silent Samuel
said, 'Well, well. You meet up with all sorts.
What did you say to them?'

'I told them that Mrs Fairbrother was out
and wasn't due back for some time, as she

was visiting her mother, who was unwell, but that I would convey their respects to her and to yourself . . . or words to that effect.'

'Aye, I know. Words to that effect. Well, they're the first that's made a move towards us. What are we going to do about it?'

'I . . . I should think it would be in order to invite them to dinner. You were talking just recently about arranging a dinner for your friends. Well, as I recall, the Hallberrys are very good mixers. And if I may make a suggestion, sir, there are two other houses to which you might send an invitation. Of course, it may not be accepted, but the refusal will be very courteous, especially from Colonel Stacey and his wife. I may add here that they are very nice people, as also are Mr Pearman and his wife.'

'Abel Pearman? Oh, I've met him once or twice at the club. I don't suppose he would refuse. Did they visit here when the old fellow — I mean his lordship — was alive?'

'Yes. Yes, they did. His wife was a friend of her ladyship, but of course that was when the entertainment was frequent. But in latter years it sort of . . . trailed off. Nevertheless, they called at times; just to visit, you understand.'

'And you think I should invite these three to mix with my friends?'

'Well, I think one of your friends, your solicitor, is well acquainted with the three people mentioned. He often came to dinner. Of course, in those days, her ladyship would vary the company. She always chose the ones who would mix well.'

'Well, what happens at dinner parties? I mean, after they've eaten? or even before they've eaten?'

'Oh well, drinks are served and there is generally much small talk, very small talk in some quarters. This used to be the time when the hostess would introduce new guests to old guests. And if she hadn't a good memory, sometimes there would be red faces. I think it was from that time that the butler took over the announcing. Now, even that seems to have died out . . . and may I say, for that mercy I'm thankful.'

'You didn't care for shouting out the names then?'

'No; because it was something out of the rule of the house. One announced the meals to the family, but on occasions of dinners and balls the guests would come in two by two. And some of them spoke so quietly you couldn't make out their names and were you to mispronounce them, oh, my! my! my!'

'Well, what d'you think is likely to happen at this do?'

'Oh, I think the guests, once in the drawing-room, will introduce themselves. It happens that way. It's done now. And, say half an hour after the last guest has arrived, I'll announce dinner, and Sarah and I will serve it while Florence carries the dishes backwards and forwards from the kitchen. And on this occasion, I think, it would be worthwhile putting young Winter into a decent suit-cum-uniform, and have him show the gentlemen to the room where they can leave their outer coats and hats, while Florence will take on that duty for the ladies.'

'Just a moment; a uniform, you say, for the lad?'

'Yes; and that's something I need to discuss with you, sir. You see, the staff have their uniform replenished every year; at least, one of their working dresses. Their blue serges may last for two or three years.'

Samuel screwed up his face. 'And I'm supposed to foot that?'

'Yes, sir, you're supposed to foot that. It's understood in such establishments as this that a servant has board, lodgings and uniform. That is why, in lots of houses, their remuneration is meagre.'

'Remun . . . eration meagre? My God! Those lasses are getting twice as much a month as I got when I was eighteen.'

'Perhaps, sir, but they don't receive enough to enable them to buy the uniform required, together with the necessary twelve aprons, four starched caps, and three pairs of sleeve frills.'

Samuel ran his fingers through his hair now while puffing out his cheeks, saying, 'Why didn't you mention this to me before?'

'I thought you would already be aware of the position, sir.'

'Aware of the position? I'm a child in this business, Maitland; you know I am. Moreover, I'm an idiot, a bumpkin, a maniac, for ever taking this place on and all it contains. Who supplies these clothes? Stanmores?'

'Oh, no, sir; they've always been made here; at least, for the female staff Mrs Talbot sees to them. She started as a seamstress here when she was a girl, then became a dressmaker.'

'Talbot? You mean Talbot the groom, from the lodge?'

'Yes, sir. Mrs Kate Talbot. She's a very good dressmaker.'

'You're pally with Talbot, aren't you?'

'We have always been friends. He took me under his wing, so to speak, when I first came into the service. He had been with his lordship since he was a boy.'

Samuel now began to pace the room; and when, at last, he stopped in front of Maitland, he said, 'You know, I live in this house but I don't know a damn thing about what goes on in it. In fact, every damn one in this place is a stranger to me, even me own bairns.'

He stared at Maitland as if expecting him to make some remark, but when he didn't, he cried, 'Well! isn't that a fact? You're not above coming out with what you consider to be the truth, so, I ask you, isn't that a fact?'

'There's a remedy, sir, at least with the members of your family: just a little more time spent with them.'

'Time? I haven't got time, man. I've got eleven shops to see to, as well as a factory, and it's a fight, Maitland. A businessman today is not just a businessman, he's a captain of industry. Business is a war. You've got to fight the next man. One time you could shake hands on a deal. You know, when my grandfather started, he not only cobbled and made clogs, but he made shoes and boots, that's when he could get the orders. And as a lad I used to go to the tannery with him and there he would choose his own hides. And you know, he used to have them hanging outside the door of the little shop. People could choose their own leather, that is the ones who could afford to have a pair of shoes or boots made. He was an artist with leather. He couldn't write his name and he was never asked to put his cross to anything. There was a handshake and that settled a deal. But now, for safety's sake, you have not only got to sign your name on a contract, it's got to have red sealing wax on the bottom of it. But me grandad had three shops before he died, although all put together they would have fitted into this room. And he was a good honest man: if a body didn't turn up for his cobbled boots within a month he would find out why. It was all right for bairns to go barefooted, but if a man hadn't any sole to his shoes it was difficult for him to travel the roads to get a job. And that period was a time of strikes and near riots for bread, and the workhouses overflowing. When I look at my lot I sometimes think of me dad, for even with the three shops me grandad only allowed himself and the family one good meal a day, and that consisted of a small amount of meat, but as many potatoes as you could eat. That was until the Irish famine, when he cut down on taties. But,' he gave a sly grin now, 'I never knew him give any to the Irish who had already got as far as here, following the famine over there. I can remember being hungry meself at times, and it wasn't because my parents were short of money. No' — he looked to the side now — 'it was because they were keeping to a pattern. Me dad and me mother had to live with the old folks because it saved rent, you see, and that was the pattern. Aye, that was the pattern; if you wanted the business to grow you had to stick to the pattern. I broke the pattern when I married, but only in a way, for I went and lived with my wife's people. And it didn't do the business any harm; in fact, it doubled it, even trebled it. Oh, God! what am I yammering on about? I know what you're thinking.' He now stabbed his finger towards Maitland. 'Common as muck, that's what you're thinking, aren't you? Common as muck.'

Maitland's tone was stiff, as was his face, when he replied, 'You are no thought-reader, sir. If you want to know what I was thinking, sir, it was, why doesn't he stop fighting himself.'

'What!'

69

'I think you heard what I said, sir.'

'Aye, I did. Why don't I stop fighting meself? You're wrong there, lad. I fight, aye, but it's others I fight. I know what I am. I know what I want. I wouldn't waste time fighting meself.' He now thrust his head forward. 'You know who I've been fighting the day?' He did not wait for an answer, but went on. 'The Japs. You know, the Japanese, that's who I've been fightin', me and fifteen other men. At least, we're making our plans to fight them. Does that surprise you?'

'It does somewhat, sir. Yes, indeed it does.'

'D'you know anything about Japan?'

'Very little, sir.'

'The Japanese are the best imitators in this world today. They've just got to see something and they can copy it, then transport it and sell it for nearly half the price we can here.'

'Can't it be stopped, sir?'

'Stopped! man? There's such a thing as free trade. One of our fellows got wind that they can make a shoe to equal anything we can do, and as I said, for half the price. And why? Because they're made by slave labour. Oh, if you've got to watch any country, it's Japan. Look what they've done to China. And just think of the size of China and think of the size of them. You'd think a wasp couldn't lay flat an elephant; but they've done it all right.'

He went round the desk and seated himself, and his voice dropping, he said, 'I was all fixed for an extension to the factory, going to make handbags to match the shoes. I'd had it in me mind for a long time; then Ryland . . . I must hand it to him, he turns out some good stuff; but there he was at the meeting and he had a handbag that had been made in Japan. It was a smart and well-finished piece of work and, as he said, in one of his shops that would have cost up to five pounds. But there it was, he had picked it up in a side street in London for twenty-five bob. Those blokes can copy anything their eyes see, he said. And shortly there'll not be a thing in this country that they haven't had a go at, except —' and now Samuel forced a smile to his face as he chuckled, 'Ryland said, the only bloody thing they didn't need to copy was copulation. And anyway, it wasn't transportable . . . Oh. Crudeness. Crudeness. You should see your face, man. His lordship wouldn't have come out with anything like that, would he now?'

It was some seconds before Maitland answered, 'You would have been surprised

71

what his lordship came out with, but in a slightly different manner,' although he refrained from explaining this difference by adding, 'His crudeness would have been expressed in wit, not coarse humour.'

'Aye, I suppose you're right. But it's odd when I come to think of it, for a short while ago I said I knew nothing about anybody in this house. I tend to think I know my business associates but it's only up to a point, for I'm sure I've learned more about that fellow, as he really was, in three months than I would have done in a lifetime's business association. He was a clever bloke, was he?'

'He had a good mind, sir. But in my opinion it was handicapped by an over-generous nature and a weak will.'

Samuel Fairbrother fell back in the revolving chair and he moved it slightly from side to side before he said, 'My stars! You do probe, don't you? I hope they never ask you to write my obituary.'

'That will never happen, sir. Those dealing with such matters would consider I wasn't even capable of writing. To you I appear knowledgeable because I'm well acquainted with household etiquette, but the men who deal with obituaries, sir, such as those on *The Times* or the *London Illustrated*

News, would have a very low opinion of my station in life.'

When Samuel began to laugh a low, shoulder-shaking laugh, Maitland said, 'You find that amusing, sir?'

'Aye, I do, because it shows you to be human. You're as testy under the skin about your position as I am about mine. D'you know something, Maitland?' He now leant forward into what had become his favourite position, his forearms on the table, his head thrust forward. 'You always manage in some way to give me a lift and you've just given me the best one so far. Because, you know, you and I are brothers under the skin . . . Look; I want a drink. Go and bring me a whisky. Bring two glasses while you're at it. And when you come back you can tell me what we're going to eat at that dinner party apart from a little bit of meat and a lot of taties.'

PART TWO

1907

Janet

1

'I'll . . . I'll pay you back, Gran.'

'I'm not afraid of that, lass; but I'll say again, what d'you want it for? You've never been an extravagant spender, except on books. You're not going to spend that amount on books, though I saw one in a shop the other day marked a pound. My! My! Sixpence is the limit I go to for one. Come on.' Then her voice changing, she said more softly, 'Come on, lass. Is it for Howard? More trouble?'

Janet lowered her lids for a moment before she explained, 'A young fellow from his school came this morning and Howard saw him coming up the drive and asked me to tell him that he wasn't in. It turned out that he's borrowed thirty pounds from him over the last couple of terms —'

'My God! Thirty pounds? Well, if I had my way I'd let the fellow take it out of his skin, 'cos somebody'll do it sooner or later. Just tell him to go to your father and ask him for it.'

'Oh, Gran. There'd be murder done. And you know, at bottom, he's still afraid of Dad.'

'Well, he needs to be afraid of some-body. But to hear him talk out of that big mouth of his you would think he wasn't feared of God Almighty Himself. Anyway, why doesn't he ask your mother? He's her golden-headed boy.'

'Not so much golden-headed of late, Gran. And I think he's already drained that particular well dry.'

'So you're the last resort. And he must have been in a bad way to come to you' — Mrs Mason now pulled a face at her grand-daughter — 'because you're not the most approachable of females, are you? Touching eighteen, you might be, but at times you frighten even me.'

Janet now almost pushed her grand-mother, and none too gently, off her straight-backed chair, and Mrs Mason yelled at her, 'Go on, knock me on the floor!'

'Well, Gran, I'm not all that unapproach-able. If you want to see someone unap-proachable you should go and meet Mother Superior.'

'Oh, aye. How's that gang going on?'

'Oh, I must tell you about my last talk with her and Sister Monica.'

'Well, there's no time like the present.'

'Oh, Gran, I must get back.'

78

'You mustn't get back and you're not going yet. Here's Kate with some hot cocoa.' She pointed to where a small elderly maid was smiling as she carried a tray on which were set two cups of steaming cocoa and a plate of buttered scones. And as she placed the tray down she looked at Janet, saying, 'My! you do grow, miss. Every time I see you, you seem to put on inches.'

'Don't be daft, woman!' her mistress cried at her. 'You've seen her at least once a week, sometimes twice, for years now. If there was any part of your description true she'd be poking her head out of the top of the chimney.'

'She's an awful woman, is your grandmother, Miss Janet.'

'Oh, I know that, Kate; I've suffered under her for years.'

'Get yourself away, woman!' The maid now made her way towards the door, laughing quite loudly, and as soon as the door had closed behind her, Mrs Mason muttered, 'She was never very bright, that one. Didn't know whether a Saturday fell on a Wednesday or not. She's dropped back into her second childhood these past few years . . . Puts on inches every time she sees you!'

'Well, everybody can't be sensible, Gran,

and she'd have to be a bit daft, wouldn't she, to have put up with you all these years?'

'Now you watch it, miss. I'm not your bead-caps and bonnet old lady. I can still use me hands to effect, and me feet on occasions.'

'Yes, and your tongue.'

'Yes, and it's asking you to tell me about the conversation you had with those frustrated dames in that convent.'

'As I've told you before, Gran, they're not frustrated; they're happier than most and, with an exception here and there, kinder than most.'

'Aye, and I suppose the exception is that . . . that Sister Benedicta or some such, the one that's not above lashing out with the back of her hand. But go on,' and her voice dropped into a conspiratorial whisper as she said, 'tell me what she said to you. I bet it was advice on your future life, telling you how to be a good woman, and if you couldn't manage that, praying to God for forgiveness.'

'Yes, Gran, it was something like that,' said Janet, laughing now. 'Well, Mother Superior sat like she always does, with her hands folded in her lap and looking you dead straight in the eye, and what she said to me was, "So you're going to be a librarian, are you?" And I said, "Yes, Mother, I hope to be." And then she said, "It will be a great responsibility, for you'll have in your power the directions that many minds will travel. It will be up to you to guide the youth with whom you come in contact along the right road. But you can only do this if your own mind is clear of impure, unkind, and aggressive thoughts." '

'Oh, well then, she's asking something. I mean —'

'Shut up! Gran, and listen, that's if you want to hear the rest. She then said, "You have been an outstanding pupil." ' Janet now preened herself for a moment before going on, " 'Such was your foresight and intelligence —" Yes, you may grin, Gran, but that's what she said. And you wanted to hear everything, didn't you? But wait for it, because she was coming to the point: "We had thought," she said, "you might tend towards our way of thinking, and if not actually join our Order then consider the attraction of our faith. But then, it is as God wills, and apparently He has other work for you." '

'Aye, such as begging for your brother to cover up his misdeeds.'

'Oh, Gran, please.'

'Anyway, what did the other one say? Be-

81

cause I don't suppose that was the end of that sermon.'

'No. She blessed me and wished me every good thing in life. And so did Sister Monica, but in a different way. Oh yes, in a very different way, because she is the sweetest but the most tactless individual, I think, in the whole wide world. As she herself says on a laugh, she is the one woman that God forgot to illuminate. In other words, she's telling you she isn't bright. But she's bright enough at English and anything to do with a tune. But there she was, Gran, during my last minutes in that school, in which I've been very happy, there she was holding my hand, shaking it up and down, saying, "It's been a joy teaching you, because I've never had to teach you, you've just gobbled up the knowledge. Now you're going out into the world, but I'm not going to worry about you, at least, where the great danger lies. You know what I mean, with men. Now if it was your sister Alicia, with her looks and sauciness, well, my words would be different at this minute. But God has given you a safeguard through your features. You might not appreciate it now, but as the years mount on you you'll see what you've been saved from on many an occasion. So, go out into the world with a brave heart, my child." '

'God in heaven! She didn't say all that?'

'She did, Gran. But I took it as it was meant. And I've got a mirror, you know. And I'll tell you one thing, I'm glad I don't look like Alicia. If I had to make a choice between brains and beauty, I'd plump for brains every time.'

'What you talking about, girl? You have beauty.'

'Oh! Gran.' It was a protest as loud as her father would have made . . .

'And don't bawl at me, with, "Oh, Gran!" You've got beautiful hair, and beautiful eyes.'

'But I've got a long face and a straight-lipped mouth and a pointed nose.'

'Oh! don't be ridiculous and stupid. There's thousands on thousands who have long faces, and they're beauties. And you haven't got a straight-lipped mouth. All right, your nose is thin, but it's better than one splashed across your face. But I'll tell you what you haven't got and that's common sense, for if you were to smile more, and with your eyes, and to lose that stiff look that puts years on you and gives people the impression that you're looking down on them, you could be a beauty.'

'Oh, it doesn't, Gran. I mean I never look down on anyone . . . well . . . not many.'

'Aye, not many, just a few, but among them are those that matter. I've seen you when you've been off your guard, and your looks could have put Alicia in the shade any day. And what's more, you know, over the years you've altered. You used to be a plain child, I'll grant you, but even when you're stiff-faced, you've got an interesting mug on you. As for that bloody nun . . .'

'Oh, Gran! you mustn't put such adjectives to women of God.'

'I'll put what adjectives I like to women of God, and to anybody else who's as bloody tactless as she is. Anyway, they wouldn't be where they are if they had any brains or weren't frightened of the world, or had not been crossed in love or some such.'

Janet was shaking with laughter when she said, 'It's odd, you know, Gran, how all those who are not Catholics, and who haven't worked with them, have weird ideas about them. There are twelve nuns in the convent, besides Mother Superior, and eight of them are teachers, the other four are domestics. But they're sweet creatures, and it's a hard life they lead, and they get no money for it.' She leaned towards her grandmother and repeated slowly, '*And they get no money for it,* Gran. Imagine you working seven days a week just for your grub. And of those seven days you can say three are spent on your knees. Now, your poor knees could never stand that, could they? Oh! that's an awful pun.'

'Give over! girl, and let's get back to normality, and trouble, and that brother of yours, because I can tell you, it's a long time since I thought of him as me grandson because every time he visits he's after something, otherwise I would never see him.'

'Well, are you going to lend me the twenty pounds?'

'I thought you said it was thirty?'

'Yes I did, but I've got ten of my own and . . . and I'll pay you back. Oh, yes, I will.' She held up a wagging finger at her grandmother.

'And how long d'you think that's going to take you out of your five shillings a week pocket money?'

Janet looked to the side now as she said, 'I know somebody who always gives me a cash present at Christmas.'

'Oh, well, me lass, that somebody might change her mind this year. You should never bank on anything. You, with your napper full of knowledge, should know that by now.'

'Oh, I do, I do, Gran; but then I take into account that some people have kind hearts.'

Mrs Mason now slowly pulled herself up from her chair, walked down the room to where a rolled top bureau stood in one corner and, pulling open a side drawer, she took out a small bunch of keys and with one of them opened a similar drawer at the other side of the knee hole. The drawer held two black tin boxes and out of one she counted twenty one-pound notes. Then, after locking the drawer, she placed the keys from where she had taken them, came back down the room and handed the money to Janet, saying, 'Now you tell him that's the last he's going to get from either of us, ever, and that if anything like this happens again I won't hesitate to go straight to your father. Now, remember that. He's not going to hide behind your skirts, nor mine, nor his mother's, not if I can help it. He'll come to a bad end, that one, and I'll live to see the day.'

'Oh, Gran, please, don't say that. 'Tisn't his fault. He should never have been sent away to that school. It's given him ideas that he's not able to live up to.'

'It's odd to hear you sticking up for him. You used to fight like cat and dog.'

'We still do.'

'Well, look, get yourself off home.' She pointed. 'It's starting to snow again. Now wrap up well, because you're all skin and bone. But you never ail anything, do you?'

'Not so far, Gran.' She now bent forward and kissed the wrinkled cheek. Then pausing, she looked round the room before saying, 'You know, I always feel comfortable in this room. I look back and know I was happy here, sitting before that fire. It always gives off a good heat, doesn't it, Gran? It doesn't smoke. The drawing-room fire back at the house puffs it out like a train when the wind's in the wrong direction. You know, I've never looked upon that house as home. I still think of this as home. Oh, Gran, why did we ever leave?'

'Because you've got a big-head for a father, that's why. Your mother didn't want to go. And it's changed her. I don't know what's the matter with her lately; but then I didn't often know what was wrong with her when she was here; she was so testy at times. Are they rowing?'

Janet turned and picked up her coat from a chair, then pushed the fur collar high up round her neck before pulling on her small felt hat. Only then did she answer, and in a low voice, say, 'Not more than usual. But it always seems like a row whenever Dad is talking. You know that.'

'Yes, I know that. But I missed his bellow when they went. By the way, are you getting the tram?'

'No; I'm on my bike.'

'Bike! in this weather?'

'It wasn't snowing when I left; it was quite bright.'

'Well, get yourself off before it comes down thick, or else they'll find you and your bike in a ditch.' Then, laying a hand on her granddaughter's arm, and in a much softened tone, she said, 'Pop in again soon, eh?'

'Yes, Gran, I will. And thanks, many thanks.' And when she bent down and kissed the wrinkled cheek again, the old woman held on tightly to her for a moment.

As Janet cycled down the quiet road of detached houses known as Sweetbanks Gardens, she thought, I'd come back here and live with Gran tomorrow if it wasn't for one thing. But her thoughts did not, even silently, voice the one thing that was preventing her from joining her grandmother in the house in which both she and her grandmother had been born . . .

It was as she neared the gates that she saw Howard's friend, Nicholas Denvers, standing to the side of them. He, too, had a bicycle, but it was leaning against the wall some little distance beyond.

When she dismounted and approached him he greeted her with, 'Hello, Janet.' And she said, 'Hello, Nicholas. Why are you waiting here? Haven't you been up to the house?'

He looked down for a moment before he said, 'Howard asked me to meet him here at twelve. It's now nearly half-past. But . . . but I must see him.'

She stared at him for some seconds before she asked, 'Is it about . . . money?'

His head jerked as he said, 'Yes. Yes. He . . . he promised to give it back as soon as we broke up. And I've got to replace it. I'm in a jam, otherwise I wouldn't.' He now started to gabble. 'It isn't fair of him, you know, Janet. He promised to let me have the money back yesterday. I got it for him as soon as I came home, and I've got to account for it. I don't know what my father will do when he finds out if . . . if I haven't got it. I get my allowance once a quarter and that's all. He's strict about it. And un-fortunately, it isn't only the twenty pounds; I've . . . I've been speculating a bit myself.

Well' — he grinned weakly — 'I put a little on a horse . . .'

'How much did Howard borrow from you?'

'Twenty pounds.'

Her lips parted slightly and she brought her teeth together before opening her bag and, taking out the bundle of notes her grandmother had given her, she handed it to him, saying, 'There, that's what he owes you.'

'Oh. Oh, Janet. Oh, thank you very much. You've no idea what a relief it is.'

He now thrust the notes into his pocket, then said, 'I'm . . . I'm going to miss Howard next term, but' — he grinned again — 'no doubt things will be a little quieter in our section anyway.' And his grin widening, he added, 'And I expect it won't take Daisy long to transfer her affections.'

'Daisy? Who's Daisy?'

'Oh-Oh.' The grin slid off his face. 'Didn't he tell you what the row was all about. I mean . . . well, I mean, why he was dismissed?'

'Not all of it,' she managed to say.

'Well, it was over the fight.'

'Yes, I understand that it was over a fight, but . . . but about what?'

'Well, as I said, over Daisy. She's the

caretaker's daughter, you know, but she was Bainbridge's property. Well, you know what I mean. She was a minx and she was passing notes to both of them, Howard and Bainbridge. But, you know, Bainbridge is senior and . . . well, he had first choice, sort of. It still might have passed off then, but he called Howard a slob upstart. That's when Howard lashed out. That was the third fight he'd had during term and the Head had warned him what would happen next time, and it did.'

Janet drew in a long breath before she asked, 'But why did he want twenty pounds in a hurry?'

'It was to pay a bookmaker. He's a nasty individual and he threatened to go to your father for the money.'

Janet gave the young man a long look before half turning in order to wheel her cycle through the gates; but straightaway she turned back to ask, 'What's happening to Bainbridge? Has he been dismissed?'

'Oh no, because he hadn't previously been in any trouble and he couldn't have let on what the fight was about. Neither of them could.' Then he said something to Janet that was very telling. 'Of course Howard didn't know then that the Head would keep his word, otherwise he might

91

have split, and then Bainbridge would have been for it too. But then, I don't think the Head would have done anything with him because his people are well liked.'

Her gaze was still on him when two flakes of snow dropped on to her face, and as her hand roughly wiped them away it was as if there was a threat in the action, for he backed from her, then turning, he hurried to his bicycle, mounted it, and rode away.

She, too, mounted her bicycle and she rode through the dim avenue of the drive and into the stable yard where, seeing one half of the barn door open, she rode in without dismounting, only to bring the bicycle to a jerking stop as she peered at her sister Alicia through the dim light, and from her to Jackie Winter, the one time boot boy who had, four years ago, taken the place of Bert Long, the stable lad who had left for another position.

Winter was a thick-set young man, twenty now, with wavy hair and a fresh ruddy complexion.

She looked from one to the other, then demanded of her sister, 'What are you doing here?'

'Nothing. I've just been helping to rub down Neptune.'

'It isn't your job to rub down Neptune

or do anything else in the stables. Get indoors.'

The girl shrugged her shoulders and flounced past Janet, saying, 'I'll tell Mam. She doesn't mind me helping with the horses. She knows I like the horses and —'

'Get indoors!' Janet said, at the same time almost throwing her bike against the barn wall before turning to face the young fellow. 'If you find you can't see to the horses yourself,' she said sharply, 'then my father must be approached to get you more help.'

'Look you here! miss,' to which Janet reacted by stepping quickly towards the young fellow and saying, 'You stop encouraging my sister, or else.'

'She doesn't need any encouragement, miss. Well, what I mean is, I don't encourage her. She just keeps coming in and I can't stop her. It's her house.'

'You *can* stop her; the same way you can stop egging on Bella when you know you have no intentions in that quarter. Bella is of a simple nature' — she did not say simple-minded — 'and she has the idea that you're sincere. But you don't know the meaning of it. Now, I'm warning you, let me catch you in here with my sister again and I inform my father.'

'You can inform who the hell you like,

miss, you're not my boss, and you don't rule my life. And while you're warnin' me off, let me warn you. I'm no fool an' don't you forget that, an' don't treat me as such. An' I'll tell you something else while you're on, an' you can go and tell your father this if you like: I consider myself as good as you any day. Now put that in your pipe and smoke it.' And with that, and a thrust of his arm, he almost knocked her on to a bale of straw as he marched past her.

She stood for a moment, her arms crossed over her breasts, her eyes screwed up tight. She was wishing in this moment that she was a man, for she could see herself running after him, pulling him about and thrusting a fist between his eyes.

She had always disliked him; she saw him as a slimy individual. She had actually seen him pawing Bella . . . more than pawing her. She had come in the back way and there they were, in the long grass by the side of the high wall that cut off the kitchen garden. A skip of raspberries lay near them. They hadn't seen her, and she had retreated, scarlet-faced and feeling slightly sick. She hadn't told her mother. She hadn't told anyone, because she knew if any damage had been done to Bella it would show its evidence.

That incident had taken place over a year ago, and now it seemed that Alicia was fascinated with him. That it was a phase, she had no doubt, and that it would soon disappear. Yet what was she talking about? She herself was still in a phase, and it wouldn't disappear. But there was a great difference between her mind and needs and that of her pretty sister, and of what might happen during Alicia's phase.

She unwound her arms, straightened her hat and the collar of her coat as if her attire had been disturbed in some way, and told herself that she must let her mother know, not about Bella and him, but about Alicia and that she must be checked, for if she didn't tell her she might be sorry later on and blame herself.

But then she asked herself why it should fall to her to have to straighten out the tangles of the house. First it was Howard, and now Alicia. What were her mother and her father doing? . . . Yes, what? Too taken up with their personal battles, as usual.

As she entered the hall she saw Sarah Johnson coming down the stairs carrying an empty brass coal scuttle, her face bright. She said, 'Going to have snow for Christmas, miss. Oh, I love snow at Christmas,' and Janet replied, 'Even if it means more buckets of coal upstairs, Sarah?'

'Oh, I don't mind that, miss; it has its compensations: we keep warm, building up the fires. Would you like a hot drink, miss?'

'No, thanks. I had one at Grandmother's.'

'I bet the mistress and the children won't say no when they get in.'

'Oh, they're not back then?'

'No, miss; but the master is.' She took a step towards Janet and, in a whisper now, she said, 'He's up in the attics. I think he's hiding things . . . you know,' she nodded, 'presents and things.'

'Really?' There was a look of genuine surprise on Janet's face, and Sarah, nodding vigorously, said, 'I saw him come in the side door and go up the back stairs. He was carrying a bag and bits and pieces along with it. It promises to be a good Christmas. If it's anything like last year, it'll be all right. We had a lovely party then. D'you remember that, miss?'

'Yes. Yes, I remember, Sarah. By the way, where is Howard?' She could never bring herself to call her brother Master Howard to the servants.

'Oh . . . Master Howard. I think he's along in the billiard-room, miss,' but then, hearing the drawing-room door open, she turned and said, 'Oh, there's Mr Maitland. Where's Master Howard, Mr Maitland?'

Roger Maitland replied, 'He's either in the library or in the billiard-room. Are you cold, Miss Janet? There's a nice fire in the little sitting-room. Perhaps you would like a hot drink?'

'I've just refused Sarah; I won't have one just now. Excuse me.' As she went to pass him he reached out and took her hat and coat from her arm, and she thanked him, then went on down the passage to the library, opened the door, saw that the room was empty, so moved on to the billiard-room, there to see Howard, not at the table but standing by the far window, looking out. He swung round, saying, 'You've got it?'

'Yes, I got it.'

'Oh.' His cheeks went into two balloons and then deflated before he said, 'Thank the Lord for that,' and he held his hand out towards her. She ignored it, saying, 'How much did you say it was?'

'You know what I said; thirty pounds.'

'*You're a liar!* And not only about that, but about everything else. You always have been, and you always will be.'

Backing from her, he hissed, 'What are you shouting about? What d'you mean?'

'I mean, you owed Nicholas twenty, not thirty. And what did you tell Father about the row at school? Oh, I can see you now, your head bowed in modesty, saying it was because . . . and you stammered beautifully, because they had called him a name.' Her voice rose to almost a shout now as she cried, 'Nobody called Dad anything. That fellow was calling *you* an upstart, and not only an upstart but a *slob upstart*. But what was all the row about in the first place? About you carrying on with the caretaker's daughter.'

'How do you know?' he growled. 'That didn't come out in the letter Dad got from the Head.'

'No; that just said you were being expelled because of your rowdy ways. You're a cheap lying coward . . .'

As he jumped towards her he cast a glance towards the door, hissing, 'Shut your mouth! or I'll shut it for you. Who d'you think you are, anyway?'

When he gripped her shoulder, she cried at him, 'Take your hands off me,' and with an instinctive movement she lifted her own hand and brought it in a ringing slap across his face.

The next minute he was shaking her like a rat; but as he lifted a hand to strike her a voice cried at him, 'Don't you dare do that!'

Janet felt herself being wrenched from her brother's grasp and pushed against the side of the billiard-table; and she stood gripping the frame in order to support herself from sinking to the floor, because her head seemed to be spinning. She heard Maitland say something that she couldn't distinguish, but she made out Howard's reply clearly enough, for it was a yell: 'She's a bitch! an interfering bitch, and I'll hit her if I like. It's got nothing to do with you.'

Maitland looked at this youth who, at eighteen, had the height and physique of a fully-fledged man, and his dislike of him came over in his voice as he said, 'That's where you're mistaken. It has a lot to do with me how the people in this house behave themselves and I consider it my business to prevent them from acting like louts.'

'Who are you calling a lout? You want to be careful. You! You've had too much say in this house. Who d'you think you are, anyway? You're nothing but a servant, a skivvy, scum of the earth.'

When the blow caught him on the chin he staggered back and saved himself from falling only by gripping the arm of a sturdy chair. For a moment he remained bent over it; then, with a shake of his head, he straightened up and, his face suffused with rage, he almost sprang on Maitland. But Maitland had the advantage of having his back against the end of the billiard-table; and as he warded off most of the blows, and his own fists worked vigorously, neither of them was aware that by now they had an audience: Sarah and Florence were both shouting. Then above their voices and the sound of the gasping and thuds came a roar of 'God Almighty!' Samuel had entered the room and immediately proceeded to drag his son aside before facing the butler and crying, 'Have you gone mad? What's all this? D'you know what you've done?'

Maitland was gasping as he said, 'Yes, I know what I've done, sir . . . and the consequences. But you can take my notice from now; I can leave instantly.'

Samuel stared at him for a moment before saying, 'Aye, well; but I've got to get to the bottom of this.'

Then looking down the room as Alice entered, still in her outdoor clothes, he said, 'There you are. A nice kettle of fish, this. Look! Clear them out. Go on! Get out!' He waved his hand wildly, shooing out the maids and the two girls who had followed their mother into the room.

Alice was now looking at Maitland as he used a handkerchief to staunch the blood that was running from the side of his mouth. Then she turned her gaze on her son, whose cheek below the right eye was a dark red, and she said, 'In the name of heaven! What brought this on?' And he, holding the side of his face with one hand, said, 'I was talking to her there. We were' — he motioned with his head towards Janet — 'we were arguing and —'

'We weren't arguing. We were fighting, and you were shaking the life out of me.'

'Yes, after you hit me.'

'And why did I hit you? Tell them. Tell them.' She swept her arm wide. 'Speak the truth for once in your life.' She now turned to her father and cried, 'Maitland came in and caught him. Then he called Maitland names, about being a servant and a skivvy and that . . .'

Samuel glanced at Maitland, then lowered his head and turned away; but Alice, addressing her daughter, said, 'Why were you fighting so much? What was it about? It must have been about something serious.'

'Well, you ask him, Mam. See if he'll tell you the truth.'

At this her father turned to Howard, and cried. 'Aye. Aye. Come here! and let's have it, the truth, mind.'

Howard stared at his father, then glanced at his mother before finally at Janet, and now he cried at her, 'I'll get even with you one of these days. You'll see. You'll see.'

His father now had him by the collar of his jacket. 'One more word out of you like that, my lad, and you'll be out of those gates on your own. You understand me? In any case, I've got an ultimatum ready for you, but that'll come later. In the meantime, I want to know the truth.' And he gave a hard jerk on the coat, and his son's head seemed to bounce for a moment; then it appeared as if the boy were beginning to tremble.

'It . . . it was nothing. You know her, Dad, and her tongue,' he said, endeavouring to sound more convincing. 'It was just an argument.'

'I think I can throw light on the reason for this upset, sir.'

Samuel now let loose of his son's coat and, turning to his butler, demanded, 'Well, let's have it.'

'It was over money. He was in debt to the extent of thirty pounds. He asked me to loan it to him, but I refused, for lesser amounts over the years have not been refunded. So now he turns to his sister and she, I'm sure, not having that amount to give him, goes to her grandmother's this morning, and — it is only a guess but I think a sure one — to ask her for the money. Your son, sir, is inclined to gamble.'

'God Almighty!' Samuel now stood almost gaping at his eldest son, who stood with his head bowed. Then he turned to his eldest daughter and asked her, 'Did you ask Gran for the money?'

'Yes. Yes, I did.'

'And she gave you the thirty pounds, just like that?' he snapped his fingers.

'No, Dad, not just like that. But she gave me twenty. I had ten of my own. But that sneaking individual' — she now thrust her forefinger out from her closed fist that had been held tight against her chin — 'he owed Nicholas only twenty. He was standing outside the gate, waiting. I gave it to him.'

'Nicholas Denvers, you mean?' Alice asked.

'Yes, Mam, I mean Nicholas Denvers.'

'Oh, my God! Why! they haven't got one penny to rub against another; they have to scrape to keep him at the school, so I understand. Where would he get twenty pounds?'

'The fact that he was afraid of his father knowing might answer that question, Mam.'

Samuel slowly approached his son, saying, 'For two pins I'd ram this fist right down your throat,' so causing Howard to back swiftly from him. Alice hastened towards them, yelling at her husband, 'Enough! Enough!'

'Aye, it's enough, woman, but it's been called too late; you've protected him all his life. I should have taken the buckle end of me belt to him years ago. But what did I get from you? Oh, he's only a lad. He didn't mean it. It's his boyish ways. But the fact is he's selfish to the core and it's almost too late to knock it out of him; but by God! I'll have a try. He's never thought about anybody but himself and his wants since he could crawl.'

'Oh, you've quickly forgotten why he was dismissed, haven't you? He was standing up for you.'

'He didn't. He wasn't.'

The words had come like pistol shots and they both turned to where Janet was standing holding her head between her hands and about to run from the room; but her father's voice checked her with a loud, 'Stay!' And as if she were a dog answering the trained call, she stopped at the far end of the billiard-table and, taking her hands away from her head, she gripped each side of a pocket and stood waiting for his approach.

'What d'you mean, he didn't?'

Her back to him, she muttered, 'It . . . it was nothing. I mean, it was nothing to do with that.'

'Turn round!'

When she did not move he turned her about, but quite gently, and, putting his hand under her chin, lifted it, saying, 'Come on. Let me have it.'

'No, Dad, no. It's no use keeping at me. It was a slip of the tongue, it meant nothing.'

For a moment he did not speak; then he said, 'He must have done something pretty bad for you to take this line.'

'No, it wasn't bad, nothing really.' She couldn't say to him, He wasn't defending your name when he fought, for that would have been the last thing he would do, because he's always been afraid of you. He's never had a good word for you. No, she couldn't say that because, somehow, inside her was the knowledge that the meaning implied by her words would have gone past the very bones of him and deep into the other man who was chained hard down but nevertheless was there, always arguing from the prison of his better nature.

'Aye well, if you won't, you won't. But I'll get to the bottom of it sometime. You know me. Well, get yourself away, and take your mother, with you,' and he held out a hand to Alice, saying unexpectedly quietly, 'See to her, will you? She's shaking.' Then, back in his normal tone of command, he addressed his son, 'As for you, get upstairs to your room and I'll be up to see you shortly with that ultimatum; but that'll come after I've dealt with you. And don't try to run off 'cos I'd only bring you back; not just bring you back, I'd haul you back. In any case, where would you run to to survive? You couldn't earn your living in a fish and chip shop at the present moment. So, go on, get out! out of me sight.'

His gesture seemed to lift his son from his rigid stand and sent him scurrying along the far side of the billiard-table and out of the door ahead of his mother and Janet.

With the room to themselves now, Samuel turned to Maitland, saying, 'Your lip cut bad?'

'I don't know, it's inside. Likely came up against my teeth.'

'Well, I'd go and have a mouthwash and take a look. But before you go, am I to take you seriously about your notice?'

'Well, sir, I not only struck your son but, I might as well tell you, the way I was feeling I would like to have killed him.'

'All because he alluded to you as a servant. Is that right?'

'No, sir, not simply because he alluded to me as a servant, but the kind of servant. And, moreover, his manner to me during the past year has been anything but civil, because I have refused to loan him . . . he called it a loan . . . any more money.'

'How much did you give him . . . I mean, at a time?'

'Oh, on each of two occasions, just about my week's wages, which I naturally expected to be returned. Prior to that, ten shillings now and again. But it doesn't matter, I can only say, sir, I have no regrets about my attitude towards him.'

'What if he had knocked you flat? He's a strong lad, and apparently, from all accounts from that school, too often ready with his fists.'

'He would not have floored me, sir. You may not know it, but over the years, for part of my day off each week, I have attended a gymnasium in Newcastle. A position such as mine encourages flabbiness; and I did not relish that.'

Samuel's eyes were wide as he said, 'You box?'

'Just a little; among other things, physical culture, weight lifting —'

'My God! You're still a dark horse after

all these years. It surprised me when I knew you went dancing with the Talbots.'

'I don't see why that should have surprised you, sir. The Talbots have been my friends from way back, when I first started in his lordship's service, as I've told you before.'

'Aye, well, dancing or boxing, or being a stiff-necked butler, things have come to a pretty pass. I've got an eldest son who is a cadger and a liar, and a bully into the bargain. By the way, was he really going to hit Janet?'

'Oh yes, sir. From what I could see when I first entered the room, he was almost throttling her. So, no matter what my private feelings were, I would have acted exactly as I did.'

'D'you want to go; leave?'

'No, sir, I don't, but the situation is untenable. Surely you see that yourself?'

'Well, I don't. We've had a domestic upset, but it'll settle down. If you change your mind I'll see he keeps out of your hair. Of course, he'll be more in mine with what I've got to say to him, but that's my responsibility. Go on, see to that mouth of yours. And think it over 'cos, you know, I don't want you to go. You run this house. You bloody well nearly run me when I'm in it.

I'd have to make other arrangements and they wouldn't be to me taste. And I've got enough arranging and re-arranging outside in my business and I don't want any more. So, see what you can do, eh?'

Maitland said nothing to this, not even, 'Yes, sir;' but he left the room, his steps still measured and stately. Samuel made his way to a chair and dropped into it and, leaning forward, he placed his forearms on his knees, his hands dangling between them, and he asked himself: what next? A bit of a family upheaval, he had said. Well, this upheaval was nothing to the one that was looming. And he'd have to do something about it. One way or another he would have to do something about it.

2

Samuel left the house, intending to return to the factory. He did not; instead he made his way down a side street and into the main thoroughfare again, crossed it and there mounted a tramcar, from which he did not alight until it reached the terminus opposite the gas-works at the end of town.

The road stretching ahead of him was bounded by green fields and led to a farm which he could see in the distance. After a while he reached a footpath that skirted the gas-works and led back to Brampton Hill.

He followed the footpath and continued walking beyond the residential area, passing a small copse until he came in sight of a cottage, the garden of which, except for the grass path that led to the front door, was heavily overgrown.

He was about to take out a key and insert it into the lock of the front door when a face appeared at the bay window to the side. It then disappeared and almost immediately the door opened and he was greeted by Geraldine Hallberry, who exclaimed, 'At last! I thought you'd gone abroad.'

'Aye; and I still might at that.' He bent towards her and kissed her on the cheek; then he threw his hat on to a chair and pulled off his coat, saying, 'Where's Henderson?'

'Oh, she's gone into town to send a wire to her sister in Scarborough to say she'll be coming through for the holidays.'

'Holidays? Why, I thought you weren't going to London till the New Year.'

'I've changed my mind,' she said, and preceded him into a small sitting-room the while he was demanding of her back, 'Why the hurry? Why the change?'

She didn't answer him until she had flopped down on to a sofa that was pulled close up to the fire. Then, looking up at him, she said, 'Have you any idea in that head of yours, Sam, what it's like to live on your own? Since poor Peter went three years ago, I've —'

'Oh! Oh!' He now went and stood with his back to the fire, his hands gripped beneath his coat tails. 'It's poor Peter all of a sudden. I've never known you mourn his loss before.'

'Well' — she shrugged her shoulders — 'it would have been rather tactless of me, don't you think? under the circumstances. There was no doubt he was a good companion, if nothing else. There was never a dull moment with Peter. He could be very amusing. You remember that, don't you?'

'Oh aye' — he nodded at her — 'I remember. He could be very amusing. But what I have a clearer memory of is that he was the most barefaced fleecer I've yet come across, for he plucked more feathers off me than I care to think about. And I won't hesitate to put the term blackmailer to him, for that's what he was, and a prime one into the bargain, smooth as silk. But I haven't any doubt now, nor had I then, that if I hadn't paid up he would have exposed me, even going so far as to say I'd raped his wife.'

'Oh! Sam, don't be so coarse. He wouldn't have done any such thing. And he never blackmailed you. You helped him out of situations, that was all.'

'Oh aye, I helped him out of situations that he was falling into every month or so. Look . . .' He went quickly to the couch and, sitting down beside her, he put his arms around her shoulders, saying, 'Why all this, anyway? And you know that whatever the price I had to pay for you, I did it gladly and would do so again.'

'Oh, Sam.' Their lips met: the kiss was long and full, and when it was over, she asked softly, 'How long have you got?'

'An hour or so. I'll have to get back. There's been ructions on in the house this morning: of all things, a stand-up fight between my lad and Maitland.'

'A stand up . . . ? You mean, Maitland struck your boy?'

'Well, I don't know who struck whom first but they both had bloody faces when they were finished, and my lad's got a black eye that'll need a steak on it.'

'But Maitland?'

'Aye, Maitland. And he's a dark horse, you know. Who would think that he could box? His normal behaviour gives the impression it would be an effort for him to bend his back but, according to his own account, he attends the gymnasium in Newcastle every week on his day off. And that's not all. He goes to dances at the Assembly Rooms.'

'Maitland? But he is the most perfect butler, and I know what I'm talking about there. I must have seen dozens in my time, and Maitland is a prize. So polite, so charming, so correct in every way, and so good looking. I hardly noticed him before that first time we came to dinner, when you were so gauche and all fingers and thumbs, and Alice was even worse, frightened out of her wits. Peter and I were the only ones of consequence there, because the Staceys, I understand, had refused, and the Pearmans . . . well, what were they, after all, but builders. I remember chuckling to myself as I imagined his lordship peering down from somewhere near the ceiling, and bristling with indignation. And, you know, the dinners you've given since, other than Peter and me, you've had no-one there of any class.'

The spring to his feet that Samuel took would normally have been made only by an athlete; and now glaring down at her, he said, 'Why, in the name of God! I feel for you the way I do, I just don't know. You are the most tactless and hurtful bitch that God ever made. And I can tell you, I remember that first dinner an' all, and I hated your guts for the way your tongue cut up Vera Pearman. And when all was said and done, Vera came from better stock than you ever did.'

'I doubt it, dear. The only claim she has of stock is that her father happened to be in the government, as was her grandfather, whereas my ancestors go back to the seventeenth century and spilt their blood all over the North in defence of their principles, although one was hanged for his foolhardiness; and that, too, has been something to brag about, depending, of course, on what one is hanged for. Anyway, you are in a very testy mood today, which is very awkward, because I've got to ask you for a little extra help. I'm going to stay with the Carters. They're down in the country and they're having a small gathering for Christmas and I haven't seen them for some long, long time now. I had a letter from her the other day wondering what was happening to me and so I told her, and in reply I received an invitation.'

'This is the first I've heard of it, or the Carters.'

'Well, the letter came only yesterday, dear, and I haven't seen you for three days. And why you haven't heard about the Carters is because I've never bothered with them very much. We are something like fourth cousins removed; and until recently they have behaved like church mice. He's on the Stock Exchange, you know.' She now lifted her face towards him and added, 'The Stock Exchange. You know about the Stock Exchange, dear, don't you?'

'*Stop it!* at once. *Stop it!*'

Her manner suddenly changed, as did her pose: she sat up straight on the couch and said, 'Yes, I will stop it. I will stop being obnoxious and face facts; in fact, talk business. You cannot keep me hanging on like this any longer, Sam. This time last year, you said let just a few more months go by and you would tell her. And you might not believe this, since you think you know all about me, but what you don't know is that I'm not enjoying this situation, and never have. I don't like being a kept woman. It was different altogether while Peter was alive, and no matter what other folks thought of us below their smiles we had keys to every house in the county: as you did, so others thought we were class, we were amusing: we made the difference between a flopped dinner, or a flopped party, and a successful one. But a widow is a different thing. To carry on repartee one needs a partner, especially when the battle of words has the basis of wit. And it is strange, but when one becomes a widow the friends who condole with you most at the funeral are the first to fade away: it seems you can no longer be easily fitted into their own do's and they discover they have so many engagements. Or they hear the whisper that the widow is associating with a . . . commoner. All right, all right!' She held up her hand. 'One imagines that word is the prerogative of Royalty, but no, it's used all down the scale of class, perhaps without the 'er' tacked on the end. I know it's stupid and unfair, but most businessmen come into this category when viewed by those up there.' Her thumb pointed ceilingwards. 'They mightn't have tuppence to their name, they even owe the servants, and the village shops have stopped giving them tick, but nevertheless, they are the gentry.'

'*Gentry!*' He turned and spat into the fire, which vulgarity made her wince. Then glaring at her, he said, 'Leeches, bloodsuckers, swollen-headed nowts.'

'Undoubtedly that's how they look from your angle, Sam, but have you thought of how they look upon you, he who has moved up to their fringe, at least with his house. They call you an upstart.'

'Oh, I'm not surprised at that, Mrs Hallberry.' He stressed the name. 'My son's just been dismissed from his school because he struck out at somebody who called me an upstart. Oh, I know what they think of me, but it doesn't bite. What does bite' — his voice dropped now and he took a step towards her until his leg was pressing against her knee — 'is that you should think the same way . . . I've been good to you, Gerry; in fact, I'm ashamed at times, for I've been a thousand times kinder to you than I have been to Alice. I've given her bairns but not much else. Nor have I given *them* much else either. But you I went overboard for, didn't I?'

'You went overboard for me, Sam, because your wife had told you plainly she wasn't having any more children. In fact, from what you said yourself, you hadn't had . . . what you call, your rights for some years previous to meeting me. So I made up for her lack, didn't I? and I was only too pleased to do so, for I may tell you now, with or without the other benefits, Peter wasn't very good in that line either. I've always had to seek my comfort elsewhere, although I never enjoyed it till I met you. And I want to go on enjoying it, I do, really I do, Sam.'

She held out her hand to him, and after a moment he took it, then sat down beside her again. And now she went on, 'But I want status, Sam. So, you've got to make your mind up, and definitely this time, so that when I return in the New Year I shall know where I stand.'

His voice was quiet as he said, 'And if you find yourself standing in the same place, what then?'

'I shall tell you that when I know what *you* are going to do. In the meantime —'

She put her fingers up to his face and gently stroked his cheek as she said, 'Do you want to come to bed?'

He looked at her hard before he said, 'It's odd, but for the first time I'm going to say no, because once in that bed I wouldn't get up for the rest of the day; I would say to hell with everything and I would wallow in you. But today of all days, I've got to get back.' He now held her face between his hands and, his voice thick, he said, 'What is it about you that gets a man? because it's attracted others afore me, I know that. You're not really beautiful, you know, but you're fascinating; and that body of yours' — one hand now slid down under her breast — 'it's almost non-existent, at least where it should be yelling out your sex; you're as flat as a pancake, back and front. So, what is it?'

She said softly, 'It's my mind.'

'Oh, no; because sometimes I hate that tongue of yours. I'll tell you what it could be though; it could be your smell.'

She reared slightly from him, 'My smell? You mean the scents I wear?'

'No. No. A woman's smell has nothing to do with scent, it's something she gives off, like a bitch on heat.'

She actually pushed him away from her

now, saying, 'If there's one thing I don't like about you, Sam, it's your coarseness, especially when you're dealing with the basic elements of the body.'

'Oh my. Oh my. Well, I'm learning something. You've never objected to them before.'

'That didn't mean that I wasn't irritated by it.'

'Aw, to hell!' He pulled himself up quickly from the couch. 'It's one of those days. Nothing's going right. I'd better be off. By the way I'll get your Christmas Box.' He marched out of the room, picked up his coat from the chair and put it on. Then, thrusting a hand into his pocket, he placed a small parcel on the side table and, looking at her where she was now standing at the sitting-room door, he said, 'Don't bother opening it until the appropriate time; I don't want to be overwhelmed by your thanks.'

'Sam.'

He was thrusting his hat on now, and he turned as she said, 'Will you please . . . ? I hate to ask you, but there'll be travelling expenses and tips and so on. You know how it is.'

'No, I'm damned if I know how it is.' But even so, he put his hand into the pocket of his inner coat and drew out a cheque book; then pushing past her as she stood at the room door, he went to a desk, picked up a pen that was stuck in an inkwell and held it poised over the book for a moment before he said, 'Fifty; that's all.'

'Oh, Sam, Sam, make it two, please. I'm on my beam ends.'

He straightened his back, saying, 'How can you be on your beam ends? You had a hundred pounds at the beginning of the month.'

'I've got to live. And there's the rent of this place and Henderson has to be paid, and she eats like a horse. Please, please, Sam, make it two.'

He bent over the cheque book again, wrote rapidly, tore the leaf out and handed it to her. After she had glanced at it, she said, 'Oh, thank you, thank you, Sam.' Then, throwing her arms around his neck, she kissed him while holding him tightly to her.

'Happy Christmas, darling. And promise me we'll spend next Christmas together, just us two. And don't say, as you've done before, that there are the children, because soon Howard will be nineteen and your clever daughter will be running the library, or all the libraries in the country, if I'm to go by you. And your young ones will be with their mother. As for the boys, they'll probably have already left home for the Army, or Navy, or some such. Anyway, they'll no longer be needing you, but I do, so bring me good news in the New Year, will you?'

She kissed him once more, then went with him to the door. And her last gesture was to rub her finger around his clean-shaven mouth, then pat his lips. After which, without further words, he turned from her to walk down the path.

At the gate he looked back towards the front door, but it was closed.

Within minutes of Samuel leaving the house Alice had gone to her son's room. He was sitting on the edge of the bed, his hand pressed tight against his ear and she said to him, 'What happened?' And he answered, 'What d'you think? He belted me on the ear.'

'Well, what did you expect? You got off lightly after what you've been up to lately. Spoiling your chances of a career and everything. And, I'm asking you now — look at me! — what was the real reason you were thrown out of that school? Janet seemed to know; and it nearly slipped out. Now what was it?'

'It was for fighting.'

'I know that, we all know that. That was the reason the headmaster gave. But why were you fighting? You said it was because somebody had called your dad an upstart, and if it hadn't been for that he would likely have skinned you alive.'

Howard rose from the side of the bed, saying, 'Tell me something I don't know and I'll tell you something that you already know: if he was going to burn in hell I wouldn't say one word to save him, never mind fight, because somebody had called him an upstart. No, it was me who was called a slob upstart, and because I had pinched his fancy piece.'

'*You what!* What are you talking about?'

'The caretaker's daughter, Mam, that's who I'm talking about. She was anybody's piece.'

'My God! boy, it's well he didn't know that or there'd have been murder done.'

'Yes, I know there would have been murder done, because he's a two-faced, big-mouthed nowt, and he's a hypocrite; he'd have murdered me for something he's at himself . . .'

Alice looked hard at her son, who was standing now, his head back as if warding off a blow. His mouth was half agape and his eyes were unblinking.

She asked him quietly now, 'What did you mean by that?'

He brought his head forward, then shook it slightly as he said, 'Nothing, Mam. I was just —'

'You were just about to spill the beans. Well, spill them. What d'you know that you think I don't know?'

'You know, Mam?' There was a tone of surprise in his voice.

'I know lots of things. But I want you to tell me what you know and how you know it.'

'It was Nicholas. He heard his folks talking. It . . . it was about Dad and . . . and that swanky piece, Mrs Hallberry. His father had said that they were . . . well, thick, and that you must be . . .'

'Blind?'

'No, Mam; that you must be, or should be, told.'

She stared at him for some time before she spoke again, and then her words surprised him because what she said was, 'Why do you make friends with weak-kneed individuals like Nicholas Denvers? He's a toady. Surely even you can see that.'

He now moved his shoulders as if he were rocking himself as he said, 'Mam, you've

124

got no idea what it was like there. It was hard to make friends. They looked down their noses at me because I didn't speak right . . . then, I mean, not like I do now, with a . . . well, a twang. You're marked when you first go in. Some of the masters were all right, but there was one I could have done for every day, because he used to split my name and say it in a funny way.' He now struck a pose, pursed his lips and said, " 'Ah, Fair . . . brother." And I'll never forget the day when I'd been there only a short time and he made the class laugh by saying, "Today we'll talk of industry. And we'll begin with the making of clogs, be- cause that is the lowest form of footwear. And we will pass on to the accessories, such as gentlemen's gaiters. Perhaps you can be of assistance in this . . . eh, Fair . . . brother?" If I'd had a knife that day, Mam, I would have thrown it.'

And he was surprised his mother did not remonstrate with him, but said, quite calmly, 'And what else did Nicholas tell you about your father and Mrs Hallberry? Well?'

'Nothing. Just that he goes up to her cot- tage, Brampton Hill way.'

'How long have you known this?'

'Not long.'

'How long?'

'Well, just before we broke up.'

'I see, or else you would have made that known to me before, wouldn't you, in some way or other?'

'No, I don't think so, Mam, because I wouldn't want you to be hurt. You've been different to me; I've only had you to turn to because he's frightened the wits out of me since I was a kid.'

'How is it he hasn't frightened the wits out of all the others? The lads are not afraid of him. They just laugh at him when he bawls.'

'Aye, well, I could never laugh at him, Mam. I could only lie to him from the beginning because I was frightened of him.'

She turned from him now, saying, 'And yes, that's your trouble, Howard. You got into the habit of lying and he knew it.'

As she reached the door, he said, 'What are you going to do, Mam?'

'That's my business, but you'll know soon enough.'

From there she went into her own room and stood for a moment, a hand gripping her throat. Why was she feeling so terrible about it now? Hadn't she known for some time he was at it with someone? And she had guessed who it was, ever since that bitch of a woman had stopped dropping in.

From the beginning she had recognised her as a snipe and out for what she could get . . . yes, what she could get. How much had he been laying out on her over the past two or three years? She would like to know that, for he had tightened the reins on this house all right. And it wasn't because he was short of a penny, even though he'd had to close two shops because they weren't paying; his coffers were still pretty full. Yet she didn't know what he was worth. Years ago he used to talk money to her but that soon stopped. She hadn't minded because he was a good provider; all she had been concerned with had been the bringing up of the family. And there perhaps she had made a mistake.

Mistake or no mistake, the time had come for changes. But what if she were to tackle him and he denied it? The only evidence would be his cheque book. But he kept that under strong lock and key in his business desk in the study, and he carried his keys on him. How many hundreds of times had she seen him passing the key ring from one suit to another when he was changing?

She stood for a further moment as if in deep thought; then she almost scurried from the room and up the side staircase to the attics. There was one room kept for lumber and among it was a box that held an assortment of keys. It had been in this room when they first came here and the desk now in the study had been one of the pieces here, too. So there could be a key here that would fit it. She pulled up the front of her dress and knelt down on her petticoats; then she sorted through at least a dozen small keys ranging in size from half an inch to an inch and a half, all of them small enough to fit the lock of the desk.

In the study, she took the precaution of locking the door; then she went to work, trying one key after another until, on the tenth, having given up hope of any of them fitting, a particular key, as if it had recently been oiled, turned the lock of the first drawer. But before pulling it open, she straightened up and drew in a long breath as a diver might take before plunging into deep water.

When she pulled the drawer open she saw that it was full of red-taped deeds of some kind or other, likely appertaining to the shops. The second drawer was full of bills. She flipped through these; they covered contracts for leather laces, nails, dyes, and such. It was when she opened the third drawer that she again drew in a long breath, and once more she was on her knees, for the drawer held dozens of cheque stubs, together with a small red notebook.

She picked up the notebook first, and the first entry read: "20 February 1893 — loaned John Ashton £200." Then she saw there was a line drawn across to the facing page pointing to: "Repaid December 1894 — no interest." Lower down the page she read: "10 June 1897 — loaned Phillip Coombes £400 @ 2.5% interest."

There was nothing on the opposite page against this entry, but she knew that he had shares in the Coombes Grocery Stores, and so likely he had taken those in place of payment. Below that, and in the same year, it stated that he had loaned Michael Riley £50 without interest. She raised her eyes from the book. Michael Riley had been a leather beater, but he was now manager of the factory. The entry on the opposite page informed her that this debt had not been repaid until four years later. She continued to turn over leaf after leaf of the little book. There were entries of premises bought as well as of further sums loaned. Then she spotted the name of Peter Hallberry, with a date of 1903: "Loaned the sum of £300," followed by another entry dated 1904: "Loaned £300." There was nothing further until an entry dated December 1905: "G — £500."

After that, she began to turn the pages more quickly, to read: "G — £200," and "G — £300," and on a separate page: "£100 monthly to G." to which had been added: "G — £200." On the page dated 1906 were listed other borrowers, but nothing more, except for a blank page headed "G". But there were no more statements.

She closed the book and sat back on her heels and stared at it where it lay across the palm of her hand. She couldn't believe it. All that money when there had been times she'd had to remind him that she needed extra to clothe the children. He had never refused her any, but she'd had to ask for it. And had he ever given her a present that was valued at more than ten pounds? Never! Never in all their married life. Or had he bought her a bunch of flowers, or given her anything, like a little surprise? All he had ever given her was children, and that had been for his own pleasure, not because she had wanted a family. What was she going to do?

As if she had been prodded in the back she almost sprang to her feet, nodding to herself: she knew what she was going to do.

She put the little red notebook in the pocket of her dress, then locked the drawer.

She had no need now to look at the bank statements for proof, she had it all nicely docketed in black and white.

In her room once again she put the book in her handbag then methodically she went about clearing her dressing-table drawers of the odd bits of jewellery and handkerchiefs and such. But as she was about to empty the top drawer of the chest she stopped herself, thinking, No; that can be done later. What she must do now was have a talk with Maitland. Oh, yes, yes, she must talk with Maitland.

The opportunity to have a private talk with Maitland did not arise before Samuel returned home. He came in puffing out his breath and seeing it evaporate in the warmth of the hall. He did not divest himself of his overcoat in his usual brisk way but seemed to take his time. And as Maitland wasn't there to take it from him, he uncharacteristically folded it in two, before placing it over the back of the hall chair, after which he unbuttoned the four buttons on his jacket and the top two of his waistcoat before making for the drawing-room. Here, he merely pushed open the door and looked in; and seeing that the only occupant was Harry, who was sitting on the mat perusing a comic, he asked, 'Where's your mother? D'you know?'

'No, Dad. Well . . . a while ago she came out of the kitchen and went upstairs.'

He closed the door, peered along the broad passage that led to his study and the billiard-room, and telling himself she wasn't likely to be in the latter, he went up the stairs and into their bedroom. And there she was. She was in the act of taking a costume down from the wardrobe and, after glancing towards him, she closed the wardrobe door and laid the costume on the bed. She had her back to him when he said, 'Alice, I've got to talk to you.'

'Oh yes? What would you like to talk about? Something special?'

He gulped before he said, 'Well, I . . . yes, it's something special. It concerns us both. Now look —' He walked up to her. She still had her back to him as he began, 'You know things haven't been right between us for a long time now; you know that, you've got sense.'

She swung round, her elbow catching him in the chest, which caused him to gasp as he stepped back from her; and now she cried at him, 'Before you start telling me what *you* want to talk about, I'm going to get in first for once, and I'm going to start by calling you a dirty, two-faced, rotten bugger. Moreover, you are what everybody says you are, an upstart. You're climbing. But you're on a greasy ladder and I'll see you fall one of these days, my lad.' She now thrust her hand into her pocket and held up the little red book before his eyes. And she had the satisfaction of seeing the colour drain from his ruddy face. And when the only words he was able to bring out were, 'Aye, well,' she repeated on a shout, 'Aye, well! A hundred pounds a month! And cheques for a hundred, two hundred, three hundred, five hundred, to that filthy lousy whore.'

'Now look here, Alice.'

'Don't you take that attitude with me, Samuel Fairbrother, because it's over. Your bullying and your voice and your chest sticking out mean nothing any more. D'you hear? Nothing! And they haven't for many a long year. But I've worked and brought up the family while you've lavished thousands of pounds on that whore. And what have you ever given me? Nothing worth tuppence: a cheap brooch, a string of imitation pearls.'

He stepped back from her, all the while rubbing his hand across the bottom of his face, and after a moment he said, 'Well, what did you expect me to do? You've asked for it.' He now pointed to the bed, saying, 'You've lain there with your back to me for years. And what happened when I last put my hand on your hip? You dug your nails into it like a wild animal. And take your mind back. Aye, take your mind back to when this all started, at least on my part, but long before on yours, when you admitted, and your own words were, because I've always remembered them, "I fell out of love with you," and that was a long time ago, Alice, a long time ago. And I was a man in me prime and I had me needs. And I can tell you now she wasn't the first to satisfy them. But she's been good to me over the years, while you looked on me as something the cat dragged in. There's many a night I felt like a leper lying in that bed. So for what's happened you've only got yourself to blame. And yes, I've kept her well supplied with money because that was her style of living.'

'*Shut up! Shut that big mouth of yours!* Her style of living! She's a slut. Going by this book' — she now wagged it head high — 'you were at it with her before her man died, in fact, you were paying him for her services. He was a ninny, and she was nothing but a high-class whore. Yes, go on, you

134

can grind your teeth. And now I don't know what you were going to say to me but I've got a good idea, and so I'm saying it to you first. Likely you want a separation, but I'm going further, I want a divorce. I've got my evidence.' She now thrust the book down the bodice of her dress, and added, 'And by God! won't I make use of it!'

He didn't speak. He couldn't. This business was nasty but she was playing it his way. She went on, 'Now to my mind that part's settled, but what isn't settled is the children. I'm taking the girls and Howard with me, because you would give him hell if he stayed here. I know you. And we're going to mother's. That's just for a short while, because she won't look forward to having us any more than I look forward to staying there. So, what I immediately mean to do is to find a house . . . a residence, some place suited to my station, one which has been upgraded over the years. You will buy it for me, and it will be in my name alone. You understand? And you will allow me a substantial weekly sum to keep myself and the children. Have I made myself plain, Sam?'

It was a full minute before he answered, 'Yes. Yes, you've made yourself plain enough. Now let me have my say. All right, you may have your divorce, because that's what I was going to put to you in any case, but you've made it easier for me. Oh, much, much easier, because you've taken the initiative. For once in your life, you've had your say. But, let me tell you something: our separation will cause talk in any case, so I don't give a damn, but I'll strike a bargain with you. You tone down all your rancour against her and I'll see that you're well settled for the rest of your life. However, you spit out your venom publicly, as you're doing now, and you'll have to fight for every penny. And I mean that. Your allowance will be a pittance and the girls' as well. No more fancy convent training for them. There's council schools running now, and anyway, you've been against the convent teaching so I don't suppose that'll matter very much. But as for buying you a house et cetera, et cetera, and you'd want it furnished, wouldn't you? well, I'll see you in hell first. It's up to you. You do things quietly and without making that gob of yours go and you can sit pretty till the end of your days. Otherwise . . . well, you've got it. And you know me, don't you Alice? If I say I'm going to do something, I do it and keep to the letter. So it's up to you.'

Neither of them was aware how long they

stood staring at each other; but he made the first move, and when he reached the door he half turned as he said, 'You said you were taking the girls with you. Well, count Janet out until I make other arrangements . . . I'll need a *feminine*,' and he stressed the word, 'presence about the place. She's got a head on her shoulders, and if Maitland decides to go I'll need to leave somebody in charge. I can tell you this much, she'll be better at it than you've been because you've never even learned how to give an order. And another thing before I finish, my allowance to you won't cover your golden-haired boy. He's eighteen and old enough to earn his living. If I had been sensible he would have been doing it for the past two years in the factory. But now I don't want him in my factory or in the shops or anywhere about me. He's on his own. You'd better put it to him, it'll soften the blow. But you'll have your work cut out, because he's a liar and a cheat. I don't know the bottom of it, but from what I gathered from the billiard-room scene, he wasn't dismissed for fighting while defending *my* name. Oh, no, I'm no fool. Anyway, there you have it.' And he made a final gesture with his hand as if wiping something away; then he went out, banging the door behind him before she had time to get her breath and yell at him, 'Your son hates you!'

As he hurried downstairs he buttoned up his waistcoat and coat; then grabbing his overcoat, he flung it on, thrust on his hat, and was about to open the front door when he saw Maitland entering the hall through the green-baized door. He paused and looked towards him as if about to speak; but then he changed his mind and hurried out.

This time he did not take the tram to the cottage but openly hired a cab, and when he alighted from it he almost ran up the path to deliver his joyous news.

The front door was locked. After knocking on it three times he went to the sitting-room window, and when he found the curtains drawn he stood looking at the blank panes. She couldn't have gone yet; she wasn't due to go until tomorrow.

He now went round the side of the cottage to the kitchen door, but before trying it he went to look in the window, but saw it was shuttered from the inside. The shutters were a relic from the old days and had never been taken down. He looked at his watch. It wasn't two hours since he had left here. He looked towards the coal-house, and the outdoor closet, and the two stables and the tack room that had once been cow-byres, all bordering the yard, and he experienced a moment of utter desolation.

He wasn't the man who owned a factory; he wasn't the owner of shops; he hadn't a wife; he hadn't really got a family; and he hadn't a mistress or a lover; at this moment he was standing in a great void and his mind seemed incapable of even asking him why this was happening to him.

Like a man suddenly bereaved, he walked back round the side of the cottage again, down the path, and jumped into the cab.

In the doorway of her mother's bedroom and with her arms stretched across the opening with her palms tightly pressed against the stanchions, Janet stared at her mother sitting facing her on the dressing-table stool: Howard was standing to one side of her, Alicia and the younger children grouped at the other. Her mother had just told them that she was leaving their father, and that the girls and Howard were going to stay with her at Gran's, while she and the boys were to remain here with their father. She could scarcely believe it, yet somewhere in the back of her mind she knew that she had been waiting for just such news. She slept on this corridor and she knew what the others did not know: that there were many nights, in fact, every night for a long time now, when her father slept in another bedroom.

She was glad she was to remain here, yet at the same time she was feeling rejected. Her mother had not said, Do you want to come? or Do you want to stay? and the next words had been ground out, 'Your father is making other arrangements.' And she had asked, 'What other arrangements, Mam?' only to be told, 'You will know soon enough.'

When Fanny began to cry Alice said, 'Now, now; there's nothing to cry about. You're going to Gran's. You like Gran, and she likes you; and anyway, we won't be there long; I'm getting a new house.'

'Where?' Alicia put in quickly. And Alice replied, 'I don't know yet, but I'll pick a nice one.'

Not one of the boys had spoken so far, but now it was Eddie who asked quietly, 'Must all this happen, Mam? Must we be separated?'

'Yes, for the time being. You know, you three boys will soon have finished at school; at least, Eddie and you, James, will. But we won't really be parted. You may come and see me at any time you like.'

Alice now looked at Janet and asked, 'What were you about to say, Janet?'

'Nothing, nothing,' Janet answered as though unmoved by her mother's statements, but then she rushed from the room with the words, 'Until your father makes other arrangements,' yelling louder and louder in her mind.

What did that mean? Oh, she knew what that meant. He had another woman, that's what it meant. But who? Who did they know? And in her mind she pictured one after another the women friends or acquaintances she knew of; then she shook her head at herself: they were all middle-aged, old or fat.

In the hall she stood looking about her as if she were lost. She was feeling cold, right to the heart of her; and so, turning, she hurried up the broad corridor and entered the library.

A fire flickered in the grate, but the room was dark except at the far end, where French doors led into the conservatory. She was just about to sit down by the fire when she thought she heard someone coming along the corridor. It could be one of the maids, but she didn't want anyone to see her like this, because she was about to cry, so she hurried up the room and into the

141

conservatory, but came to a halt when she saw Maitland clipping pieces of greenery from a tubbed bush near the drawing-room door. He stopped what he was doing and glanced in her direction; and after a moment she continued her way slowly between the tall and leafed plants on the slatted racks, until he said, 'What is it, Miss Janet?'

She put her hand out as if for support and gripped one of the racks, and she rubbed her lips together before she said, 'I . . . I can't believe it.'

'What can't you believe?' He laid down the secateurs, 'Are you in trouble?'

'We're all in trouble. She's . . . she's going . . . Mother. They are parting. She's . . . she's taking the girls and Howard and leaving me behind with the boys. She says I've got to stay and run the house because, so she indicated, you'll be leaving . . . will you?' She did not wait for his answer, but went on, almost in a gabble now, 'I . . . I had wanted to start in the library, either that or take a teaching course. Why must they do it? And if Dad was to bring someone, I mean, marry again —' She stopped and hung her head for a moment, then muttered, 'Oh, Maitland; why do these things have to happen?'

'I don't know, miss. The easy answer

most people give is that it's life. But that's really no answer. People do these things through motives that concern themselves, and only themselves, without thinking of the effects on others. But don't worry, at least try not to —' He broke off when the drawing-room door opened and his name was called: 'Maitland. Are you there, Maitland?'

Janet's reaction was to take a step backwards; but Maitland calmly called back as he stepped into the drawing-room, 'Yes, madam? Can I help you?'

Alice was dressed for outdoors and standing with her hands joined, and she moved a step closer to him and said, 'It's happened.'

As if he were at a loss, he said, 'To what are you referring, madam?'

'Oh! Maitland, don't act blind. You knew it was coming. You know everything that goes on in this house and, in fact, how everyone in this house feels.' She paused and her eyes widened as she stared into his face before she said, 'I'm divorcing him, Maitland, and you know why; it's that filthy slut of a Mrs Hallberry. You warned him about them when they first came to dinner; at least, you hinted to him that the fellow might want to borrow money. And did he borrow it? You'd be surprised, or perhaps you wouldn't. Hundreds and hundreds that pair have got out of him, and right up till this very week. It makes me ashamed. And yet, why should I be ashamed? Why should I?'

'No, madam, you need not be ashamed; you've nothing to be ashamed of.'

'Oh, Maitland' — she shook her head — 'drop the madam. For goodness' sake drop the madam. Let's come into the open. You're leaving, aren't you? and . . . and you've understood how things were with me for a long time, haven't you?' Her eyes were still wide, her lips moist, and she repeated softly now, 'Haven't you?'

'Madam, I would say no more because . . . because I don't wish you to be embarrassed. And in my position.'

'Damn your position!' Her voice was still low, but harsh now. 'We've talked, haven't we? many a time, not as butler and mistress but as man and woman, and we're of the same age. Yes, just think of that, we're of the same age. Anyway, you mustn't take another position when you leave; we'll work something out.'

'*Madam!*' His voice was loud, his tone a command. 'I am not leaving this situation. Your husband may not have all the attributes of a so-called gentleman and he may have deceived you, but this is not an un-usual occurrence. It happens in many fami-lies. But his trust in me is such that I would never consider breaking it in any way. And I'm deeply sorry, madam, if you've misun-derstood my attitude when we have hap-pened to talk. I feel all that I have implied in my part of our conversation has been to aid you in your running of the house, such as the reception of guests, and small matters of etiquette. Please, madam' — he put out his hand towards her but did not touch her — 'please, I beg of you, don't be upset. And I consider it an honour that you should . . . well, consider me as a close friend, but —'

'*Shut up!*' It was a whisper, but, like an echo, it had a ring to it, and it reached Janet where she stood one hand gripping a hand-ful of her luxuriant hair as if she meant to pull it out of her head, and her whole body trembling as, with her other hand, she clung for support to the rack, the while she moaned inwardly, Oh! Mam . . . Mam. Oh! dear God. Stop it! Go away! Go away, be-fore you shrivel up with shame. How could you! How could you! Yet at the same time her mind was yelling at her, You've known this all along. And remember the dream, and the end of it that you would never let yourself think about, because it pictured her all dressed up putting her bags on top of his luggage, then flinging her arms around his neck and kissing him . . .

The banging of the door startled her and brought her from the rack. One of them had left the room; it would be her mother, because Maitland would never slam a door like that.

Minutes passed before she sidled along by the racks and looked into the drawing-room, there to see Maitland sitting on a chair, his body bent forward, his head resting on his hands. She couldn't face him.

She turned and, staggering now, made her way back through the conservatory to the library, and then into the hall, there to see Edward closing the front door.

'Where's Mam?' she asked.

He thumbed over his shoulder: 'She's gone to Gran's.' Then letting out a long sigh, he said, 'What d'you think about it?'

When she didn't answer he walked up to her and asked quietly, 'Did you see it coming, Janet?'

'No.'

They walked together down the passage and, as if of one mind, turned into the bil-liard-room; and there, he took up a cue and stabbed aimlessly at a red ball before turning to her, commenting, 'It's going to be hard lines on you: we three will be out of it, at school for most of the time, but you'll be stuck here — with Dad and whoever . . .'

As his voice trailed off her eyes widened just the slightest. There had never seemed much love lost between her and Eddie, but now his concern touched her.

'Mam went out in a blaze,' he said; 'I've never seen her like that. She had told me before she was going to Gran's; but she never spoke after coming out of the drawing-room. It seemed she had been telling Maitland off. But I couldn't imagine her doing that because she's always relied on him. And that's another thing: if he goes you'll have to see to everything yourself. D'you think you can manage it?'

She couldn't say, He's not going, so what she said was, 'I don't know.' Then she spoke in a most un-Janet fashion, at least to his mind, for she said, 'I don't know how I feel, Eddie; it's dreadful. And this is only the beginning. What about you?'

'Oh, I feel the same; it's knocked the wind out of me. And she said divorce, not just separating. That'll cause a scandal. There must be another woman. D'you know who she is?'

'Mrs Hallberry.'

'Good God! Huh! That slinky piece. And she's . . . well, I mean, she's uppish. You know what I mean, not Dad's type at all, I should have said. What if he marries her?'

But he did not wait for Janet's opinion on such an eventuality; he went on, 'Well, we'll be getting out anyway. Jimmy and I are going for the Navy, in any case, so I can tell you, we'll jump this boat if that does happen. Education or no education, I couldn't stand her in the house. Holy snakes! no. And I bet you couldn't either. But then, if it was to happen it would relieve you: you could go in for your library business and go and live with Gran. She would like that; Gran and you have always got on.'

Janet looked at this brother of hers. She had never imagined he was so observant. But then she had never thought of him in any other way but as an irritant.

He asked now, 'Are you going to miss the girls? I know you won't miss Howard; nor shall I, or the others. He should join the Army; that would sort him out. But will you miss the girls?'

She answered truthfully when she said, 'Not as much as I would have missed you and Jimmy and Harry, were you going.'

He smiled at her now, saying, 'It's funny, isn't it? Remember how we used to fight?

You nearly throttled me once, didn't you? more than once, but I know I deserved it, because I was always thinking up things to irritate you. And d'you know why?' He grinned widely at her as he waited for her comment, but when she didn't speak but only made a slight movement with her head, he went on, 'Because I realised you were clever. You had a lot up top and I resented it. But mind you didn't forget to let me know and everybody else that you had a lot up top, did you?'

Leaning against the side of the billiard-table, her body was slightly slumped, for the tenseness had flowed out of her as she had listened to this brother of hers revealing himself in a new light, and her, too.

He now said, 'Aye, well, these things happen, but one's still got to eat. Are you coming for some tea?'

'No, not yet, Eddie. You go along. I'm going up to my room for a while.'

About an hour later she heard her father's voice outside her bedroom door, calling, 'You in there, Janet?' Which made her spring from the bed and pull the skirt of her dress straight, smooth her hair back from her brow, sweep the bunch of long ringlets from her shoulders, then tighten the bow that held them together at the back.

As she unbolted the door she herself called, 'Yes, Dad?'

'You busy?'

'No, Dad.' She opened the door wide and he stepped into the gas-lit room and looked about him as if he had never been in it before. And he had to admit to himself it had been a long, long while since he had seen it.

'You all right?' he said, and she answered, 'Yes. Yes, Dad.'

He now walked to the bed and gripped the brass rail at the foot of it and, for a moment, it seemed that he was about to shake it. Then turning abruptly towards her, he demanded, 'What d'you make of it?'

'That's a silly question to ask. It's really, what d'you make of it? You're the instigator of what's happened.'

'Oh, now, now. Women to the fore again. There's always two sides to everything. You haven't been married yet; you know nothing about it; but you're a young woman on eighteen and you've got enough sense and knowledge to know that bairns just don't come through kissing. And a man needs to be . . . well . . . loved . . . and cosseted a bit, and what's more, not to have his bad points served up to him on a plate every day. I know my bad points. I've always known them, and I've taken pride in some of them, and some of them have got me where I am today, especially in business. Tenacity, bull tenacity is what pays off if you want to survive out there. But that isn't the whole of life. A man needs a woman. And let me tell you, girl, and you remember this, a man needs a woman and something more than just the mother of his children, and that's a fact that I've worked out through experience. Every time you give a woman a child she takes something from you and never gives it back; it goes into that child and you are the loser. The first child comes first with her, and the second child comes first with her, and the third child comes first with her. What have you got of her in the end? Nothing. That's unless a woman is wise and knows the place the children have in her life and makes sure it's not the first place. You know, Janet, it's very odd — in fact, it's bloody odd — that we pity the gentry's bairns who are kept up in attics and left to nurses and that some are not brought down to the drawing-rooms to meet their people until they are able to wipe their noses themselves. In these cases the wife has more time to see to her husband even if it's just playing hostess to his friends, or travelling with him wherever his work takes him. By God, they know a thing or two, the upper class. They ignore their young and the young respect them for it.'

'You ignored your young, Dad.'

'What d'you say?'

'I said, you ignored your young. You never bothered with us, did you? You never played with us. I was just on ten when I came into this house and I can't remember you ever lifting me in your arms or hugging me, or even kissing me good night. Never that, no, never that. It isn't all Mam's fault.'

He opened his mouth twice to speak but no words came. And then he turned about again and once more he was gripping the rail and staring towards where the bracketed globed gas-mantles were making plopping sounds. Then, as if it was a matter of importance and needed attention, he went up the side of the bed, turned the gas jet down low before turning it up quickly again, thus stopping the plopping sound. Then he walked round to the other side of the bed and did the same to the other mantle.

Again he was facing her, and now he said, 'What a man sows so shall he reap: that's what you're saying, isn't it?'

'No, Dad. I'm only pointing out that it isn't all Mam's fault.'

'I never said it was. But at the same time,

and I'm stressing this, I'm not entirely to blame. When I seemed to be neglecting you lot I was building up a business. Oh, aye, it seemed good to start with, but I soon learned that you could have four or five little shops one week then you could find yourself pushing a barrow the next, roughly speaking.'

They stared at each other in silence for some seconds before she asked softly, 'How long does a divorce take, Dad?'

'Oh, I'm not quite sure, but a long time, a year . . . maybe two or more.'

'Really?'

'Oh aye, aye: you can't jump in and out of divorce. There's a lot of dirty washing an' all going to be hung on the line. You see, she's got to prove that I've been a bad lad, and she's got to name names. And she's got the evidence. Oh aye, she has. Your mother's clever: she got the evidence before she opened her mouth.'

At the look of enquiry on her face, he said, 'She must have managed to break open my desk in some way and find a little book in which I kept my private accounts.'

'Mam did that?'

'Aye, your mam did that. But don't blame her; she had her suspicions and she wanted them verified. And she got them verified all right. But God! it's an awful business.' He put his hand flat across his eyes, then drew it slowly down his face before he muttered, 'There's one thing I stuck out for: she wasn't going to have you. She could take her blue-eyed boy with pleasure, but not you. Somehow, in a very strange way, you're like Maitland, you know. You're somebody that I need . . . I feel I can't do without.'

'Oh! Dad.' For the first time in her life she put her arms around his neck and he held her close, saying, 'There, there; it's all right. Everything'll work out all right. You'll see.' He held her from him, his own lids moist as he looked into her tear-stained face, and said, 'I should have added there, with the help of God, shouldn't I?'

Forcing herself to smile back at him, she agreed, 'Yes, Dad, with the help of God, and Maitland.' And at this he actually laughed and, again pulling her to him, he kissed her. Then he hurried out.

For a time she remained still, her eyes on the door; then turning swiftly around, she again threw herself on the bed and, grabbing a pillow towards her, she wept into it, not because her mother had shamed herself offering herself to the butler, and so was leaving the house, but because for the first time her father had, to her knowledge, held her in his arms and kissed her.

3

There had been no party at Christmas; in fact, it had been a sad and worrying time, especially for the staff because, knowing all the circumstances now, they dreaded the thought of having to work under . . . that slinky piece, as the cook referred to Mrs Hallberry. And Mr Maitland had been very reticent, refusing to discuss it or even refer to it, except to remind them that the master's and mistress's business was theirs, and that it was the duty of the staff to refuse to gossip about things that didn't concern them. But as Sarah Johnson pointed out forcibly to him, it *was* their business, it *was* their business who they worked for, happily or unhappily. But, she had added hopefully, 'It may never come off, for she's a skittish piece, that Mrs Hallberry.'

Everyone in the house knew where the master had gone today, for besides a new bowler hat, he was wearing a new overcoat with a fur-trimmed collar, and as well as a walking stick he was carrying black kid gloves. Previously, he had carried a walking stick, but never black kid gloves.

His usual cab driver drove him to the cottage. Just before arriving, Sam had told him that he would want him back within a couple of hours. But after alighting and before he was halfway up the short drive, he noticed that the curtains of the lower windows were still drawn, and so he called over his shoulder, 'Hold your hand a minute . . . wait!' Then, as he had done before, he examined the back door and the window and, as he had also done before, he stood in the yard and looked towards the outhouses. She was due back yesterday; she had said she would be back on the third. It was now the fourth and, what was more, she had left a day earlier than she was supposed to do.

He returned to the cab, was driven home, divested himself of his new apparel, got into a less fashionable suit, coat and hat, then went out again and visited the factory . . .

He did not begin really to worry until he had made three such journeys and felt he was becoming a laughing stock, if not of the cabbie, then of his staff.

The next morning he was up long before the post came, but there was no letter from her, and there was no way he could get in touch with her. All he knew was that she had joined these friends named Carter. He had never thought to ask her for the address.

For the following ten days he existed in a private hell. Then a letter came. He took it upstairs and into the bedroom he had once shared with Alice. And he sat on the dressing-table stool, where she had sat when she explained to her family the coming events.

He had split open the envelope by inserting his forefinger, so leaving a roughly scalloped edge; and now his fingers actually trembled as he withdrew the pink and scented missive. And then he read:

Dearest Sam,

This is going to be a very difficult letter to write. But I can now see its inevitability right from the beginning of our acquaintance. For my part, I know the years are mounting on me: charm needs youth to support it and I know from experience that a lone, middle-aged widow has few doors open to her. Women are tigresses at bottom and they protect the male, especially from . . . widows, more so if they happen to exude that unknown quality, charm. So, dear, dear, Sam, in self-defence, I am protecting myself from the horrors I've described by marrying an old friend who happened to be a guest at the Carters'. He had just retired from abroad where I met him many years ago in India. He had lost his wife about the same time I lost dear Peter. And so after we commiserated with each other we discovered that we had still a lot in common . . . we'd had a great deal in common those many years ago when I was young and he perhaps not so young. He is naturally still not so young, being all of twenty years my senior. But we talk the same language; you know what I mean. So we are being married quietly quite soon and intend spending some time travelling on the continent.

I'm sure when you have time to think calmly you will be happy for me. And, my dear Sam, do believe me when I say, I appreciate your kindness to me over the past years, though I did try to repay you in my own way. I have already contacted the agent of the cottage. Wasn't it a good job you never bought it for me?

Anyway, now there will be no need for you to upset poor Alice, for divorces always leave a nasty taste in the mouth. Don't you think?

Do wish me luck, Sam, as I do you.

My very warm regards to you,
                    Geraldine.

The letter dropped from his fingers and on to the glass tray; then he looked at his reflection in the mirror. The winter's sun was streaming through the window and was touching one half of his face. He saw the man looking at him, one eye bright staring out of his head, the other in deep shadow seemed to be dropping back into his skull. One side of the face was black compared with the other, which had a bleached look. He saw the mouth wide open, the tongue moving in and out, and part of it was coated with a gray-white substance. He saw a deformed face, that of a grotesque idiot, an idiot possessed of a heart that no-one knew about, a heart that a writer of a novelette might describe as breaking. But his heart wasn't just breaking, it was being torn into shreds, not only by lost love, not only by deception, but also by the scorn that had dripped from the ink of that letter. Moreover it had stripped off all his skins: it had ripped off the skin that showed to the world the businessman; then it had ripped off the skin of the man who would stand no nonsense from anybody, whose word was law, in business and the home; finally it had ripped off the skin of the climber who wasn't fitted out for the climb. And what was left? Nothing but a raw creature whose inferiority was known only to himself.

There arose in him a feeling of such rage that nothing but physical force would alleviate, and so, with his fist doubled so tightly it became a bloodless driving pile, he rammed it into the face in the mirror.

As the cry escaped him the blood sprayed the breaking glass, the pink-shaded notepaper, and the front of his face and shirt. And then he was holding the doubled fist tightly to his chest.

He groaned aloud now as he fell forward on to the dressing-table, unaware for the moment that his chin had been pierced by a piece of broken glass.

It was the chambermaid, Florence Furness, who entered the room to do some tidying up, then ran back downstairs, crying, 'Mr Maitland! Mr Maitland!'

Before she had finished gabbling out what she had seen, Maitland was taking the stairs two at a time, Florence following him. And when he reached his master it was to see him sitting before the broken mirror attempting to wrap his bleeding hand in a handkerchief.

'Oh, sir! Oh, sir! Come along.' He put his arm under Samuel's oxters and helped him to his feet, then led him to an easy chair while saying to Florence, 'Bring me a bowl of water and some towels and bandages, quick!' The next thing he did was to tear off his house coat, which was already splattered with blood, and to roll up his sleeve.

The blood was still flowing freely from the knuckles, and when Maitland went to straighten the fingers and place them on a small head pillow he dragged from the bed, Samuel let out a long agonised moan.

When Florence brought the bowl of water and the hand was immersed in it, the water almost instantly turned scarlet; and when Maitland, having gently laid the hand on a pad of towels, went to bandage it, Samuel spoke for the first time: 'Broken, I think,' he muttered.

'Yes, sir, I think it could be. You'll need the doctor.' And turning to Florence again, Maitland ordered, 'Go downstairs quickly and tell whoever's in the yard to go for Doctor Campbell. Tell him it's urgent.'

As Florence was running across the hall towards the green-baized door leading to the kitchen, it opened and almost knocked her backwards and Janet said, 'Oh, I'm sorry, Florence.'

'It's all right, it's all right, miss. I've . . . I've got to get the doctor for your . . . the master.'

'Father? What's the matter?'

'He's . . . he's hurt his hand.'

'Where is he?'

Florence was halfway along the passage towards the main kitchen door and she called back, 'Up in the bedroom. Mr Maitland's there.'

Janet was pulling off her coat as she ran up the stairs and when she entered what had been her parents' bedroom, she stopped for a moment and took in the whole scene: the broken, blood-spattered mirror, the blood-stained towels on the floor; her father's face looking colourless except where a red streak of blood was slowly dripping from his chin, and Maitland, with a pair of scissors, cutting her father's coat and shirt-sleeve right up to the shoulder.

'What on earth's happened? Oh! Dad; what . . . what is it?'

She was about to put her hand out towards her father when Maitland said quickly, 'Hand me one of those towels,' and he pointed backwards. She jumped to the

162

table, picked up a towel and brought it to him.

'Tear it down the middle.'

'What?'

'I said, tear it down the middle.'

On another occasion she might have said, 'Don't speak to me like that, please;' this time, however, she straightaway made an attempt to do as he had bidden her, but the huckerback towel resisted her attempts, and Maitland pulled it from her, gave the hem a twist and tore it straight down. Then, rolling one part up like a cord, he tied it round Samuel's upper arm, saying, 'This will feel a little tight, sir, but it will stop the bleeding.'

'What . . . what happened?' asked Janet.

'Your father slipped and fell against the mirror.'

'Slipped and . . . ?'

Maitland turned towards Janet, and there was something in the look he gave her that checked her further words. Slowly she turned from him and went towards the mirror. Her father had slipped and fallen against it. What a ridiculous thing to say. She stood looking at the broken glass. The sun had caught a piece and was sending a shaft of light up into her face.

Just as she noticed the envelope and the

sheet of pink paper, she heard Maitland's voice saying to Sarah, 'Bring a dustpan and brush and clear up the glass.'

'Dearest Sam.' Part of the third line was blotted out with blood, but a number of lines following were clear and as her eyes scanned the words, she muttered, 'Oh, dear God! Oh Dad!' and within seconds she had taken in the gist of the letter. Immediately she grabbed it, folded it up and, with the envelope, thrust it into the drawer.

A voice behind was saying, 'I'd mind the glass, miss.' It wasn't Sarah but Florence. 'I'll pick the big pieces up, they're too big to go in the dustpan. Sarah has gone for it.'

She turned away from the dressing-table to where her father was now speaking hesitantly to Maitland, saying, 'A drink. Get me a drink.'

'Yes, sir. But . . . but I don't think you should have whisky. I'll bring you a little brandy.' He took a clean towel and wiped his hands; then, glancing at Janet, he said softly, 'Stay with him. I won't be a minute.'

Standing by her father's side, she put her hand on his brow and stroked his hair back, and as she did so he lifted his good hand and pointed across the room, saying, 'Get . . . get rid of them.'

She bent close to him now, saying,

'They're clearing up the glass, Dad. They'll be gone in a minute.'

'There's . . . there's a letter on the . . .'

She touched his cheek now, tapping it gently as she said, 'It's all right. I've put it away.'

His gaze held hers; then he sighed and his head fell back against the upholstered pad of the high-backed chair.

The two maids had left the room by the time Maitland returned, and when he held the glass out, saying, 'Drink this, sir,' Samuel peered at it, questioning, 'Milk?'

'It is well laced, sir. It's the best way to take spirits when you're suffering from shock.'

Shock? Yes, by God! he was suffering from shock; and not only from that letter, but from that terrible, terrible feeling that had overpowered him and caused him to break his hand, because his hand was broken. He knew instinctively that more than one finger had gone, for the pain he was experiencing at the moment and which reached his shoulder was excruciating. But even this pain was nothing to the emotion that had caused it. God Almighty! If she had spoken those words to him instead of writing them he would surely have killed her. Oh, yes, yes, he knew that, he would have murdered her on the spot, because a man could stand only so much humiliation.

He finished the glass of milk in order to get the brandy into him. He was feeling terrible. It was as if he could pass out just like any woman.

He closed his eyes and muttered something, and Maitland said, 'He won't be long, sir. Winter's gone on horseback for him. If he's not in, his assistant is likely to be, and he's a good man, too. The bleeding has eased, sir; only don't try to move your hand in any way.'

Don't try to move your hand, he said. He couldn't move any part of his body if he tried. Was this what you called shock? He had never in his life before wished to be dead, but now he didn't care if it happened at any minute. He wouldn't have believed that any woman could be such a bitch, such a devil. For three years he had kept her living a life she was used to. And what had he got for it? An hour in bed when he could manage to sneak off. And then she wasn't always willing: it wasn't convenient; or she had never indulged in that kind of thing before lunch. What in the name of God! had he seen in her, anyway. She had fascinated him like a snake; and he had loved her. But then, had it been love? Oh aye; don't let him kid himself, it had been love all right. Yet, how could you love anyone who belittled you? And she had belittled him countless times, but in such a subtle way. And at those times when he had come back at her she had been hurt and said she couldn't understand his attitude, because she was merely talking as she always did and as had all those she had mixed with during her lifetime. Aye, that was one of her ways of pointing out the difference between them, insults with a smile, insults with a soft kiss, her lips moving around you like a cat purring and rubbing itself on your bare skin. What was the matter with him? He blinked his eyes, then muttered, 'Doctor?'

'What have you been up to? Drinking first thing in the morning, eh? and falling about, breaking mirrors. Ah, well, let me have a look. But let's have that tourniquet off first.'

Although Dr Campbell gently undid the towel around Sam's arm, and the bandage around the fingers, he could not prevent the groan coming through his clenched teeth.

'Oh my! Oh my! Did the mirror hit you with a sledge-hammer? Dear! Dear!' The doctor now looked up at Maitland, saying, 'Would you come round this side and grip his wrist as tightly as you can for a moment?'

When this was done, the doctor felt the bones of the four fingers. And then he nodded to Maitland to release his hold on Samuel's wrist and to place the hand gently on the towels again. And now straightening up, the doctor said, 'Well, I'm afraid it's hospital for you; you have three fingers needing more attention than I can give them. I would say the knuckles of the first and second fingers are broken, likely splintered. The third one I'm not sure about, but it's all out of line. I'm afraid it's going to be some time before you hold a glass in that hand. Are you still using your carriage?'

When Samuel made no reply but continued to lie back with his eyes closed, Maitland answered, 'Not for some time, sir. The master generally takes the cab. There is a particular one he hires when necessary.'

'Well, you had better order it at once. I'll notify Doctor Crabtree at the hospital. Then if you'll get me a piece of linen to make a sling for his arm, and a piece of wood to which I can strap his hand, we'll be all set and ready to go.'

It was twenty minutes before they were ready to go, and just before the doctor left the room he looked at Samuel and said, 'Well, I'll drop in tomorrow and see how you're faring. They'll have likely fixed it up by then, and you can return home for nursing.'

On the landing, the doctor turned to Maitland, speaking quietly, 'What happened?'

'I really don't know, sir. I was called up by one of the maids and there he was, covered with blood and the mirror broken. It . . . seems clear, and I'm sure it is evident to you, how his fingers came to be in that state.'

'Oh, yes; yes, it is evident enough: he punched the mirror. But why? No idea?'

Maitland looked innocently back into the doctor's eyes, saying, 'No; none whatever, sir. I can't understand it.'

'Oh, well, there's something behind it. Anyway, those fingers are in a bad way. If he ever moves them again he'll be lucky. But then,' — he smiled — 'he doesn't need to work for his living, does he?' a statement rather than a question, one to which Maitland did not respond, but repeated in his mind: He doesn't need to work for his living, does he? Strange how little one man knew of another. If there was anyone who worked for his living, it was that man back there, he who must have been rejected yet again to cause him to fight himself with such vengeance.

Back in the room Sam beckoned Janet. She was sitting on a chair quite close to him, but she stood up and bent towards him to hear him whisper, 'Where is it . . . the letter?'

'In the top drawer of the dressing-table.'

'Take it . . . take it out of there, and . . . and lock it up in your room. Will you do that?'

'Oh, yes, Dad; yes. Don't worry about it. Don't worry about anything any more. It's over. She wasn't worth your spit.'

Sam gazed at this daughter of his, this correct, stiff-necked young lass who had just said that that woman wasn't worth his spit. Sounded odd coming from her. If there had been a smile in him he would have smiled at her or even laughed. But no, he could never see himself laughing again, for, from this day, no matter what he did he'd be conscious of what he really was, what they all said he was: an upstart. But more so he would know himself to be a man without any guts left in him, what his granny used to call boast, and his granda a nowt.

As if he had spoken his thoughts aloud, Janet said, 'You'll come out on top, Dad. You'll show them that you're somebody, her and everybody else, Mam and all. Oh yes, Mam and all. She should never have left you like that.'

God! he was going to cry. Shut up! girl. Shut up. There was a lump in his throat. Dear Jesus, don't let me give way. I couldn't bear that. No, I couldn't bear that.

'Are you ready, sir? Do you think you could stand? By the time we get downstairs and get you wrapped up, the cab will be here. Will you go with your father to the hospital, Miss Janet?'

'Oh, yes, yes. Just let me get my coat; it's over there. I had just come in when I heard.' And she nodded, then ran across the room and put on her coat and hat without bothering to look in the long wardrobe mirror, a most unfeminine action, Maitland remarked to himself.

As he was about to help his master from the chair, Sam looked up at Janet, who was standing to his other side, and said quietly, 'Do that little job for me before you come downstairs, will you?'

She paused a moment before saying, 'Yes, Dad. Yes, I'll do it.'

Maitland showed no interest in this exchange but, linking his arm in Sam's good one, he brought him up from the chair; and although Sam now said, 'I can manage, thank you,' he did not relinquish his hold as he led him from the room.

The moment they were gone Janet dashed to the dressing-table, pulled open the drawer and took out the letter. And now, pushing it back into the envelope, she put it in the pocket of her coat before running out and into her own room; and there she unlocked the 'secret' drawer in her bureau in which she kept her diary. However, before she put the letter into it, she withdrew it from the envelope again, and read it word for word. When she was finished reading, she had the desire to crush it in her hand or to tear it into shreds; but instead she replaced it in the envelope and put it in the drawer. She then pressed a button in the side of the bureau, which caused the door to close and, to a cursory glance, merge itself into the framework.

In the hall, Maitland was helping her father to put one arm into his overcoat, and he was saying, 'Would you like me to come with you, too, sir?' and Sam paused for a moment before answering, 'No. No, thank you. Stay and hold the fort.'

'Don't worry, sir, I'll do that.'

The cab was drawn as near to the front door as was possible and after settling them both in it, Maitland closed the door and, looking up at the cabbie, said, 'Take it easy.'

And the cabbie, looking down at him, answered, 'I'll do that. Leave it to me; I'll do that.'

Not until the cab had disappeared out of sight down the avenue did Maitland close the front door. When he turned, it was to see Florence standing there and when she enquired, 'What d'you make of it, Mr Maitland?' he answered quietly, 'I don't know, Florence; in fact, I could ask you that, because you know more about it than I do. You were the one to find him.'

'Yes. Yes, I was.' She came a step nearer to him. 'And I can tell you this, Mr Maitland, I'm sure it was about the letter he got. He'd been waiting for a letter for days. You were upstairs when the postman came and he sorted through them before I could get me hands on them. And there it was, on the dressing-table.'

'What was on the dressing-table?'

'The letter. I caught a glimpse of it just before Miss Janet pushed it into the top drawer. That's where it likely is now.'

He looked at her hard before he said, 'If that's where you think it is, Florence, then I should leave it there, and not attempt to open the drawer or enquire into the matter further. You understand me?'

Her head twitched as though it were saying, 'Huh!' But then she said, 'Yes, Mr Maitland, I understand you,' and she turned to go about her duties.

Maitland made his way to his room, and there he took off his coat and shirt. He poured cold water into a basin and washed his hands and arms up to the elbow. After donning a clean shirt and a different coat, he picked up the soiled one and went to the kitchen and spoke to the cook, saying, 'Would you see that this coat goes to the cleaners, Cook, please?'

'If it's not much, I'll have it sponged down, Mr Maitland.'

'That's very kind of you, but I doubt if you'll get the stains off.'

'By the way, how is the master?'

'He's not in a very good shape at the moment, Cook. I would say he is suffering as much from shock as from broken knuckles. He must have fallen very heavily against the mirror.'

Mrs Wilding stared straight at the butler as she said, 'Yes, I'm sure he must. He would fall heavy an' all, being a big man.'

'You're quite right, Cook, you're quite right. Anyway, we'll keep things going as usual until he returns.'

'Yes, yes.' She was still staring at him as she added, 'It's a funny house without the mistress though, isn't it, Mr Maitland?'

He returned her look and seemed to consider her question before he answered, 'Yes, Cook, as you say, it's a funny house without the mistress. But we must all remember that Miss Janet has, in a way, taken over. And as young as she is, she has a very sensible head on her shoulders. The master thinks she'll be equal to it.'

'Yes. Yes, Mr Maitland, I'm sure she will . . . in time. But still, I thought she was going in for a career in the library?'

'Oh, she still may do that, but it's all in the future. We'll have to wait and see, won't we, Cook? Wait and see.'

'Yes, Mr Maitland, that's all we can do. That's all anybody can ever do, is wait and see.'

'You're right, Cook, you're right.'

On this the cook returned to her work at the table and Maitland left the room.

He straightaway mounted the stairs and went into his master's bedroom. And there, he went to the dressing-table, opened it, and when he found it entirely empty, he nodded as he said to himself, She did what he asked. But I would dearly like to see what that bitch wrote that would make a man smash his fist against a mirror with such force as to shatter it and break his own bones. Then he nodded to himself as he thought, Perhaps time will prove that, after all, it was a light price to pay for a life that would have been one of torture . . . refined torture that only women such as she are capable of handing out.

PART THREE

1911

The Inheritance

1

Sam, emerging from his bedroom, was just in time to see his daughter, as she made for the head of the stairs, pulling on a pair of grey cotton gloves, and he said, 'My! My! How d'you expect your boss to take to that rig-out? Grey from top to bottom; not even a black band on.'

'Dad, the library staff must be the only people in the town who are still dressed in black. The King's dead; Long live the new King. And anyway, if they can hold Ascot during their mourning, my attire pales into insignificance.'

'Ah, but lass' — he was wagging his finger at her the while he smiled — 'don't forget, they were all in black, dead black.'

'A lot of hypocrites.' She went down the stairs before him and stopped at the foot to fasten the last button of her glove.

'Still, lass, you must remember you are a public servant. What d'you think the town will say?'

'What can they say? The only thing in black outside the library is the soot in the chimneys.'

He laughed at that. 'Well, I'll look forward to hearing about your reception by Mr Stanford . . . oh, and not only Mr Stanford, but also Miss Rose Stillwater. My goodness! What will Miss Rose Stillwater say?'

'Dad, listen to me for a moment. I've got something to say to you and it's serious, and it must be said soon. I'll talk with you later about it, and you must listen.'

'Serious?' The smile slid from his face. 'Something to do with your mother?'

'No; not really.'

'What d'you mean by "not really"? Come on, out with it.'

'I can't, Dad, there's not time now; I'll be late, and that' — she smiled now — 'added to my appearance, anything could happen should I step in through those portals one minute after the half hour.'

During their short discourse Maitland had come across the hall and was now holding the front door open, and as they went to pass him he said, 'May I expect you in to dinner, sir?'

'No, not the day, Maitland. I'll have it later on, around six.'

'Very well, sir. It's a lovely day.' He addressed this last remark to Janet, and she answered, 'Yes, isn't it? Oh, by the way, tell Cook that I, too, will have my dinner this evening, and just to make me a snack for around twelve.'

'Very good, miss. Very good.'

'Look, if you're worried about being late, get in the car with me, and Talbot will have you there in five minutes.'

'Talbot won't have me there in five minutes, or fifty. And anyway, I prefer my bicycle; it's safer, and I don't get held up in traffic.' She smiled at her father now; then turned to look back towards Maitland, and when she smiled at him, he returned the smile; then he watched her as she walked swiftly towards the yard, her long skirt swaying from her narrow hips, her shoulders straight, her head held high. Then the sound of Talbot swinging the handle to start the car brought his eyes back to his master sitting waiting. And he remained waiting without further recognition from his master, until the car disappeared down the drive.

He did not immediately close the door but stood waiting until Janet and the bicycle came abreast of him; but, like her father, she made no sign and nor did he. Since she had taken up her new position in the library, each morning he had stood at this door and watched her ride away, and had to resist raising his hand to wave as one would to someone held dear.

After closing the door he made his way to the kitchen. Mrs Wilding was sitting at the table finishing her last cup of tea. She did not get to her feet but looked towards him and said, 'They're both off then?'

'Yes. Yes, they're both off. And the master won't need his main meal until this evening; and Miss Janet too; but she'll have a snack at midday.'

'Huh! Shortly it won't be any use cooking a decent meal at all.'

'Well, there's always us, Cook.' He smiled at her and she jerked her head and said, 'Yes, and we're going down an' all, aren't we? Who would have thought Jane, at her age, thirty-five, going off to get married. I wouldn't care if she was bettering herself; but I told her, yes, I told her she would find out before long that she had laid her egg in the wrong nest, him a bricklayer and never knowing if he's in work or not two days at a time. Only Master Harry left, and I'd like to bet as soon as he's finished in that school, it'll only be a month or so before he'll be off to join the other two, in the Navy.'

'Oh, I doubt it. No, I don't think Master Harry is inclined towards deep water. As he said himself, he only bathes under protest.'

'Did he say that?' The cook was grinning now.

'Yes; and that was only last week when I put your very words to him: did he think he would be joining his brothers? I asked him, and that's what he said. His limit was a paddle, he said, and a bucket and spade.'

'He didn't!'

'He did. He's a very quiet boy, but he's got a sense of humour. By the way' — his voice dropped and he leaned towards her — 'how is Bella really faring?'

The cook's voice was equally low as she answered, 'You wouldn't believe it; you wouldn't believe the change in that girl since Jane went. It's as if she had got some sense into her head at last. And she scurries round and nothing is too much trouble.'

'Oh well then, Cook, I think if Bella is making such a good effort then she should have the position of kitchen maid, and a young girl could be engaged for the scullery.'

'Yes. Yes, I agree with you there. When I tell her she'll be over the moon.'

'Well, do that. Yes, do that, Cook.' And he was about to turn away, but talk of the recently observed growing changes in the two young people in the house brought a further observation from Cook: 'It's a quiet house these days, don't you think? After the explosion three years ago it's sort of settled into . . . well, middle-ageness is the only way I can put it. D'you hear anything of the other house, Mr Maitland?'

'No. No, Cook. Except that I think they are all doing well.'

'I've never seen the mistress for — oh, what is it? — two and a half years. Not since that time she came barging back and there was a shindy. Did you ever get to the bottom of it, Mr Maitland?'

'No, Cook; no, I didn't.' With a small smile on his lips he added: 'That was one shindy I couldn't work out.'

She laughed and he laughed; then he left the kitchen to go to the dining-room, where he gathered up the silver and took it into a small room along the corridor. He made three journeys before taking off his coat and donning a green linen apron and settling down to the cleaning task that would normally have been allotted to the footman, or some lesser menial. But he enjoyed cleaning the silver: every piece was like an old friend. He actually enjoyed all his duties in this house now; but for how much longer he could go on enjoying them he did not know. He was approaching forty years old, and although he knew he looked nothing like his age, that he could still pass for middle-thirties or less, nevertheless he was nearing forty, and his manhood was not only making demands on him now, but had been for many a long year. Was he to go on denying it permanent release? Mike Talbot's niece was thirty. She had been waiting some years now for him to say the word. He had really given her no encouragement other than to dance with her when accompanying Mike and Kate and her to a ball in the Assembly Rooms, or to the dance at the Queen's Hotel, but she always happened to be at the lodge when he would call in on his way back from Newcastle on his day off.

He had always assiduously practiced routine in his work in the house, and so it was natural for him also to practice it on his day off: two hours in a gym in town, followed by a lunch; in the afternoon a walk round the galleries or a seat in the picture-house, followed by high tea in the hotel . . . owned by his friend.

There was a club in Newcastle frequented by men of his standing. It was run by a retired butler, but he had not considered joining it: at some time or other he would have been encouraged to relate the happenings of this house to outsiders. And how would he have described them, anyway? A mediocre family; not working class, no; middle class? yes, but without status, except in the business world. The master? What was he? An arrogant man through his ignorance because he was, you could say, a widely *unread* man, except for his perusal of the newspapers. And this consisted mostly of the headlines whilst he was eating his breakfast, and remarks addressed to whomever would be at the table with him, or to himself, more often to himself. Remarks such as, 'They are calling themselves the Labour Party now. What next? I'm all for bettering everybody, but what will that result in? Strikes. Oh aye, strikes.' And on other occasions, 'Look at this front page. It's that Malthus man, mentioned again, and some fellow named Mendel, both long dead. Why bring them up again, and their theories? D'you know anything about this Mendel fella, Maitland?' He recalled he had been forced to smile as he had tried to explain through his own small amount of knowledge garnered from his reading of newspaper articles about Mendel and his theories, from which had recently been developed The Chromosome Theory. And for his thanks on that particular morning his master had pulled him up, saying, 'Aye, well; wipe that smile off your face. You've got time to sit on your backside and delve into stuff like that. You might be knowledgeable, aye, but you've got me to thank for it, because you've got the run of the library in there.'

At the time such remarks would make him want to retaliate, but gradually he had got used to them. However he still found it a tongue-biting business and was prevented from making tart rejoinders only by realising that his position in this house was similar to that of a split personality: on the one hand he was butler-cum-housekeeper, on the other, a mentor to his master. It was knowing what he had himself obtained or supplemented by making use of the library and which he had, in subtle ways, passed on to this man who owned the library but who hadn't taken from its shelves half a dozen books during the ten years he had been in the house, which made him angry. Nevertheless, his daughter had made up for him, because she was in the literary position she held today because of that library, for it had taken her far beyond her convent training. And he had to admit to himself that it was her search for knowledge since she was a child that had furthered his own desire to know, for he wanted to meet her on her own level all the way.

Lately, a new tangent to the situation had revealed itself: his master would become irritated should his daughter use him as he himself was likely to do and draw him into conversation as he waited on breakfast- or dinner-table.

He recalled the morning when the non-intellectual subject of dress had come up. The master, eating while he talked, said, 'What are they at now? Getting us out of black frockcoats and top hats and putting us into what they call lounge suits. Aye, well, that's all right for them that's got time to lounge about. And look here, they've got an advert for a silk hat. Well, we know what happens to those, don't we?' He had nodded towards his daughter. 'A shower of rain and it's finished. Who's behind this change of style, I wonder? The same blokes who are dressing the soldiers in khaki? Did you ever see anything like them? Dull as dish water. Why?'

It was at that stage that he had put in, 'There is some deep thinking behind that, sir. I imagine men would prefer to wear a dull uniform and remain alive, to a bright red one that would act as a target. In my opinion, it is something that should have been put into action, so to speak, a long time ago. It might have saved many lives.'

It was when Miss Janet had said, 'I agree with you, Maitland, you're perfectly right,' that her father had rounded on him, saying, 'Look! Maitland. When I want your opinion I'll ask for it.' And with that he had risen from the table and had stumped out of the room.

It was that same morning that she, too, rose from the table, came round to the sideboard and put her hand on his arm. It was the first time he could recall having personal contact with her. And her voice had been soft as she said, 'Please don't take any notice. He doesn't mean it. His hand is still painful, and being unable to bend the first two fingers, he has trouble handling his knife. I know that's really no excuse and it sounds so ungrateful after what you do for him, and for this house. But he's not ungrateful, believe me. He thinks the world of you. I don't know what he would do if you ever left him.' She had paused before she had added, 'I don't know what any of us would do, Maitland, if you were to leave.'

It was then he had turned and looked at her, not only looked but gazed at her. Then they had gazed at each other, and there was the same look in her eyes that had been in her mother's the day she had offered herself to him. And whereas, if he'd had a mind, he could have accepted the mother, he could do nothing about her daughter. He was forty years old and she but twenty, and she was the daughter of his master, and more and more that man was depending on her as he had never seemed to depend upon his wife.

He could imagine what would happen should he make his feelings known to him: I would like to propose marriage to your daughter, sir. Yes, I know I am forty years old but I have long held a deep affection for her, and I hope that she has an affection, however slight, for me.

The likely response to this rang loud in his head.

'What! You, and my lass? By God! you've got a nerve. Then you always have had. But this is the limit. *Out!* Talk about taking advantage. Look how I've treated you over the years. You've had a free hand running this house . . . *Out!* No . . . shut up! I don't want to hear another bloody word out of that smarmy mouth of yours . . . *Out!*'

Yes, that's how it would be; in fact, that would be putting it mildly. There was little doubt that, in that case and if his right hand had not been damaged, he would have instinctively used it on him.

His thinking was interrupted by Sarah pushing open the door and saying quickly, 'You're wanted on the telephone, Mr Maitland. It's . . . it's Miss Janet.'

He pulled off his apron, rolled down his sleeves and picked up his coat, which he put on as he made his way to the hall and there he picked up the receiver now lying on the small hall table and said, 'Yes, Miss Janet?'

'Maitland.' Her voice was a whisper; and after a pause, he again said, 'Yes, Miss Janet? Is anything wrong?'

Her voice still a whisper, she said, 'Will you go to the stables, or look around and see if Miss Alicia is about? The convent has just informed Mother that she hasn't turned up for school. Both Jessie and Fanny said that she was with them in the corridor and that's all they know . . . And Maitland?'

'Yes, Miss Janet.'

'Will . . . and will you see if Winter is there?'

'*Winter?*'

'Yes. Yes, Winter. He has been seen talking to her. Oh the fact is, I've warned him, and her, too, that if it didn't stop I would inform Father. And I really would have done tonight. I don't altogether blame him . . . Winter. Anyway I'm greatly worried, and so is Mother. Will you phone me back?'

'Definitely. Definitely. I'll go straight out now.'

He hung up the receiver, and surprised both Sarah and Florence as he ran through the hall towards the kitchen door. The cook, too, jerked her head in surprise to see Mr Maitland, who had been known to hurry, but never to run, dashing down her kitchen and out of the back door as if he were partaking in a race.

Mike Talbot, who was lying flat on his back under the end of the car, jerked his head up, saying, 'Yes, Roger? What is it?

'Is Winter about?'

'Aye, yes.' Talbot pulled himself to his feet. 'What's up?'

'Where is he? D'you know?'

'Is he not in the stables?'

'No, the doors are wide.'

'Well, he'll be in the barn. If not, he'll be down helping Tom in the greenhouses. There's not so much to do up this end these days. Anyway, what's the matter?'

Maitland paused before he said, 'Miss Alicia; she hasn't turned up for school.'

'Oh that. Good God! Don't tell me that's starting again. But look, Roger, it isn't all his fault. Oh, I know what kind of a fellow he is, but she's doing the running like a bitch on heat. I thought Miss Janet had put a stop to her gallop, and his an' all, just before the mother left here. Aye, as far back as that. Now go careful with him, Roger, because he's pretty handy with his paws.'

At this, Maitland made no comment, but he hurried away, not running now, down through the ornamental gardens, to the walled kitchen garden.

It was in the vinery, running along one wall, that he saw Winter, and there was no conversational lead up when he confronted him, for he said straightaway, 'Have you seen anything of Miss Alicia this morning, Winter?'

Jackie Winter, who was now twenty-four years old and heavily built, though in no way flabby, brought his head forward as he said, 'What did you say?'

'This is no time for parleying; you heard what I said, and you know what I mean. God help you if the master has to deal with you.'

'Huh! I'll tell you something, *Mr* Maitland. *God help you and the master* if you as much as lift your hand towards me. Just attempt it. Now, I'll answer your question. No, I haven't seen her this mornin' nor yesterday mornin', nor the mornin' afore that. But I'll tell you what she did say the last time I saw her. She said, "Will you marry me?" Aye, she said that . . . I warned you, didn't I? Just a little further with that hand

and you'll find yourself flat on your back. And I'll tell you something more she said, that her dear dad would come round and put me in a good position, and if he didn't her mother would. We could get married on the quiet, she said. D'you know what she is? She's a menace, she's a slut. Poor dizzy Bella inside there' — he jerked his head backwards — 'is worth ten of her, an' the lot of them, your Miss-Nose-in-the-Air Janet, an' all . . . Oh her! I could tell you what I'd do to her —'

The next thing to jerk was his body, as one fist caught him full in the stomach and the other on the side of his chin. As he went sprawling backwards he grabbed at the thick branch of the vine, only to miss it and tumble among some boxes and lie there for some seconds with utter astonishment showing on his face. Then he was scrambling to his feet, and going at Maitland, his fists flailing, and finding their target here and there, while his own face was pummelled. Then suddenly he stepped back gasping and, one hand held tightly around his waist, he said, 'Dark horse, aren't you? Clever bugger,' before he turned and lumbered down the vinery to where his jacket was lying over the bench. And as he picked it up he said, 'I'll get me own back, so look out,' then turned about and went through the far doorway.

Rubbing his knuckles, Maitland leaned back against a rack for support. He was shaking visibly. For years he had practiced self-defence: he had lifted weights, he had punched at a bag; he had worked his legs out on a treadmill machine; he had skipped; he had done physical exercises, and not all in the gym, but some exercises, such as bending and stretching, he had done in his room first thing in the morning before taking a cold wash down. But never, not once, had he exchanged such blows with another man. The encounters he'd had those years ago with Howard were mere taps compared with this bout.

He now stretched his fingers. They were paining. Exercise was one thing, but when it came to the real thing, it hurt. Two of his knuckles were skinned but they weren't bleeding; nor was his face, although it was sore.

He stayed in the vinery a further five minutes; but before he reached the gardens he was met by Mike Talbot, saying, 'You all right? You've knocked his face about. How, in the name of God! did you manage that?'

Maitland could feel his jaw stiffening now, and he moved it from side to side and made a sound in his throat that could have been a laugh as he said, 'I suppose with the help of God and a lot of weekly practice.'

'Oh aye, your gym. Well, if you managed to get the better of him you should go in the ring. He's a tough, that 'un. He's gone up into the loft to get his things. I think he means to be off.'

'Well, I hope he doesn't change his mind before the master comes in, for, from what he let drop, there's trouble ahead, I think.'

'With the lass?'

'Yes, Mike, with the lass.'

'Well, that's not surprising. Mind, I've wondered for many a year how Bella's escaped. But of late she seems to have got a bit of sense an' stopped running after him. As for Miss Alicia, Roger, I hope there's not that kind of trouble with her. Aye, I do.'

'Well, we'll only have to wait and see, Mike.'

'Your jaw hurting?'

'Yes; and I think I have a tooth loose.'

Mike looked more closely at him, saying, 'Well, there's no sign of blood.'

'No, perhaps not, but I can feel something wobbling,' and he ran his tongue round the inside of his jaw; then smiled and said, 'I didn't realise that I'd always wanted to hit that fellow.'

'You are a funny bloke, Roger. I've said it again and again, I can't make you out. Well, it's your day off the morrow, so why not rest up in the lodge? I think you've had enough physical culture for this week. What d'you say?'

'We'll see . . .'

From the yard they went their separate ways, and once again Maitland was speaking to Janet: 'She's not here, Miss Janet. I spoke to the person in question and it seems that it's some days since he last saw her; but from what I understand transpired between them, there could be' — he paused — 'consequences.'

'Oh, no! Maitland. Oh, no!'

'When your father comes in you must talk to him and put him in the picture.'

There was silence on the other end of the phone.

Samuel came in earlier than usual, marching in demanding immediately, 'Is she here?'

'No, sir; she's not here.'

'My God! Where's the young bitch got to? She stormed in — the wife — into the office at the factory putting the blame on me: If it hadn't been for my exploits, she said, they'd all be together under one roof, and protected. Then she tells me I should have sacked Winter years ago. What d'you make of it? Where's Janet?'

'She isn't in yet, sir. It isn't yet twelve.'

He stamped towards the drawing-room, saying, ' 'Tisn't yet twelve? She shouldn't be in that bloody library; this is her place, seeing to the house; never here when she's wanted. Get me a drink, will you?'

A few minutes later, the drink in his hand, he was sitting in the drawing-room and, his voice a little calmer, he looked up at Maitland, saying, 'What's it all about anyway? Can you throw light on it?'

'Yes, sir. I think there has been an association between Miss Alicia and the man Winter. I had an altercation with him a short while ago —'

Samuel was peering up at him now. 'Altercation? Your chin's all bruised. D'you mean to say you had a fight?'

'One and the same thing, sir.'

'You fought Winter?'

'Yes, I fought Winter.'

'And you've lived to tell the tale?'

'Sir, I have, over the years, as I think I have told you before, kept myself in trim, at least by taking vigorous exercise once a week, and at other times whenever the opportunity has presented itself.'

'How did he come off?'

'Much worse than me, sir. He is what you call a basher; he has no idea of self-defence. What he and his kind do is strike out blindly. Of course, they put a lot of weight behind it.'

'You never cease to amaze me, man. You know that? But tell me, why did you hit him? Come on, come on. Don't turn away, the fire can take care of itself. Why did you hit him?'

'Because of something that he implied, sir. And what I gathered from his words is that Miss Alicia has run away because she is afraid. She is afraid because . . . because after having gone to him and asked him to marry her, he must have rejected her offer —'

'*She what?*'

'You wanted to know why I hit him, sir. I am telling you, and using his own words, she asked him to marry her.'

Samuel was on his feet, the remains of the whisky swirling round in the bottom of the glass. For a moment it was as if he was going to throw it from him with the same force as he had used with his fist three years previously.

'*The bloody little hussy!*' The glass was

banged down on the table. 'Lowering herself. Wait till I —'

'Sir, your daughter has run away because she must be fearful of the consequences of that association. If this is the case, the damage is done, and harsh words and similar treatment are not going to help her, or the situation. I think what we have to do now is to find out where she has gone.'

Samuel dropped back into his chair, growling, 'Under me bloody nose.' Then, glancing up at Maitland again, he said, 'Had you any inkling of this? I mean, them meeting?'

'No, sir; until just recently, when I think Miss Janet must have been aware of the situation in some way.'

'Janet? Then why the hell didn't she tell me?'

'I . . . I think she intended to, sir, and . . . Oh! Here she is now.' He went quickly towards the drawing-room door and opened it, and stood looking hard at Janet as if to warn her of the onslaught that awaited her.

She hadn't to wait any time because her father's words hit her straightaway, saying, 'Why the hell! girl, did you let this happen? Why couldn't you have put me wise? Have you heard anything more? Have you seen your mother?'

She did not answer him, but slowly un-buttoned her coat, and when she took it off, Maitland was waiting for it. Next, she drew the hat pin from the back of her flat-brimmed straw hat, and this, too, he took from her. And then her father yelled, 'Come on! open your mouth, woman. You're ready with your tongue every other minute of the day. Tell me what you know.'

'Not until you stop yelling.' She turned now and looked at Maitland and said, 'Do you think I could have a drink, please?'

'Yes, miss, what would you like?'

'I'll have a sherry.'

'God in heaven!' Samuel was now beating his forehead with the palm of his hand. 'We're in a bloody play. We're all acting. "I'll have a sherry," she says, and the butler goes and gets her one. But, go on, go on, I can wait. Get the woman a drink.'

As Maitland went from the room Janet looked at her father and said quietly, 'One of these days you'll yell too much. You'll go too far, and he'll have had enough and walk out.'

'Look' — he twisted round in his chair — 'what's the matter with you, woman? We're not talking about my manner, or Maitland's reaction to it, we're talking about a sixteen-year-old girl who's run off.

And why has she run off? Because, from what I understand so far, the odd-job man in the yard, Winter, has refused to marry her . . . Oh, yes; now that surprises you. It must have surprised his lordship, because he's lowered himself to use his fists on the fella. Did you notice his chin and his knuckles? Oh, I always look at people's knuckles. It's a failing of mine now because it tells me what people do with their hands, bloody fools like me —'

'Dad, stop it! please.' She lowered her head and leaned forward. 'I've . . . I've had an awful morning with Mother. Mister Stanford let me off and I went to the house. She was nearly demented. And, of course, Howard and I had a go at it, too. Mother, as usual, took his part. And there we were, the three of us, like cats and dogs at each other's throats, while all the time the main issue was, where was Alicia and what had happened to her? Well, I dashed out of the house. I rode round the park, Brampton Hill, everywhere I imagined she might be walking or hiding. Anyway, we've got to face up to the fact, Dad, the reason why she ran away is because she's afraid.'

'Aye, and she has a damn good right to be, by all accounts, because Maitland said that swab had said she had come and asked him to marry her. What d'you think of that? Aye; you can widen your eyes.'

Maitland was entering the room carrying a small tray on which there was a glass of sherry. And when he handed it to Janet she said, 'Thank you,' and straightaway put the glass to her lips and took much more than a sip of it before she said, 'Should we inform the police?'

'God damn! no. Police? Well, let's wait and see if she turns up this afternoon,' and looking towards Maitland, he added, 'Don't you think that's the best plan?'

'I'm at a loss, sir, to give an answer to that. But to my mind I think all possible steps should be taken to find her, and as soon as possible.'

'And that includes the police, you mean?'

'I still don't know. When you begin with the police you're inviting the newspapers.'

'Aye, well, that's what I'm getting at. So, we'll leave it for an hour or so. Who knows, by this time she may have returned to her mother. Oh, that woman! There's no reason' — he was looking at Maitland again — 'or what you would call logic, in anything that she says. Her saying that if we hadn't broken up this would never have happened, when all the time she was responsible for any breaking up that was done.'

'Dad!'

'Yes, yes; I know I keep on. But with one thing and another, girl, it's enough to drive a man round the bend.' He rose to his feet and started to march out of the room, but stopped as he came opposite where Janet was sitting and, stabbing his finger at her, he admonished her, 'You're drinking too much of that stuff. You want to put a stop to it.'

She could say nothing, only stare at him. But after the door had closed on him she turned to Maitland, saying, 'Drink too much of that stuff. I have one glass a day, don't I? one glass a day. And that's in the evening with my dinner. Does he ever see himself, I wonder? Two double whiskies in the evening when he's at home, sometimes three, one after the other, and I'm drinking too much with one glass of sherry. You know, this is the kind of thing, Maitland, that would make people, as Cook says, take to the bottle.'

Maitland smiled tenderly at her while saying, 'Oh, I shouldn't worry. I don't think there's any fear of that.'

'You never know, you never know.' She now drained her glass and as she handed it to him she said, 'Wherever she is, she must be in a state. We never got on very well, she and I. I suppose because she was so pretty . . . jealousy.' She smiled weakly, and he shook his head vigorously, saying, 'To my mind there was no need for jealousy. None whatever.'

'Oh' — she made a small flapping movement with her hand — 'you would lie to the Pope of Rome, Maitland;' then somewhat sadly, she added, 'It's odd. I dislike my elder brother and I've never got on with my sister, who is next to me. And according to the book, this position in the family usually forms a close trio against others, as if they were intruders. But there, I love Eddie and James, odd' — she smiled now — 'particularly Eddie, because you remember, it didn't stop at a battle of words with him, did it? It was fists, feet and anything goes. Yet we are the best of friends now. I had a letter from him yesterday. He's enjoying his training, and still has a year to go at Greenwich. His only regret is he doesn't see as much of James as he had thought he would. He says that if they had been twins they could have asked to be together. And there's Harry. Could you find a nicer boy than Harry?' and straightaway Maitland said, 'I agree with you. He's a charming young man, is Master Harry. And Miss Jessie, and

Miss Fanny have their own share of charm, don't you think?'

'Yes. Yes, especially Jessie' — She smiled — 'She's the only one in the family who takes after me, at least in character . . .'

They both turned and looked down the room. Having tapped the door, Florence entered and almost tripped towards them. Then, glancing from one to the other, she said, 'Can I have a word?'

It was Janet who said, 'Yes. Yes, of course, Florence. What is it?'

'Well, miss, I was passing the foot of the attic stairs and I thought I heard what sounded like a cough. It was just a small noise. And then there was a slight squeaking sound as if someone was walking quietly across the boards in the lumber-room. You know, it's the only room up there that hasn't got any lino. Then I thought it might be the cat; but then again I'd just left her downstairs sleeping in the basket chair in the conservatory.'

Janet and Maitland exchanged quick glances and, without a word, they hurried from the room, Florence following. On the attic landing Maitland pushed open the lumber-room door. It was a long room running more than half the length of the house, and it was packed with oddments of all kinds, from a three-legged chest of drawers to an assortment of children's toys. The room was dimly lit, but straightaway Janet made out the huddled form crouched on an old mattress in the far corner.

Quickly now, she made her way towards her sister, and there, dropping down on to the mattress beside her, she pulled her into her arms. No word was spoken between them. And with the girl clinging to her, Janet looked up at Maitland, saying, 'Go and tell him, and try to calm him down . . . you know.' And to Florence, she said, 'Would you make some tea, Florence, please?'

'Yes, miss. Oh yes, miss.'

They were alone together now; but when she tried to raise Alicia's head from her shoulder and her arms from about her waist, the girl still clung to her; and she continued to mutter: 'Janet. Janet.'

'It's all right. Come on. Come on. Sit up, and tell me what's happened.'

It was some seconds before Alicia eased herself away, but her shoulders were hunched and her head down, and what she said now was, 'I'm . . . I'm frightened, Janet.'

'Yes, I know, dear.'

'I'm . . . I'm going to have a baby, Janet.'

'Yes. Yes, I know that, too, dear.'

The pretty tear-stained face was now turned towards her and the voice came as a whisper, saying, 'They'll kill me, both Mam and Dad.'

'No, they won't. But you should have told Mam.'

The girl now shook her head as if in desperation, saying, 'I couldn't. I couldn't. And anyway, all she thinks of is Howard, and getting him settled. It's always Howard, Howard.' The tears now were raining down her face. 'He's in and out of jobs and she gives him money. But not me. It was the same when we were here, it was always Howard, Howard. I hate him.'

'You're not the only one.'

Alicia sniffed, blew her nose, then said, 'Yes, I know, you've never liked him . . .' Then the tone changing, she said, 'What am I going to do, Janet?'

'You're going home. And don't worry, I'll talk to Mam.'

'Couldn't . . . couldn't I stay here, if Dad would have me?'

'Yes, you could stay here, and Dad would have you, but Mam wouldn't hear of it, would she? Look, come on, get up, straighten your hair.' And Janet stroked the hair back from her sister's wet brow, and lifted the ringlets gently over her shoulders. Then she asked a question, but diffidently, 'When is . . . I mean, how long have . . . have you been in this condition?'

'Three months . . . more.'

Janet's voice was loud as she repeated, 'Three months, over?' Then, biting on her lip and in a lower voice, she said, 'Why on earth have you kept it to yourself . . . and how?'

Alicia's head remained bowed, and she muttered, 'Well, being plump . . . you know how I like sweet things, you all know, and when I've felt ill, Mam has put it down to eating. And I've been wearing corsets . . . Oh Janet, what am I going to do?'

'Come on; it'll all work out. Come on downstairs.'

'No. No, he'll go for me.'

'Well, what did you expect?' This was the old Janet that Alicia remembered, and she was about to turn away when Janet's voice softened as she said, 'You must have known, and anyway, I warned you all those years ago. You must have known he was up to no good. He was a swine.'

'No, he wasn't, Janet, no, no! Roughish, but he was all right; and' — her head drooped — 'and . . . and I love him. I've loved him for years and years. He . . . he

209

was to me what Maitland is to you. Well, what I mean is, he was good to be with. And . . . and we laughed and he . . . he said he loved me, and . . .'

Janet took a step back from her sister: it was as if she had been shot; and mentally, she had been, for her sister had said, *'what Maitland is to you'*. Her heart was racing; but she checked it by telling herself: she only meant that I have chatted to him since I was a child. Yes, because nobody else would imagine . . . No. No; of course not. She put out her hand now and said, 'Come on;' then added, 'things will be all right. But you've got to make up your mind that that business is over. That man was only making use of you. You know that now, don't you?'

There was no acknowledgement from Alicia; but what she had to do now was to put her arm around her sister's shoulder and ease her towards the door, then press her down the attic stairs to the landing. From there she took her hand and together they went down the main staircase and into the drawing-room, where their father was sitting in the chair, looking as if he hadn't moved out of it since coming into the house.

Samuel did not look at his daughter as

she was being drawn up the room towards him, but kept his gaze directed to the side as if he were interested in something on the carpet. And not until she stood about three feet away from him did he turn his head towards her and say, 'Well! What have you got to say for yourself? And all the trouble you've caused. You should be at school, shouldn't you?'

He knew it was a silly thing to say. They all knew that, but it seemed to dampen the fiery atmosphere; apparently though, only for a moment, for, being Samuel, his voice had to rise and demand again, 'What have you got to say for yourself?'

'Nothing.'

Janet looked at her sister in surprise. This was a different attitude from that which Alicia had shown only a few minutes earlier up in the attic. It was defiant, it was like meeting like, for behind that soft exterior there was a lot of her father in Alicia.

'Nothing? Oh, well, if you've got nothing to say then everything's all right. You can go back to school this afternoon, can't you? and everything is as yesterday, and the day afore that. No scandal, no bairn in the offing. Bairn, did I say? A bastard!'

'Dad! Please!'

'You shut up!' He rounded on Janet. ' 'Cos

that's what it's going to be, isn't it? That's the word for it, because even if I would allow it, that dirty, low-down, stinking scum refused to marry her.' His head now swung and he was glaring into the startled face of his daughter. 'Yes. Yes, that surprises you, doesn't it? You went and proposed to him, didn't you?'

In the silence that followed Maitland turned away and moved towards the window and stood looking out, while Janet sat with her head bowed; but not Alicia. After the revelation — which had astounded her, for she couldn't understand how her father had come to know this, unless Jackie himself had told him, but she couldn't imagine that — the next minute the room rang with her voice, almost as loud as his, crying, 'I hate you! D'you hear? I hate you!' And at this she swung about and ran from the room, with Janet after her.

Maitland had turned from the window and Samuel, looking at him, and in a voice that trembled, said, 'Go and ring her mother and tell her to come and fetch her.'

2

'Don't talk, Gran; it tires you.'

'If I don't talk now, lass, I won't get the chance again. So listen to what I'm saying. Put your head down.'

Janet leant from her chair and put her face close to the pale wrinkled cheek and listened to the muttered words.

'There'll be a lot of surprises when I'm gone; and mind, you mustn't give in in any way, or let anyone attempt to take back what is yours. You understand?'

'No, Gran,' Janet whispered back at her. 'But don't worry yourself about wills or anything else; you're going to be here for a long time yet telling me what to do.'

Mrs Mason turned her head impatiently on the pillow before saying, 'Look, lass; I've always thought you had a head on your shoulders, not only thought, but know you have. Now, you know as well as I do that time's running out. It's been running out for me these last three years; in fact, I thought me number was up then. It was just after the split when those two pig-headed individuals you have for parents went their own ways. Well, no matter what your dad seems to be, he is a fair man, and he bought that house for Alice, furnished it and allowed her twice as much as anybody else would have on a legal separation; and,' she now gasped for more breath before she went on, 'what has she done with it? Kept that great big lazy good-for-nothing in comfort. He's never been able to keep down a job. He's in the shipping office now, but how long will that last? You know, she was so worried last year that she even asked me to suggest to your dad that he give him a chance and take him on as a traveller, or have him in the office or some such. But after what I said to her she didn't broach the subject again because that lad's called your dad worse than muck in this town; and the different tales he's spread around of why he was thrown out, you wouldn't believe. But people are getting to know him.'

When Mrs Mason again gasped for breath Janet said, 'Stop nattering, will you, and go to sleep.'

'I'm not going to sleep, lass; I'll be sleeping enough very shortly. But you know, there's two things I'd like to have seen before I went. I would like to have been here to see me great-grandchild. She's a stupid, empty-headed little madam, but nevertheless she's going to be a mother shortly. But just think, lass, what a mother. Bringing an illegitimate child into the world, not only into the world, but into this family! Well, as I said, that's one of the things I'd like to see, illegitimate or not, my great-grandchild. The other is, lass, I'd like to see you happily married. That Mr Stanford seemed a nice fellow, the little I saw of him when I used to pop into the library. Oh, he's a bit older than you, I know, but what does that matter? And you've told me yourself you've been on a number of jaunts with him.'

'Oh! Gran. Gran. Together with those other maiden ladies. One of them has had her eyes on him for years but she's older than him, another thinks the sun shines out of him, and then Phoebe Carrington. Well, you know her, and among the staff she's just like a cheap bound book, and she's scared to death of him. So, yes, dear Mrs Mason, I've been out with Mr Stanford a number of times but, the sad truth is, never alone.'

'Aye, well, you can laugh, but he didn't ask them to a ball in Newcastle, did he?'

'No, he didn't, Gran, but if he had asked either of the first two, in fact, any of them, he would have had a partner straightaway. Now will you stop talking? Anyway, I'm going to the kitchen to say goodbye to Mam. She is talking to the three witches.'

'Aye, well, witches they may be in your eyes, but they've been good to me, and I'm being good to them. They'll have no complaint.'

As Janet backed towards the door her grandmother lifted her hand, saying, 'One more thing. Come here.'

Sighing, Janet returned to the bed, saying, 'They'll blame me for tiring you.'

'You know what I've often thought?'

'No, Mrs Mason, I don't know what you've often thought.'

'Well, it's just this: it's a pity that Maitland is double your age, because servant or no servant, he's a gentleman, and one with something up top. And you've always liked him, in fact you were a disgrace when you were a bit of a lass, trailing round after him. Oh, you can blush red; I know what I know. 'Tisn't done, is it? 'Tisn't done. But have you asked yourself why a presentable fellow like he is has stayed there all these years if he hadn't something in the back of his mind?'

'*Gran! Please. For goodness' sake!* And don't you dare, d'you hear me? — don't you dare say anything like that to Mam.'

'Oh, no, I wouldn't do that, lass. Here.'

'No, Gran. Go to sleep.'

'Bend over. What you mightn't know, my dear, is your mother would have had him like a shot. You should have been here the day she left your dad. Her tirade, you know, wasn't so much against your dad, but against *him,* and what she called the harm he had done to that house. Now think on it, and ask yourself why he stays on as he does, 'cos a man like him could get a job like a shot in any of the county houses, and with somebody different from your dad over him. Aye yes; somebody different from him.'

'Good night, Gran. I'll be in in the morning. And you know something? You see more than is good for you, and you imagine the rest. Maitland, indeed!' And on this she actually flounced out of the room, if any walking of hers could be called flouncing.

Her mother was coming out of the kitchen and she said, 'You're off then?'

'Yes.' She fastened the belt of her coat, then pulled on her gloves before she said further, 'She's very tired.'

'She's more than very tired; she's on her last legs, and has been for some time, and I'm worn out running backwards and forwards. What with one thing or another I don't know where I am, and I haven't any help, at least at my end.'

Janet could not bite back the words: 'Well, whose fault is that?'

'Now, now! Don't you start again, I've got enough on my plate. You've got it easy.'

'Easy? I'm working all day in the library, Mam, and in the evenings, at least on four nights a week, I keep Dad company.'

'Oh, that'll be very hard.'

'Yes, it is, when I want to go out and have a game of tennis or go to a meeting, or enjoy myself like working women of my type do.'

'Really! Really! Working women.' Alice's mocking tone changed. 'You don't know when you're well off, girl. And let me tell you, you are only in the position you are because things happened when they did, and as they did. You're playing the lady of the manor now, aren't you, with your henchman?'

'Mother! I'm warning you: you be careful what you're saying, because if you don't, I'll say things that I'll be sorry for, but for you more so. Do you understand what I mean?'

Alice did not reprimand her daughter; she made no reply at all, but her face flushed red and she turned from Janet and made her way towards her mother's bedroom.

Janet went out and took her bicycle from where it was resting against the creeper-covered wall, but instead of mounting it, she pushed it down the drive and on to the road.

With her foot on a pedal, she paused and wondered how it was that everybody seemed to surmise her connection with Maitland to be something deeper than it was. At least, in its outward show, because their hands hardly ever touched.

Everybody seemed to suspect something in her connection with or attitude towards Maitland. No; there was one exception: her father. He saw her still as a young girl and Maitland as a middle-aged man, but more so he saw him as a servant, in spite of his knowledge that the man was superior in many ways to himself.

The situation, she thought, was like the story of the boy who was hanged for stealing the apple: he had admitted taking it from the tree but someone had stolen it from him, he had never eaten it. Well, in a way, Maitland and she were being hanged. They hadn't even reached up and taken the apple because both of them were well aware of the danger. And there was another danger outside, someone she might succumb to in desperation at the thought of empty years ahead, for Mr Stanford had shown more than once the light in which he held her. And who was the danger in Maitland's life? She didn't really know, because he did not discuss his off-duty time with her. She knew only that he did gymnastics, and went dancing and, lately, had taken up tennis. Well, you could do gymnastics by yourself, but you couldn't dance or play tennis by yourself. With the latter you could have a male partner but not with the former.

Still, these things were of no account at the moment: her gran was dying and she would miss her. Oh, how she would miss her. Because her gran was a mother to her as her own mother had never been.

Even the necessary facts concerning the beginning of womanhood had been gently explained to her by Sister Monica, an unmarried woman, and a nun, and it had been she herself who had passed her knowledge on to Alicia, then to Jessie, and to Fanny.

She had once complained to her gran about her mother's reluctance in this matter, and her gran had said, 'Well, some women find it difficult to talk to their daughters; and anyway, nature takes care of itself; it really tells you everything you want to know.'

Did it? Did it tell you the result of what

would happen if you gave way to the rising tide of desire that swamped you from the age of fourteen onwards? Did it explain itself to Alicia, when she gave herself to that beastly fellow, that the result would be the swelling of her abdomen, until she now saw herself as something ugly, and cried over the fact? Oh, let her get home . . .

She had hardly got in the door when Maitland said, 'The master would like to see you, Miss Janet. He's in the study.'

Without verbally acknowledging this, she gave him a look which he translated as a battle warning; naturally, he did not take it that her opponent was to be himself. And he certainly did not realise how near she had been to crying at him, Do you know what they are saying about us? So, in my opinion, if they are saying it, why don't you do something to confirm it? I've always hated to be blamed for anything I haven't done.

She did not immediately enter the study, but drew in some deep breaths and told herself to calm down. Her father was not at his desk but sitting to the side of the fire in the high-backed leather chair, and the first thing he said to her was, 'How is she?'

'Not good,' she answered.

'D'you think she knows how bad she is?'

'Of course she does.' Her voice had an impatient note in it. 'She's known, as she said, for the past three years.'

'I know that, miss. And take the edge off that tongue of yours. What I'm meaning is, does she know her time is drawing nigh?'

And so it was more softly that she answered, 'Yes, Dad; she knows it, and speaks of it. And I found it unbearable to listen to her.'

'But she's still clear-headed?'

'Oh, she'll be clear-headed until her last breath goes.' She sat down opposite him, saying, 'You wanted to see me?'

'Yes, you'll never guess what the latest is.'

'Not until you tell me.'

'I've had a visit from a Catholic priest, the one that sees to the convent.'

'The Catholic priest? What does he want?'

'Only the adoption of my daughter's coming child.' He stressed the last words.

'Adoption? That's the first I've heard of it.'

'And me. But not your mother apparently; she's got it all planned out. So has dear Alicia.'

'Really?'

'Yes, really. But by all accounts it wasn't his idea, it was your mother's. And, you know, right from the beginning she wasn't for any of them going to the convent school, was she? But what does she do? She goes and sees him. The Church, I understand, has an adoption society, and they've got people waiting for bairns. Of course, they're not short of them. Two of my lasses in the factory had bairns last month. They worked up till they nearly had them on the factory floor. They'll be starting back next week again, 'cos I said I would keep their jobs open. They were good workers. And you know something? I had to laugh at one. She's twenty-eight or so, and she said to me, "I'm an unlucky sod, mister." Those were her very words. "I came from across the water to avoid it. I thought, not for me; I want a different life. And what happens? I go to a hop, and I was taken on the hop, and not by an Englishman either, but by a smooth-tongued Irish bugger. Ever heard anything as daft as that, mister?" '

As her father laughed at the memory Janet was forced to smile, but only for a moment, for now she said, 'What did you say to him, the priest?'

'Well, you would think I'd have gone for him, wouldn't you? But he was a civil enough bloke and he said that my wife was for it, and the mother of the child was for it, but that he felt it was only right to know if I was for it. Now I thought that was fair, don't you? And I told him in plain but simple unvarnished language what I thought; which meant, no way would I stand for that. She'd got herself into this trouble so she had to face up to it. And as it's my grandchild, bastard or not, it wasn't going to be adopted by anybody, working, middle, or upper class. He had already stressed that he could arrange for it to be adopted by a good middle-class family, oh aye, seeing who we were, et cetera. Well, I gave him a message to take back to my wife. It was polite, oh yes, it was polite, but definite. But I'll tell you something more, and this is worrying me more than the talk of adoption. He kept on about Jessie, what a good child she was, and that he knew of course that she was of a different denomination, but he was so pleased that she liked coming into the chapel. And did I realise what a beautiful singing voice she had? I had to admit that I didn't. Oh, yes, he said, and she often joined in the chants . . . Now I wonder if your mother knows this and I should be the one to go and ask her. But then you know what happens. We had our arguments when

we were living together here, but not half
as many as we've had since we've been
parted. It seems that every time I go to that
house my son is either coming in or going
out. And at that particular time of day it
points to the fact that he's out of work
again. And I, being tactful, as you know I
can be, bring it straight up. And naturally
she defends him to the hilt. D'you know,
Janet, I look back and I see that that boy
has acted like the tinder that sets the explo-
sives off. All right, I know, I know I was
carrying on, but it wasn't always like that;
I started to carry on with someone outside
because I had no-one to carry on with on
the inside, if you follow me.'

'Yes, I follow you, Dad.'

'Well, I can say this to you: even before
I went off the rails, so to speak — that's
the term they give it, isn't it? — Well, even
before that it was Howard needed this and
Howard needed that, and Howard wasn't
getting enough pocket money. And I
shouldn't speak to Howard the way I did.
And Howard didn't lie. Oh, that used to
get up my nose, Howard didn't lie. That
boy couldn't tell the truth if he had been
actually paid for it. And you know something? I learned the other day what he's up
to. Oh, friends are always forthcoming when

they want to pass on bad news. They're not so quick with the congratulations on good ones, like when I've pulled off another deal. But you know Teresa Phillips?'

'Yes. Yes, I know Teresa Phillips. I should do, for they've been your friends for years.'

'Well, her mam and dad have. But I had to push her off at one time, and she hasn't forgotten it. She was man-mad before she got herself engaged recently. She even made eyes at Maitland. Oh, she would have had him like a shot. Well, that will tell you what some women, so called "ladies", will do, when they'll pick up a servant —'

Her words and voice, raw and harsh, shocked him as she cried, 'Why must you always refer to Maitland as a servant? I should have thought by this time you would have considered him a friend, because that's what he's been to you, and to this house. All right, you pay him wages, but the Prime Minister gets wages, the Archbishop gets wages. It doesn't say that because you pay a man wages that he is a servant, or that because he opens a door for you and attends to your every wish that he is a servant. I mean, men like Maitland. Why! he looks after you and this house like nobody else would do. Why he stayed here, God alone knows.'

He was gazing open-mouthed at her, and he said, 'Well, well! Defending the servant class now, are you?'

'I am not defending any servant class. And there's no servant class as such now; we're not in the last century. And you of all people should not keep yammering on about the servant class. What were your father and your grandfather? Low . . . working-class cobblers.'

He too, was on his feet now, crying, 'Shut your mouth! girl.'

'I'll not shut my mouth. I get tired of listening to you and your bigotry. Who d'you mix with, anyway, at your so-called club? Greengrocers, drapers, fishmongers. Oh, it's a wonder you associate with them; fishmongers. Well, let me tell you, Dad, that Maitland and such as he could buy you and your lot at one end of the street and sell you at the other, where intelligence matters,' and she finished her tirade by bouncing her head at him. She had almost reached the door when his yell nearly lifted her from the floor. But she didn't stop, and the crashing of the door drowned his words.

He remained standing and staring at the door for some time. When he sat down he put his hands on his knees and bent forward as if he were listening to someone speaking.

Then suddenly flopping back in the chair he declared aloud, 'No! No! But what if . . . No! No! No!' He would not stand for that. By God! No! 'But what if . . . ?'

He was on his feet now. There was going to be no 'if' about it. He was half-way across the room to the door when again he stopped. He couldn't send him packing without giving a reason . . . And could he do without him?

For a moment his mind presented him with a clear picture of the house without Maitland. And what if, she being the temperament she was and now turned twenty, she decided to leave, too, and he could do nothing to stop her? What then? Again he had a flashing picture of what this house would be like. He'd be alone with two maids and a cook, people he hardly ever saw except in passing, because Harry, if he passed his last exam, would be for the university at Oxford and would move out of his life as if he had never been in it. The Navy had claimed his other two sons, and his wife had claimed his other three daughters. He'd have to think. Oh, aye, dear God! he'd have to put his thinking cap on here.

He went back to his seat and sat down; but although he sat for some long time, his thinking cap seemed not to have settled on his head. What came to mind was Willie Phillips's oft-used saying about status quo, leave things as they are.

3

Mrs Mason died on the second of January, 1911 and Samuel's grandchild, a boy, was born on the fifth, and he and everyone in the family, particularly the child's mother, wished it too had been born dead.

When Janet first looked down on the child, set apart in a cot in the spare bedroom, she put her hands to her head and closed her eyes against the sight of the little face which seemed to be grimacing in pain, for every part of its head was misshapen, from the top of its quite bald head down to where the chin should have been. Also, she had been informed, it had one leg shorter than the other, and it was twisted. And further, Dr Campbell had told Alice that its heart was very weak and for that, all should be thankful.

When Alicia had first caught sight of her son she had screamed, and her screaming had continued until she was given a sedative.

These things happened, the doctor had said to Alice. There was no accounting for them. But the nurse said: tight corsets, that's what could have caused it. She had seen cases like this before. And, of course, it stood to reason that if you pulled your steel-laced stays in against what was inside you, it would get all twisted up.

Alice had stood in the kitchen wringing her hands and making the same remark her husband was wont to make: 'What next!' she said. 'What next! There's a curse on us.' And she had pointed at Janet as if she were responsible, saying, 'Nothing has gone right since we went to that house. Ten years or more in Sweetbanks Gardens and life was good. Everybody was happy. But from the day we stepped into that house things began to happen. And I look back and ask myself, why? And the answer is, there are evil genies about.'

Once again Janet had to bite on her tongue. Maitland was the evil genie. There was that saying, Hell hath no fury like a woman scorned. Yet her mother was a sensible woman. Why should she still be feeling like this?

Then there was her father. What were his feelings? Suppressed rage, indignation and shame as if he had been personally insulted. His rage was directed against Winter. He had even made enquiries with regard to the fellow's whereabouts. It would seem that he had left the town, which was as well, or murder could have been done.

But the poor child relieved them all of anxiety when, on the day Mrs Mason was buried, he too died. And Alice was able to leave the house and attend her mother's funeral with a feeling of relief on both counts. For she had convinced herself that she had become worn out not only with the trailing backwards and forwards, but also because her mother had become more and more an irritable old woman. And she could date it to the day that she had left Sam, for it was on that day her mother told her she was a fool and she would live to regret it.

Howard, Jessie, and Fanny were with her when she returned to her old home to join the cortège. Sam, Janet and Harry, were already there, as was her mother's own solicitor, Mr Winterbottom, a round pudding of a man with a pleasant countenance which seemed to indicate that it was constantly on the verge of merriment. And Mr Winterbottom was aware of this, and therefore he found funerals very trying, for he was that rare of all creatures in his profession, a happy soul, very content with his lot, and his aim in life seemed to be to make others appreciate theirs, whether good, bad or indifferent, as being the result of the carefully thought out plan of God. You could say that at heart Mr Winterbottom was a merry religious.

He greeted their arrival, Alice thought, as if they were strangers to the house. She didn't like the man, never had, and she summed him up to be smarmy. She watched him now beckon the pallbearers; and from that moment the funeral started . . .

In the cemetery, Maggie, Annie and Kate cried openly and genuinely, for they all knew they had lost a good mistress . . . and a friend; and each wondered what her future was to be, for she was getting on in years.

Jessie and Fanny, too, cried openly. Their gran had been kind to them. There had always been a little extra pocket money when they visited her, given with the admonition: 'Keep it under your hat.' Harry didn't cry because he was a seventeen-year-old, but there was a deep pain in his chest and a restriction in his throat. He had loved his gran. After his mother left the house, his gran had seemed to take her place. As for Howard, he stood with his head bowed most of the time; he definitely was not crying, nor did he feel like it. To him his gran had been an old bitch. She could have helped him if she liked, because she was rotten with money, so his mother said; but it was years now since she had given him a penny. Nevertheless, he wondered how he would fare in the will. She had no-one else but the family to leave her money to and there would likely be a sum shared out equally among the children. Well, let them hurry up and get back and hear what that solicitor had to say, because if he didn't have some cash soon he would be in trouble, and he didn't want another up and downer with his mother.

As for Samuel, his thoughts were sad. Poor old girl. She had always been decent to him. Of course, he had been decent to her, too. He had never wanted to start his married life in her house, but she was on her own and it was a big place for one person; at least, with its ten rooms and offices it had seemed big to him in those days. And life had been easy at first with three servants in the house; he would never have kept three servants eating their heads off, although he could have well afforded it, even in those days.

He remembered they used to talk business together. She had a head on her shoulders for business. She had kept the two coal depots going, one in Fellburn, down in Bog's End near the river, the other in

Gateshead; there were six dray carts and the accompanying horses.

Altogether she was employing twenty men when she sold out to Dickinson, who must have paid her well for the business. She never told him how much she received. No; she was cagey. But that was to be expected. Her upbringing had been similar to his: his father was a cobbler, hers a coalman. Anyway, he'd no doubt there would be plenty of money she would have spread around, and he was interested to see how.

Janet was not crying, but her eyes were burning and her heart was heavy. Even more than Harry she had looked upon her gran as a mother, because they could talk and they could laugh together. There were so few people she could laugh with. She could tell her gran funny incidents that happened in the library, such as a woman coming in for a book but ashamed to mention the title, even going so far as to say she wanted to loan it to a friend. Perhaps it was a novel by Elinor Glyn who, to most people, was a shocker. And then there was the man who sidled in and said to Miss Barker that he wanted a book, but that he wanted to see the man who served. Miss Barker had said the librarian was out at the moment, but could she help him? Well, he wanted a book on marriage, he said; but when she asked him the title, he snapped at her, 'How do I know?' And Miss Barker had come to her, saying, 'There's a difficult customer here, and I don't think Miss Stillwater is up to managing him. Would you come and help?'

'Have you any idea of the title of the book, sir?' she had asked him.

And to this he had answered, 'You're a bit of a lass. Are you married?'

No, she had told him, she wasn't married; and on this he had turned and hurried out.

The bed had shaken under her gran. She had laughed so much that day. And she recalled her spluttering, 'You should have sent the poor fellow to me, I would have sorted his problem out for him.'

Oh, she was going to miss her gran.

She walked between her father and Harry from the grave to their separate car, and they drove back to Sweetbanks Gardens, where the girls had set out a cold buffet before leaving the house. But it would seem that no-one was very hungry; at least, for food. Instead, a number of them were hungry for the contents of the will . . .

Mr Winterbottom sat in a chair behind a sofa table that had been placed for him in the middle of the room. From a folder he took out a document and a sealed letter; then, adjusting his glasses, he glanced over the folded parchment, as though taking in those sitting and waiting before him.

He began: 'Always sad, but interesting business, this. But seeing it is the last will and testament of Mrs Mason, it echoes her conversation, which was always brief and to the point.'

He now read out the usual preamble concerning being of sound mind et cetera. But when he came to, 'On this day, the second of June in the year nineteen hundred and seven,' he raised his eyes from the page, saying, 'Mrs Mason dictated her will on that date, but there is a codicil attached which was written three months ago — I will come to that later — in which she endorses all that I am about to read. Apparently, she did not alter her mind in any way. Well now, to get on.' He adjusted his glasses once again and then began to read:

To Maggie Fawcett, Annie Garrett, and Kate McPherson, these three women who have looked after me so well for years I leave, first to Maggie Fawcett, because she's been with me the longest, one thousand pounds. And to Annie Garrett and Kate McPherson

I leave five hundred pounds each. This should set them all up in whatever they should decide to do. And now to my family. Because I consider my son-in-law Samuel Fairbrother a wealthy enough man to take care of his wife . . . under any conditions . . .' Here Mr Winterbottom gave a little cough before proceeding, 'and with the exception of his eldest daughter, Janet Fairbrother, the other members of his family. To Janet Fairbrother, because I hold her in deep affection, I leave this freehold house together with its contents, and because I feel that at some time in the future she will be in need of a home of her own. I also leave to her the rest of my monies, which are spread over bonds and securities and are at this day worth in the region of thirty-two thousand pounds. This will no doubt cause arguments in the family, but it is my wish and I want it carried out to the letter.

Signed this day the second of June, nineteen hundred and seven.'

Mr Winterbottom took off his glasses, wiped them and peered at the amazed faces staring at him in varying degrees of disbelief. No-one moved or made any remark when he said, 'The codicil, dated the twenty-second of November, nineteen hundred and ten reads: Time is running out. I don't change my mind about anything I have said in my will. And the family know my mind is very sound and will remain so till the last, I hope. There will be some bitter words said but in making my choice as to who has my fortune, I know what I'm doing. Don't think too badly of me, Alice. Your husband will always look after you. But if, by some unfortunate turn of event, he shouldn't, your daughter will'.

After a pause Mr Winterbottom folded the parchment, coughed deep in his throat, rose to his feet, then made to walk towards the door and, as he did so, nodded to Samuel. At this, Samuel made as though to follow him, but then turned and, as if marshalling a flock, indicated with a sweep of his arm that Jessie, Fanny and Harry should leave with him. He did not look at Howard. When the door closed on them Janet, her mother and her brother were left standing in the room. And it seemed as if Janet and her mother could collapse at any moment, for different reasons, but Howard's expression was neutral. He stared at his sister, repeating to himself over and over again,

Thirty-two thousand and this house. Thirty-two thousand and this house. And he hardly recognised his mother's voice when, thrusting her face out towards her daughter, she growled so deeply as to make her words almost unintelligible: 'You sly, sneaking bitch. You'll not get away with it. I'll . . . I'll appeal. It's mine. It's mine. Everything. I . . . I was born in this house. It's mine by rights. And all I've done for her. You know what I could do? I could throttle you, girl; and not only today — no, not only today. You've been a thorn in my side since you were born. I tell you that now. An oddity in short clothes. But you won't get away with this. I'll burn the place down first before I'll let you come and live here.'

Her voice had risen from a growl to almost a screech, which brought the door open and Samuel striding in, the while shouting, 'Shut up! woman. Shut up! You've only got yourself to blame for what's happened,' only to stop by the side of Janet, who was stepping back from her mother's verbal onslaught. Enraged by this seeming alliance, Alice whipped around and grabbed a vase from the mantelpiece and flung it at them; and only Samuel's hand forcing Janet to bend low caused it to miss them.

The vase hit the wall and its crashing into

pieces moved Howard to his mother's side as her arm was lifted to repeat the process. He was shouting, 'Give over, Mam! Stop it!' and he pulled her close to him. Then, turning his head towards his father, who was now advancing on them, he cried, 'Don't you start! She's . . . she's had enough. We've all had enough.'

'Enough is nothing to what you'll both get. Get out! the pair of you! Quick!'

Howard had to drag his mother from the room and it seemed that her fury was so great she could no longer speak.

Samuel stood with his arm around Janet's shoulders and they were both silent as they listened to the bustle coming from the hall. Then a door banged, and all was quiet for a moment.

'Sit down.'

Janet sat down; then they both looked towards the door, where Harry was edging in Maggie and Annie. And it was Maggie who said, 'You all right, miss? Oh, my goodness!' She spotted the remains of the vase. Then, shaking her head, she said, 'I never thought to see the day. It's been a shock all round, pleasant for some, unpleasant for others . . . Would you like a drink?'

'No, thanks, Maggie,' Samuel said. 'We'll be on our way home in a minute.'

Apprehensive at seeing Janet seated, Harry hurried to her, saying, 'Did it hit you?'

She shook her head. She was unable to utter a word, although inside her head her thoughts were moving rapidly. She wasn't at all surprised at her mother's reaction; in a way it was natural, but the things she had said to her, especially about her being odd since she was in petticoats. Was she odd? Was she different from anyone else? The answer came clearly now. Yes, she must be, else her gran wouldn't have left her that fortune. It sort of indicated that she had no future, not as ordinary people would have. Was she so plain? No. No. She had changed during her teens. She was still plainish but not plain, and she carried herself well, and she dressed well. What was more, she had a mind. Was it that that made her odd? Was it that that had infuriated her mother all these years? . . .

There was a knock and the solicitor entered the room and diffidently approached Janet, saying, 'I have a letter for you, Miss Fairbrother. I did not mention it during the business as I wanted a private word with you. But that will be later, of course, when you can come to my office. There will be papers to sign and matters to discuss. But this is the letter left by your grandmother.' He now handed her the envelope and her voice was a mere whisper as she said, 'Thank you.'

She made no attempt to open the letter and Mr Winterbottom said, 'I will leave you. Try not to worry about your good fortune. Reactions to it weren't unexpected; they were natural.' He now turned to Samuel. 'Under the circumstances I think you would agree, sir, they were natural.'

On this, he bowed slightly from one to the other, then turned and went from the room.

Maggie now approached her and she said 'What are we going to do, miss, I mean, the three of us?'

Janet was saved from answering by Samuel saying, 'Leave it, Maggie. Just carry on as you've always done, as if . . . Mrs Mason was still here. My daughter will sort things out when she's feeling a little better. But now we'll all get off home.'

As they went to leave the room, it was Harry who turned to the women and said, 'It was a very nice meal, thank you.'

In the motor car on the way back to the house Janet recalled that her brother had thanked the girls for the meal. He was thoughtful, was Harry. He was nice. It was strange: he had come from the same stock as Howard, the same stock as herself. How could individuals coming from the one stem be so different? She had always been different, but she would be more so now because she was a rich woman. She could almost hear her father striding into the house and proclaiming it to Maitland. Oh yes, because whatever barrier there had been before, she hadn't seen it as eventually insurmountable. But her gran, in all her thoughtfulness, had now erected a wall around her, a fortress that a man like Maitland would never deign to breach. So her future was all planned out: she would spend her daytime energies in the library and her evenings in Sweet-banks Gardens, with one or other of the girls for human though mindless contact. The pattern seemed set.

4

Janet hung on to the handle of the door with one hand as she turned one shoe this way and that on the iron shoe-scraper so as to rid it of the caked snow. And she was about to do the same with the other shoe when she almost fell sideways into the hall as the door was pulled open.

'Oh, I'm sorry.' Maitland's hand steadied her, then he added, 'Don't worry about your other shoe. Come in, come in; you must be frozen. I was just about to come and meet you. You're early.'

She peered at him through her snow-tipped eyelashes and saw that he was in his overcoat with a scarf wound about his neck. And she muttered, 'Thanks,' before dropping down on to a hall chair. As she pulled off her woollen hat and shook it, he knelt down on one knee and went to unstrap her overshoes, but she pulled her foot away, saying, 'It's all right, it's all right. I can do it.'

But when he grabbed her foot, and none too gently undid the buckle before pulling the rubber shoe off her foot, she made no protest. The other rubber shoe was also taken without her protesting in the slightest, not even when, saying, 'Let me have your coat,' he placed a hand on her arm to help her up from the chair. And when she slipped her arms from the coat, he turned and called to Florence, who had just emerged from the corridor, and ordered, 'Take Miss Janet's things and put them in the airing cupboard, and tell Cook Miss Janet will be ready for a meal in ten minutes.'

'Yes, Mr Maitland . . . Isn't it awful?' This last was addressed to Janet. 'How on earth did you make your way from the tram, miss? Thank goodness you didn't try to cycle. It must be nearly up to your knees out there.'

Stroking her hair back from her face, Janet smiled as she said, 'It's up to your neck where the drifts are, Florence. My father's going to have a job to get back. The car'll likely get stuck.'

As she made for the stairs Maitland said, 'The master phoned earlier on, miss. He has an appointment that will keep him busy until about eight o'clock, he said. This being so, I've taken the liberty of setting your meal in the morning-room. It's much warmer in there.'

'Thank you.' She did not look back as she spoke, but as she reached the top of the stairs she repeated to herself: 'I have taken the liberty.' Why, oh why was he so stiff and proper? Yet, when they were together, at least, when there was no-one else present . . . No, together was the wrong word to use with regard to them: it spelt closeness, companionship, and understanding, and there was no closeness, or companionship. But yes, oh yes, there was understanding.

The bedroom was warm; the fire must have been going for some time; and so she quickly divested herself of her serge skirt and white blouse with the black bow at the neck. Then she washed her face and hands in the hot water from the steaming jug that always awaited her. Following this, she changed her shoes. She had two rows to choose from and all made from fine leather. And why not? Her father made them . . . or had them made, not only for her but for every member of the family.

Lastly, she took down from the wardrobe her latest purchase in the way of clothes, a midnight-blue velvet dress, which daringly reached to just below her calves. It was the fashion at the moment and was causing comment.

She hadn't worn the dress before and,

doubtless, if her mother had still been living in the house she wouldn't have been wearing it now; although it was dark, it wasn't black. And, after all, it would have been said that if anyone should show respect for the dead, she should be the one, for look what she had gained from it.

Oh, she knew what she had gained from it: the hate of her mother, because she knew that her mother would never forgive her. In her mother's eyes she was a usurper, a creep, a crawler, everything that was bad.

Since gaining her inheritance the reactions of the family had been varied: Alicia had come to the library yesterday and their conversation over the counter had been brief. 'I think you should share it,' she said. 'It isn't fair.'

She didn't say to her, I've already shared it where I want to. She hadn't even told her father what she had sent Eddie and James, and they, because she had asked them not to speak about it, had kept quiet. So her father would never know. Harry, too, had received a thousand pounds. His reaction had come over the phone and he had said, 'Bless you! Janet. And I'm saying that for the three of us. Eddie and James have phoned me. As Eddie put it, "You're a bit of all right." '

Her eyes had been wet when she had left the phone.

As yet, she had given nothing to either Jessie or Fanny, because whatever she offered them, she knew that her mother would make them give it back.

And then there was Howard. She had recalled a number of times her surprise at his reaction on the day of the funeral, for he, unlike her mother, had not turned on her, in fact, he had not said a word one way or another. His silence had really surprised her, because, of them all, he was the most money-conscious.

She surveyed herself in the long mirror. She looked smart, different. The square neck of the dress showed up her skin to advantage, at least that part which was exposed. But her face was colourless. She turned swiftly and went towards the dressing-table and from a drawer took out a small round box and almost guiltily she opened it, pressed a piece of cotton wool on to the pink powder, gently applied it to her cheek bones, then put her face closer to the mirror. Was it too much? Was it noticeable? She made a small defiant move, wet the side of her finger on her tongue and applied it with an upward movement to her dark lashes. Again wetting her finger, she went through the same process with her eyebrows. Lastly, she drew the comb through the waves of her hair, not pressing them down as she usually did before leaving for work in the morning, but raising them into their natural folds.

This done she swung round and for a moment stood with her buttocks pressed tight against the edge of the dressing-table, and, her head bent slightly, her teeth clenched, she said one word: 'Why?' But the answer remained in her head. What she did say to herself was, Get yourself down.

When she reached the foot of the stairs it was to see Sarah carrying a tray to the breakfast-room. And Sarah, who was now in her forties and a staid quiet woman, almost stopped in her tracks, and the tray wobbled in her hand for a moment before she exclaimed, 'Oh, my! You do look bonny, miss,' but she did not give voice to her next thought: Fancy her leaving off the black so early, and after all she's got from her granny.

'Bonny?' Janet gave a little derogatory laugh, which Sarah brushed aside as she walked on, saying, 'Yes, miss, bonny.'

She could have accepted smart, but never bonny, nor pretty, nor beautiful. Yes, and perhaps, in a way, attractive.

If she had expected some exclamation from Maitland she was disappointed for, after glancing towards her, he pulled out a chair, and when she was seated he turned to the sideboard and took up a hot plate and with a white napkin he dusted it before placing it before Janet. Then from the tureen which was already on the table he proceeded to scoop the soup on to her plate. After the second spoonful she raised her hand and he returned the ladle to the tureen and, in the act of lifting it from the table, he said, 'Would you care for a little wine tonight?'

She paused. 'Yes. Yes, I think I would,' she said, the pause having been engendered not because she was making a decision about the wine but by her realisation that he had omitted the 'miss'.

After eating her way through what was an ordinary four-course meal: soup, fish, roast lamb, and now a chocolate pudding with wine sauce, she laid down her spoon and fork halfway through it and speaking to Maitland over her shoulder, said, 'I'm sure you are acquainted with the saying, "Living like lords"?'

'Yes. Yes, I am,' he replied. 'It's a very common saying, but only among the poor.'

'Is that so? Well, has it ever struck you

as odd that I should be working in a library all day, and half . . . oh yes, a good half of our customers, so called, are of the poor, and I'm dealing with them, yet I come back here every night and live like a lord . . . or a lady. And speaking of ladies, her ladyship would have dressed for dinner every evening, wouldn't she?'

'Yes, her ladyship always dressed for dinner.' His voice came from behind her and she put her head back now as she said, 'And you took that as natural . . . normal?'

'Of course.'

'So that is why you made no remark when I, for the only time in your experience, came down dressed for dinner? Or was it that you were astounded as Sarah was to see that I have discarded black? Does it appear to you as a lack of respect for the dead, especially one from whom I have benefited so much?'

While she waited for an answer she heard him arranging the dishes; then he was at her side, his hand on her pudding plate and he was saying, 'Have you finished, miss? Would you like your coffee in the drawing-room?'

When she looked up at him, their gaze held; but she was the first to look away. Then, as he moved from her, she only just managed to check herself from bursting out laughing when he said quietly, 'Ladies should never pose questions to butlers, especially when other servants are likely to pop in and out of their presence. In the drawing-room it would be different, for there, the poor butler would be able to defend himself; he might even dare to ask the reason for his mistress's tirade.'

Her head was slightly bent as she rose from the table, and it remained so as she made her 'ladylike' way from the room without uttering a word.

In the drawing-room she sat on the chintz-covered chesterfield couch opposite the blazing fire and smiled to herself. He had unbent for the first time since her grandmother's funeral. The stiffness went out of her body, she lay back on the couch, arranged her velvet skirt around her knees and did not pull it down any further over her calves.

It was a good five minutes later when he entered the room, carrying a tray on which there were two silver jugs, a silver sugar basin, and a small coffee cup and saucer. And she watched him place the tray on a side table, pour out the coffee as she liked it, half black, half white, add one lump of sugar, then come towards her; and as he handed it to her, he said, 'I think you should always wear velvet. It enhances your skin colour.'

Her eyelids blinked, she swallowed, took the cup from his hand, and said, 'Thank you.' Then she nipped at her lip before adding, 'Sarah told me I looked bonny. It was the wrong word to apply to me, wasn't it?'

'Yes. Yes, indeed it was, for you are neither bonny nor pretty. At times your face can appear beautiful, very beautiful, at others, plain. This is when you are in an aggressive mood, especially during a meal, and the most beautiful attire can be overshadowed by a dour countenance . . . Ah,' his hand came out and steadied the saucer, and he said, 'There are other means of spoiling a beautiful dress.'

As she pulled the saucer away from his fingers the coffee spilled over from the cup, and she straightened up, and almost glaring at him, she said, 'Do you know what? I have the strong desire to throw this coffee over you.'

'I have no doubt of that, miss; nor would it be the first time. But at this moment I have a strong desire to put you right about something. You have acquired, of late, the unfortunate habit of prefixing what you are about to say with, "Do you know what?" It is most unlike you.'

Her mouth was agape and her breath came from it in a gasp as she said, 'I do not.'

'Oh yes, you do; and you've just this moment said it.'

And now she had to quell the desire to get to her feet and say, You are being rude. How dare you! But this was what she wanted, wasn't it? An exchange, an ordinary exchange, an argument, a battle, anything to get back on to the old footing. So now, her voice as ordinary as she could make it, she said, 'Ah well, if I am speaking colloquially I am only reverting to breed.'

'Nonsense.' His hand came out again towards the cup as he added, 'Let me have that. I will get you a clean cup.'

She let him take the cup from her.

It was when he was again pouring the coffee that he changed the conversation altogether by asking, 'Have you decided what you are going to do with your grandmother's house?'

The question surprised her, and it was a moment before she replied, 'Oh, that has been decided for me. She left me a letter, you know, asking me not to sell the house for at least five years. I was surprised that she hadn't stated that in the will. But no, this was a special request, and also that I would keep on any of the girls who wanted to stay. Well, it should happen Maggie is getting on in years and is glad to retire. She is going to live with a cousin of hers. And Kate, the youngest, is about to achieve a dream that she's always had, of having a wool shop, but Annie has asked to stay on. She has no relatives, and I'm glad it is she who is going to see to the place, because I am rather fond of Annie and she loves the house. And do you know what?' She turned towards him, her hand over her mouth while her eyes laughed at him. And he smiled broadly down on her as, laughing outright, she nodded at him before she said slowly and emphatically, 'And . . . you . . . know . . . something? What d'you think? That's Miss Barker's favourite introduction, and generally said in a whisper. We are all copycats aren't we? Except for you.' And the smile slid from her face as she now asked, 'How d'you manage, I mean, to keep so correct all the time?'

'Oh, I don't keep correct, not all the time. When at work my business is to be correct, but I have my off duty, and then you'd be surprised . . . By lad! ya would, ya would that.'

The last was said in pure Geordie. But she did not let out a laugh as she might have done at one time; and her voice was serious as she asked, 'If you were to leave here tomorrow, what would you do?'

'Oh, that is an easy question to answer. I would start a training school for butlers and footmen, and perhaps upper house-maids and such.'

'Really?'

'Yes, really. It has been in my mind for a long time, because butling is a career. To fill this position properly a man should not only know the rudiments of how to see to his master's wants, to receive guests, to order a staff, but also keep up with the affairs of the day. His lordship taught me that, and I'll be forever indebted to him, if only for the compliment your brother paid me when he got his open scholarship in English Literature, for I was able to discuss the papers with him, at least in part, and I recall that he looked at me and said, "Maitland, you could have sailed through this, given the chance." And I, lacking in humility' — he now pursed his lips — 'replied, "Yes, I think I might have . . . given the chance." And I might add that up till now I've envied no-one in your family, but I shall envy Master Harry when, in October, he goes up to Oxford.'

Both her voice and her glance were soft

as she looked up at him and said, 'I was just on ten years old when I came here and you were thirty. You appeared to be an oldish man to me then. Now, eleven years later, you appear to me younger than when I first saw you. And here am I just under twenty-one, and I feel old, so old. I —'

She broke off abruptly and turned and looked towards the door, as did Maitland, for the sound of her father's voice could be heard coming from the hall.

Before Maitland reached the drawing-room door it was thrust open, and as her father burst in Janet thought, I wonder when he'll ever enter a room like an ordinary human being.

'You look frozen, sir.'

'Well, what d'you expect? It's bloody awful out there. You don't know when you're well off, stuck in here all day, the house like an oven. Get me a drink.' Then his voice softened as he added, 'A hot drink, soup or something.'

'How about a hot toddy, sir?'

'Oh aye; that would be better still.'

He now walked to the fire, bent his back, lifted his coat tails and let the flame thaw him out for a number of seconds before he said, 'How did you manage?'

'Much worse than you I should say; I had

to walk from the tram,' replied Janet.

'That's your own fault. You should get yourself a motor car. You can afford it.'

'Did your motor car get you to the door?'

'Not quite. I had to leave it at the lodge. I'm going to find out what those buggers are up to during the day; that drive should have been swept.'

'It was already clear at dinner time. There's a wind, perhaps you noticed, and drifts.'

'Yes, I noticed, miss. I went into one at the gate.'

'Well, you don't expect the men to work outside with lanterns, do you?'

'I expect them to keep that drive clear, knowing I'll be home.'

'They've kept the drive clear all day —'

'All right, all right! D'you know where I've been?'

'To a meeting, so I understood.'

'Aye, a meeting with your mother. And what d'you think the latest is?'

'I wouldn't know. I can't even guess.'

'She's back on the divorce trail again.'

There was a pause before she said, 'Why now?'

'Aye, why now? You may ask. And she's demanding it on her own terms. Either she names the person in question — or rather the person who used to be the one concerned — or I give her the evidence in another form, like they do now with a bedroom and a hussy stripping off and the door bursting open and a camera pointed at you.'

'She didn't suggest that!'

'Oh, but she did. Oh, yes, she did. Anyway, I'm going to see about this. I haven't had time to think, but I should imagine there's a time limit of separation that can form grounds for divorce.'

He now came and dropped down on the couch beside her, and as he leant back he cupped his maimed hand with the other and shook it a number of times before he said quietly, at least for him, 'You know something, Janet?' As she waited for him to go on, she would have liked to have said in jocular fashion, You shouldn't start a sentence with that; it'll be picked up by you know who. But her father was in no jocular mood and his next words surprised her: 'I've always had the idea, Janet, that she would come back.' He brought his face round to hers. 'D'you know that? I never doubted it somehow. I thought, She'll be back one day; she's bound to forgive and forget. But no; she wants a divorce, really wants a divorce. She always threatened it but I know women do that, especially when they're separated. It's to get the man to go back on his knees. Well I've tried that already, verbally, but even so, it's always ended with a loud-voiced battle. My fault mainly, I know, but I used to think, Well, she knows me by now, nobody better. She knows I don't mean half what I say, that is when dealing with the family. Business is a different matter altogether: I mean what I say there, every word of it.' He nodded at her now. 'That's why I am where I am today. People know that I am as good as my word. When I say something, that's that. You know, I couldn't believe it at first when she told me, and she said it quietly, too. So I thought she was just saying it because I still refuse to give that lazy, sly tyke a job. If ever a man has rejected his son, I have him; and I won't take him on, not even if it means her going through with it. And oh, she means that all right. I've been trying to think if she might have somebody in her eye, because, you know, she lives a separate life now, has done for nearly four years.'

'Have you ever thought of marrying again, Dad?'

'*What! Marry again?* No! Not me. I burned me fingers once, and me hand, so to speak.' He now grinned at her, saying, 'What is the word you would use to explain that sort of pun? I've heard you use it . . .'

'Metaphorically speaking.'

'Aye, that's it, metaphorically speaking.' He now held up his misshapen hand and stared at it. And his voice, although quiet, held a deep bitter note as he said, 'I punched marriage out through a mirror the day I did that. I also punched some sense into me head, and that boiled down to two words: never again. No, lass, no more marriage for me. That isn't saying, no more women.'

'Oh, Dad.' She shook her head in mock horror; and he laughed and leant his shoulder towards hers as he said, 'As long as I've got you to come back to in this house.' And putting his mouth to her ear, he whispered, 'And the wizard who keeps us all in our places and who is the real boss of the house. You know that.'

She pushed him gently away and smiled at him as she said mockingly, 'But just let him get that idea into his head and he would get the boot, wouldn't he, dear?'

Leaning towards her again, his voice still low, he said, 'That's what worries me about you. You know too much about me.' . . .

Maitland was now handing him a small salver on which there was a pewter mug, steam rising from its rim, and he was saying,

'Your meal is ready whenever you are, sir.'

'Thanks. As soon as I've drunk this I'll be in.'

While Samuel took a long draught from the mug, Janet got to her feet, and as she smoothed down the front of her dress her father looked her up and down and remarked, 'That's the difference, is it? I knew there was something wrong with you the minute I came into the room. Well, I wouldn't say wrong, but when did you get that?'

'Recently.'

'You're quick out of your black, aren't you?'

'Gran would have had it this way.'

'Aye, well, so you think; but you can't speak for her, yet others will speak of you, especially if you go out with something light on.'

'Well, they'll have to speak, because that's what I mean to do.'

'Suffragette side coming up again, eh?'

'Yes, you could say that, Dad.'

'What d'you think about this, Maitland?'

Maitland was at the drawing-room door, in fact, he had already opened it and he turned and said, 'If you're alluding to Miss Janet's attire, I would say it's very becoming, sir.'

When the door had closed on the man, Samuel said, 'Has he remarked on it before?'

'Yes. Yes, he has.'

'What did he say then?'

'Much the same as he's just said now.'

'Aye, because he's an old softie and . . . he's looking old these days, don't you think?'

'No more so than you, Dad. In fact, I would say he's not aging so quickly.'

He drained the mug, then got to his feet and, wiping his mouth with the side of his finger, he said, 'You know what?' And she repeated, 'Yes, I know what.'

'There are times when I'd like to slap your little face for you, because you're a cheeky bugger, you know.'

'Yes, I know, and I really must take after you because just a little while ago I said something similar to Maitland: "I'd like to throw this coffee over you," I said.'

She watched her father's eyes widen and his chin being pulled into his neck; then after a long moment he muttered, 'You said that? Why?'

She answered, 'I have my reasons;' and she turned from him, her back straight, her head high as usual as she walked from the room. He followed her quickly, calling,

'Here! a minute. Here! a minute. I want to hear more of this.'

They had entered the hall when she turned to him quietly, saying, 'Well, I'm afraid you're going to be disappointed. Now what you've got to do is go and have your dinner, and I'm going into the library to study. I shall see you later.' She put out her hand and patted his cheek before walking away down the corridor towards the library, and he was left standing open-mouthed and troubled, deeply troubled; and in a way which out-did any trouble his wife was causing him.

5

Arthur Stanford was a very presentable man of thirty-six years and was almost six foot in height, fair-haired, blue-eyed and altogether what you would call a handsome man, and being such he could not at the moment accept the fact that his second assistant was wavering, no, not even wavering, but almost refusing his proposal of marriage.

He now took hold of Janet's hand, saying, 'My dear, this couldn't have come as a surprise to you. I've always held you in high esteem, and I'm sure that my intentions over the last year or so have shown you to be more than friendly.'

Janet lowered her gaze. In a way he sounded very much like Maitland, precise, correct. But what else did she expect? Was she waiting for someone like her father to come and sweep her off her feet? Loudmouthed, brash, intelligent but not educated. No, she wasn't waiting for anyone like that. She knew whom she was waiting for and that she would likely have to go on waiting until something drastic happened.

'And what is more,' went on Mr Stanford, pressing his case, 'my mother likes you very much, as does my sister; they would welcome you into the family. Of course, I am well aware that you have a very good family of your own and also that people would consider your status, monetarily speaking, far above mine, but that makes no difference to me, because I am sure you were aware of my feelings long before you came into your inheritance.'

'Arthur, I . . . I do like you. We get on very well together, we are of similar minds, but as for marriage, I have never . . .'

He put out a hand and placed his finger on her lips, 'Don't say it, my dear. Give yourself time. I'll wait. As long as you wish, I'll wait.'

She had to remove his fingers from her mouth by taking hold of his wrist, and as she began, 'But Arthur,' she was stopped by a knock on the door, and he, leaving her side and going swiftly around his desk, sat down, before he called, 'Come in.'

When Miss Phoebe Carrington, who had been promoted from the basement to the counter, said, 'There's a young gentleman wishing to speak to Miss Fairbrother, sir,' Mr Stanford said, 'Oh. Oh, well then, of course, show him in.'

Janet turned towards the door, her face bright. It would be one of the boys; they must be on leave; and she was in the act of moving towards it when there, on the threshold, she saw Howard. The bright look slipped from her face and she turned to the librarian, saying, 'Will you excuse me? I will talk with my brother outside.'

'No need. No need.' Arthur Stanford looked from Howard to her, saying, 'Make use of the office for as long as you like,' and appeared to be waiting only for Janet to make an introduction. But she didn't, and he went out and closed the door behind him.

And there stood Howard with his back to it and saying, 'I . . . I knew you would expect to see one of the others, but . . . but you're the only one I could come to.'

'Come to for what?'

'Well' — he moved a step from the door towards her — 'I've . . . I've never asked you for anything before, and . . . and I know you've been generous to the others. Oh, it doesn't matter how I know, I know. Well, they visit Mam, you know, and when she starts upbraiding them things slip out. Anyway, Janet, I'm well aware of what you think of me and I'm not making any excuses. I . . . I know it's been mostly my fault. But now I would ask you for help, because I'm in a hole, a bad one.'

She had never seen him like this: he was almost cringing and she wondered which Howard she disliked the more. She said, 'Why don't you ask Mam? She's not badly off.'

'No; I daren't. Anyway, we are not seeing eye to eye because . . . well, once she marries Jock Dickinson I'm leaving. I've told her.'

'She's going to marry Mr Dickinson?'

'Yes, that's the idea; and she'll be pretty well off when she does. And she means to live in his house in Newcastle. And there'll only be Fanny to go with her because Jessie is determined to go into the convent, and that's causing ructions at the present moment. But if Mam doesn't let her go she says she'll just wait until she's of age and go in then. But now, she says, they can't stop her being a Catholic. It's hell in that house. You're lucky you're out of it.'

She continued to look at him as she thought, Yes, I am lucky. In all ways except one I am lucky. And it was true she had helped the others but not him, which, in a way, she felt was unfair, because if her gran had left her money to be divided among them he would have had his share. But she did not say to him: How much do you want? but, 'How much are you after?' It was as her father would have put the question.

She watched him wet his lips before answering: 'Five . . . five hundred.'

'What! You say five hundred when you mean four or three. Remember Nicholas Denvers.'

'It is, it *is* five hundred, Janet. It's been mounting up and they've threatened what they'll do to me.'

'Who has?'

'The bookies.'

'Betting?'

'Aye.' His head drooped. 'I don't seem able to stop. I always think: next time. And I *have* won. Here and there I *have* won . . . three hundred last year.'

'But now you owe five hundred?'

'I'm sorry, Janet but it's . . . it's taken a lot for me to come here and ask you.'

She stood looking at him. She never thought she would consider her eldest brother pathetic; but in spite of his good looks and being well dressed he appeared to her at this moment like a man who had lost his grip on life. He looked older than his twenty-two years.

She said now, and harshly, 'If I let you have this money that's the end, mind. You needn't come again, because —'

'I won't, Janet, I won't. I promise you that once out of this mess, I . . . well, I . . . I mean to make an effort.'

She wanted to say, I've heard that before. But she couldn't, because, looking at him, she experienced an unusual feeling, at least connected with him. She was pitying him, and her mind took her back to a time when she didn't dislike him. That was when they lived with their gran. It was with Eddie whom she then fought. Yet now, of all of them, she thought she loved Eddie the best. Well, she loved them all, James, Eddie and Harry. But she couldn't remember when she first hated Howard. 'You may have it,' she said brusquely. 'Drop in in the morning, and I'll give you the cheque. But mind, no more. That's the first and the last.'

'Oh, Janet. Thanks. Thanks.' He took three steps from the door and gripped hold of her hand. 'I can promise you I'll never trouble you again, because I mean to take a pull at myself once I get out of this hole.'

She withdrew her hand from his, saying, 'Well, I hope you stick to that. Does . . . does Mam know, I mean, about the fix you're in now?'

'No. No.' He shook his head; then sadly he said, 'Mam's changed. She should never have left him, you know. And . . . and I thought she'd go back. I used to dread that at one time, but not any more. I . . . I would have been better on my own. I know I would.' He was looking to the side now, his head moving in small jerks as if to emphasise the statement to himself.

Of a sudden she wanted to end the interview, to see him gone. She could not stand his abasement any longer. She said, 'I've got to get back on duty.'

'Oh yes, yes. And what time shall I come tomorrow morning?'

'It would be best if you meet me outside at about ten minutes to nine.'

'I'll do that. Yes, I'll do that, Janet. And thanks, thanks again.' He backed from her before turning and going swiftly out.

She was standing where he had left her when Arthur Stanford came back into his office, saying now, 'Is . . . is everything all right? No bad news?'

'No; no bad news.'

'Good. Now, Janet, where were we?'

'Please. Please Arthur. I must tell you . . .'

'No. No, you mustn't. No, you mustn't.' He was wagging his forefinger at her. 'As I said, give yourself time to think. Consider everything. I know I am fifteen years older than you, but that being so I am more able to take care of you. And we *are* of a like mind and —'

'*Please.*'

He stopped and with raised eyebrows and an expression of surprise on his face, he said, 'Very well, as you wish,' and he stood aside to allow her to leave the office.

She went into the cloakroom and stood leaning against the door. A proposal of marriage and a plea for five hundred pounds. She could comply with the second but never with the first. Married to Arthur? Oh, no, no. Not even out of desperation. She knew there was another side to Maitland, she had seen it in action. She had also listened to it. But there was only one side to Arthur and she got enough of that during working hours. She had made the mistake, she knew now, of accepting his invitation to their Sunday jaunts and games of lawn tennis, even though the others were with them. But her final mistake was to take tea at his home. Dear! dear! what a beginning to a Monday morning.

It was the following week when Janet's hatred of Howard returned twofold. The snow had disappeared except for the dirt-capped mounds that still lay here and there on the roadside and on the grass verges. The sun was shining brightly, there was even a touch of warmth in the air.

When Janet cycled from the library back home to lunch her journey took her down Baintree Road, past the convent and the Catholic church next door to it. And on this day, when she saw Jessie coming down the steps, she dismounted, and they hailed each other smiling.

'Isn't it wonderful to see the sun?' Jessie greeted her sister, and Janet replied, 'Not before time. Hasn't it been dreadful?'

'Yes, it has; but then we're used to the weather.'

More for something to say than anything else, and because she couldn't ask after her mother or Fanny, Janet said, 'Been to church again?'

'Yes, I've been to church again. It's the only peaceful place in my existence now I've left school.'

'Are you still bent . . . well, on going in?'

'More than ever, Janet, more than ever. It's so peaceful; and inside the church too. Have you ever been inside?'

'No.'

'You should pop in some time; the door's always open.'

'Tell me something' — Janet now leant

over the handlebars — 'were you pressurised into this? I mean, did they talk you into it? Keep at you?'

'No. No.' Jessie shook her head. 'Not at all. No; but I myself took to it right from the beginning. I loved going into the chapel. I loved the routine and . . . and the serenity. Not that they're all angels in there, not by a long chalk.' She laughed now. 'Sister Benedicta, she's a holy terror. She had me frightened to death at times; but then I stood up to her when the rubber came across my knuckles.' She chuckled now as she went on, 'I said to her, "Wouldn't you find a whip handier?" She gave me an imposition that took me nearly a week to get through. As Father Connell says, "There's some good 'uns and there's some bad 'uns. And the good 'uns are as bad as the bad 'uns and the bad 'uns are as good as the good 'uns, but all in different ways." '

Janet said, 'Perhaps it's as Dad says, "They're clever, they can laugh you in." '

'Oh, Dad says things he knows nothing about. But then, he's not as bad as Mam. Oh Janet, life's been awful there lately. Mam's so changed and she's going to marry Mr Dickinson. Well, I told her that the day that happens I walk out and into the convent with or without her permission; and it will then be up to her to get me out again. But when I'm twenty-one, I'll be able to please myself. And she's had trouble with Howard again. He's left, you know.'

'Howard's left? You mean he's left home, left Mam?'

'Yes, he's left home, left Mam. She's got him out of trouble so many times. But this time two men came to the house looking for him; he owed them three hundred pounds. I think it was for gambling. But that's not all. He's been going around with a married woman . . . her husband goes to sea. Mam said she would put him out if he didn't stop. He said he had. Well, she found out that he hadn't. The job she had got for him was travelling, but he was spending most of his time with her. So, last Wednesday she told him to go to her. And when the men came she told them to go and find him.'

She couldn't believe it. Three hundred pounds. The Nicholas Denvers business over again. My God! and she'd fallen for it. But he had sounded so sincere . . . 'What did you say?'

'I said, I pray for him but it doesn't seem to do much good. I don't blame him really. If there's any blame to be attached, it's to Dad. He should have taken him in hand years ago. But then he was never at home to take anyone in hand, was he?' She gave a shaky laugh before adding: 'The prospective nun condemning her father who, after all, was just working for the lot of us. Funny about our family, isn't it? Half of us have made good and the other half have done nothing, nor likely to. You and the boys are doing something with your lives, but there's Howard and Alicia who are really two hopeless cases . . . and Fanny. Well, Fanny will trail along holding Mam's skirts. And there's the one called Jessie' — she pulled a face at herself now — 'throwing myself away, so I'm told.'

'I don't think you're throwing yourself away. The only thing is, I don't know why you're doing it.'

'Oh, I can tell you that, Janet, quite simply, because I can't help myself. If I wasn't becoming a Catholic nun I would have become a Church of England sister, or gone into training to be a missionary. I'm made that way. But I'm glad I'm going into the Catholic Church. It's warm, it's enfolding, and you know where you are.'

'Have you thought that it will be a very hard life?'

'The harder the better, that's how I see it.'

'Do you really believe in God all that much?'

'Well, Janet, I wouldn't be doing it if I didn't. Now would I?'

'You're so sure, I mean, that there is one God?'

'Oh yes, yes. As sure as I'm standing here looking at you and loving you. I've always loved you, you know. And now' — she wagged her finger towards Janet's face — 'that isn't holy-Joe talk. It's got nothing to do with priests, nuns, or the Pope.' She laughed outright now. 'But yes, I've always loved you.'

'Oh, be quiet!' The words seemed to be wrenched from Janet's throat.

'Oh, Janet, Janet, don't cry. Please, it's the last thing I would do is to make you cry.'

Janet sniffed, blew her nose, then turned from the gaze of a passer-by who was looking intently at her.

'You know what you are, Jessie Fairbrother, you know what you are already . . . you're a barmy nun.'

'Yes. Yes, I know. Well, the first part, barmy, yes, but not the second yet. But that's what I mean to be —' she ended on a solemn note, 'a barmy nun.'

'When are you going in?'

'Well, I hope to go at the beginning of September when I'll be sixteen, but that will depend on whether I can get them both to agree about the same thing for once. Mam blames Dad for sending me to the convent in the first place, and Dad blames her for not keeping me clear of priests and nuns. And they want to know how it is that the other twenty-seven in my year haven't got the bug. Oh, it's because I'm weak-minded and they've got at me. And so it goes on. But anyway, dear Janet, we'll see. And if I can, or when I can, convince them both, I'll slip into the library and let you know the latest. Bye-bye, dear.' She bent forward and kissed Janet on the cheek, then turned and ran down the road like the schoolgirl she really still was; yet a schoolgirl with a mission firmly implanted in her mind, and for a moment Janet envied her, for this young sister of hers knew exactly where she was going, and even what she would find at the end.

She was sitting at the library table, books and papers spread out before her. For the past three hours she had been studying for her assistant librarian examination, which was looming up. She raised her head and glanced at the lantern clock on the mantelpiece. Five minutes to eleven. She leant back in the chair and put her hands palm downwards on the table and stretched her fingers wide. She did not realise she had been working for so long. Her father hadn't come in yet; but then some nights it was twelve when he returned, and she would hear his heavy tread across the landing, very often an uneven tread. Where did he get to these nights? He always said it was a meeting at the club, but the meetings surely wouldn't go on till nearly twelve. Still, that was his business and one she wouldn't care to probe.

It was also Maitland's day off. He usually got in about eleven. She wasn't often up when he returned but she knew he always did a round of the house before making for his room in the annexe. Her hand stretched out towards the wine glass: there was still a drop in it. As her head went back and she drained the glass the library door opened, and she swung round, to see Maitland standing there. She blinked twice before she realised it was he. He was dressed in a light grey suit and as he came towards her she saw with some surprise that his shirt was blue and his tie sported a pattern.

'You are up late.' No miss to her name.

'I've been working.' She now pushed the

glass back onto the table, and when his eyes followed her actions she nodded at him, saying, 'Yes, and that was the second one tonight.'

'Dear, dear; things are getting worse.' He was smiling at her. He looked entirely different. He sounded entirely different. She turned in her chair, asking now, 'Have you had a good day?'

'Yes, excellent; ending in a very good evening.'

'Did you have two glasses of . . . whatever?'

'Oh, more than two, four, and of . . . whatever.'

'I can tell by your eyes.'

'Indeed. Am I not the same Maitland I was yesterday, and the day before that?'

'No; I would say you are more of a human being.'

'Ah well, then I must follow the pattern of today more often and you will always view me as a human being.'

'What do you do with yourself all day?'

'What did I do once I left the house?' he asked the question of himself. 'Ah! well —' He looked up towards the chandelier, then said, 'Of course, I went to the gym. I couldn't possibly miss the gym, could I?' He was shaking his head. 'From there I went to an hotel and had a good lunch. And sitting in the smoke-room later and reading the paper, I saw that there was an antique sale that day in Newcastle. So I walked leisurely down Grey Street, viewing the shops on my way; then I entered the Chambers situated near the Courthouse where the auction was taking place. And there I found myself standing amid a galaxy of dealers, and my amazement grew at the prices furniture and effects went for. And my mind travelled back to this house and I thought that there is more than a small fortune in furniture alone here. Do you know?' He leaned towards her. 'A Victoria rosewood davenport of no particular appearance went for thirty pounds, and a piano-front one brought in fifty pounds. Also a brass skeleton time-piece. That was very sweet, four pounds ten —'

'Didn't you buy anything?'

'Yes. Yes, I did.'

She waited, then said, 'Well, what was it?'

'Oh, I can't tell you that. You see, it is a present for a lady.'

'Oh.'

'But to get back to my day. Following my time in the saleroom I went down to the quay. I'm very fond of Newcastle quay; there's so much of interest there: ships of all kinds loading and unloading, and the men from them, all nationalities. I sometimes think I would have liked to go to sea. But then we can't have everything we like in this life, can we?' And he waited for an answer, but when it wasn't forthcoming, he went on, 'But to get on with my day. Following my stroll on the quay I had a light evening meal before going to the theatre.'

'Oh,' she put in with raised eyebrows; 'you didn't dance tonight?'

'No. No, you could say.' He pulled a face at her, a funny face, and repeated, 'No; I didn't dance tonight. I went to the theatre, but I didn't enjoy it. No, I didn't enjoy it. So I came out during the interval and went back to the hotel. It's a very fine hotel and it's owned by a friend of mine. I think I've mentioned it before. Yes, yes.' He was nodding at her. 'Nothing to do with butlers, footmen and menials of any kind, because the waiters are not even menials. So, after a drink, or perhaps two or three, and some very good sandwiches, and of course conversation, I took the train from Newcastle and alighted in Fellburn, from which station I decided to walk back to this abode.'

'In order to sober up?'

'No, miss; I never take on so much alcohol of any kind that I need to sober up. My intake of liquor spreads a warmth through me which enables me to enjoy . . . just walking . . . just walking on a hard surface.'

She stared at him. She wanted to laugh at him and at the same time she wanted to cry. This twisting of her emotions not only troubled her but puzzled her. Her emotions of tears and laughter seemed closer than those of love and hate and only a thread held those two apart at times.

'Now, that was my day. What has yours been like? But before you tell me, as it is still my day off, I'm going to seat myself, and don't try to stop me' — he wagged a finger at her — 'I have my rights.'

She watched him pull out a chair and sit down at the end of the table, then place one elbow on it and cup his chin with his hand. He looked so different, so satisfied with himself, so pleased with life, his way of life, she wanted to startle him, burst the bubble, so she put her head back as if she were thinking, then said, 'I won't only tell you what's happened today, but also what's happened this week. Starting with Monday morning . . . I had a proposal of marriage.'

He did not blink an eyelid, nor did his expression change. He said simply: 'Yes, and what happened next?'

That her news apparently had no effect

on him caused her jaws to tighten now as she said, 'My brother, dear Howard, came to me in a pitiable fashion. He was in dire trouble, and needed five hundred pounds or else, from what I could gather, he would be beaten up by bookmakers.'

'Did you give him the five hundred?'

'Yes, I did.'

'I am surprised at that; but go on.'

'I was again pressed for an answer to the proposal of marriage.' And she waited some seconds for a reaction; but still none was forthcoming, and so she went on, 'Well, in between times I learned that my mother is still wanting a divorce; then later that she is going to marry the son of the man to whom my grandmother sold her family's business. I learned from my father that this came as a bit of a shock. He had expected my mother to come back to him; and he became incensed. Myself, I can't see why. Then today it comes to my knowledge that my dear brother, Howard, has left home. He has been turned out by my mother, because two men called and demanded that her son pay up the three hundred pounds he owed for his betting . . . *Three* hundred, mind you, not the five that he had so pathetically begged from me to pay these same men. Also that he is living with a married woman whose husband is at sea. And lastly, I learned that nothing is going to deter my young sister Jessie from entering the Catholic Church and eventually becoming a nun. That was my week . . . Oh, but that is not all. No. My father has decided that his life is worth living only if I will always remain at hand for him to come home to. So, I have a choice! I can accept the proposal of marriage, or I can remain in this house living only to welcome my father when he deigns to return from whatever night pursuits with which he fills his life; and oh yes, as the song says, gradually watch myself . . . withering on the vine.'

Maitland's hands went across the corner of the table and grasped hers tightly now, and his voice was low when he said, 'You will do neither, my dear. Do you hear? Neither. You will soon be twenty-one: you can please yourself then; no-one can stop you. Three weeks ago I thought the barrier to be insurmountable, but today I made up my mind to climb it.'

He now drew her hand towards his face and, turning her palm upwards he laid his lips on it. When the tears sprang to her eyes, and she muttered, 'Oh, Maitland,' he got to his feet, saying, 'Not Maitland; Roger, and . . . Janet.'

They both realised what was about to happen next, but at that moment they were checked by the sound of a door opening and banging closed. And when the library door was thrust wide they were both standing looking towards it.

Samuel was well into his cups but he wasn't so drunk as not to sense an unusual atmosphere, and more so when he came up and saw his daughter dabbing her face with her handkerchief.

'What's this?' His voice was thick. He turned now and looked at Maitland. 'Thought it was your day off. No place for you at this end of the house on your day off.'

'I always do a round, even on my day off, sir.'

'Aye, well; but what's this? What are you crying for?'

'I am not crying. I have a slight cold.'

'Oh aye? You hadn't a slight cold at dinner-time when I last saw you. Full of temper you were then. Couldn't get a word out of you. Anyway, what's going on? It's well after eleven.' He pointed a waving hand towards the clock. 'You been saying something to her?'

'Yes. Yes, I have. I've been telling her she's a highly intelligent, beautiful woman, and there's a different life before her if she has the mind to choose it, and that it is entirely up to her what she does with it.'

'Bugger me! But you have, eh? And who the hell d'you think you are to tell her what to do?'

'I am a friend. I always have been.'

'A friend? Well, friend, get to hell out of it and about your duties!'

'My duties do not commence until after twelve o'clock, sir, but good night.' Maitland inclined his head towards Samuel, then smiled at Janet before turning about and walking slowly from the room.

'That bugger'll have to go. D'you hear what I said?'

'Yes, Dad, I heard what you said; that bugger'll have to go. And now you hear what I have to say. You're drunk, but you're not all that drunk. If he goes, I go. Good night.'

In one sweep she gathered the loose papers from the table and into her arms; then she, too, left the room.

Samuel stood for a moment staring after her. Even when she had closed the door behind her he still kept his gaze directed down the room. Then with a plop he sat down on the chair she had vacated and, resting his forearm on the library table, he slowly looked about him. The racks were filled with books, and he had never read one of them, hardly taken one from the shelves, but that bugger had. He had had the run of this house. He had educated himself from this room. That was just since he had taken over the house, because the other lot, they wouldn't have given him any free hand. He'd been too bloody lenient with him, too soft. But he'd put a stop to that. Aye; aye, he'd put a stop to that. What had she said? If he goes, I go. She couldn't mean that. Oh, but it was Janet who was talking, not Alice, or that silly bitch Alicia, or the come-on nun, or the one still clinging to her mother's skirts. No, it was Janet, who had a man's mind and a man's determination while still being very much a woman. And all of a sudden she seems to have become very attractive. And look how she was rigging herself out! All since she came into her gran's money. Her pittance from the library never stretched to her buying the sort of clothes she was wearing now. It was a pity she had got that money and the house; it was the worst thing that could have happened — the house. And what had she said? If he goes, I go. Where would she go? Well, need he ask? My God! Yes. Need he ask? She had got him in a cleft stick. And if that fellow left this house to the women, what then? The place would be adrift: they were so used to taking orders. It would mean that he would have to employ somebody else. And where would he find another Maitland? He'd been all through this before, hadn't he? He'd have to think. His head was buzzing. He was tight. He knew he was tight, but he wasn't all that tight, but they weren't to know that. He could be so tight that he had no memory of what happened. Aye, likely that was the best plan. Forget about it for the time being, but make sure that he kept his eye on both of them. It would mean staying at home more nights. Well, that wouldn't be a bad thing. And if he went out he could always come back on the hop.

He got to his feet and brought his left hand down hard on the table. Anyway, what was the matter with him? What was he worrying about? She would never marry Maitland. Twenty years older than her and him a servant. No, of course not. She had more in her head than that. And anyway, there was the librarian. She had been to tea with his people, played tennis, and one thing and another with him. What was he worrying about? But, nevertheless, he'd keep a lookout on both of them. And she wasn't twenty-one yet, anyway.

God! he was tired. Aw, to blazes with everything. Sometimes he wondered if life was worth living.

The next morning, when Janet entered the breakfast-room a few minutes after her father and heard him talking to Maitland, she said to herself, Oh, so that's how it's going to be, is it? For Samuel was saying, 'I'll have coffee this morning, black. I've got a head like a stairhead. I must have had a skinful last night. Yet I can't remember having more than usual.'

Maitland made no response, but he greeted Janet in his usual way: 'Good morning, miss,' and she answered briefly and rather hoarsely, 'Good morning.'

'You got a cold?' was Samuel's greeting to her.

'No . . . not that I'm aware of.'

'Then what you croaking for?'

'Was I croaking?' She looked across the table to where Maitland was now placing a cup of coffee before her father, and she said, 'Coffee this morning? Why the change?'

'Well, if you want to know, I've got a thick head.' And it was no lie, Samuel had a thick head; but what was more to the point, since wakening up and remembering most of what had transpired last night in the library he had a worried mind.

When he said, 'No bacon this morning, just a piece of toast,' Janet thought, Oh, he's playing it well, for there was one thing he enjoyed and would have under any circumstances and that was his breakfast. She couldn't ever remember him going without his bacon and eggs, often accompanied by a sausage and kidneys, washed down by two, sometimes three, cups of tea, ending up with toast, the butter on it almost as thick as the bread.

As if she had said aloud, Two can play at your game, Dad, he raised his head sharply when she said to Maitland, 'I'll have the lot this morning; I'm feeling rather hungry.'

'Sausage and kidney?' Maitland enquired of her now.

'No, not both, just a sausage.' She had almost added, 'Have you any black pudding?' That would have been showing her hand too much and turning the situation into a farce. But it was no farce. Oh no; there was nothing to laugh at in what was taking place: her father's determination to thwart any plans of hers and to keep her tied to him whatever the cost.

There was a knock and Sarah entered the room with the mail on a silver tray, and

Samuel greeted her with, 'That's late this morning. Give it here.' But Sarah was already handing it to Maitland, who took it from her and, after swiftly sorting through the small pile, as he always did, he placed six letters by the side of Samuel's plate, and one by the side of Janet's. And she, recognising Eddie's handwriting, slit open the envelope and began to read.

Across the table, Samuel laid aside five of the letters, knowing that they were dealing with business, and he too slit open the envelope that he knew would be from one of his sons. And he had hardly begun to read when he lifted his eyes from the page and, his face bright, he said, 'He's passed. He's a sub-lieutenant. My! My! What d'you think of that?'

He was addressing Maitland, whose reply was immediate and genuine: 'Splendid sir. That is the beginning,' only for it to be dashed as being luke-warm.

'What are you talking about, man, beginning. He began two years ago. He's halfway there.'

'Well, I don't suppose they'll make him captain of a battleship in four years, sir.'

'No, nor do I. But I thank you to keep your bloody sarcasm to yourself.'

'It was merely a statement, sir. No sarcasm was intended, for I'm sure Master Edward will soon be first officer on the upper deck, but naturally it will take time. That was what I was implying. He has just finished being a mid-shipman, and now he's a sub-lieutenant. In two years time he'll likely be a lieutenant. But it might take longer to become a lieutenant-commander. And then who knows. He could be in charge of a frigate.'

'God Almighty! You rile me at times. You think you know every bloody word in the book, don't you?'

'No, sir, only what I read in your library. It is all there. When I knew the young men were going into the Navy I looked up the procedure, that is all. Such as, now he will likely sign on for seven years.'

During the one-sided discourse Janet had been watching Maitland while still holding her opened letter and she was smiling so broadly she was on the point of laughing outright. And now her father turned on her, crying, 'You think that's funny? I call it —'

'No, I don't think it's funny. Maitland was just passing on information that he had read. What I am smiling about' — and now she pointed to her father's letter which was lying open on the table — 'is what Eddie says about marrying the girl.'

'*What? What you talking about?*' Sam now lifted up the letter from the table, glanced over it, then looking at her again, he said, 'Marrying what girl? All this tells me' — he shook the sheet of paper — 'is that he had got through. To put it in his own words —' he now read from the letter, ' "It was a hard swim. Not the dog paddle I imagined it would be. We had a great night in the mess. I think I must have got drunk." ' He looked at Janet again. 'So what's all that twaddle about?'

'Oh, I don't think he got drunk on whisky or wine; although perhaps he did, but what he is telling me here' — she now tapped her sheet of paper — 'is that there was a dance and he met this girl. She's an Australian. She was visiting her aunt, who was the wife of one of the instructors at the college. And he danced with her three times.' She glanced at the letter again, then repeated, 'Yes, three times. I'll read it to you:

"I waited until the third dance to tell her that I was going to marry her. I didn't ask her, I just told her. And she laughed so much that we had to stop dancing and sit it out. And she couldn't stop laughing. When I told her that I'd give her two years to get her bottom drawer ready, she practically stopped the dance. Oh, it was a great night. But I'm serious, Janet. I mean to marry that girl one day." '

'Bloody young fool! I'll have something to say to him.'

Janet folded up her letter, placed it back in the envelope, then said, 'He is a man. He is in the Navy. He has his own life to lead and you can't do anything about it.'

'Oh, can't I?'

'*No.*' The laughter had gone from her face, and she had accompanied the 'no' with a thud of her fist on the table. And now she cried at him, 'Get it out of your head, Dad, that you can run people's lives. You have lost Mam, you have lost three daughters, and a son. You have three sons and a daughter left. Now you will be well advised not to interfere with their lives, and that includes mine. Do we understand each other?'

And she thrust her chair back, grabbed up the cup of tea that Maitland had placed to her hand, and stalked out of the room, leaving a silence behind her in which the two men neither spoke nor moved: Samuel sitting at the table, one hand lying flat on the open letter, his injured one pressed against his chest, and Maitland standing at the sideboard, his back to him, his hands resting on the open-worked lace runner on which the breakfast dishes were spread, together with the spirit-heated, double-shelved and lidded meat tray.

'I don't deserve this, you know.'

Maitland turned slowly and looked at the man who was addressing him. He watched him. Sam's head was shaking slowly now as he said, 'I've worked hard all me life. Oh, I know I keep saying it, but I have, and right up to this very day. And what for? I've been asking meself that a lot lately — what for? This afternoon I might pull off a deal with the Army: I'm to meet three men in Newcastle. If they have accepted my estimate then I'll have an order for a thousand pair of boots, and I don't think they would have asked to see me if there wasn't something in the wind as regards clinching the deal. And I'll make a pretty penny out of that lot if I sign on the dotted line this afternoon. And that could be the beginning of a contract worth thousands of pounds. I only thought yesterday, if there was a war I could become a millionaire. But at this minute I'm asking myself again, what's it all for? She was right, you know. I've lost half me family besides me wife. Why?'

He drew in a long breath, then he pushed

his chair back and got to his feet. And now, his voice changing, he said, 'But that's as far as it's going to go. What's left I'm going to hang on to. There's more ways of killing a cat than banging its head against the wall. D'you get my meaning, Maitland?'

'No, sir, I don't.'

'Then you're not as bright as I thought you were.'

He walked along to the end of the dining-table and there pointed to the hot plate, saying, 'You can take that lot back into the kitchen and they can give themselves a double stuffing. You're all damned lucky, you know, to be in this house, so you should tread carefully. You should all tread carefully.' And he walked to the door.

With the closing of the door Maitland brought his doubled fist up to his mouth and pressed his knuckles tightly across it. His clenched teeth were stiffening his cheeks and for a moment he had the unusual urge to lift up the hot plate and splatter its contents across the room.

It had to end, soon; he couldn't stand any more of this. He must see her, and alone. It must come into the open. He had been a fool not to speak sooner. But he hadn't wanted to take the girl, he was waiting for the woman; and she was a woman now, every inch of her. The only thing he regretted was that he hadn't spoken before her grandmother died. But what did it matter? He had enough saved of his own to start him up in business; he wouldn't need to touch a penny of her money. But he must get her alone, and somewhere out of this house.

6

Janet did not know how she got through the following week without exploding, for life seemed to be closing in on her from all sides. She loved her work in the library and, in a way, she had looked upon it as an escape from the house. That was, until ten days ago, when she had given Mr Arthur Stanford a definite 'no' to his proposal. He had been so disinclined to take it that she had been obliged to raise her voice, and only this had seemed to convince him, when he came back at her with, 'Then you should not have led me to believe otherwise.'

She had never led him to believe otherwise, she stressed, and for the first time in their acquaintance he spoke to her as he might have done to Phoebe Carrington when she first started, or to the young boy who was now down in the basement. And this attitude had continued up till today; in fact, up till this very minute, because here she was in his office, together with Miss Stillwater, Miss Carrington, Miss Barker and young John Inness. It was the monthly meeting and discussion, always held on the last Friday evening of the month, after the library had closed, of course. And he was saying, 'There is a matter being discussed at the present moment among librarians with regard to uniform. It concerns a suggestion that all library assistants should wear a certain type of overall. And I think I favour this suggestion, because, as you yourselves know, dark skirts show the dust.'

'But we wear a kind of uniform now, don't you think? A white blouse, black bow, and dark skirt constitutes a uniform, surely,' said Janet.

Arthur Stanford, the man who had professed his love for her only a short while ago, looked at her coldly, saying, 'It is only a uniform, Miss Fairbrother, by the fact of the white blouse and the dark skirt, and these, I can see, in your case are of a different material, being your personal choice. A uniform would be in the form of an overall of one colour and shape.'

A diversion was caused here by the young male daring to laugh and say, 'But they're all different shapes, sir.'

Young John should have become frozen by the look the librarian cast upon him; but he took heart from the smothered giggles and Janet's suppressed smile as she glanced sideways at him.

Choosing to ignore the remark, Arthur Stanford went on, 'Anyway, the matter is under consideration.'

'We might as well be shop assistants, or work in a subscription library,' Miss Barker dared to put in now. 'I for one wouldn't wear an overall.'

'If it became compulsory you wouldn't have any choice, Miss Barker. There are rules, you know . . . rules.'

Miss Barker stared back at him. Oh, she had the choice: she was going to be married soon. That's why she had dared to stand up to him and say what she thought.

Janet put in now, 'Did you see Miss Read's article in *The Librarian*, Mister Stanford? about the hundred and twenty pounds a year offered by the London County Council for a woman librarian, when a Mr MacKnight, through whose departure the position was becoming vacant, was earning fifty pounds more a year than was being offered, as Miss Read pointed out, and angrily, because it was a woman and so wasn't worth as much as a man, even though she would have had to go through the necessary examinations to be eligible for the position. And Miss Read was given credit by the Library Assistants' Association for calling attention to this injustice . . . Did you see the article?'

The question was too innocently put.

'Did you happen to be at the conference at Exeter, Miss Fairbrother?'

The sarcasm was evident to them all and she retorted stiffly, 'I would have been, Mister Stanford, had I been given leave. But I follow Miss Margaret Read's articles closely. I think she keeps us so in touch as to what is going on and how we could, if we were so mindful, help ourselves, generally keeping us up to date on lectures in English Literature et cetera. But now she says there are to be courses arranged in various areas, to include classification and Library Administration.' She stressed the latter words. 'And I am thinking about asking for leave to attend them.'

Such a request had not previously crossed her mind, nor had she intended to spread the knowledge she had gained from reading Miss Read's articles, but the man's attitude towards her in the past days, and openly now in front of the others, had riled her.

She had the satisfaction of seeing his face redden and the effort being demanded of him to keep his voice level as he replied, 'If you put your request in writing, I shall see it is passed on to the committee. Whether they grant you leave or not has to be seen.'

'I have already applied to the committee and to the council stating my wishes.'

Why on earth had she said that? Oh dear! There was nothing for her now but to get a letter off as quickly as possible to both parties. Anyway, that had settled it, now she would have to make a move. Well, there were other libraries.

She was aware that her audacity had put Miss Stillwater's mouth into a gape, and brought Nancy Barker's and Phoebe Carrington's eyes wide, while young John Inness dared to grin at her. She couldn't stand any more of this. She looked straight across at the man who, since she had first come into the library, had shown her favour, with one thought in his mind, but which had held no reflection in hers; and in an even tone she now said to him, 'If you will excuse me, I must go. I have an appointment,' and she stood up and had begun to walk to the door when he retorted: 'This is very bad form and shows a bad example, Miss Fairbrother.'

She turned slowly and looked directly at him as she replied, 'Well, Mister Stanford, you know quite a lot about both those faults, as you have demonstrated over the last few days.'

She could hear the echo of the gasps when she was halfway down the library. She had burnt her bridges all right now. Anyway, she'd have to work out a month's notice. But first she must see Maitland, privately. Why must she always say Maitland? His name was Roger. She thought of him now as Roger. But how were they going to meet? . . .

As if she had actually just asked that question of Maitland, he answered it almost immediately he opened the door to her: he gave her no greeting, but as he helped her off with her coat he said, 'Your father's in the billiard-room; he's been in an hour or more. I will be at the station waiting, just after four tomorrow. I have changed my day.'

She turned from him. He had her coat over his arm and was holding her hat and she looked at him softly and said, 'Thank you, Maitland.' He inclined his head towards her, and as he walked away her father emerged from the corridor.

'You're late, aren't you?'

'It was the monthly meeting. I'm not as late as usual; I walked out.'

'What d'you mean, you walked out?' He was now following her into the drawing-room.

'I had what you would call a stand-upper with my boss.'

'The librarian?'

'Who else? I've only one boss.'

He smiled at her now as he said, 'As you say, as you say. But that man Stanford, I thought . . . well, I thought —'

'Yes? What did you think?'

'Well, I thought he was gone on you.'

'Yes, he's gone on me, and he's gone too far. He proposed marriage and I refused him.'

'Well, well! That was your first proposal, I suppose?'

'Yes, Dad, my first proposal, but, I hope, not my last.'

He had taken up his usual position with his back to the fire and there was a thin smile on his face as he said, 'You've got hopes then?'

'Oh, yes; a woman is never without hopes, not in that line anyway. You should know that from your experience.'

'You're in one of those moods, are you? What was the row about?'

'You wouldn't understand if I told you.'

'Oh, I'm dim now, am I? Besides being a loud-mouthed bully, I'm a loud-mouthed dim one.'

'No, Dad; you're not dim. You're uneducated in the real sense of the word, an uneducated but highly intelligent man with a one-track mind. And that track is so narrow that you won't let anybody pass you.'

'You know something? I don't like you when you talk like that; in fact, I could slap your face for you.'

'I know that, because you recognise the truth.'

'Truth? Truth? What d'you know about truth? It can be a killer in lots of ways. If I was to say to you that you're a plain-faced, unattractive sourpuss, but you're highly intelligent, what would you think of that?'

'The first I'd admit to, but I'm neither unattractive nor a sourpuss. And I'll ask you this. If you think I'm unattractive and a sourpuss, why do you seek my company?'

'Simply because I've got no-one else I can talk to.'

'You were never at a loss for someone to talk to up to this last week or so, because you were never in; you had all your business associates, and in the evenings, your club, or your other attractions. Dad —' her voice was lower now and more intimate as she said, 'I wish you would stop your acting and come out into the open. It would be better all round.'

'Better all round, you say. You don't know what you're asking. Do you want murder done? 'cos I'm quite capable of it, you know.'

'Dinner is served, sir.'

They both started and looked towards the door. There was a pause before Samuel exclaimed, 'Those are the best words I've heard today, so let's get at it.'

As he walked quickly towards the door, Janet stood, with her head lowered and staring at the floor. Her whole body seemed to have shrunk because for the first time in her life she was experiencing real fear; she was recognising that her father was a dangerous man.

On Saturday afternoon, she did not ride her bicycle to the library; she walked to the main road and took the tram into the town. It was a miserable day; sleet was falling and the sky seemed to be lying on top of the building; but her world was bright. At ten minutes past four she would be at the station and they'd be together, alone. Even in a train load of people, and a town full of people, they'd be alone. For once they'd be alone . . .

She was clearing her desk when Arthur Stanford came to the counter and, in a low voice he said, 'I wish to speak to you in my office before you go, Miss Fairbrother.'

She glanced at the clock. It was four minutes to four, the last two customers were going out of the door and John Inness was standing at the side of it ready to push the bolts in.

'I'm sorry, Mister Stanford,' she said; 'I have a pressing appointment. I must leave at four o'clock.'

'Miss Fairbrother,' his voice was low and his words were slow, 'this is an order: I wish to speak to you before you go.'

She now leant slightly forward towards him across the counter and her voice, too, was low and her words slow when she replied, 'Mister Stanford, I wouldn't obey that order tonight, not from God Almighty or the devil. So you have my answer. Is that clear?' And on this she turned and, almost at a run now, moved along by the counter, lifted the flap at the end, let it down with a bang, made her way to the cloakroom, grabbed up her coat, hat, scarf, gloves, and bag, and was dressing herself as she crossed the library towards the door, past the white-faced librarian and a grinning boy, who quickly pulled the door open for her.

John Inness did not know what had passed between Miss Fairbrother and the boss; he only knew that . . . she had given it him again. Oh, he did like her. 'Good night, Miss Fairbrother,' he called after her into the darkening street. And she half paused and shouted back to him, 'Good night, John.'

At the end of the road she boarded the tram. The station was four stops away, and when she alighted she had to prevent herself from running across the open cobbled yard. In the lamplit booking office she looked around, to see a number of people standing in a queue at the ticket window. He wasn't among them. But . . . there he was at the entrance to the platform, dressed in a grey suit and a darker grey overcoat.

They walked along the platform, neither of them speaking; and when he took her arm, it was to say simply, 'It's due at any minute.'

'Oh,' she answered.

The train came in and he drew her further along the platform looking for an empty carriage; but at last he had to open a door and help her into the company of two old men both smoking very old pipes, and a husband and wife, the woman nursing a young baby who kept whining. But they were sitting down together.

The train made three stops before it entered Newcastle Central; and then they were walking through the station and out into the city. Now he was holding her arm close to his side and he said, 'We'll have some tea at the place where I usually have dinner. It's . . . it's very nice. They are friends . . . I know I've mentioned them before.'

She made no reply; she felt unable to talk. There were no words tumbling about in her mind; it seemed blank, empty.

They walked up Northumberland Street, across the Haymarket. The shops were all lit up, the streets crowded with scurrying people, seemingly all hurrying to get out of the sleet and the cold.

Now he was leading her into an hotel. The lobby was warm and brightly lit. At the reception desk the young man smiled at Maitland, saying, 'Oh, good afternoon, sir. What a day it is! Shall I ring and tell Mister Crawford that you are here?' Then he stopped and pointed, adding, 'Oh, there he is, sir. There he is.'

Maitland now turned to where a small, smartly dressed man was coming towards them and exclaiming, 'Well, well! You're before your time, aren't you? Oh.' He stopped and turned his gaze on Janet as if just recognising that they were together; and Maitland said, 'Donald, this is Miss Fairbrother. Janet, my friend, Mister Crawford, who owns this hotel.'

As she said, 'How d'you do?' the man took her hand and shook it, saying, 'I am delighted to make your acquaintance, Miss Fairbrother. But come, get out of that damp coat. And it will be tea you're wanting?' He had turned to Maitland. 'Too early for dinner.'

'Yes, just tea, Donald.' Maitland helped Janet off with her coat, then took off his own and handed them to a porter who was standing by. And as Mr Crawford led them towards the dining-room, he said over his shoulder, 'There's quite a crowd inside. We've been very busy since before three. It's the weather, I suppose. But we'll find a place for you even if I have to give you my alcove.' He turned and nodded his head at Maitland; and Maitland said, 'That would be nice.'

'Yes, why not? You may take the alcove and poor me will go and sit in the kitchen and have my tea amongst all the clutter and busy-busy.'

'I'm very sorry for you, Donald.'

'I appreciate that.'

They were now wending their way between tables, some holding four, some six, and some only two people. And when Mr Crawford ushered them into a panelled-off section that held a table for four with a 'Reserved' card on it, Maitland said, 'Thank you very much indeed, Donald. It's very kind of you.'

'Nonsense, it's nothing. Anyway, I've got to go now. I'll send Frank to see to you. But come and have a word before you leave.'

'Yes. Yes, I will.'

There was a velvet-covered rail attached to the partition of the alcove and she leant her shoulders against it and gazed at the man she had seen nearly every day for eleven years, yet who appeared as an entire stranger to her at this moment. Here he was, a man on friendly terms with the owner of this lovely hotel, and the staff treated him as if he was someone of importance. Yet, after all, he was Maitland the butler.

'Come back.'

'What?'

'Come back from where you'd gone. You looked miles away. Give me your hands. It doesn't matter who sees us. Those people across there' — he moved his head towards the opening of the alcove — 'they're concerned with their own lives. Let us be concerned with ours. Oh.' He now held her hands tightly before saying, 'Oh, Janet,

Janet. You've got no idea what this moment means to me. That we can sit together here like two ordinary human beings . . . say something to me.'

'I . . . I can't. I can't. Not at the moment. I'm . . . I'm so overcome.'

'Oh, my dear, dear, Janet. Just to hold your hands, to be able to sit and look at you without being on my guard, without waiting for the drawing-room door, the library door, the breakfast-room door to open, and the look that says "What are you up to? What have you been saying to my daughter? How dare you look at her? Who are you, anyway?" It's been a kind of hell lately, you know; but you do know, don't you?'

'Oh, yes, yes —'

'Good evening, Mr Maitland,' a voice broke in.

'Oh, good evening, Frank. How are things?'

'Splendid, sir, splendid. Business is brisk. This is the weather for it.'

'Has the new waiter arrived yet?'

The man laughed now, saying, 'No, he keeps hanging on. It should have been the middle of last week.'

'Yes. Yes, of course.' Maitland now looked across at Janet, saying, 'Frank is waiting for his third son to arrive. It's going to be a son because he's going to make them all waiters, but in his own hotel, of course.'

The man now nodded his head at Janet as he placed the cup and saucer to her side. 'He's a great kidder, is Mr Maitland. But you know, there's lots of truth spoken in jest, miss.' He now bent towards Maitland as he took the last plate from the tray, saying quietly, 'It could come about too, if the customers would only double their tips,' then turned quickly away on a laugh.

She was again leaning back against the velvet pad, her eyes closed now, and he said, 'What is it?'

After swallowing deeply she said, 'I want to laugh, not just a polite laugh, a real, real, belly laugh. I want to stand up and laugh.'

'Go on, do it then. But before you start I think you had better pour the tea . . . and oh! look at those cakes! oozing cream. Well, I'm going to indulge. And you must too; you need to be fattened up . . . No; no, you don't, you've got a beautiful figure.' His voice dropped. 'You're beautiful altogether. If only you would realise it. You're beautiful altogether.'

She poured out the tea and handed him a cup, but she did not speak or make any remark, not even as she took a piece of bread and butter from the plate he was handing her; and his voice was full of concern now as he said, 'What is it, my dear?'

She swallowed again before she answered, her eyes cast down: 'How is it that every time I desire to laugh I also want to cry, because now I'm making a great effort not to burst into tears.' She blinked her eyes, looked up at him and smiled, then said, 'And if you don't want that to happen, you'd better stop telling me lies.'

His voice had a serious note to it as he now said, 'I don't think I've ever told you a lie in my life, not from the day you came into it, a very plain scraggy little girl, who would keep talking to me, talking at me, hounding me. I think you must have crept into my heart then although I wasn't aware of it, because at that time my heart, to use a novelette phrase, was broken, as I'd had designs on Miss Cissy Moore, the nurse to Lady Irene Boulter's little girl. And I would have thought that in the servant class we were on equal terms; but apparently not so, for she was entertaining other ideas well above her station, for she dared to have her eyes on Colonel Stacey's nephew. Yet, didn't I follow in her footsteps? And all through a pestering little girl who would follow me about.'

'I did pester you, didn't I? I sometimes wonder what I would have done if you had left, because I used to go through agonies fearing that something would happen. I wanted to say to Dad: Stop yelling at him, he'll walk out.'

He smiled gently now as he said, 'I look back, too, and I often thought about leaving and wondered why I stayed on, because your father used to irritate me more than a little at times with his unnecessary bombast. I was bumptious enough to think, when I first took him in hand, I could alter him, or at least file down his rough tongue and manners. But no, he takes pride in being what he is. And when you were sixteen and I knew how it really was with me, oh, I went through the mill then. I thought the best thing I could do was to get out, at the same time knowing I couldn't leave you. And in a way, cursing you. Yes,' he nodded at her, 'because there was a woman of my own age, just down the drive, the Talbots' niece, Sally, whom I am still big-headed enough to think was just waiting for me to pop the question. I had never any affection for her, although she was a very nice girl. And I suppose I used her in a way. I danced with her, went to the pictures with her, took river jaunts with her, but of course, Mike and Kate were always there, too, and I know they were waiting for me to say the word. At times I felt awful about it.'

'Is she still waiting?'

'No. Her mother died and her father moved South and she went with him . . . But look; come along and eat something. We must clear at least one plate, or Donald will be popping in and asking if things were not to our satisfaction, ma'am and sir.'

She selected a cream cake; then looked beyond the cubicle, to where four people were leaving a table. She broke the cream cake in two with her fork but didn't attempt to eat it. And when he said, 'Isn't it nice?' she looked at him, and very quietly she said, 'I can't remember a moment in my life when I haven't loved you. I don't remember anything that happened before I was ten and I stepped into that house and first saw you. I love you so much it has become a daily pain. It has brought me no happiness, no joy, nothing but an ache and lately a great want. I . . . I've always felt older than my years and I feel that I've been loving you for a number of lifetimes . . . Oh! please don't.'

He had left his seat and walked round the table and he was sitting close to her, her hands held to his breast, and there were tears in his eyes as he said, 'I want to kiss you, the first kiss. I want to hold you so close that you will sink into me and be there forever. And I shall, but it can't be here. Oh! my dear.' He was now cupping her face tightly between his hands and his voice was thick as he muttered, 'I'm drunk. I'm drunk with love of you.'

She glanced over his shoulder to see a waiter was showing a couple into the seats at the empty table and she said, 'There are people sitting down now. Let . . . let us finish the tea and then go.'

He slowly took his hands from her face, then rose and went back round the table and seated himself opposite her again.

She began to eat the cream cake, and he didn't speak until she had finished, when he said, 'Help me to clear this.' He was holding out the plate of bread and butter again. And she took a piece and nibbled at it; and after a moment she asked softly, 'What are we going to do?'

He replaced the half-eaten piece of bread and butter on his plate before he said, 'Candidly, dear, at this moment I couldn't give you an answer to that. All I can think of is that you are sitting there and that you love me, and that you have sliced the years off me. I am no longer forty-one. I am right back to the day when I first set eyes on you.'

'To me you have never changed from that moment, and you still look like a young man; and you must never wear anything but grey. From the day you leave the house you must never wear black again.'

'We are leaving the house . . . when?'

She now closed her eyes tightly before she muttered, 'Tomorrow. I wish I could say tomorrow, but Roger . . .' she put her hand out across the table where his was already awaiting hers, and she said, 'I'm afraid. I must admit it, I'm afraid of Dad. But whatever we decide we must get quickly away out of the town, far away, for some time, until he can accept the idea of us being married. And . . . and we *will* be married, won't we? Straightaway?' It was like a plea from a child and he answered, 'This very night. If it were possible I'd ask Donald to ring for a minister, and we'd have it done here and now. Oh, yes, here and now.'

She was nodding at him as she said, 'I know. I know. But I can't get Dad out of my mind. He's become dangerous. It is because he, too, is fearful. He's afraid of being left on his own. He knows the boys will never come home. So out of the eight he has bred, there is only me left. If . . . if they hadn't separated it might have been different. Yet, I don't know.'

'Listen, my dear; I am not afraid of him, and he or no-one else is going to stop us coming together. Never!' His jaws stiffened and he jerked his head and his words were even a growl as he repeated, 'Never! So let's make it tomorrow, for knowing now how you feel and fear him, I'll not be able to stay in that house any longer and listen to his abuse.'

She said, 'I can't sell Gran's house for five years. And we couldn't stay there anyway; he'd come. What would we do?'

'Take a house somewhere else in the meantime. And I would start my little business of training butlers and so on. There's a big market, you know, for butlers in America. They are transporting them by the boatload.' He laughed gently now. 'But it's true, the Americans like English butlers. And there's a great many wealthy people there.'

'And what would I do during this meantime you mention?'

'Well' — he sat back — 'you could help to instruct my numskulls in the correct use of the English language, the while you study to become a head librarian.'

'You would still like me to go on with my work?'

'Of course, my dear. And you love it, don't you?'

'Oh yes, yes. But it wouldn't matter.'

'It would matter, it would. You must continue to use that mind of yours, that is important. Your father, unintentionally' — he now pulled a face at her — 'provided me with the wherewithal to use mine. I've learned so much from those shelves that my confidence is unbounded; at least, in the fact that I can start a business on my own.'

Leaning forward again across the table, his voice a whisper, he said, 'Donald and his brother were both in my business, you know, both butlers. His brother has now established a home for elderly gentlemen.'

'Really?'

'Yes. How old d'you think Donald is?'

'Oh, sixtyish.'

'He is seventy-four; and he didn't start this business until he was near sixty, when his mistress died and left him a nice little sum. So you see, my dear, what one can do so can another. And I will . . . I will provide for you in exactly the way you have been used to. Oh, I know, I know' — he wagged his hand across her face — 'but what's yours is yours, my dear, and what is mine is yours also.'

'Oh, Roger.' Her voice was thick. 'What a pity we've only one life ahead of us.'

'Yes, isn't it? But you know, I think we've had many lives before. I have often wondered about this, especially when I questioned what was holding me to you, you a young girl and myself a settled man. I never thought of you as a daughter, and you could have been. I only know that when you were a small girl and your continued demands irritated me, I realised the situation was unusual. Oh' — he made an impatient movement — 'let us go, let us get outside, because there is something I want to do, something I must do.' With this he rang the small bell on the table, and when the waiter appeared he said to him, 'A lovely tea, Frank. But now we must be off.'

Janet said, 'Thank you,' and Frank bowed to her, saying, 'My pleasure, miss, my pleasure.' And as she passed into the main restaurant she heard him say, 'Oh, sir, there's no need for that now. No,' and Maitland reply, 'It isn't for you, it's for the coming waiter.' And at this there was an unusually loud laugh and Frank's voice saying, 'I'll give it to him, I will. I'll give it to him, sir.'

When they were in the hall and dressed,

Maitland said to the receptionist, 'Mr Crawford is likely busy, but tell him I'll pop in later in the week.'

'Yes, sir, I'll do that. Good night, sir. Good night, miss.'

Outside in the street, Maitland took her arm, saying, 'It's eased off, so we'll walk to the station, taking the long way round. There's a garden I'd like you to see.'

'In the dark?'

'Yes, in the dark. It's an open garden. I often go there when I'm doing my rounds of the city. I've sat and dreamed there.' He pressed her arm closer into his side, and they walked on, their steps matching, until they came to a short street that was clear of people with, at the end of it, a tall gas-lamp shining down on two stone pillars that at one time must have supported gates. And after walking her between them he said nothing for some time until he stopped, and this was in the dim light from another lamp some distance away. And now he slowly drew her into his arms and just as slowly laid his lips on hers. And so they stood, for what length of time neither of them knew.

When their faces drew apart they peered at each other through the dim light; then, as if a great wave had swept them together, they were enfolded again. Now his lips, smothering her face, finally came to rest on her mouth again and, their bodies so close as almost to become one, they swayed where they stood and, like the wave breaking itself on the shore, they lay spent against each other.

Her head was now resting limply on his shoulder, her hat just being saved from falling off by the pin caught in the bun of her hair.

'Oh, my darling.' He stroked her brow, saying, 'A little while ago I said I didn't know what we were going to do, but now there is one thing sure, we must be married, and soon.'

She raised her head and said, 'Yes, my dear, dearest . . . Maitland, soon.'

Then she dropped her head onto his shoulder again and began to laugh. Her body lying against his shook them both until the laughter was punctuated by a sob and brought him holding her tightly again, saying, 'There, there! my dear. Please! Please! don't cry. Don't. That will break me up.'

'I'm . . . I'm . . .'

'What? What d'you say?'

'I'm so happy.'

'You're happy? Oh, my dear, and you're crying so.' He, too, was laughing now.

After a moment she drew herself from his

arms, straightened her hat, and as she wiped her face with a handkerchief she said, 'I must get back to . . . to arrange things,' and he said, 'Yes, we must get back.'

'No, Roger, please. Don't come in with me. Not this night, my last, I hope, in the house. I want to remember this as a night apart, not broken by my father yelling and doing God knows what else. Oh, yes, God knows what else.'

'I'll come as far as the lodge, where I'll call in on Mike.'

As of one accord now, they walked out of the gardens and back to the station, caught the local train to Fellburn, and then the tram, which left them with quite a walk to the house, and throughout they exchanged hardly a dozen words. But before they reached the gates they were once again enfolded, their lips together, but gently now. Then he said, 'I'll pack my belongings tonight and stay with Mike and Kate in the lodge until you come.'

She paused a moment considering, then said, 'No, no. Go straight to the house. You know it. I'll get in touch with Annie and tell her to expect you. But we mustn't stay there; we must get off as soon as possible.'

'I'll do that. Yes, as you say it would be better that way. Yes, I'll do that.'

Once more they embraced; then she broke away from him and hurried up the drive. She couldn't explain to herself how she was feeling, only that her mind was repeating, It's happened. It's happened at last. At last it's happened.

She didn't go to the front door but made her way to the yard, intending to pass through the kitchen and take the back staircase that led to the gallery and the bedrooms. But on entering the kitchen, she was greeted by Mrs Wilding with: 'Oh, miss. Oh, miss.'

'What is it? What's the matter?' She turned now to Florence, and when Florence shook her head, she said, 'Fa . . . Father?' And Florence shook her head again, saying, 'He's . . . he's in the study, miss. He's in the study.'

'He's ill?'

'No. No, miss, he's not ill.' She glanced at Cook, but Mrs Wilding was staring down towards the table. So now she ran through the kitchen to the passage and into the hall, pulling off her hat, gloves and coat as she went.

At the study door she paused, and drew in a deep breath; then she pushed open the door and stood gaping at the sight of her mother seated to one side of the fire and her father to the other.

Her whole body seemed to deflate. She hadn't known what to expect, except perhaps bloodshed of some kind; yet, here they were, sitting as they had often done before when she was small and had come in to say good night.

Her father was on his feet. 'Where have you been?'

'Out. What's the matter?'

'You would be out at a time like this, wouldn't you? Well, in your travels, have you come across him? D'you know anything about this? Has he been to you?'

'What are you talking about? Or who are you talking about?'

She turned to her mother, who lifted a hand and pointed to a newspaper lying on the table. She picked it up, and there, in bold black type, half an inch high, she read the dramatic headline: MURDER IN THE EARLY MORNING. After staring at it she turned and glanced at her mother, then at her father, before reading,

'Around seven o'clock this morning, William Mailston was stabbed to death in front of his wife, at 49 Pike Street, a boarding house run by Mrs Mailston. Mrs Mailston, who was greatly distressed, could only say that one of her boarders, Howard Fairbrother, broke into her room and attempted to assault her. She was saved by the return of her husband. There ensued a fight in which Howard Fairbrother stabbed Mr Mailston in the neck. Mrs Mailston's screams brought another boarder from his room. According to Mr Norman Wilmer, he was woken up by screams; and when he opened his door he saw the man, Howard Fairbrother, rushing from his landlady's room. He was only partly dressed and when he ran past him and into his own room he noticed there was blood running down one arm. Mr Wilmer then went to the assistance of Mrs Mailston, who was in a hysterical state. And when he looked into her room and saw her husband lying on the floor and covered in blood, he himself immediately got dressed and called the police.

He said that Mr Fairbrother had been lodging at the house for some weeks and, as far as he understood, he was on friendly terms with Mrs Mailston. The police are now searching for Howard Fairbrother who, it is understood, is the son of Mr Samuel Fairbrother, the shoe manufacturer, well known in the town.'

The paper was shaking like a fan in her hand, and as if it had suddenly burned her, she dropped it and leaned back against the table, staring at her mother and father. But she wasn't seeing them or, for the moment, taking in the immensity of this tragedy. Instead, her mind was crying, Oh, Roger; Roger. Their beautiful day was blotted out. Their glowing future was gone. The wonder that they had exchanged in each other's embrace was now like the remnants of a dream that was slipping further and further away as consciousness took over. And this was consciousness, this room, her parents, the paper lying on the floor.

She felt she should say something, but what? She glanced from one to the other. They seemed changed. There was no aggressiveness in her mother's expression, whereas over the past weeks when she thought about her, her mind had presented her with the expression on her mother's face as her father had dragged her from the room in the house she considered to be hers.

And her father: he looked deflated; he seemed to have shrunk. Yet, when she almost croaked, 'Have they found him?' his voice was in a tone that was very recognizable: 'I don't know,' he said. 'They hadn't by four o'clock, when they came and scoured this house.'

'They've been here?'

'Of course they've been here; and they've been to his mother's.' He now flung his hand towards Alice. 'Practically took up the floorboards. My God! When is it all going to end? I often say, what next? to the things that happen in this house, but God in heaven! I never thought it would come to this pitch. And here I am, here we both are' — he again gesticulated towards Alice — 'on pins and needles, because they said they would be back, the police. As the inspector pointed out, if he's wounded, he's got to hide up somewhere . . . Funny about people.' He shook his head. 'Inspector Tipple, I know him as well as I know you. You could say I grew up with him; and when we meet at the club every now and again, it's back-slapping: Good old Sam. And he'll tell me the wife and the bairns are going into one of my shops tomorrow. Yes: that'll be in Bailey Street, the high class one. And more slapping on the back for good old Sam. And good old Sam gets word to Mrs Castel that when Mrs Tipple and her tribe visit the shop, they are to be offered the best and be given a good discount. But what a difference when Tipple becomes the inspector. Well, as he said, it's the first murder they've had in the town for fifteen years, and it'll hit the Sunday nationals by tomorrow morning.'

Janet again took in her father and mother. Alice was holding a handkerchief tightly across her mouth, her head was bent, and the tears were dropping off the end of her nose. She left the support of the table and went to her and she put her hand on her shoulder; but she could say nothing, for what was there to say? He's always been in trouble and you have cosseted him? If you had let Dad do what he wanted many a time and given him a hiding, he might have been better? . . . But would he? . . . What was bred in the bone . . . Yet there wasn't his kind of badness or weakness in her mother, or in her father. Her father was a selfish, domineering man, a possessively domineering man, but he wasn't a murderer. He wouldn't stab anyone . . .

Wouldn't he? What had she been afraid of for weeks now? Just that. She feared for Roger's life should he dare come into the open and express his feelings, or indeed for her own, should she do the same. He might live to regret what he had done, but there was no doubt in her mind that he would do it in a blaze of rage. So who could blame Howard?

'Crying won't get you anywhere.'

She looked at her father, and Alice looked at her husband, and gulping and spluttering, it was she who said, 'What d'you expect me to do? Have a good laugh? I'll get the blame anyway, won't I? for being soft with him. But when I follow your pattern, the one that you've used all your life, and show the heavy hand, what happens? He goes and lives with that woman: that is, when her husband's at sea. Well, by all accounts her husband had come home from the sea. In a way, it's a pity for him that he did. And it's a pity for me that I ever bore your first son, or any of them, if you ask me. For where am I now, while you are still where you always wanted to be, playing the big fellow?'

His hand to his brow, Samuel turned away, muttering, 'For God's sake! Alice, don't start that again, not at this time, not with this on our hands. D'you know what this means?' And he swung round to face her again. 'He'll swing. It's murder. Tipple says the man must have died almost immediately, the knife went into his jugular vein. It's murder, and he'll swing. Now we've got that to think about; but at this moment, let me tell you, I could put a rope round his neck and pull him up meself. By God! I could —'

Of a sudden he stopped and turned about to see Maitland standing at the door.

Janet watched her beloved walk slowly up the room. He did not look towards her but straight at her father, saying, 'I called in at the lodge. They told me. Is . . . is there anything I can do?'

Samuel sighed now and his voice sounded ordinary as he replied, 'No, there's nothing any one of us can do at the moment, Maitland, only wait until they find him. God knows what'll happen then. Oh, but yes' — he was now nodding his head violently — 'as I've just said to my wife, there'll be a hanging.'

'There may be extenuating circumstances, sir. It could have been self-defence.'

Janet gazed at the man who was still dressed in that grey suit, even though it was now worn by the butler. For a moment she couldn't decide if she was vexed or pleased by the dual personality. Then she knew she was pleased. He was admirable. He was acting as he knew she would wish him to in the circumstances. But there would be no leaving the house for them tomorrow, no starting up this glorious new life with what she had tasted in the park. Would it ever come now? Yes. Yes, it must, it must. She had to check herself from moving towards him, for she could sense he was purposely avoiding her glance. He was addressing her mother now and saying, 'Good evening, ma'am.'

Alice did not answer him, but she inclined her head by way of acknowledgement, then wiped her face with her handkerchief. Maitland was about to speak when the door opened again and Sarah Johnson came into the room. Looking towards Janet, she said, 'There's a call on the telephone for you, miss. It's . . . it's Annie from your house.'

Janet glanced from one to the other before hurrying down the room and into the hall. And there, picking up the receiver, she said, 'Yes, Annie?'

Annie's voice was usually loud when speaking on the phone, being unused to such an instrument, but now she was whispering and Janet said, 'Speak up, dear. I can't hear you.'

'I'm afraid, miss. I mean, I went out to the coal-house and . . . and I heard something tumbling about in the store-house next door. I . . . I think there's somebody in there, you know, miss. And I didn't get the coal, I just rushed back in. I've locked the door. It . . . it could be, you know who, miss. But I'm on my own, you know. And you see —'

'It's all right, Annie, it's all right. I'll be over directly. Just stay where you are. Keep the door locked.' She put the phone down and hurried back into the drawing-room. They were all waiting for her, their eyes fixed on her. She said, 'It was Annie. She thinks there's someone in the outhouse.' She turned to her father, and after a second added, 'They wouldn't have thought of searching there . . . Did they?'

'Not that I know of,' he answered; but nothing more, just stood staring at her, and she almost barked at him now, 'Well, hadn't you better go and find out, or at least come along with me?'

As if coming completely to himself, he barked back at her, 'You stay where you are, miss. Stay with your mother . . . Maitland, come on.'

She was about to protest when Maitland's eyes met hers for the first time, and he gave the slightest shake of his head, and as if he had given her an order she stepped back, let out a long slow breath, went to a chair and sat down.

Alone now with her mother, she felt ill at

ease. She looked at her: she was sitting staring towards the fire. Why wasn't she kneeling by her side, her arms about her, comforting her? Simply because there was no feeling of affection to impel her to do that. There had never been any real affection between them; she had always been closer to her father. She felt she understood him more, at least that she was more in sympathy with him.

The silence was weighing on her. She'd have to say something, or do something.

Suddenly, her mother was addressing her: 'You never liked him, did you?'

Janet was on her feet now and walking to the fireplace. She put both hands out and gripped the mantelshelf before she gave her answer, and grimly, 'No, I never liked him, because he was a liar and a cheat; and also perhaps because he was the one on whom you bestowed all your affection. In your eyes he could never do any wrong. And I wasn't the only one who missed your care; the other three boys did too.'

'Never!'

She swung round now and, looking down on her mother, she said, 'Yes, and they've spoken of it. And I'll tell you something else: you took it out on us all in retaliation after Dad insisted on him going to that private school. Nobody could please you for a time.'

She watched her mother now slowly shake her head and then pronounce: 'Dear God! my whole life was given to bringing you all up.'

'Yes. Yes, bringing us up, seeing that we were fed and well clothed: but lacking the one necessity to make us whole . . . love.'

'Well, let me tell you something, girl: you weren't a lovable child: you were the least lovable of the lot. The only thing you had to recommend you was your tongue, and you used it in the wrong way; and then acting like a little slut, and not only a little slut, but a young woman slut, trailing the butler.'

Janet was holding her throat tightly and the words were spilling out of her mind into her mouth, but she knew that if she were to utter them the rift would never, never heal, for she, as a child, might have trailed the butler, but even as a young woman she did not openly offer herself to him as her mother had once done. Without another word she swung round now and left the room and hurried upstairs and into her bedroom.

Oh! her mother, her mother. The bitterness of her: you weren't a lovable child, she

338

had said; and not only a little slut, but a young woman slut . . .

The fire was glowing bright in the small grate; the bed was turned down and her nightdress case was lying on the top of the padded quilt. The water in the jug was covered with a thick fleecy towel. It would be cold now, for it would have been placed there for her return shortly after four.

She stood in the middle of the room looking about her. This was to have been her last night here. The bedrooms in Sweetbanks Gardens were comfortable, but in an old-fashioned way. By comparison, this, her bedroom, and everything else in this house was luxurious. The life she had led in this house was that of an upper-class lady. Would she miss it in taking up life at Number 19 Sweetbanks Gardens? That's if she would ever have the chance to live there.

'No! No! Never!' She had spoken the words aloud. All she wanted to do was to throw off this luxurious bedroom, the whole house and this way of life and begin a real life with Roger . . . not Maitland. No, she never wanted to see Maitland again, nor the black suit; she wanted the man in the grey suit. But she couldn't have him. Well, not for a time, because he wouldn't walk out and leave her father until this matter was settled. But how did you settle a matter of murder? Only by the gallows. Oh Lord! Lord! And this was only the beginning. He'd have to be found, captured, tried, then sentenced.

She sank down on to the edge of the bed. The wardrobe mirror was opposite her. She should have seen her reflection in it but instead what she saw was her brother's face as it had been the day he came to the library begging the money from her. He had gained her sympathy, although he was lying. He was a born liar. Yet there was something else in the face that she was seeing now, and that was fear. Yes, it would be fear. He must be petrified because this was something he couldn't coax or lie his way out of.

It was almost twenty minutes later when she went downstairs again, and as she reached the hall she heard the car grind to a stop on the drive. She had the door open ready for her father and Maitland to enter. And to her look of enquiry her father said, 'He wasn't there. But there were signs that he'd been there.' He paused before adding, 'There was blood on some packing stuff he had been lying on.' He now asked, 'Has anybody rung?'

'No; no-one.'

When Maitland went to take his coat he said, 'No, leave it. I'll —' he paused again, before saying, 'I'll have to take the missis home.' It seemed that he did not know whether to address her as his wife or as Mrs Fairbrother, although she was still entitled to be addressed by either title.

He went on and into the sitting-room, where Alice, standing as if she was waiting for him, said, 'Well?' and he shook his head and answered, 'He had been there, but he was gone.'

'Dear God!'

'It's no use worrying more than you can help. Come on, I'll take you home.'

She passed him to go into the hall. Her coat and hat were lying on a chair and it was he who helped her into her coat. She ignored Maitland and Janet and left the house.

After a moment Samuel followed her, but not until he had turned to Maitland as if he were about to say something, only to think better of it. However, Maitland immediately followed, then held the car door open until they were both seated and Arthur Mears had again taken his place at the wheel. He did not watch the car's departure, but hurried back into the house to see Janet about to enter the drawing-room, and he followed her. And when, a moment later, they were standing on the hearthrug facing each other, he did not put his hands out towards her but quoted, 'The best laid schemes o' mice an' men gang aft a-gley. But don't worry, dearest, this is only a pause. We can't do anything at the moment, can we?'

She shook her head and, her voice breaking, she said, 'It was such a wonderful evening: it was like a glorious lifetime while it lasted.'

Now his hand did come out and take hers and, holding it tightly, he said, 'Our life together has been postponed. Get that into your head, my dear. Nothing or no-one is going to separate us. But for the time being I can't walk out, and you wouldn't walk out. So there we are. But we must be on our guard, because on top of all this, it would be disastrous if he became aware of our situation.'

'But this business could go on for weeks, months.'

'Yes, perhaps; but there is my day off, and my nights off. And you will have library meetings.'

'I'm leaving: life is unbearable there. I meant to tell you about it.'

'Well, there are other libraries. In fact, I

came across an advert in the local paper only yesterday. There's a new stationer's and bookshop opening in Gateshead, quite a big place, I understand. They will be running what they call a subscription library.'

'Yes, I know about them, but they are quite different from a public library. They don't have the range of books.'

'But any port in a storm.'

'I love you.'

'Oh, my dear, dear, my very dearest; and how I love you! I want to take you in my arms again but I mustn't, not tonight.' He stepped back from her, saying, 'Florence is crossing the hall; she'll likely be making her way here to see to the fire.'

'How d'you know that?'

'Oh, because of the sound of her feet. They always go flop, flop, flop, flop, when they leave the carpet and come on to the parquet floor before reaching the runner.'

'Oh, Roger, that is really funny and I should laugh. Is there anything you don't know about everyone in this house?'

The door was opening when he said, 'Not much, Miss Janet,' and he bent down and picked up the poker and put it into the fire, and Florence, hurrying up the room, said, 'Oh, Mr Maitland, I was just going to see to that.'

'It's all right, Florence.' He put the poker back on to the stand, adding, 'I'll leave it to you then,' and turning to Janet again, he asked, 'Is there anything I can get you, miss? A hot drink?'

'No, thank you.'

He bowed slightly towards her before turning away and leaving Florence to replenish the fire.

When the door had closed on him Florence, dusting her hands one against the other, said, 'Terrible business, miss, isn't it? We're all upset. Who would believe it? What d'you think will happen to him, miss?'

'I don't know, Florence.'

'They say he's wounded, miss, and if it happened early this morning he could be bleeding to death.'

Oh, if only he would . . . Good lord! she shouldn't be thinking like this. But it would solve his problem, and everybody else's.

'Are you all right, miss? D'you feel faint? Will I get you a cup of tea?'

'No, Florence; I'm all right, but . . . but it's been a very trying evening.'

Had it been a very trying evening? Not until she had returned to this house; the first part of it had been a fairy-tale evening. She must sit down.

She said, 'Yes, I think I will have a cup

of tea, Florence.' It was one way of ending the conversation and of getting her out of the room . . .

After she had drunk her tea, she hadn't long to wait before she heard her father's voice in the hall. And then he was striding into the room.

On reaching the hearthrug, he bent forward and held out his hands to the flame, and from this position he said, 'She's in a state.'

When Janet made no reply, still bending, he turned sharply towards her and repeated sharply, 'I said, your mother's in a state.'

'I heard you, Dad. What can I do about it?'

'You can answer me when I speak to you.'

'You made a statement; it wasn't a question.'

'Oh God above!' He stood up now. 'Don't you start on me with your grammar at a time when I'm nearly out of me wits. Have you thought about the scandal? The town's on fire with it.'

'You haven't murdered anyone, nor have I.'

'No,' he was thrusting his head towards her now, 'but he's my son. There it was in the paper: "Howard Fairbrother, the shoe manufacturer's son". How many friends will this leave me, eh? My so-called friends will skitter away like frightened rabbits. Oh, I know them. Has Joe or Martha Atkinson rung up? Or Jim Dawson? And I helped to start him up in his drapery business, don't forget that. The only one who's phoned up is Willie. Of course, he would; he wants the business, he's my solicitor. He can see the trial coming; there's big money to be made at trials. He'll engage a barrister. Oh, there's big rake-offs looming ahead for all of them. But what about me?'

She had risen from the chair and, standing facing him, she said, 'Yes, what about you, Dad? 'cos you're the only one concerned, aren't you? Even Mam doesn't come into it, nor I, nor the boys, nor the girls, just you.'

'It's me that'll have to carry the can, miss; it's me that'll have to fork out; it's me that'll have to bear the brunt of the sneers, because you nor none of the others are in business. You're not facing the lot of them every day; you're not sitting on a committee with them. Yes, there's only me concerned as I see it from where I stand. The upstart who took on a gentleman's residence, the home of a lord and lady, and who kept on their butler and staff, who brought his family up to believe they were somebodies. Yes, it's me that'll have to bear the brunt.'

He turned to the fire again and stood staring down into it and more to himself now than to Janet, he said, 'One son a murderer, the other three not giving a real damn for me. Oh, I know, I know how they feel. One daughter a young scut; and it wouldn't surprise me if she ended up on the streets; another going to closet herself in a convent, so she might as well be dead. That leaves Alice with one; and she's a dim one. If ever I've seen a simple-minded lass, she's one. Nearly sixteen now, and still talking and thinking like a precocious six-year-old. She'll be on her mother's skirts for life. But still, she'll be left with one and I'll be left with one.'

His tone had changed on the last words. He was no longer just thinking aloud. There was a question in these words and he turned now to her and added, 'Won't I?'

She stared him out before she said, 'It will all depend, Dad. If you loosen the reins you will still hold my love and affection, but if you pull on them you'll lose me altogether . . . D'you understand me?'

'Aye, I understand you. But I'll tell you something else. I'll see you dead before I let you belittle yourself. So, *d'you* understand *me?*'

'Yes, perfectly. And I'm going to tell you something more. If it wasn't for the trouble we're in at this minute, and that it's now nearing ten o'clock at night, I would walk out of here for good, because I have a house waiting for me and I have enough money to keep me for life, if I don't choose someone else to keep me. So you think on that, Dad. You can't keep me here against my will. You can't rule my life. If I stay with you it will be of my own free will. But that will only be for a time. Now we're in the open, and again I say, d'you understand me? And don't you try any heavy-handed stuff with me . . . or mine, for it's you who will suffer in the end. If you've got any sense at all left in that big bragging head of yours, you'll do as you've been doing for months past; walk softly.'

That she had shocked him, even staggered him, she was fully aware, because he did not say a word, not even when she passed close to him as she made to leave the room. No hand came out and clutched her and swung her round to show who was boss.

Her legs were trembling as she went up the stairs.

On the landing, Maitland was lowering the gas-lamp and he turned swiftly towards her, but she only paused for just a moment to mutter, 'We're in the open. Be on your guard.'

He noticed her pale and strained face, but said nothing. But when her door had closed on her he went slowly down the stairs and made for his own room. And there, taking one of the two cases from the top of his cupboard, he began to place in it things that were not necessary to his daily living, such as an excess of handkerchiefs and ties, cuff-links and studs, because he felt sure that when the time came for his leaving, there would be little time for packing.

7

Janet had slept fitfully. It had been a long time before she had first fallen asleep; and then she had been troubled by nightmarish dreams in which she was trying to stop her father from stabbing Maitland through the neck.

On a Sunday, breakfast was at nine o'clock, but she was up and dressed before eight, and wasn't at all surprised to find that her father had been about before her.

Samuel greeted her quite civilly. 'Bad night?' he said.

And she answered in an equal tone, 'Yes, nightmarish.'

'Not surprising. The breakfast's ready if you want it. They've pulled it forward.'

'I'm not hungry . . . are you?' She looked at him enquiringly, and he answered, 'No, but we've got to eat if we want to live.'

When she made her way to the breakfast room he followed her, and there Maitland greeted her in his usual manner: 'Good morning, miss,' he said.

'Good morning . . .' She just stopped herself from adding, Roger. He had asked her never again to call him Maitland but that was going to be difficult if this charade were to continue for long.

As she sat down she said, 'I'll just have coffee and toast, please.'

'The same for me,' her father said. Then pushing the toast rack towards her, he asked, 'What are you going to do with yourself?'

'I'm going to ride over and see how Annie is. She was very disturbed last night.'

'Aye, she was that. She wouldn't let us in at first. I had to bellow before she recognised me.' He now pulled a slight face at her as if she had confirmed his statement that he could be recognised by his bellowing voice. Then, quite abruptly, he said, 'He's got to be somewhere. He wouldn't risk travelling; and if he's in a bad way, he couldn't travel. Well, he's not here and he's not at your granny's . . . oh, I forget at times, your house, miss. So the only place I can think of is some of his bookie friends have taken pity on him and are hiding him up.'

When, after a short while, she rose from the table, he said, 'You going now? I mean, out?' she replied, 'Yes, I'm going out.'

'Are you going to stay long?'

'I don't know. It's such a nice day I might take a run out into the country, or I might sit in the park and watch the ducks.'

'I don't need any of that, not this morning, miss.'

'Then you shouldn't ask for it, Dad, should you?' With that she walked out of the room.

'I'll have another cup of coffee,' Samuel said.

As Maitland refilled the cup and put it to his hand, Samuel looked up at him and said, 'What d'you make of all this? Have you any idea where he'd make for?'

'No, sir. No, I'm sorry, but I haven't. In fact, I've not seen him since he left the household.'

'Aye. They're all leaving the household. I'm thinking about selling this place, you know.'

'No, sir, I wasn't aware of that. But of course, you'll have your reasons.'

'Of course I've got my reasons, man. Two of us in this bloody great place; five indoor servants, and four out. Nine to look after two folks; it's ridiculous. And I know that Janet won't mind leaving; and I'll go and pig in with her in the house in which I lived for so many years. Anyway, I'll save a lot of money and be a damn sight happier.'

Maitland made no response but busied himself arranging the cutlery in the green-baized drawer of the sideboard, while Samuel gulped at his coffee, then drained the very hot liquid before, pushing his chair back and getting to his feet, giving Maitland a long cold stare before leaving the room.

In the meantime Janet had put on her coat and hat and gone out to the yard to collect her bicycle. This was stored in one of the three empty stables, now put to other uses. And it was as she was about to wheel it out into the yard that she was checked by the cat scurrying past her. Yet it wasn't the noise made by the cat that had checked her; and now she quickly glanced upwards. There it was again, faint, yet it was as if someone had spoken.

The stable was the end one of the three and was situated next to the barn, and above the barn was a hay-loft. Cut off from this were two rooms that used to be the stableman's quarters, but which hadn't been in use for some time because now there was only Mike Talbot, and he occupied the lodge, and Arthur Mears, who, from being coachman, had become chauffeur and odd-job man and lived out, as did McBrien and Younger, the two gardeners.

As she was again about to push her bicycle into the yard she was brought to a halt by the noise, which wasn't really a noise, but more like, as she had first thought, a voice. And then she was leaning the bicycle against the wall and staring upwards and saying, 'Oh no, no.'

She was in the yard now looking one way, then the other. But it was Sunday morning; there was no routine on a Sunday. Mike and Arthur now had alternate Sundays off. The car was rarely used on a Sunday, and anyway it was Arthur's Sunday off. She was about to run to the house, then paused: she might be imagining things, but without hesitating now, she turned and ran into the barn, and straightaway looked to the ladder that led up to the hay-loft. Then her gaze swung to the end of the barn where the brick wall formed part of the last stable. To the side of it was a door which opened on to rickety stairs and led to the first of the two rooms that had housed the stableman.

Quietly she lifted the sneck of the door, then treading softly she groped her way up the dark staircase, and when her head came above the well of it she was looking onto a bare room that held an old kitchen table and a broken-legged chair.

Standing up now, she went cautiously to the door leading to the other room. Her hand trembled as she gently pushed it open, and what she straightaway saw caused her to gasp, for there, in the dim light afforded by the cobwebbed and dust-covered little window, and lying on a shake-down that hadn't been slept on for five years or more, was her brother.

Howard was lying on his side. His eyes seemed to be staring out of his head, and on the sight of her he made an effort to raise himself on one arm, but fell back.

She was on her knees beside him now, staring in horror at the blood-soaked shirt front and coat sleeve.

'Janet.'

'It's all right. It's all right.' What a thing to say, it's all right. How stupid! But, oh dear God! she must find out which part of him was bleeding or had been bleeding, for the blood on his shirt showed a great black stain.

'Janet.'

'It's all right. It's all right.'

'Can . . . can I have a drink?'

His lips looked dry; then she put her hand on his brow, to find it running with sweat. He had a fever. It must have been twenty-four hours since the event had occurred. She said, 'Can . . . can you get up?'

'I . . . I didn't mean it. He went for me . . . he meant to kill me. It . . . it was on the floor: we fell on the floor.'

'All right. All right. D'you think you can stand up?'

'Janet. Janet, don't . . . don't leave me.'

'All right, I won't leave you. But can you stand up? Could you make the stairs?'

'I feel rotten . . . bad . . . What'll they do? She screamed. She screamed, Janet, that he was dead. What'll they do to me? Can I . . . have a drink?'

'Look. Listen. I'm going down to the house; somebody will come and help you. You've got to be seen to; d'you understand?'

'Don't . . . don't leave, Janet. I'm sorry. I'm sorry about the money.'

'It's all right. It's all right.' She was stroking the hair back from his brow again. 'Don't worry about anything. Just lie still until I come back.'

'You won't let them do anything? You can stop them? I'm sorry, Janet. I'm sorry about the money. I've . . . I've been rotten. I've been thinking.'

'Lie still. D'you hear? I'll be back.' She rose from her knees and walked a few steps backwards, nodding at him all the time; then she turned and hurried as well as she could down the rickety stairs, and across the yard. Not towards the kitchen quarters but towards the drive and the front door. And she burst into the hall, crying, 'Dad! Dad!'

When Maitland appeared at the far end of the hall and hurried towards her, exclaiming, 'What is it? What's the matter?' she stammered, 'Where's . . . where's Dad? Oh, Roger!' and she shook her head, 'Where's Dad?'

'I'm here, what is it?' Samuel had appeared from the corridor, and she hurried towards him, crying, 'He's up in the loft. He's . . . he's in a state, a bit delirious; and . . . and he's covered with blood. He can't stand. He'll have to be brought . . .'

'Steady. Steady.' Samuel was holding her by the shoulder now, and he said, 'Howard?'

'Yes. Yes, of course,' she cried, impatiently now. 'Who else? But he can't stand. I think he's badly hurt.'

'God in heaven!' Sam looked towards Maitland and said, 'You'd better come along. I might need a hand.'

The three of them hurried out now, but when Samuel came to the foot of the stairs leading to the loft he stopped and bit tightly down on his lip before he said, 'How am I going to keep me hands off him?'

At this Janet hissed at him, 'He's hurt, Dad. He's wounded, and badly, I should say. And what's more, he's terrified.'

357

'Aye, well!' he hissed back at her; 'he's got a damn good right to be terrified, hasn't he?'

'Oh, you!' Janet jerked her head and actually ground her teeth before almost thrusting her father aside and hurrying up the stairs.

When the three of them were standing by the shake-down, Howard looked up at them and, his gaze coming to rest on his father, he opened his lips to say something, then closed them again; and he also closed his eyes. And at this Janet said, 'We'd better get him up.'

It was Maitland who put his arm beneath Howard's shoulder and raised him into a sitting position; then with a slight jerk pulled him to his feet. But immediately, Howard's legs gave way, and Samuel's hands, seemingly with an effort, reached out to help hold him upright. And so, between them, they got him to the top of the stairs; and there they stopped and Samuel said, 'How are we going to get him down the stairs? They're hardly wide enough to take one.'

Maitland paused a moment, then said, 'I'll put him over my shoulder, but we'll have to go down backwards. You,' he addressed Samuel not as Maitland but as the man Janet knew. 'You go down backwards and steady me. And you, Janet, come behind, but hold on to his hips, pull them towards you so that I won't overbalance. D'you understand?'

As she nodded, her father cried, '*You* carry him?' He was about to add, You've never carried anything heavier than a hot water jug in your life, when Maitland rounded on him: 'Yes, I'll carry him. And don't waste any more time,' which brought a muttered 'My God!' from Samuel, but then silence as he watched the butler put his arms around his son and hoist him up on to his shoulder. Then he himself was gripping the banister with one hand while pressing his other into the back of this man to whom he'd have something to say later. By God! he would.

At the foot of the staircase, Maitland gently lowered Howard to his feet. Then, supporting him on either side, they slowly led him, his feet almost trailing the ground, across the drive and into the house. And once inside the hall, Janet cried, 'Put him in the study. There's a couch in there. You'll never get him upstairs.'

By the time they had laid Howard on the couch, he appeared to be already unconscious, and it was Maitland who, now returning to his butler role, said, 'Before anything else is done, sir, I think we'd better phone for the doctor.'

'Aye, well, I suppose so. And then it'll be the police, because we can't hold him here, can we? Go on, you'd better do it.'

But before Maitland turned away he pointed down to the arm that was now hanging limply over the side of the couch, and he said, 'The coat will have to be cut off. Perhaps you would do it?' He had turned to Janet, and she, looking at her father, said, 'Get a knife and some scissors then, Dad, please.'

After her father had gone from the room, she knelt down by the couch and again her hand was on Howard's forehead, when he opened his eyes: 'Janet,' he said.

'Yes? Yes, Howard? It's all right. You're home.' Why on earth had she said that? Well, it was his home, wasn't it? She was surprised at the pity that was flowing through her for him. His trouble had been through weakness, there being no real guiding hand to turn it from the way it had been fostered by their mother.

'Janet.'

'Yes, dear?' She had called Howard 'dear'.

'Stay . . . with me.'

'Yes, I'll stay with you.'

'Dad. Don't let . . . Dad . . .'

'No, I won't let Dad do anything.' She wasn't aware that her father was at her side handing her the scissors; and she didn't look at him as she took them from him and immediately slit up the torn coat sleeve to expose the ripped shirt sticking to a long blood-caked slit. 'Oh, dear God!' she said; 'It'll have to be cleaned,' and she glanced up at Maitland.

'He must have lost a great deal of blood,' he said; 'his clothes are soaked with it.' Then turning to Samuel, who for once seemed lost for an exclamation of any sort, he said, 'The doctor will be here very shortly.'

He now put a hand under Janet's arm and raised her to her feet, saying, 'Will you please go and tell one of the girls to bring in a bowl of warm water and towels and some bandages from the medicine cupboard?' and she obeyed him immediately.

Then to Samuel, he said, 'I think we had better get the coat off him altogether and the shirt. Will you hold him up, sir?'

Without comment, Samuel now took his son in his arms and held him upright while Maitland drew off his coat, then gently eased his left arm out of the shirt before cutting around it where the material was adhering to the dried blood.

'Good God!' Samuel was looking down on the long black gash, and his voice was a whisper now as he said, 'It's all of six inches.'

'Yes, all of that, sir, and more. I think once the arm is seen to he must be changed. His underwear is badly stained.'

'Janet.'

They both looked at each other; then Maitland, bending over Howard, said, 'She'll be back in a minute.'

'Janet. Don't leave me, Janet.'

Samuel stood staring down on his son in something akin to amazement; then looking at Maitland, he said, 'He's asking for Janet. Well! Well! They never got on, you know; fought like cat and dog, both of them.'

'Very likely he recognises strength when he needs it.'

'Strength? What d'you mean by that?'

'Well, sir, I don't think you need to be told that your daughter is of a strong character; and your son was somewhat lacking in that way, but he seems to recognise it now. I don't know, not really, it might be just surmising, because he is slightly delirious, and he is definitely running a temperature.'

When Florence, followed by Janet, arrived carrying a bowl of water and almost dropped it when she saw the sight of the man on the couch, Maitland rounded on her, his voice stiff, saying, 'Pull yourself together, Florence! and listen to me. Go now and tell Cook to say nothing; and no chat to the milkman. You understand? Has he been?'

'Not yet, Mr Maitland, 'tis Sunday.'

He nodded at her, and she almost scurried from the room. And now he turned to where Janet was wetting some squares of linen in the warm water; then he made room for her as she knelt down by the couch and began to wash the blood from her brother's chest and waist, then from around the wound. But when she came to the wound itself she looked up from one to the other and said, 'If that is made wet it will likely start to bleed again. What shall I do?'

'I would leave it until the doctor comes.' It was Maitland who had answered her.

Almost following on this there was the sound of a slight commotion in the hall, and the door opened and Florence let the doctor into the room.

'Good morning.' He nodded from one to the other. And as Maitland said, 'Good morning, Doctor Campbell,' Samuel said,

'A nice kettle of fish.' But Janet just looked at him, then stood aside, and the doctor gazed down on the arm for some seconds before he pronounced, 'Nasty! Nasty!' Then, noticing the bowl of reddened water, he said, 'Could I have a fresh bowl of water, please, cold?' and began to take off his coat. Then after rolling up his sleeves, he lifted the limp arm and gently pressed his thumb down each side of the wound.

When Howard opened his eyes and looked at him, Dr Campbell asked quietly, 'How do you feel?'

'Not . . . not good.'

'That's understandable,' he said, as he grasped Howard's wrist and felt his pulse. He pulled down his lower lids. Then he sat back as though trying to determine his further actions.

When Maitland returned with a bowl of water the doctor sponged the dry blood from the wound to reveal a deep jagged gash which immediately began to ooze blood again, and after dabbing something that smelt like Lysol on it he turned to Samuel, saying, 'I'm afraid I can do nothing with this. He'll have to go to hospital. It's very deep and I should imagine there is damage to the muscles, and possibly the bone.'

'Dry, Janet. Dry.'

'I'll get you a drink, dear.' Janet hurried away from the couch; but outside the door she stopped for a moment and covered her face with her hand. Why was she feeling like this? For the first time in her life she was being swamped by pity for him.

Both Florence and Sarah were standing at the end of the passage and they came towards her and Sarah said, 'Is there anything we can do, miss?'

'Yes . . . Yes, please. A glass of water; he's dry.'

'Immediately?'

'Yes, directly.' They both turned and hurried away, and she returned to the room, thinking, Mam . . . If he's sent to hospital the police will be there. Nobody will be able to see him without the police.

She went straight to her father and in a low voice she said, 'Mam should see him before he goes.'

'Aye. Yes. Yes, you're right. I'll phone her.' Then he turned to the doctor, saying, 'There's no great hurry, is there? His mother would like a word.'

'Well, I think the quicker he has attention the better; or on the other hand . . .' He did not go on to say what was on the other hand; but nodding now, he said, 'Ask her

365

to be as quick as possible.'

Fifteen minutes later, Samuel was waiting in the hall when Alice arrived. Neither spoke; they just stared at each other before Samuel turned from her and walked down to the study, and she followed him.

Maitland was supporting Howard with one arm while holding a glass to his lips. He did not turn his head to see who had entered, nor did he even look up until Alice was standing by the couch; then he laid Howard back on the cushions, straightened himself and stood aside. And Alice, now kneeling by her son, said, 'Howard. Howard.'

Howard opened his eyes and stared at his mother for some seconds before he muttered, 'Mam.'

'Yes, dear; yes, I'm here.'

'Feeling bad.'

'Yes, I know. But you'll be all right,' she said, and placed her hand on his forehead. She turned to Samuel and said, 'He's . . . he's in a fever.'

'Aye, he's in a fever; he's lost a lot of blood. He's been on the run, you know, for twenty-four hours, so he's bound to be in a fever. But that's nothing to what —'

'Don't say it, Sam! Don't say it.'

'Janet . . . Janet,' muttered Howard.

Alice had been looking at her son, but now she turned quickly to her husband again and said, 'He wants Janet.'

'Aye; it's strange, isn't it? she's the only person he seems to want; Janet. Of course, he's half delirious, but nevertheless it's been Janet all the time.'

Alice turned round now and gave her daughter a glare.

'Janet.'

'Yes, Howard; I'm here.' Janet gently eased herself between her mother and the head of the couch and she put out her hand and stroked Howard's brow, the while her mother gazed up at her again, open mouthed now, as her daughter said, 'It's all right. It's all right. Rest now.'

'What . . . what are they going to do, Janet?'

'Nothing. Nothing, dear. You're just going into hospital to have your arm put right.'

'Oh, no, no, Janet.'

Alice rose abruptly to her feet and walked towards the fireplace, where she stared down into the bright flames, acknowledging to herself that her son was delirious, but nevertheless questioning, delirious or not, why he should be calling for somebody he could not stand, and never could; and then her talking to him like that, calling him 'dear'.

The doctor came back into the room now, saying, 'An ambulance will be here shortly.' Then, addressing Samuel, he stated, 'You will want to phone now, Mr Fairbrother.'

'Aye, yes.'

The doctor followed Samuel out of the room, leaving Janet with her mother. And now Alice confronted her, saying, 'What's all this "dear Howard" all of a sudden?'

'I don't know, Mam. I don't know why he should be calling for me.'

'Nor do I. My goodness me! nor do I; except that you might have been getting at him on the quiet; taking another one away from me.'

'Oh . . .' Janet's head slowly bowed until her chin was on her chest: the word had come out as a groan. Then she muttered, 'There must be something wrong with you, Mam. Go back to what you said: he and I couldn't stand each other, but for some reason he thinks he needs me now. And I might as well tell you this: for some reason I can't fathom myself, I find I want to help him. So there you have it, woman!'

'Don't you dare call me woman.'

'What else can I call you, until you act

like a mother? Not some spiteful . . .' she just stopped herself from adding, bitch; but, her voice breaking, she said, 'What have I ever done to you to make you treat me this way? I ask you.'

'You want to ask yourself, girl. It's your manner. You've been too big for your boots. You're like him' — she jerked her head towards the door — 'a servant. There's a pair of you: you think you're superior.'

'I don't! I never have. I've never felt superior to anyone; just the opposite.'

They were hissing at each other, their voices hardly above a whisper; but then they turned as one towards the couch when Howard croaked, 'I . . . I can't . . . I can't go home . . . Janet.' His voice trailed off now, saying, 'She'll . . . she'll . . .' And at this Janet turned and stared at her mother before hurrying from the room . . .

The St John ambulance and the police arrived almost at the same moment.

When the inspector and the two constables entered the hall and the inspector immediately said to Samuel, 'Where is he? What's the ambulance for?' it was the doctor who answered him, saying, 'The ambulance is to take the patient' — he stressed the last two words — 'to the hospital. He is a very sick man. He is wounded and has lost a lot of blood.'

'I must see him,' insisted the inspector.

The doctor glanced at Samuel as though for his approval and it was he who answered, 'You may see him.' And he turned and led the way down the corridor to the study there to find Alice kneeling by the couch.

When she rose to her feet, the inspector, bending slightly over Howard, said, 'Mr Fairbrother.'

'You won't get any sense out of him. He's delirious. As the doctor said, he is a patient and he's going to the hospital,' Samuel said, which caused the inspector to turn sharply to him and in a low but gritty tone, say, 'He's also a prisoner, Mr Fairbrother. A man was murdered yesterday morning. Your son will be under police surveillance while he is in hospital.'

As Samuel stared at the officer he was telling himself, My God; and I know him . . . Well, I'll remember him, an' all. By God! I will.

There followed the usual procedure of lifting the patient on to the stretcher, with Howard repeating, 'No. No,' as if by way of protest.

In the hall one of the ambulance men said, 'Is someone coming with him?' and

Alice immediately, answered, 'I am.' On this Samuel looked at the inspector, who said, 'You may come with us if you wish.' And Samuel nodded his acceptance then glanced towards where Maitland was already holding his coat and hat.

From the doorway, Janet watched the stretcher being lifted into the ambulance, and then her mother being helped in; she saw her father take his seat in the back of the police van, and lastly the doctor step up into his trap; and one following the other, the small cavalcade proceeded down the drive.

After closing the door she turned swiftly and hurried across the hall and back into the study. Maitland followed her, and putting his arms about her shaking body, he drew her to him, saying, 'There, there, my dear.'

Only seconds passed before she drew herself from his embrace and, wiping her face, she whispered, 'They . . . they might come in.'

'Does it matter any longer? It doesn't to me.'

She now withdrew from him and sat on the couch, and when he stood by her side she said, 'I . . . I can't understand it, but I feel so terribly sorry for him. It is as if I had always liked him, even knowing him to be a cheat and a liar, and I still know it. But somehow I would give anything for him not to have done it, and to have to face the consequences. Do you think it dreadful of me if I say, I know he won't, but I could hope he dies.'

'No. No, my dearest, of course not. I feel as you do. He's in a bad state, and the longer he is without medical attention the more in danger he is. And if I could have possibly delayed things I would have, because . . . well, there is little hope for him, either way.'

'Don't . . . don't you think it strange that he's kept asking for me?'

'Yes, perhaps. But, like you, he's had a change of heart. Your pity for him must have got through and touched something in him. I . . . I don't know . . . but what I do know is that it upset your mother.'

'Yes, and that's another awful part of it. He was lying there in such a state, and we almost came to blows, all because he kept calling for me.'

'She's an unhappy woman, my dear. She should never have left your father, no matter what he had done. She should have understood him more than anyone else; she's known him longer, lived with him longer.'

'Yes, perhaps; but on the other hand she must have got tired of his bullying and his rough ways. That's why she fell in love with you . . . Oh, don't look so surprised or shocked, she did. She wanted you to go away with her, didn't she? It was at the time she found out about my father and was leaving him, and you said you were leaving, too. You had just left me in the conservatory.'

'Oh, my dear.' He bent down and held her hands now. 'It was only because she was lonely.'

'No, it wasn't. She had been in love with you for some time and I had sensed it. And that's one of the things she seems to hold against me, because she knew I'd loved you since I was a child, and that it hadn't fizzled out.'

When the door opened abruptly and Florence stood there, Maitland did not release her hand but, turning to address her, said, 'Will you get Miss Janet a strong cup of coffee, Florence? She is not feeling at all well.'

'Yes, Mr Maitland. Yes, yes.'

When the door closed Janet said, 'Oh, dear me!' and he replied, 'Now don't worry. Don't worry. They're bound to find out sooner or later.'

'Yes, I know; but it will be very awkward

373

for both of us if it comes to light, I mean, just now. I . . . I want to get out of the house, away from it, before they know anything for sure.'

'I understand, my dear, and I too want to get out of this house. But I think, for the time being, we must remain here, don't you?'

'Oh, yes, yes. But Roger . . .' she pulled herself to her feet, and she now gripped his hands, saying, 'What if he is found guilty and is hanged? Or, if not that, given a long sentence, perhaps life, how . . . how is Dad going to react to it? If I walk out, he . . . well . . .'

She released her hold on him and turned from him, and he said, 'Janet. I told you last night that nothing is going to separate us. In the end we will be together. I'm as certain of that as I am of standing in this room now. Let things take their course. You know how I feel and I know how you feel. Nothing on God's earth can alter that. Except if one of us were to die. In any case, alive or dead we'd be together, dear. I haven't waited for you all these years just to lose you now. Whatever the outcome of this affair it's not going to alter our lives, believe me.'

8

Samuel was not, as he had feared he might be, startled by the headlines in the local paper, for they were more concerned with reports of the preparations by Germany for war. Apparently, yesterday, he read, Sir Edward Grey had astounded the House of Commons by his accounts of what was happening in Germany. It wasn't, he said, so much a question of if there would be a war as when it would begin. And would Europe be for her or against her? The whole world was seething, proclaimed Sir Edward. Hadn't France taken Morocco? Taken it? They had seized it; as Italy had seized Tripoli. The poor Turkish Empire had been divided up. And there was that man, Lloyd George, with his proposal for a National Health Insurance that was upsetting all the doctors; just for the benefit of working class people, so that they could be taken care of if they fell sick. Were they not already taken care of? After all, they had their sick clubs. What was all the fuss about?

But there it was, on page two, introduced, as it were, by, of all things, the Suffragette

Movement, of which the members had gone so far as to refuse to pay taxes, and who were attacking property, smashing windows, upsetting businessmen by the score. Many were being imprisoned, with some of the more fanatical among them refusing to eat and, as a consequence, being forcibly fed. It was a dreadful state of affairs in this England, where women were happy to take a lead from the dear, dead Queen and act as she did, as a loving wife and mother. What were things coming to? One such woman was at the centre of a murder, committed by the son of an industrialist in this quiet north-eastern town, and creating as great a storm as Crippen did the previous year, when, after murdering his wife he tried to escape with his paramour, Ethel le Neve, on a ship to America, but had been apprehended, as it were, by a device called wireless telegraphy, and was later hanged. But Crippen had been an American. This man in question, as had been stated, was the son of a wealthy shoe manufacturer. As far as could be ascertained he had murdered his mistress's husband. That, of course, was one story; but another story, according to the wife of the dead man, was that this man whom she had taken as a guest into her boarding establishment had pressed his attentions on her, and she had repulsed him, and not for the first time. But on the day of the tragedy he had burst into her bedroom and attempted to have his way with her; but fortunately, or unfortunately for him, the husband had returned and confronted the boarder, Howard Fairbrother, only to be himself wounded.

Samuel's reaction after reading the report was to crumple up the newspaper and throw it into the fire, exclaiming, 'Whore!'

Janet had been standing by the window in the drawing-room as he had come in opening the newspaper and not until he spat out the word 'Whore!' did she say, 'What's happened now?'

His response was to draw in a deep breath, and say, 'I think he's going to lose his arm. They worked on him for a couple of hours or more, but the doctor says that with the amount of blood he had lost, it is a wonder he is still alive. And as well as the dreadful cut, he must have been battered by blows from a very heavy hand. Well, he would be, wouldn't he? The fellow was a sailor and a big burly one into the bargain. From what I gathered from the inspector his ship came into the Tyne for repairs. She hadn't been expected, and so neither had he. Because the ship had to go into dry dock he was given a short leave, and it turned out to be his last.'

She asked quietly now, 'Is Mother still there?'

'No. I took her home. It was no good her staying. No good anybody staying apart from the police. There's an officer sitting by his bed. It's ludicrous when you think of it. Is he going to run away? Besides everything else, he was running a high temperature. He could be developing pneumonia. Anyway, he'll still be under the influence of chloroform. The fact is, from what I understand, they were in two minds whether to do anything or not. Yet, as the surgeon said, they didn't want to deal with gangrene later on, because then there wouldn't be any hope of saving the arm at all. As it is, it's slight now. Well, anyway, he won't need two hands to work with where he's going.'

'Dad, please!'

'*Oh, miss, please,* face up to facts.'

'I have, before you did. But you needn't be so raw about it; he's still your son.'

'You don't have to remind me of that.'

'Sometimes I wonder.'

'Yes, you may; and I'll tell you that sometimes I wonder an' all why the hell I put up with you, what makes me care two hoots whether you stay or go. But I'm going to tell you, miss, this hasn't changed me mind about anything. You can say that my son has disgraced me in one way, well, I'm going to make damn sure you don't disgrace me in another and lower yourself.'

'Oh my God!' She flung round from the support of the back of a chair, crying, 'If it wasn't that I know you'll regret what you're saying and be sorry for it later, I'd walk out now, this very minute. I don't have to remind you, do I? that you can't keep me here, and that I have my own house and money to support me. I've told you this before. I'm telling it to you again. Now be careful, Dad. Just be careful.' Then moving two steps towards him and quietly, she said, 'Just ask yourself, who d'you think you are? And how high up in the hierarchy in the town did you imagine you were before this latest business hit you? You are living in a lord's establishment, you've been waited on hand and foot for years, but that hasn't made you a person that anybody looks up to. You're still the son of your father and your grandfather, a cobbler. And I'm still the great-granddaughter of a cobbler. And you'll never get it into your head that you're inferior in many ways to those you look down on. Why do you look down on them? Because they show you up in breeding, intelligence, the lot. Now why don't you hit me? I've said enough for you to want to commit murder, so why don't you have a try?'

Of a sudden her hands went out and on to his shoulders and almost around his neck; their faces were close, and her voice now almost a tearful cry as she said, 'Be fair, Dad. Be fair, please. I love you. Don't you know that? I love you. I don't want to hurt you in any way, but I do because you're so unfair.'

When her arms now actually did go around his neck and she fell against him he slowly put his hands on to her back and, his head dropping on to her shoulder, almost like a child he whimpered, 'Don't leave me, lass. Don't leave me. Don't do that to me.'

And her voice as low as his, she muttered, 'I don't want to, Dad, I don't want to. Only try to see it my way . . . our way.'

She felt him stiffen; then his arms dropped away from her and he pushed her gently from him and turned away.

Despondently, she left the room and went upstairs to stand shivering in her bedroom, her feeling of fear, revived by the stiffening of his body and the look on his face, sapping from her again.

* * *

On the Monday morning she arrived at the library at her usual time and went straight to Arthur Stanford's office There, after knocking on the door and being bidden to enter; she faced a rather surprised librarian, who rose slowly from behind the desk.

'Good morning,' she said coolly.

'Good morning, Miss Fairbrother,' he replied. His voice, too, was cool, and when he added, 'I did not expect to see you on duty this morning,' she put in quickly, 'Why not?'

That was a stupid thing to say, for perhaps he was trying to be kind; and yet she doubted it after Saturday's encounter.

'I wish formally to tender my resignation, Mr Stanford, and I wish to leave this afternoon . . . I mean, today.'

He made no objection to this, but said, 'May I say I'm sorry for the tragedy that has come upon your family.'

Was he sorry? Very likely he was now congratulating himself on his escape from marriage to her, for apart from himself, his mother would have been horrified that her future daughter-in-law was the sister of an accused murderer.

She said no more but inclined her head

towards him and left the office; and it was soon apparent to her that the members of the staff were tentative in approaching her, and when they did it was as though they were dealing with someone far from well.

Young John Inness was the only one who appeared to be his usual self, but there was no grin on his face when he said, 'Don't take it on yourself, miss; you can't help it, it wasn't your fault. People do what they have to do after all, don't they?'

She actually smiled at him as she put out her hand and ruffled his hair.

The morning seemed interminable, even though they had never been so busy. At one time there was a queue at her counter and Miss Stillwater in passing remarked, 'I've never known so many people all at once enquiring about joining the library.'

Janet discovered that she didn't like Miss Stillwater, that she had never liked her, and that Miss Stillwater reciprocated this feeling. Naturally, being so fond of Mr Stanford, she would do.

At last it was the dinner break and, taking her bicycle, she made her way straight to the hospital.

At the desk, when she asked if she could see Mr Fairbrother, the nurse said, 'It isn't visiting hours. What's your name?'

'Janet Fairbrother.'

'Oh, I see. Go down to ward six and ask for Sister Birkett.'

Sister Birkett also asked her name, then said, 'You are a relative?' and looked searchingly at her.

'I am his sister.'

'Oh.' And now, perhaps more compassionately, she said, 'Well, come this way. Your mother has only just left.'

'How is he?'

'He has recovered from the operation remarkably well, and his temperature has gone down a little, but' — she paused — 'he's a very sick man. I would ask you not to stay more than five minutes or so.'

'Thank you.' And she followed the sister into a long ward in which most of the beds were occupied. At the far end was a bed around which curtains were drawn.

When Sister Birkett gently pulled the curtain aside a policeman rose from his chair, and the sister said to him, 'This is the patient's sister, constable. She may stay for five minutes.'

'Very well, Sister.'

Janet walked slowly along the side of the bed and gazed down on Howard. The whole of one arm was swathed in bandages, the other was lying limply by his side. There was not a vestige of colour in his face apart from his eyes, and even their blue seemed faded.

When he gently moved his hand towards her and whispered her name, she had the feeling he appeared more rational than he had done the day before. She did not say, 'How are you?' because that would have been pointless. And anyway she could find no words to say, for pity for him was tearing at her.

She lifted the wavering fingers from the bed and held his hand gently within hers. But when his lips moved and again he said her name, she bent over him and was not surprised when she said, 'Yes, dear?'

And now he whispered, 'Mam . . . keep her . . . off . . . away.'

She did not say, I can't do that; instead she said, 'She's . . . she's worried for you, dear.'

'Cries . . . cries. Made . . . made a scene.'

He moved his head a little and glanced to where the policeman was sitting, his gaze centred on the curtain opposite as if his action would obliterate his presence, or at least take away his hearing. But then he looked quickly across the bed at Janet, and in a low voice, he said, 'People get upset, naturally, miss; but . . . but it's my duty. I don't like it any more than . . . well, people do.'

She nodded at him understandingly. Her mother had likely ordered him out and, in a way, that would have been natural, too.

'Janet.'

'Yes? Yes, dear?'

'Sorry . . . sorry . . . the money, very sorry.'

She bent closer to him, saying softly, 'Now I've told you, you've got to forget about that, it doesn't matter. Nothing matters . . .' She stopped herself from saying, Only you, and you must get better.

Get better? What for? My God! What a situation.

'I . . . I didn't, Janet, not what . . . what I said.'

'Now be quiet. Be quiet. Don't talk about it any more. I know what you did and it doesn't matter, I tell you.' She stressed the words softly.

The curtains were drawn aside slightly and Sister Birkett looked at her meaningfully. And now Janet, most unusually for her, bent over her brother and kissed him, not on the brow or on the cheek, but on his quivering mouth. And when she straightened up he had his eyes tightly closed; in fact, screwed up. She laid his hand gently back on the bed, then left the cubicle.

The sister walked with her down the ward and in the corridor she said, 'Your distress is quite understandable. It's a very, very sad case.'

Janet choked, then coughed before she said, 'How . . . how long will they . . . I mean, do you think they will allow him to remain here?'

'Oh, only until he is fit to be moved to the . . .' and the sister paused, before adding, 'the prison infirmary.'

'How long will that be?'

'Well, his condition at the moment is very poor, so I should say in about ten days, perhaps more, but at least ten days.'

'Thank you. And thank you for allowing me to see him out of visiting hours.'

'Oh, that's all right. But will you do something for me? Will you ask your parents not to call in again today? He's had rather a trying morning.'

'Oh, sister, you have set me a problem. I . . . I can ask my father not to come but . . . has he already been?'

'No; but I thought he might be coming.'

'Well, he may or he may not. As regards my mother, though, I'm afraid she would not take any notice of what I might say in that direction. It would be more definite coming from yourself, or someone in authority.'

'Oh, I see, I see. All right, I'll deal with it should I have to. Goodbye.'

'Goodbye, Sister.'

Outside, Janet hesitated before mounting her bicycle. She couldn't go home, not in the state she was in: if her father was there and she had to tell him not to visit the hospital he would likely respond with, 'If I want to go to the hospital, I'll go; at visiting time. Nobody can stop me then,' even though she would know that the last thing he wanted to do was to visit his son with a policeman sitting by his side.

She would go to Annie's house, as she had come to think of the property which she now owned and which might indeed become home to her soon . . . But how soon? And how was it to come about? Oh, that must wait now.

When she arrived at 19 Sweetbanks Gardens, Annie opened the door to her with a welcoming smile: 'Oh, come in, miss,' she greeted her. 'You do look froze. I've kept the fire going in the sitting-room just in case. I always do. Have . . . have you seen him? How is he?'

She didn't immediately answer any of Annie's questions. She went straightaway to the sitting-room that remained just as it had been before they made the move. She had always liked this house, even though now, eleven years later, her gran's taste was still evident. That was one thing her mother had never been able to do — change any part of the house in which she had been born and brought up. She could recall the niggly little rows between her gran and her mother about proposed changes. But it was comfortable; it was home.

When she sat on the couch Annie bent over her, saying, 'By, you look peaked, miss. You all right? But that's a silly thing to ask, if anyone is all right. Now what can I get you? I've put some chump mutton chops in the oven.'

'Just some soup, please, Annie. I think I'd enjoy that. I haven't eaten much these last couple of days.'

'Well, look . . . lift your feet up,' Annie said, at the same time giving her words action by grabbing Janet's legs and swinging them round on to the couch, saying, 'There! You rest yourself and I'll be back in a minute.'

When she was alone Janet smiled to herself. She hadn't answered Annie's questions, and Annie hadn't really expected an answer.

She was garrulous, and like many such people, kind and caring. She was just like the house — homely. Oh, wouldn't it be wonderful if she and Roger and Annie could live here! Roger and she never to be parted again. Odd, but for so long now, she had experienced any kind of happiness only when he was within her sight. Why then had she chosen to come here instead of going back to the house? Oh, she knew the answer to that. At this moment she craved for the comfort that he would give her, and she knew deep down inside her, that once she entered the house, feeling as she had done when she left the hospital, she would seek that comfort, no matter who saw her, be it even her father. At the same time she also knew that she must not add to the tension that was still gripping him at the moment for, as he had subtly threatened, anything could happen.

When Annie re-entered the room carrying a tray holding a bowl of soup and a plate of new bread, she sat up and said, 'Oh, that smells good, Annie.' And after she had tasted it she looked at the woman waiting for her verdict and said, 'Lovely. Really lovely.' With a smile, she added, 'But then you were always a good cook . . . when you were given the chance.'

'You said it, Miss Janet, when I got the chance. Oh, aye, Maggie was a stickler for keeping her place. The only chance I got to go near that oven, except to carry things out of it, was on her day off, or when she wasn't up to it.'

'D'you miss the others?'

Annie seemed to consider for a moment before answering, 'Aye, sometimes, at night. But, you know, miss, I don't mind being on me own; and it's nice to have only one boss.' She grinned now. 'But mind, we all got on very well together. Well, we had to, working as we did. How many years? Eeh! I don't like to count up. But I came here as a bit of a lass when the missis was first married. I was twelve at the time. Fancy that, twelve! Maggie was here then, but Kate wasn't. Oh, no, I don't mind being on me own. Yet, when I say that, miss, it would be nice to see you back here, I mean, living here altogether. D'you think you ever will?'

'Oh, yes, yes, Annie. You may get a surprise one of these days, and not so far away.'

'Will I, miss? Oh, well, that's given me something to think about. And I won't ask you if you'll be by yourself. Anyway, I suppose whatever you do you'll want things to settle back to normal, you know what I mean, miss, before . . . ?'

'Yes, I know what you mean, Annie.'

'Have you heard how he is, miss?'

'I've just come back from the hospital. He's very poorly.'

'It's very sad, sad. But he frightened the daylights out of me. I was silly I suppose. But, you know something, miss' — she bent down towards Janet again — 'I heard a bit from the milkman this morning. He knows that piece . . . well, he knows of her. He's not on that round, he's too far away, but his cousin is, and his cousin says she's a proper tart. And the young lad isn't the first one she's hooked. It's supposed to be a boarding-house, and as the milkman said, "It could be a shipping office the way the fellows sign on to board there." And her saying that Master Howard was going to rape her! As the milkman said his cousin said, and the other boarder said an' all, "The first time she was raped she hadn't heard of bloomers." Eeh! miss, the things they say.' She put her hand over her mouth. 'But if you keep your ears open you hear lots from the milkman.' And then she grinned widely as she added, 'And not forgetting the paper man and the coalman.'

Janet was actually laughing: the half

empty bowl of soup wobbled on her knee, so much so that Annie bent quickly and lifted the tray to one side. And as Janet put her hand across her eyes a voice inside her head shouted at her, Stop it! don't cry.

She swallowed the lump in her throat, took in a deep breath, then reached for the tray again, saying, 'You always had the power to make me laugh, Annie.' Then she smiled at the plump, middle-aged woman, saying, 'D'you remember the day in the back-yard when you cowped your creels to make Eddie laugh because he was crying with the toothache?'

'Oh, aye, aye, miss, I remember that. And oh, didn't I get it off Maggie, because me skirt fell over me head and showed me petticoats and the bottom of me drawers. But you know, as a bit of a lass, I was always cowping me creels. Me mother told me I could do it as soon as I could crawl. But go on, miss, finish that soup before it gets cold. It'll do you good. Then I'll bring you in a bit of apple tart. And would you like coffee or tea?'

'I think I'll have tea, Annie.'

'Well, tea it is, miss. I've never been a coffee person meself . . . Oh, it's nice to see you sitting there. Are you likely to stay a bit?'

'Yes, Annie, yes, I'll stay a bit. I feel . . . well, I'd like a rest.'

'Good. I'll get the tart.'

As Janet watched the happy woman hurrying from the room she felt more than a tinge of envy. Wouldn't it be wonderful to feel like Annie, someone who was just willing to work for others twelve hours a day or more for what was really a meagre wage, and be satisfied that life was providing you with a roof, a comfortable bed, and plenty to eat; with a highlight now and again of going to a variety show or the new cinematograph picture show? She would exchange her own life for one like that any minute . . . But would she? Had Annie ever read a book other than one of those paper novelettes? Had she ever loved anyone with a consuming passion that filled consciously and subconsciously every minute of the twenty-four hours of the day? Had she for years looked in the mirror and asked: Why am I so plain, and Alicia so beautiful, and Jessie so pretty? Fanny, too. But then she had looked again and said, He thinks I'm beautiful. He says I'm beautiful. So I *am* beautiful. Inside, I am so beautiful: I'm a starlit night; I am the full moon; I am the glorious dawn; I am a leaping young fawn; I am all the poetry that has ever been written;

I am Beatrice; I am . . .

'Oh! Did I startle you, miss? You were nearly asleep. It's that broth and the fire. But look; you eat this pie, and I've put some cream alongside it. And I won't bring your tea for a while, because as soon as you finish that, I'd put your feet up again and have a nap, 'cos you look whacked.'

'Thanks, Annie; but I feel I must get back to the house.'

'The house can wait. I'm sure there's nothing spoiling in the house with that butler there. He sees to everything. A fine man that. You were lucky to get him.'

'Yes. Yes, Annie, we were lucky to get him.'

'Well, there now, I'll leave you. And I'll give you half an hour, then I'll bring your tea in.'

She ate the pie and the cream and once more she put up her feet on the couch and lay back against the cushions, thinking: Yes, he is a fine man, and we were lucky to get him . . . I was lucky to get him.

She was brought out of her sleep by the sound of her father's voice. 'A cup of tea'll be fine, Annie,' he was saying. She forced her eyelids open and there he was looking down on her.

'What's this?'

'What's what?'

She slowly pulled herself up into a sitting position.

'Asleep at half-past two in the day?'

'I've got to sleep some time. I didn't sleep last night.'

'You're not the only one. But why couldn't you let me know?'

'Let you know what?' She blinked her eyes. 'That I was going to have a nap?'

'When you didn't come home for your lunch I . . . I phoned the library at one; then I even went to the hospital.'

'Oh, you *even* went to the hospital?'

'Yes, I did *even* go. Because as far as I can gather they don't want anybody there for the time being, especially your mother. They wouldn't let her in again, and there was high jinks. And it was a good job that I happened to be there; I was about to come away when she landed. But you saw him, didn't you?'

'Yes, I saw him; but only for five minutes.'

'What's he like?'

'He's ill, Dad.' She pulled herself to her feet. 'He's very ill.'

He did not respond to this but, dropping into an armchair, he asked, 'Why didn't you come home then, if you didn't want to go back to work?'

'Because I wanted a little peace, that's why. And anyway, this *is* my home. Don't you remember? This *is* my house.'

'Oh, aye, aye.' He turned his head to look one way, then the other, as if he had never seen the room before, then continued, 'Aye, it's your house, but it isn't what you've been used to for the best part of your life. And you'd take badly to it if you made the change, and —'

Now she was bending towards him, her voice slow, low and firm: 'Oh no, I wouldn't, Dad,' she said. 'I can tell you in truth that I'd be delighted to make this my real home tomorrow. In fact, from now on, from this very minute; then I needn't move a step out of it except when I wanted to.'

He stared at her, then sighed as he said quietly, 'Why d'you keep on, lass? You know what I'm going through; but you keep hitting below the belt. I need you back there. If ever I needed you before, I need you now. D'you know you're the only one I've got that I can talk to, let off steam to?' He turned to look towards the fire as he said, 'At one time I could natter away to Alice — not that she listened to half of what I said, but she was a kind of focal point, she was there, she was somebody to come home to. But, oh my God! how that woman has changed. I think she's going round the bend, because there we were, in the car; I took her back, at least to *her* house. Funny that, my house, her house, and your house. Anyway, what did she start on about but the divorce, at a time like this! She realises she's not going to find it so easy. Apparently, it's a question now, her solicitor said, of whether I threw her out, or if she went of her own accord. If she left of her own choice, it's going to be difficult for her, I gather. So, she wants me to say I threw her out. I have three options, I'm told. If I throw her out, she's got a case against me; if I name the woman I had an affair with, she's got a case against me; if I don't do that, but set up the pantomime of hiring a whore and a photographer and going through all the paraphernalia of booking a room at an hotel, then acting out the part, then whatever has to follow, she might get a divorce. But it isn't going to be as easy as she thought. If I said she walked out on me and her home is there ready if she cares to return she won't have a leg to stand on. Well, in any case, it would take her a long time to prove her case. But that's what she was on about in the car and when we got into the house she sat down and howled like I've never seen her cry before. But you know something, lass? I came out almost laughing, and you know why? My God-seeking daughter, the future nun, swore at me.'

This last remark made Janet turn round and say, 'Jessie? Jessie swore at you? Never!'

'She did. And you know what she said . . . her very words?' He grinned slightly. ' "You know what you are, Dad, you're a damned menace. You breed chaos, you and that bloody voice of yours." '

'She didn't say that?'

'She did, every word of it. I'll never forget it. I could have laughed at the damn and the bloody, but I didn't like the bit about me breeding chaos. Oh, I know all about me voice; but to breed chaos. No, I won't have that. Still, that's what my young daughter thinks of me. I'm going through a very enlightening time, lass, a very enlightening time . . . Ah' — he turned round — 'a cup of tea.'

As Annie handed him the small tray on which was a cup of tea and a sugar basin, he looked up at her and said, 'How's things? Finding it lonely here?'

'No, sir, not a bit of it. I'm in me element, to tell you the truth.'

She bobbed her head at him before turning away, and as she closed the door he turned to Janet, saying, 'In me element. It's strange when you come across a happy person, isn't it?'

'You're spilling that tea.'

'Oh, aye.' He took two gulps at the cup before saying, 'What I really wanted you to know was that Harry phoned from Oxford just after you left. I was on the point of leaving the house. He was setting off and should be home around six tonight. He had been rowing or some such all day and he didn't get in till late and his room-mate told him first thing this morning.'

'It's . . . it's very good of him to make the journey, but what can he do?'

'Nothing. No more than any of us. But I was pleased he's making the effort to come. I don't suppose we'll hear anything from Eddie or James, 'cos Eddie was expecting his ship to go to the new Naval yard at Rosyth in Scotland, wasn't he? As for James, well, as he said the last time he was home, and he made a joke of it, if I remember, you don't get leave from the college except for the death of a close relative.'

There followed a silence, before he got to his feet, muttering, 'Well, are you coming or are you staying?'

She did not answer him, but walked out of the room, picked up her coat and hat from the hall stand, then went into the kitchen.

'Well, you're off then?' remarked Annie. 'Oh, it was nice having you, miss. Look in soon again, will you?'

'I will, Annie. And thank you for letting me nap; it did me good.'

'You need something to do you good by the look of you. You're all skin and bone. If I had you here I'd fatten you up.'

Janet leaned towards her, and whispered, 'Who knows, Annie? You might get the chance one of these days.'

'Speed the day then, miss.'

'Yes, Annie; speed the day.'

'Miss, before you go, would you mind if I had me friend staying with me for a weekend? She lives in Gateshead, and she's blind.'

'Not at all, Annie, not at all. But she's blind? Poor soul.'

'Oh, she doesn't need to be pitied, miss. She makes you split your sides at times. She's full of life.'

'Well, you have her any time you like, and tell her I hope to meet her one day.'

'I will that, miss. I will that.'

As Janet went out to join her father, she

thought, She's got a friend and she's blind. How little one knew of another's life. And she had known Annie for years; as far back as she could remember, she had known Annie. But she hadn't known she had a friend who was blind and who could make you split your sides.

Harry arrived at half-past six. Samuel met him at Newcastle Central with the car, and when they reached the house it was evident to Janet that her brother was very shaken by the news.

After a quick wash and a meal he mentioned that he must return to Oxford the following day, because on the Wednesday there was an important lecture that he did not want to miss. And at this, Samuel came back at him characteristically, saying, 'Why did you trouble to come then?' and Harry replied, 'Well, I hoped I might see him, just for a word. I suppose it's natural, he being my brother. And anyway, when you said he was in hospital, I thought there'd be more chance of a meeting; when he —'

But only for Samuel to interrupt his excuse by saying, 'All right, say it, say it: When he goes along the line.'

'All right, I'll say it,' Harry said. 'When he goes along the line there'll be very little chance of any of us seeing him except on special visiting days. And as I can't arrange my time —'

'All right, all right' — Samuel raised his hand — 'but you've little chance of seeing him tonight. They wouldn't let your mother in this afternoon.'

'I'll go along with you,' said Janet, 'and we'll explain to the sister, at least to the one that's on. It won't be the same one as I saw at dinner-time, but we can but try.'

'You can't have the car. Arthur's gone this hour or more.'

'So we'll go by tram, or I'll ring for a cab.'

Janet now rose from the table and went into the hall and there picked up the telephone and ordered a cab. And a quarter of an hour later they were on their way.

'He doesn't change, does he?'

'No, he doesn't change, Harry. Well, that's wrong; he's getting worse, I think.'

'How d'you stand it every day? A while back it came to me that we three fellows were at school most of the time and so we were out of it altogether, but you're still stuck there.'

'Not for long, Harry, not for long.'

'No? You have something up your sleeve?'

'Yes. Yes, I have something up my sleeve.

I'll tell you about it another time.' . . .

It was a different sister on the ward. She approached them as they stood in the corridor. What did they want? This was no visiting time. Saturday, Sunday and Wednesday . . .

'I am Howard Fairbrother's brother,' said Harry in a most charming manner. 'I've just travelled from Oxford and I have to return first thing in the morning. I . . . I was greatly troubled to hear the news of my brother and I wondered if you could stretch a point and allow me to see him for a few minutes. I know it is asking a great deal, but in the circumstances I fear this is the only time I shall see him for . . . well . . .' he paused and made a slight movement with one shoulder, then looked hard at her.

He had had no need to stress the fact that he had come up from Oxford: his manner, his tone, everything about him spoke for him and the image of that university these had implied. Under other circumstances, this class attitude would have immediately activated Janet's critical mind, but on this occasion she awaited the reaction of the sister: she pursed her lips, drew in a breath that raised the medal hanging from the breast of her blue serge dress, then quietly said, 'Well, just for a minute or two, mind.

Of course, you know there is someone sitting with him?' She had turned to address Janet now, and she answered, 'Yes, Sister, we know.'

And Harry said, 'Thank you. Thank you very much indeed, Sister.'

Almost on tiptoe they followed her up the ward and into the curtained cubicle. The patients had not yet settled down for the night and their concerted gaze followed them.

A different policeman was seated by the bed. He had been reading a paper but on the sight of the sister he immediately stood up, and she, in a whisper, said, 'His brother and sister; just for a few minutes.'

He inclined his head towards her and when she drew aside a curtain Harry walked to the bed and looked down on to his brother's face. Howard had his eyes half open as if he had been wakened from a doze. And they remained like that until Harry said quietly, 'Hello there, Howard.'

'Oh. Oh. Harry.'

'How are you?'

'All . . . all right, Harry. All . . . all right.'

'I . . . I just popped down when I heard you . . . you weren't very well.'

Janet, standing to the side, bowed her head: the suave Oxford student had gone;

404

here was her young brother overcome by the same kind of emotion as she herself had felt when she first discovered Howard injured.

'In . . . in a mess.'

When Harry could say nothing to this, Janet stepped to his side, and Howard's eyes turned to her as if he hadn't noticed her before, and he said, 'Oh, Janet.'

'We are breaking rules, Howard, but Harry wanted to see you.'

'Eddie and James . . . they all right?'

Harry swallowed, then glanced at Janet and she, now bending over Howard, said, 'They phoned; they are going to try and get leave.'

It was as well he was in no shape to question if his brother was able to phone from a battleship or even from a Naval Training School. Anyway, likely neither of them would as yet have heard of the trouble.

Looking at Harry now, Janet could see that he was becoming more overcome by the sight of his brother, a brother for whom, like herself, he had never cared until this moment.

'Come . . . to . . . morrow?'

'Yes. Yes, I will.' For the second time that day she bent over and kissed him, and Harry, lifting up the hand from the bed, held it tightly for a moment. Then, laying it back on the counterpane, like something lifeless, he touched his brother's cheek and stroked it twice with his fingers, then muttered, 'Goodbye, fella. I'll be seeing you.'

'Bye . . . Harry . . . thanks.'

They walked out of the ward and into the corridor. The sister seemed to be waiting. Her eyes were on the smart young man who spoke so nicely, but it was Janet who thanked her. Then they were outside and walking from the hospital into the town, and to the cab rank. Only then, as Harry helped Janet step up into the cab, did either of them speak, when he said, 'My God! It's awful. Terrible. What a way to end a life. And either way it goes, it will be ended for him. I . . . I never thought I'd feel like this about him, Janet.'

She took his hand and held it as she said, 'I know exactly what you mean. As you know, I never liked him. Although looking back, I recall that before he went to the private school he used always to come to me when he got into a scrape. But from then we fought like cat and dog.'

'Oh God!' Harry bent forward, his head shaking as he muttered, 'He'll hang; if not he'll die in jail. He's weak, always was, and he wouldn't be able to stand a long term.

It would be better if he went now.'

'I think the same, Harry, I think the same. As for Dad, he's not only wishing he goes but he's praying for it; that's if he ever prays for anything.'

As the cab neared the house she said, 'I want to have a talk with you about something private. Would you stay up? I mean, after Dad goes upstairs.'

'Yes; yes. I wouldn't be able to sleep anyway if I went to bed.'

But Samuel had already gone to bed, as Maitland told Harry as he helped him off with his coat, saying, 'The master has retired and he wondered if you would drop in and have a word with him before you go to your room?'

For the first time since coming home Harry smiled and answered, 'That's a wonderful translation, Maitland. The original would be more like, "Tell him I want to see him as soon as he comes back." Isn't that so?'

'Not quite, not exactly word for word, Master Harry.'

Janet had gone ahead into the drawing-room, and when Harry followed her, saying, 'He's unique, is Maitland,' she turned to him and said, 'Yes, I agree with you; he is unique.'

They were both seated on the couch when Janet said abruptly, 'I'm going to be married, Harry.'

'What! Married? Who to? The librarian?'

'No, no.' She shook her head. 'Not the librarian.' She gave a small smile. 'I refused him and he didn't like it, and so I've left there. No; I'm going to marry the . . .' she pointed towards the door, inclining her head in the same direction as she said, 'the unique one.'

He had been lying back on the couch, but now he was sitting upright, half turned towards her, and his voice was a whisper as he queried, 'Maitland?'

'Yes, Maitland.'

'But . . . but he's twice your age, over forty. He's —'

'Yes, I know all that. But he doesn't look over forty, does he?'

He flopped back into the cushions again, his head towards her, a smile on his face as he said, 'I should say I'm amazed . . . well, I was surprised by your announcement; but at the same time I shouldn't be, because you've trailed him for years, haven't you? from when you were a kid.'

'Yes, I've trailed him for years and he's loved me for years, too.'

'Really?'

'Yes, but he kept it hidden.'

'But Janet, his . . . his correctness, his polite manner, his —'

'That's Maitland. There's another Maitland named Roger who's different altogether and so good to be with, you have no idea.'

'No! Really? That a fact?'

'Oh yes, really; that's a fact; and I don't think we should be here now if Howard's problem hadn't happened. Just last Saturday we . . . we arranged things. It meant going off secretly because — you won't believe this, Harry — I'm practically a prisoner here. Dad watches my every movement.'

'He knows?'

'Yes, he knows; but he hasn't actually come into the open, instead he's cajoled and threatened, and I believe his threats. Oh, yes. And I know that had it been only ten or twenty years earlier, he would have had me locked in my bedroom and kept on bread and water until I should swear on the Bible that I'd give up this mad idea. And, of course, Maitland would have been kicked out. But now things are changing, and he can't actually do that. But he never leaves me alone for long.'

'He's out all day, or at least he used to be.'

'Yes, he used to be, but he arranges his hours differently now. And I know this, Harry: should I come into the open he'll do something drastic. Perhaps not to me, but to Roger. And yet, I don't know: he's told me he would rather see me dead than lower myself. And I certainly don't consider it lowering myself by loving or marrying Maitland. He is highly intelligent and well read. Hardly any of you bothered about the library, did you? Well . . . you were at school, I suppose you got enough of reading there. But every spare minute of his time, I should imagine, not only since we came into the house but when he was with his lordship, he has used that library. And that's only one side of him. He's a bit of a gymnast, too.' She now pursed her lips at her brother as he made a small derogatory sound in his throat, and she emphasised, 'He is a bit of a gymnast. Once a week for years he's attended the gymnasium in Newcastle on his day off and there has done all kinds of exercises. Can you imagine him hoisting Howard, who's no small weight, on to his shoulder and walking backwards down the stairs from the room next to the hay loft where I found him?'

'He . . . he carried him?'

'Yes, he carried him, and as if he was

410

used to doing it every day.'

'Good gracious! You do surprise me on that score. I would have thought this kind of life would have made him soft. Well, you know —'

'Yes, I know; and likely he, too, was aware of that years ago.'

'But . . . but what'll you do for a living? Oh I know you've got money; but he wouldn't want to live on that.'

'He's got it all planned. In fact, he's had it planned for years what he was going to do when he left here. He had an offer, you know, to join his lordship's family in America and refused it. That was just a few years ago. But he's going to start a school to train butlers, footmen and so forth.'

'A school for . . . ? Is there such a thing?'

'I don't know, but that's what he's going to do. If not that, he has another string to his bow. With or without me he had meant to do this. But I'm all for it; in fact . . .' she turned from him and clasped her hands tightly on her knees as she said, 'I'm all for anything he'd ever want to do, because, Harry, I love him so much; and I feel I'm so lucky in that he loves me, so very lucky.'

'Oh, I wouldn't agree with you there. The thing is, you're a very attractive girl, Janet. You used to be a plain kid early on, in your teens. But these last few years you've changed. You're different, particularly when you smile. You know, Eddie said that, the last time we were together when we were talking about you. Beautiful, he said you could be . . . and he's right.'

'Shut up! I know what I look like.'

'Does . . . does anyone else know . . . well, about this?'

'Oh, no, no. And I've only spoken to you because . . . well, you're different: you're not talkative, and I knew I could trust you and you wouldn't chip me as Eddie might have done in his fun-making way. You know, I was surprised when I first knew that Jessie wanted to go into the convent and be a nun, but somehow I would never have been surprised if you had wanted to go into the Church.'

He stared at her for a while before he said, 'You know, that's funny you saying that, because I've been thinking a lot about that same thing lately. So, who knows?'

'Oh, no, you wouldn't, would you?'

'Why not? Why not? Lately, I've got to asking: why am I here? Where am I going? And, when I die, what becomes of this little grey matter up here?' He tapped his brow. 'Will that be the end? Or will that merge into the power from where it came? And what is the power? Or who is the power? If there is an end there has to be a beginning. You know, going back, it was man who first created gods, because in his groping mind man knew there was something bigger than himself, more powerful than him, something that had put him on the earth. So he picked the sun because that was powerful, and there could be no voice more powerful than thunder, and there was an arm that shot across the sky and lit up all his world. And . . . have we advanced so much since then? Every colour and race in the world have chosen a god. Oh goodness me! and so it goes on, never-ending, and I tell myself to shut up.'

Of a sudden she leaned her head against his shoulder, saying, 'I can see you plainly in the pulpit now.' And he, putting his arm around her, laughed as he answered, 'Well, I can promise you one thing, dear, it won't be a Roman one because I want a wife.'

'Oh yes, you must be married, Harry, and have children, lots of them, just like you.'

They drew apart self-consciously as there came a tap on the door, and Maitland entered the room. 'Your father would like you to call in and see him as soon as it is convenient,' he said to Harry.

Recognising the glint in Maitland's eye,

Harry said, 'You wouldn't like to go back, Maitland, and tell him it isn't convenient, and that I'll come when I'm ready?'

'I would, Master Harry, I would very much like to do just that.'

Janet rose quickly to her feet and hurried towards Maitland and, clasping his hand, said, 'Roger, dear, I've told Harry.'

Maitland looked at her, then looked at Harry, and after puffing out slowly, he said, 'Well, now you know.'

Harry, too, had risen to his feet and, moving towards them, he held out his hand, saying, 'I wish you both much happiness, and I mean that. And when I have time to think, I know I'll come to the conclusion that I know of no-one else I'd welcome more as a brother-in-law.'

'Thank you . . . Harry.'

'You're welcome . . . Roger.'

And at this exchange they all three laughed. Then Harry said, 'I felt so sad a while ago about Howard — I still do, but I really think that an occasion like this calls for a drink; so look; I'll dash upstairs and see his lordship, then I'll be down again.' And at that, smiling from one to the other, he hurried from the room.

They stood gazing at each other for a moment before their arms went out and they

414

held each other tightly as Maitland said, 'I don't know what the response will be from the others, but that's a good beginning. At least —' he smiled into her face now as he added, 'from the sidelines.'

She did not return his smile but said, 'Oh, if only Howard —'

And at this he interrupted her by repeating, 'Yes; if only Howard; but I have a strange feeling that he is but a part of the pattern of our future life together. I can't explain it except to say, it's a sort of . . .' He did not go on to explain further, and she asked, 'What kind of feeling? Sort of what?'

He tweaked her nose, saying, 'I don't know. But what I do know is I want a drink, and Harry will be back in a minute. He's a nice fellow. Now, now, no more probing. Come on.'

9

It was visiting time on Saturday afternoon and Janet was making her way to the ward when, in the corridor, she came face to face with the inspector. Simultaneously they stopped, he saying, 'Good afternoon, Miss Fairbrother.'

When she made no response he said, 'I . . . I have just been to see your brother and . . . and to tell him he will be moved on Monday.'

'But he is still ill.'

'I'm acting on the doctor's opinion of his condition. He'll continue to have nursing attention, but the situation as it is . . . well, it's very awkward.'

The look of consternation on her face caused him to add, 'Don't worry over much; I've had a long talk with him. It appears there's something on his side, after all. He tells a different story from Mrs Mailston, which is somewhat corroborated by the evidence of the other lodger, and so things are not as black as they might have been.'

'When . . . when d'you think the trial will be?'

'Oh, I can't put a date to that at the present moment. There's a lot to go into, you know. But, as I said, try not to worry, because . . . well' — his voice sank low in his throat — 'self-defence is bound to be brought in, and if this is upheld . . . well, the outlook may not be quite so bleak. You know?'

Yes, she knew. But the present looming up still made her sick at heart. 'Thank you,' she said, and they parted.

The curtains were still drawn around the cubicle and Howard was sitting up; at least, he was not lying flat. The policeman half rose and nodded to her as she entered. She had not seen this one before. When she went to Howard's side his hand came up and caught hers in a weak grip. He seemed to be finding it difficult to speak, his agitation no doubt caused by the inspector's visit and the coming move to prison quarters.

She reached out with her other hand and pulled a wooden chair close to the bedside. Sitting down, she leaned towards him, saying, 'It'll be all right. It'll be all right. There's another side to it, they all know that.'

He closed his eyes now and shook his head; then in a whisper he muttered, 'Either way, I . . . I can't stand it, Janet. I can't.'

'Now, now.' She put her hand up and stroked his hair back. 'Dad is hiring a good lawyer and barrister.' She now glanced at the policeman, but he was looking straight ahead as the other had, as if he were deaf and blind. And when Howard said, 'It'll make no difference,' the hopelessness in his tone seemed to infect herself and she thought, No, it won't make all that difference for, however long or short, he'd have to serve a sentence, and that is if he is lucky enough to live.

So, in an effort to take his mind off the consequences with which, every minute, he must be living, she pointed to the basket resting on the trolley at the foot of the bed, saying, 'Cook's made you some nice tidbits, custard tarts and things. You used to like those, she remembered.' She glanced again at the policeman as if she were wanting him to take note of what was in the basket, although she knew that later he would not only take note, but would probably go through each item before Howard would be allowed even to see what she had brought.

She said now, 'James said he was writing to you. Have you had a letter?'

Nodding towards an envelope lying on top of the bedside cabinet, he said, 'Yes.

418

Yes, he's . . . he's going to try and get leave and come and see me; but' — he shook his head — 'he needn't go to the trouble, because I won't be here.'

'Well, he can always come.' She hesitated, then she added, 'He's concerned; as we all are, dear.'

As she looked at him his lips moved into a smile, although the smile did not touch his eyes, and then she bowed her head against his next words, 'You know, Janet, I'm having more kindness and concern shown to me now than I've had in all my life before. Dad never bothered, did he? And Mam's concern was . . . well, always filled with anxiety and threats of what would happen to me if . . . if. And she was right about the "if". Oh, she was right. But it's odd, don't you think, Janet? it's odd that there could be something I'm glad about, and that is that you . . . well, you above all people seem to understand. And I was thinking just last night, it is as if we were back in Gran's. You used to look after me there. But after we moved, things were different. They were different for all of us, don't you agree?'

'Yes. Yes, Howard, you're right; they were different for all of us after we moved.'

'Talking of moving, they'll be moving me on Monday.'

He looked fully at her, and she made a little motion with her head as she said, 'Yes, I know.'

He lay back, quiet now, his eyes closed. The policeman suddenly spoke. He said, 'Nice to see the sun, isn't it, miss?'

'Yes. Yes, it is, constable.'

'Spring'll soon be here.'

'Yes. Yes, it will.'

'I like the spring. Not so fond of the summer. Don't like the heat very much, but I like the spring and' — he smiled across the bed at her — 'and the autumn. But . . . but you can keep the winter and the summer.'

The cubicle became quiet again, a silence made more noticeable by the muted buzz of talk from the visitors in the ward. But when Howard said, 'Have you got a file with you?' the policeman seemed to swivel round on his chair, only to see Howard withdrawing his hand from Janet's and spreading it wide, saying, 'Would you file my nails for me?'

'Yes. Yes, I have one in my handbag.' She bent towards the floor and picked up her handbag and from a little case that held scissors, a comb, and a cuticle presser she drew out the file, then slowly began to file her brother's nails.

The policeman had settled back, almost to his original position, but not quite. He was now sitting in such a way that he could see what Janet was doing. And he sat like that until he saw Janet return the file to its case and replace the case in her bag.

It was at this point that the curtains opened and the nurse beckoned the policeman towards her, and when she backed into the ward the policeman stood half in and half out of the cubicle, his hand holding the curtain. It was only for a matter of seconds, but it was long enough for Howard to grip Janet's hand and, bending towards her, whisper, 'Slip me your scissors.'

'What?'

'The scissors.'

He pointed to the mattress. 'The case, push it in there.'

Janet hadn't time to reply, but her chair scraping back on the polished floor, away from the bed, gave Howard his answer. And at the sound the policeman turned and stared at them and they both returned his look.

Whatever the request the nurse had made of the policeman, he said, 'Thanks. I'll see to it. Don't worry.' Then he was again sitting by the side of the bed.

Janet was staring at Howard and he at

her. Why did he want her scissors? But need she ask? Oh, no, no, he wouldn't. Yet, why did he ask?

She glanced at his hand, which was now hanging over the side of the bed, below the hard mattress, and was gripping convulsively at the iron framework that held the slotted ends of the meshed iron springs. It was as if he were talking to her with his hand. She now took hold of the hand and brought it to the top of the counterpane and there she stroked it as she said, 'It'll be all right, dear. Things will pan out. I promise you.'

He lay looking at her, his expression beseeching help.

Her throat tight, her eyes moist, she muttered, 'Mother should be here in a minute. I'll leave as soon as she comes. But I'll be in tomorrow.'

'Janet.'

'Yes, my dear?'

'Sorry . . . sorry about the money.'

'Oh, Howard, I've told you and told you, forget about it. It was nothing, nothing . . .'

The curtains were suddenly pulled aside and as her mother entered Janet got to her feet. Then, bending over Howard, she said, 'I'll be in tomorrow, dear.'

'Janet. Goodbye, and thanks.'

She wanted to take his face between her hands and say, What is it? What d'you mean? But she straightened up and their gaze held for a moment, and then she was passing her mother without an exchange of words. But while she held the curtain open she turned and looked towards the bed again. Howard's gaze was on her and she lifted her hand towards him. He couldn't raise his in reply because Alice was holding it now, but he moved his head twice.

She went down the ward with her head bent. It was still bent when she reached the corridor, where her father's voice broke into her thoughts. 'You going?'

Startled, she blinked as she looked at him. When she made no answer, he said, 'It's no use being upset, 'cos there's more to come likely.'

Her voice low, she said, 'Mother's there.'

'Yes, I know she's there. I brought her. They only allow two in at a time. Look, I'll go in now, but I won't stay; and if you wait, I'll run you back. I can always come back for her.'

'There's no need, I've got my bicycle.'

'You going straight back, then?'

'Yes, I'm going straight back.'

He stared hard at her for another moment

or so before he turned abruptly and walked into the ward.

During her cycle journey home, she must have said at least twenty times, He wouldn't! Surely he wouldn't!

It would seem that Maitland had been waiting for her: she had hardly rung the bell before the door was opened and he said, 'You're back early.'

'Yes. Yes.'

'Something's gone wrong?' His voice was low and his hands lingered on her shoulders as he helped her off with her coat.

She did not make for the drawing-room but went down the corridor and into the library. And when, a moment or so later, he followed her, she did not immediately go to him, but sat down in the leather chair before the fire and held her hands out to the blaze. And when he stood by her side, he said, 'What is it, dear? Has something else happened?'

She looked up at him and said, 'They're moving him on Monday. He's in a state, and . . . and he asked me for scissors or a file.'

'Scissors?'

'Yes.' She nodded up at him, then told him briefly what had happened, adding, 'But . . . but I can't imagine him doing it.

He's . . . he's not strong enough; I mean, in his character. But he seemed desperate. And the look on his face! Oh, the look on his face.' She now closed her eyes and shook her head slowly. 'I'll see the look on his face for the rest of my life. Even when I was going out and mother was holding his hand he was silently pleading with me. It was as if he were saying goodbye. But he won't be able to do anything, will he?'

'I shouldn't think so. Apart from the policeman sitting with him all the time, there's the nurses. As he has the use of only one hand, they will wash him, and anyway, how could he get hold of an implement? That's one of the reasons why a policeman must always be close enough to watch, in case he should attempt anything.'

'He'll never survive prison, Roger.'

'It's amazing what the human frame and mind can survive. And, as we've said, if it's self-defence, he will likely just get a short sentence; a few years, not life.'

'Life. The very sound of it makes me feel ill. And you know, he seems to be worrying about the money I gave him; He said again that he was sorry. I keep telling him that's the least of his worries, or words to that effect.'

'By the way, there was a phone call from

James just after your father left. He wanted to know how things are.'

'Did he say he was coming home?'

'No. He didn't mention anything about leave.'

'Odd. He's not a bit like Harry or Eddie. If Eddie had been ashore, he would have made sure he got leave, at least for a day or two. Still, what could he do? What can anybody do? I feel so sad, Roger. Right to the very depths of me.'

He dropped on to his hunkers before her and, taking her hands, he said, 'I know, dear. And it's strange that all this sorry business seems to have fallen on you; the main emotion of it all, I mean. Your father is taking it as a personal insult, and I think your mother, by the sound of it, is bent down with humiliation. And that's understandable, for he's her son. But it's you, the last person you would imagine he would turn to, he's found solace with.' Then he added, 'Did your father know you were coming straight home, not going to Annie's as you've been doing?'

'Yes, I told him so.'

'Then,' he pulled a rueful face, and rose to his feet adding, 'I had better be about my duties in the hall, because the last thing we want at the present moment is a show-

426

down, isn't it, dear?'

She looked up at him, saying, 'Yes. Yes, you're right there. I don't think I could stand much more today. But you know what I'd like?'

'Yes. A nice cup of tea. And you'll have that within minutes, my dearest.' Quickly now he bent and kissed her softly on the lips, then hurried from the room, and the man who went out was not Maitland.

10

As of long habit Sarah Johnson, Florence Furness, and Bella Forbes rose at six o'clock. Sarah and Florence both took their rising slowly, whereas Bella still scurried a little, although, as she would have said, not so much as in the old days when, first she was the scullery maid and then, after Jackie Winter left the kitchen quarters to go into the yard as a stable lad, when she had had to clean and polish all the boots for the family. There being now only three pairs to do, although she saw to Cook's as well, she was able to have the kettle boiling and the tea brewed before half-past six, when she would take a cup in to Cook, just as either Sarah or Florence would knock on Mr Maitland's door and call out that his tray was, as usual, resting on the dumb waiter that stood in the passage connecting the annexe with the house.

Roger had initiated this procedure many years ago when, as a young man fresh to the post of footman, he had to fight off the early morning attentions of an amorous housemaid.

His arrival on duty was at seven prompt, by which time the main grates had been cleared and the fires lit. Following this, one of Sarah's first duties was to clean the breakfast-room; afterwards, he himself would lay the table for the family breakfast.

But this particular morning's routine was changed. It should happen that Bella, from the kitchen, heard the distant ring of the telephone bell. Now, she had never touched the phone — she was afraid of it — so she scurried to Florence's bedroom and, knocking on the door and in a hoarse whisper, she cried, 'The telephone bell's ringing, Florence.'

Florence opened the door, then finished fastening on her starched cap before saying, 'What? Telephone bell ringing? Not at this time of the morning; you must be dreaming.' Then putting her head on one side, she said, 'You're right,' and hurried along the passage and into the hall and there, picking up the earpiece, she said, as she had been taught, 'Yes? This is the Fairbrother residence.'

'I would like to speak to Mr Fairbrother. This is the night sister.'

'The night sister from the hospital?'

'Yes, the night sister from the hospital.'

'He's . . . he's still in bed, but I'll get

him. Can you wait?'

'Yes. Yes, I can wait.'

Florence did not run up the stairs to Samuel's room but almost flew to the annexe and there, knocking rapidly on the door, she cried, 'Mr Maitland! It's the hospital; they're on the telephone. It's the matron, she wants to speak to the master.'

Maitland appeared in his dressing gown. He strode straight past her and into the hall and there, picking up the phone, he said, 'This is the butler speaking. The master is still in bed. Can I give him a message?'

There was the sound of mumbled conversation, and then a man's voice said, 'This is Sergeant Baker. There . . . there has been an accident. Mr Howard Fairbrother . . . the prisoner, is . . . is very ill. I can say no more, but I would advise Mr Fairbrother to get here as soon as possible.'

'Yes. Yes.' Maitland slammed down the phone, then ran upstairs and, after one brief knock on the door, he entered Samuel's bedroom, and going straight to the bed, where his master was lying on his back with his mouth open and emitting a none-too-gentle snore, he shook him by the shoulder, saying, 'Sir! Sir! Wake up!'

Heaving himself up on to the pillows,

Samuel demanded, 'What's the matter? What is it now?'

'There's word come through from the hospital, sir. I understand there's been an accident, and they say that Mr Howard is very ill, and suggest you had better go quickly.'

'What . . . what kind of an accident?'

'They didn't say.'

'How could he have had an accident with a policeman sitting by his side all the time?' He was getting out of the bed now.

'I wouldn't know, sir. It's early; and so while you're getting dressed, I will order a cab.' As he made for the door, he added, 'Shall I see that Miss Janet is informed?'

'Yes. Yes. She'd better come along.' Then, as Maitland was about to leave the room Samuel called after him, 'Get Florence to wake her.'

Maitland went out, closed the door and stood for a moment as he repeated to himself, 'Get Florence to wake her.' He hesitated a moment, deciding whether to defy the order, but seeing Sarah coming on to the landing he said to her, 'Go and wake up Miss Janet. Tell her to get dressed quickly; she's needed at the hospital.' . . .

Ten minutes later Samuel and Janet were standing in the hall drinking tea as they

431

waited for the cab. Janet had not spoken to her father, even when he greeted her with, 'What's happened now?' She felt she knew what had happened: in some way he had attempted to put an end to himself, but exactly how, she did not know.

Maitland was dressed now, and when the cab arrived on the drive he hurried out and spoke to the driver as he opened the cab door, saying, 'Don't get down, but drive as quickly as you can to the General Hospital.'

At this, Samuel put in, 'No. I must first pick up my wife; I'll direct you.'

They had been sitting opposite each other for some minutes when Samuel said, 'Why can't you say something, girl?'

'What is there to say?'

'Anything, rather than sit there like a dummy. You could wonder what's happened or something.'

'I don't need to wonder what's happened; I know.'

His face stretched and he said, 'You know? What d'you mean, you know?'

'I know that he must have tried to commit suicide if he's so bad that they need your presence there.'

'Suicide? How could he with a policeman sitting by him twenty-four hours a day?'

'Yesterday, when the policeman happened to be speaking to the sister, half in and half out of the cubicle, Howard was quick to take advantage of that, asking me for scissors or a file.'

'Did you give him the scissors?'

'Would you have given him scissors?' she retorted.

He turned his head away before saying, 'I don't know. I don't know.' Then looking at her again, he demanded, 'Did you?'

'No, I didn't.'

'No, of course you wouldn't. But all I can say now is, if he's tried it I hope he's done the job properly, because if not, he's only extending the agony.'

She stared at him for some time before she said, 'You are a hard man.'

'No, lass, I'm not; I'm just a practical one. And I've realised for a long time that this particular son of mine wasn't much good, not to himself or anybody else. Who he takes after, God alone knows. It isn't me or anybody on my side. And from experience of them both I know it wasn't your granny or your grand-dad. Somewhere along the line he's inherited his character from a weakling.'

'Weakling? I would say it takes courage to try and commit suicide.'

'No, I don't think so, lass, not when

you've got the picture of a rope hanging before your eyes; or, if not that, a long stretch in prison with the dregs of the earth for company, and under the supervision of bullies, in the main.'

Of a sudden he pulled down the window, thrust down his head and yelled up at the driver, 'Can't you make that animal move?' And when he dropped back on to the seat he nodded at her: 'I'll have to learn to drive that bloody car or get a driver who'll live in. They used to at one time.' . . .

In answer to Samuel's heavy banging on the door with his fist, Alice appeared still blinking the sleep from her eyes, and straightaway he said, 'You'd better get your clothes on, woman, and quick. They've phoned from the hospital. It sounds as if' — he paused — 'well, something's happened. He's in a bad way.'

When she put her hand to her head, saying, 'Well . . . well, I've got to get dressed and see to the girls and —' he said abruptly, 'How long is that going to take you?'

'Ten minutes or so. I . . . I don't know where I am; I've . . . I've just woken up.'

'Well, in that case, we'd better get on. I'll send the cab back for you.'

'Can't you wait?'

'No, I can't. I know you when you start

dithering.' And at this he turned about and went back to the cab and said to the cabbie, 'Make it as quick as you can, man, will you?'

There was still no retort from the cabbie and when Samuel took his seat opposite Janet again, he jerked his head backwards, saying, 'He's tarred with the same brush as you; he only speaks when he wants to.'

She said nothing to this, for she knew that he was under stress: he always shouted and blustered when he was faced with trouble.

Later, standing in the hospital corridor with the night sister, his voice was low and his manner was even gentle as he asked, 'How is he?'

Her voice, too, was soft as she explained Howard's condition. 'He is unconscious. But he is still alive. We did not expect him really to last this long.'

'How . . . what happened?'

'He attempted . . . in fact he practically succeeded in taking his own life by cutting his wrist.'

'But how did he get hold of . . . ? Did he have a . . . well, a knife?'

'No; 'tis amazing how he did it. Of course, he wouldn't have had the opportunity to get a sharp instrument of any kind, but he did it by goring his wrist with a piece of wire attached to the bed. It was little over a quarter of an inch long and was protruding from where the mesh was joined; it was part of the spring. And, of course, the result wasn't detected for some time. He must have kept his hand under the bedclothes and the night nurse imagined he was asleep, as did his guard. I'm . . . I'm very sorry it had to happen this way.' She turned from them and slowly walked up the ward, and they followed her.

Activity in the ward was subdued. Some patients were being washed, others were making their way to, or returning from, the washroom.

When the sister parted the curtains, the two officers rose from their chairs, and one, coming forward, said, 'Good morning, sir. I am Sergeant Baker.'

Samuel inclined his head, and stood for a moment looking over the foot of the bed at his son, before moving slowly up the side of it.

The sergeant now motioned to his companion and they went outside, and the night sister, addressing Janet, said softly, 'I'll be outside if you need me.'

And there they were, one at each side of the bed, Samuel gazing at his first born and Janet at the brother whom she had actually hated, and again she was swamped by a feeling of pity; yet strangely, not so much for Howard, because he would soon be free, but for the man who was gazing down at him, because she was witnessing a very rare sight, her father was crying.

Slowly she walked round the bed and, standing by his side, she put an arm around his shoulders, and he turned to her, and she held him. Then, as if disturbed by a sigh, they turned hastily from each other and looked down at the figure on the bed.

Samuel was rubbing his face vigorously with his handkerchief when he muttered, 'Call the sister.'

Leaning over the prostrate form, Sister gently lifted an eyelid. Then she placed a hand inside the bed cover and on Howard's chest, after which she straightened up and, looking from one to the other, she said, 'I'm very sorry.'

It was at this moment that Alice made her appearance She paused by the curtain, her hand gripping her throat; then almost pushing the sister aside, she leaned over her son and cupped his face in her hands, muttering, 'Oh! Howard. Howard. Oh! My boy. My boy.'

When her body began to shake, Samuel went round to her and, taking her arm gently, made to draw her away from the bed. But she shrugged off his hold and hissed at him, 'Now you're satisfied, aren't you? You're satisfied. And you let him die here in this ward . . . a public ward. You wouldn't put him into a private ward, would you? Would you?'

'Quiet! Alice. Come on.'

To Janet's surprise she watched her father now put an arm around her mother's shoulders and her submit to being led outside.

Janet remained standing by the bed. She was looking down on her brother's white face: his expression was sad, yet at the same time peaceful. Inwardly, she told herself, You were very brave, Howard, and you did the right thing, for you would never have been able to stand what was to come. I'll always remember, Howard, that we were friends at the last, and that you needed me.

She did not turn to her father, although she was aware that he had come back into the cubicle; not until he laid a hand on her arm, saying, 'Come on; there's nothing more to be done; his battle is over,' did she turn from the bed and allow him to lead her out, as he had done her mother. But in her mind she wasn't submitting. To herself she was saying, Yes, your son's battle is over, but your daughter's is just about to begin. My brother is lying dead, and this man who is being so tender towards me now is not a little to blame, for his son's life had been patterned through fear of him, and lately I have experienced that same fear. But it isn't going to rule my life, nor is pity for his loneliness that he aims to evoke in me going to keep me by his side.

When, in the corridor, he muttered, 'My God! Why did he have to do that?' she pulled her arm from his hold and hissed at him, 'Don't be such a bloody hypocrite. You've been praying for it.'

And she stalked away from him towards the main exit, leaving him standing speechless, for he could find no words that would have enabled him to contradict the truth with a lie.

11

The next morning Maitland himself took delivery of the newspapers from the wide-eyed paper boy. One seemed to raise the status of the tragedy by referring to it as 'The Fairbrother Affair'; the other was much more dramatic:

Unable to take the consequences,
Howard Fairbrother takes another life.

For once Samuel did not ask for the papers; and throughout the day he appeared to be very subdued; and even on the Monday, when he went out to make arrangements for the burial, he was still not himself; only much later did he return to normal when, hardly in the door, he exploded with, 'Bloody authorities! Unconsecrated ground, be damned!' His eyes were blazing as he looked at Maitland, whose response did nothing to soothe him: 'Well, weren't you aware of this, sir?'

'No, I wasn't aware of it. It's not something that happens every day. I don't think about these kind of things, but apparently you do.'

'Well, it's a known fact, sir, that anyone taking his own life cannot be buried in consecrated ground.'

'Well, it wasn't a fact known to me. I'm an ignorant slob, you know.' He turned now to walk towards the drawing-room, saying, 'Where's Miss Janet?'

He always made a point of stressing the 'miss' when speaking of her to Maitland.

'She's out, sir.'

'Where?'

Maitland paused before he answered, 'I don't know, sir.' . . .

In the drawing-room, Samuel did not take up his usual position with his back to the fire, but dropped heavily on to a chair facing it, and in a voice from which all the spirit seemed to have gone, he called to Maitland who was about to close the door, 'He's not to have a Christian service either. I knew there was something about that, but when they slap you in the face with it . . .' he was subdued again and added simply, 'What's to be done?'

Maitland, walking slowly towards him, said, 'I don't know, sir, except that perhaps some minister of a lesser denomination would officiate.'

'Aye, of a lesser denomination. But why can't a Church of England minister do it, I ask you? The C of E covers all kinds. Ask anyone who hasn't been inside a church in his life, ask him what he is and he'll say, "Oh; C of E." And what's more, having a son who has killed a man and then committed suicide, I've disgraced the town. You certainly find out who your friends are, don't you? I could have laid my life down for Joe . . . Joe Atkinson, you know. I put him where he is today by getting him contracts, and I did the same for his son an' all. I put him into his posh solicitors' office and kept him there by getting him well-oiled clients. And what d'you think Joe said to me? "It was such a pity for the town because, like the murder, it was the first suicide they'd had in years." Gateshead and Newcastle could have them; oh aye, they could have them every other day; but Fellburn no; not in Fellburn. And you know something else he said? He said it was a very strange thing for Howard to do, to take his own life, because, as he remembered, he wasn't of a very strong character. Talk about tact. You think *I'm* tactless. Huh! Well!' And he tossed his head. But after a moment, he added, 'But I have one friend, at least, because Jim Dawson was there at the time and he nearly swallowed Joe Atkinson whole. For once in me life, and just when I should have, I hadn't been able to open me mouth . . . Anyway, what am I going to do about this? It's just a thought, but I was wondering if one of those priests would stretch a point, a Catholic priest. They're going to have me daughter in their convent, and I've paid through the nose for me three girls to go there; and I've given generously to all their off-shoots, and mind they've got some. Well, what d'you think?'

Maitland didn't say what he was thinking, that they were the last people who'd break the rule. But you couldn't squash this man's last hope, and so he said, 'You can but try. You could speak to the priest.'

'Oh, I couldn't, not me; I'd have to send Janet.' Such was the state of his mind that he had omitted the 'miss'. 'She could go to the Mother Superior and the old girl could act as a liaison officer. The sooner he's put to rest the better, for his mother's nearly going round the bend. You know what she wants now? She wants to bring him home. But I've put me foot down on that. And she insisted on going to the mortuary again.'

He sat back in his chair, put his hand over his eyes and said quietly, 'Maitland, get me a drink, will you please? And as soon as Janet comes in, at dinner time, tell her I want to see her. I'll be in my office.' He

443

now rose slowly from the chair, waited for Maitland to hand him a glass of whisky, then went out, followed by Maitland. He was thinking, as Janet had done, that this was the other side of the man. But his thoughts went further; that this was the side that could break down Janet's resolve.

Janet looked at her father. He wasn't sitting at his desk but by the window. He had told her what he wanted her to do and her immediate feeling was to say, 'Don't be ridiculous, Dad! They're the most stiff-necked of the lot.' She didn't, and when she remained silent he said, 'Say something, girl!'

'I can but try, but I wouldn't hold out any hopes.'

'Take Jessie along with you,' he said. 'That should put a bit of pressure on them, 'cos I could put me foot down, couldn't I? and not let her go in, at least until she's twenty-one, when she can please herself.'

'What would you do with her in the meantime, Dad? Tie her up, or leave her at home with Mam, which would drive them both mad, because, you know, Jessie's got a bit of me in her: when her mind is set on something she won't be side-tracked. Anyway, that's in the future. I'll see what I can

444

do about the burial.'

As she went to turn away he said, almost in a whisper, 'Awful state of affairs, lass, isn't it?'

'Yes, Dad, it's an awful state of affairs, but it'll soon be over. And, as Gran used to say, nine-day wonders don't last more than nine days, or words to that effect.'

'This business'll stay in my mind until the day I die.'

She said nothing, but turned to walk towards the door where again he stopped her, this time with, 'You got in touch with the boys?'

'Yes. Harry said he'll be here tomorrow. There's nothing certain about Eddie except that his ship should dock tomorrow. And James said I had to phone him back when I knew the details of the funeral.'

Sam's reaction was to mutter, 'The funeral. Well, there's one thing you can be sure of, the kitchen lot won't need to make a big spread for the mourners, for they'll be few and far between on that day.'

12

Howard was buried on the Thursday; and Samuel had been right in that the mourners were indeed so few and far between as to seem almost non-existent. Jim and Gladys Dawson were the only people who joined the small cortège at the cemetery.

But there *was* a minister at the graveside.

Janet's approach to the ministers of various denominations proved to be a lesson that she would always remember as one portraying the love and charity of the Christian Church. But of the various responses she had received to her request, that of Sister Mary Terese would stand out.

Sister Mary Terese was deputising for the Mother Superior who was ill in bed, and to whom Jessie, much against the grain, had taken her request. The Sister had stared at the sisters aghast before saying, 'It would be no earthly use, my child, your going or my speaking to Father McTaggart, or even to Father Connell, who has the softest nature in the world, because your own sense should tell you, child, that your brother has upset God so much he cannot hope ever to see His face, or find redemption of any kind.'

The minister at the graveside was a Unitarian. He stood among the small group and spoke words of comfort, and as they lowered the coffin into the unhallowed ground, his voice low but clear, he ended with, 'Go in peace, brother. Rest easy. God understands your needs.'

Later, when they were about to enter the cab, Samuel thanked the man and tried to push some crumpled notes into his hand but the young minister pushed them away. Samuel said in some surprise, 'Well, well! sir, all I can say is, thank you. And I'm glad to find one Christian outside the main churches.'

And to this the man replied, 'We're all Christians who follow Jesus, under whatever banner.'

There had been some heated discussion, at least between Samuel and Alice before the day of the funeral, as to which house her sons would return to after the burial, because there was one thing certain, Alice said, she wasn't going back to his place. And she felt she was entitled to see something of her sons; at least, of two of them.

So here they were in Alice's house, standing by the dining-room table, spread with enough food not to have disgraced a birthday party or even a wedding reception. And it was Samuel who expressed aloud not only his own thoughts but also those of the rest of the family by saying, 'Alice, it looks grand, but one bite would choke me. What I would like is a drink and then perhaps a cup of tea. All right, lass?'

Alice's head was bent deeply on her chest, and when she didn't answer, his voice rising, he said, 'Well, do you feel like stuffing your kite at this minute?' Then turning to Eddie and Harry, he asked, 'You . . . are you hungry?'

'No, Dad,' they answered simultaneously, 'we too would like a drink, or a cup of tea.'

'All right, then. What I say is, let's go into the sitting-room where there's more comfortable chairs. Well, Alice?'

'As you wish, as you wish.' She led the way out of the dining-room, across the small hall and into the sitting-room where, pointing to a side table on which had been arranged some bottles and glasses, she said, 'You can help yourselves;' then immediately turned about and went out, followed by Fanny.

Eddie went to the table and poured out three whiskies: then, after handing one to his father, then another to his brother, he looked at Janet, saying, 'Did you want something?'

'Yes. Yes, I would like a sherry, please.'

'Oh, a sherry? Oh, all right.'

As he somewhat reluctantly handed her the sherry, he looked towards Jessie and, on a half smile, asked, 'Water for you, miss, I suppose?'

And she, bobbing her head at him, said, 'Wouldn't it surprise you if I were to ask for a sherry too!'

'Yes, it would; and you wouldn't get one.' This came from her father. And she, looking at him, said gently, 'Who's to stop me when there's no-one here, Dad, eh?'

'Well, you'd better not let me or your mother catch you.'

'Oh, I wouldn't, Dad; I'm very clever at being underhand.'

'You can say that again, miss, and in all honesty.'

Janet found herself standing apart from them all, not only physically, but also in her mind.

There was a strange feeling of numbness on her. She had shed no tears at the grave; her mother had done enough for all of them. She looked from her brothers to her father and then back to Jessie. This was a divided house, a divided family, if ever there was one. It could be said that James had already left it never to return. He had told her plainly on the telephone that he couldn't see any sense in his attending the funeral: Howard had done this mad thing because he was a coward. No talking on her part had convinced him that, to her mind, no-one who took his own life as Howard had done could be termed a coward; his reply had been: that anybody who couldn't face up to the consequences of killing another person was a coward.

Harry caught her attention now by asking, 'What's this about Alicia and her cold? She was in bed, too, the last time I came,' and Janet replied, 'I don't think she has ever got over the baby business.'

But no further comment on this statement was made by anyone.

From the direction of the kitchen there now came the sound of raised voices, which prompted Jessie to remark, 'Oh dear! There they go again,' and Janet to walk out of the room, immediately to be followed by her father.

'I'm off home,' he called to her. 'I can't stand any more of this. What about you?' She answered, 'I'm off home, too,' but she didn't add, And I won't be able to stand much more of you when I get there.

Maitland wasn't able to get a private word with her until they had been in the house for half an hour, when he said, 'How did it go?'

'Awful. Terrible. But I think it was worse when we got to mother's than at the cemetery. He bounced out of the kitchen yelling that he couldn't stand any more of this, and I wanted to say, neither can I. And I can't, Roger, although I agreed that I wanted to be off home too.'

'Oh, my dearest, I know how you feel.' And he pulled her to the door of the breakfast-room and stood with his back to it; then he took her in his arms and kissed her. And afterwards, he murmured, 'I too can't stand much more of this. I feel I've got to come into the open and face him and tell him that we are going . . .'

'I know, I know.' She stroked his cheek with her finger. 'I dream of that, of us both going out of the door and getting into a cab and it galloping to the station and you buying two tickets to just anywhere.'

'It'll come. It'll come soon; it must. This very minute I would really like to go to him and tell him straight —'

'No, no.' She pressed him slightly from her, repeating, 'No, no; he would do something quite desperate. He would become physical.'

'Well, he would get the worst of that, my dear.'

'Yes; but I don't want that.'

'No, of course not. Neither do I. But he's got to be made to see that he can't keep you chained up, nor can he play on your sympathy any longer. He's a man still in his prime. As soon as the divorce goes through, he can re-marry. But in the meantime he takes his pleasure . . .'

He stopped and half turned from her, and she said, 'What did you say?'

'It doesn't matter, dear.'

'You said, he takes his pleasure. You mean . . . ?'

'Yes, I mean just that. Your father is a man of strong passions; you must realise that. And when Geraldine Hallberry left him, you know what happened then.'

'Has he got another woman?'

'No; nothing permanent. I don't think. He would never let himself in for that again. I'm only trying to point out he's not the lost and lonely man he makes out to be. What he is is a possessive father where you are concerned. I think if your mother had still been here it would have been the same: he would still have wanted to hold on to you. These things happen. Anyway, let us say that we will wait until Monday, but no longer.'

She nodded; then, closing her eyes, she smiled softly as she said, 'Monday. It's like looking towards a star and knowing you can grasp it.'

'We'll grasp it, dear,' he said; 'we'll grasp it.'

They had just moved from the door when Florence entered and, addressing Maitland, said, 'Oh, Mr Maitland, will you come and see Cook? It's about the meal. You know, she thought you'd be having . . .' she was nodding towards Janet. 'Well, she thought you and your father would be having a meal out, miss. But she wanted to know if she can knock something up now or —'

'All right, Florence,' Maitland interrupted her. 'I'll be there in a moment.'

'Yes, Mr Maitland.'

When the door closed again, he said, 'Didn't you have a meal of any kind?'

'No. Mother must have done a lot of cooking, and Annie had laid a spread in the dining-room, but there wasn't a thing touched. Nobody could eat, and it's understandable.'

'In that case, I'll see about something

straightaway. Will the boys be back soon, d'you think?'

'Oh, yes. Then they'll be leaving about four o'clock. It would seem that they both can't get away quickly enough. And I don't blame them, not really.'

'Nor I. Still, I think it's a pity they're not staying with him tonight.'

When Maitland had gone she nodded to herself, repeating, Yes, it *is* a pity they're not staying with him tonight. But it was evident that even her nice brothers were not going to shoulder the responsibility of sympathy due to a bereaved parent. As James had said on the phone, something like this took living down, and he was glad he was out of the town. Eddie wouldn't have said that.

Anyway, it was over. Howard was at rest and, as that man had said, at peace with God. She hoped so. Yes, she hoped so.

13

She had been to the solicitor's office to sign a form concerning bonds her grandmother had left her, and she was taking the tramcar back home. She had just taken a seat on the upper deck when straightaway she was on her feet and twisting round to gaze over the heads of the two passengers seated behind her.

As she sat down again with a plop on the slatted seat, she told herself she couldn't have been mistaken; it was Alicia and that man Winter. But one thing she was sure of: she wasn't going to be the one to bring this into the open. Anyway, if it *was* Alicia they would all know soon enough. But dear lord! What next . . . ?

Maitland was already in the hall when she opened the door; and as he took her coat from her, he said softly, 'Your father has gone out for a short while. He will be back for lunch' — he glanced towards the hall clock — 'in half an hour. I have some news. Come into the dining-room presently, I'll be busy there.'

She gave him no answer — Florence was

just coming out of the drawing-room with an empty coal scuttle — but as she made her way towards the stairs, he said, 'It's a beautiful morning out.'

'Yes. Yes, it is. Nice for walking.'

She spent some ten minutes in her room before coming downstairs again and entering the dining-room, where Maitland was putting the last touches to one end of the long dining-table, which was set with two places.

He immediately approached her and, taking her hand, said, 'I had an idea this morning. You remember the Unitarian minister, Mr Hatton? I phoned him. The Unitarians are a very moderate sect. So I wondered how they managed their wedding ceremonies.' As his grip tightened on her hands she pulled them together and he went on, 'It is all very simple, he tells me. What we need is a certificate from the registrar; not a special licence, just a certificate. Then he will marry us at any time.' And now he added on a broad smile, 'As long as we've been living in the district over a specified period of weeks.'

'Oh, Roger. Roger. We could do it, even if we had to come back here for a time.'

'I was thinking that too. Yes, yes. But I don't want to come back here after we're

456

married, and I'm sure you don't, do you?'

'Oh, no, no. But as long as we are married; that is really all I want at the moment; to be married to you.'

Such was the appeal in her face that he dropped her hands and took a step backwards and, adapting the Maitland stance, he said, 'You had better keep your distance, miss, or I won't be accountable for the liberties I shall take, even though your father is due.' Then his manner reverting once more, he bent towards her, saying, 'First thing tomorrow I'll go to the Registry Office and find out the correct procedure. And we'll take it from there.'

Janet now turned her head quickly to the side, then said, 'That's Dad; I'd better be going.' Then on reaching the door, she turned for a moment and, looking towards him, she said, 'I hate this scurrying.'

'And I hate the fact that you have to do it.'

She reached the hall to see her father about to go up the stairs. He turned in some surprise and said, 'You back, then?'

'Well, if I'm not, this must be my apparition.'

'Flippant, aren't you? Well, what happened at the solicitor's?'

'I signed a form.'

He had come down from the bottom stair and was now following her into the drawing-room, saying, 'You've got your library manner on again.'

'I haven't got a library manner, Dad. You should recognise that it is my usual manner.'

He looked hard at her; then, a small smile parting his lips, he said, 'Aye, I should. You're a funny lass. You take some getting to the bottom of, an' all.'

He was standing in front of the fire now, one hand on the high mantelshelf, and he put his foot out and pressed a lump of black coal away from the top bar of the grate and into the heart of the fire before he said, 'How are you feeling?'

'What d'you mean, how am I feeling?'

'Well' — he half turned towards her — 'don't tell me you haven't had a reaction after all this business.'

She thought a moment before she answered him: 'Yes; yes, I've had a reaction, but it came the day he died. And it was the same as yours, relief that there would be no hanging or, at best, a long term of imprisonment. Yet, it mightn't have been all that long because, being made as he was, he couldn't have borne it. He'd have likely done what he did sooner or later.'

'You've got a mind like a razor, haven't you? So logical, so practical. And knowing this, I cannot for the life of me understand the other side of you, because to me you've got all your values mixed up. And whether you like it or not we've got to talk about values sooner or later, haven't we?'

'Yes, Dad; we have to talk about values. And for my part the sooner the better.'

'Oh, is that it?'

'That's it.'

'D'you know what you're saying?'

'Yes, I know what I'm saying.'

'Well, have you thought of the consequences? And my reaction?'

'Oh yes, yes, I've thought of the consequences. For my part they're good. But as for your reaction . . .'

She stopped at that and turned towards the door, and Samuel did, too, for they could hear the sound of Alice's voice. Hers was a distinctive voice: the tone was high when her voice was normal, but emotion of any kind heightened the pitch still further. And as she listened to her mother saying, 'I know my way, thank you,' Janet knew that she hadn't been wrong: it *had* been Alicia she saw in the bus.

When Alice entered the room she didn't pause, but hurried towards Samuel who had started to move down the room towards her.

'What now? What is it, woman? What's happened?'

'She's gone. Alicia's gone.'

'Gone? What d'you mean? Where?'

'*Gone. Gone.* She's run off with him. Not only that —' She now turned to Janet: then she gazed around the room as if searching for a place to sit, before making for a straight-backed chair. When she was seated Samuel seemed unable to say anything for the moment: and when, at last, he said, 'With Winter?' she barked at him, 'Who else? Who else? And not only that. She's . . . she's taken' — she gulped now — 'every penny out of my drawer.'

'Every penny? What d'you mean, every penny?'

'Your cheque; I'd cashed it. The two hundred was there and another seventy-five pounds. She's taken the lot. And she left that.' She now pulled a sheet of paper from her coat pocket and thrust it at him. It was folded in two, and slowly he opened it and read:

Don't try to find me because you won't be able to. I'm going with him and we'll be married somewhere. If not

460

it doesn't matter. If Dad tries to bring me back I'll only do the same again at the first opportunity. I love him and that's all about it; and he's all right, no matter what you say or think. You've never got it into your head that I'm not a girl any more, I've had a baby. I'm taking your money because it would be no use asking you for it. And anyway, there's plenty more where that came from. And I'm not sorry for what I'm doing because I would likely have done something the same as Howard if I'd had to stay because nobody had a good word for me, apart from Jessie. I was the black sheep.'

There was no signature.

Samuel did not give the letter back to Alice but silently handed it to Janet. And after she had read the last words she looked up, first towards her mother, and then her father, and she said quietly, 'She was right: nobody had a kind word for her. It must have been awful.'

Then she was surprised when her mother looked at her and asked quietly, 'What can be done?'

'I don't think you can do anything, Mam, because, as she says, if you did find her and bring her back she would just do the same again; perhaps if not with him, with somebody else. But there's one thing certain, she cares for that man. No matter what he is she cares for him. And it may . . . well, it may work out.'

'Cares for him, be damned! A yard man, the scum of the earth, who had his way with Bella for years.'

'Why did you employ him then? And why did you not keep an eye on him when you knew what he was? No, you were too busy out and about your business. You had to make money, be a big noise in the town. One of these days you'll wake up and see yourself, and you won't be able to stand the shock.'

As Janet marched past him he did not say a word, but his gaze followed her to the door; then he turned and looked at Alice saying, 'What did you think of that?'

Alice did not answer for a moment, but reached out and picked up the letter Janet had thrown on to the table to the side of her. And after she had replaced it in her pocket she rose to her feet, and then she said quite quietly, 'She has a point. But it's only what I've said to you before.' Then, his outburst being checked by her hand going to her mouth and the tears spurting from her eyes, she muttered unintelligibly, 'I can't stand much more. I can't. I can't.'

'Aw, lass.' His hand was on her shoulder, and when she fumbled in her pocket for a handkerchief, he handed her his own, and after she had rubbed it roughly around her face, she said, 'First Howard, and now Alicia. And Jessie might as well already be in that convent, because she lives there most of the time. She'll go her own way, too, with or without permission from either of us. And where does that leave me? With a grown-up baby, for that's all that Fanny is.' She stared at Samuel now, then nodded and said, 'I've had to face up to that. She'll never develop more than she is now.'

'But you'll be marrying Dickinson, and if you feel as badly as you do, well, I'll try to hurry things through for you.'

She turned from him, her voice low now as she said, 'I won't be marrying Dickinson. He's another one that's walked out on me.'

'He walked out on you?' His voice was high. 'You mean he . . . ? Well, tell me what you do mean, walked out on you.'

'He . . . he couldn't stand the scandal of Howard. It was on the first day, when the newspaper came out. He said he'd have to think about our future. And I told him . . . Well, you can imagine what I told him:

463

there was no need to take time to think.'

'I'm sorry, lass.'

She turned now and looked at him, saying, 'I'm not. It really didn't upset me, except my vanity. He and all he stood for paled into nothingness with what's happened since. And now this. It's bad enough her running off, but to steal every penny I had in the house.'

'Well,' his voice was soft again as he said, 'there's more where that came from, as she said, so don't worry about that. You can have what you want any time, you know that. And I'll be as good as me word, what I said a few minutes ago, I'll hurry things through, make them as easy as possible.'

'You want it that way?' She had her back to him.

'Well, it's what you want, isn't it? 'Tisn't what I want, it's what you want. I'll not marry again. I learnt me lesson more than three years ago.'

He walked slowly up to her now and turned her about to face him; then after a moment's pause he said, 'Would you come back, Alice?'

She seemed to have some difficulty in getting the words out: 'Yes, Sam.'

'Aw, lass.' His hands were on her shoulders now. 'That's the best thing I've heard in a long time. We'll make it, older and wiser. We've both had lessons to learn, I think.' He bent forward now and kissed her gently on the lips; and when, for a brief second, she laid her head on his chest, he sighed and smiled as he said, 'We'll be a family again. The house will take on its old feeling —'

'Oh no, Sam.' She drew slowly away from his hold. 'I couldn't come back here.'

'You couldn't? You mean . . . ? But Alice, I love this place. Well, not love it, but I've got used to it. And it's your home, really your home.'

'I couldn't, Sam. It was never my home, never. I didn't fit in. I knew I wasn't going to from the beginning. I loved Sweetbanks. I was born there, and if I'd got my rights I'd be there now. And you know that, Sam. All that money to her, the results of my great-grandfather's efforts, my grandfather's efforts, and my father's, and all of them thrifty, mounting up the profits. And they were, they were big profits, as thirty-two thousand signifies.'

'Oh, be fair, Alice. Your mother got a big slice of that through doing a deal with the firm you were going to marry into. You know yourself they had been in competition for years and they had their eyes on both depots, because it would have taken a lot of ordinary profits to reach thirty-two thousand. Still, it's no use being bitter about it. Your mother left it to her and she's been generous with it. She even helped Howard, and you know there was no love lost between them; that is until the end, when she was more sorry for him than any of us were.' He put his hand out now to silence her as he said, 'Oh, yes, she was, because your sorrow was tinged with bitterness and the disgrace of it all, as was mine. She has two sides to her, has Janet.'

'Well, Sam, that's one too many for me. That's another reason why I couldn't come back here. We never really hit it off before I left so what it would be like with the new arrangement, I dread to think.'

'Well, what would you want me to do?' His voice was harsh now. 'I couldn't go and live in that house of yours after the years I've spent here. Sweetbanks . . . well, that would have been a different kettle of fish. I lived there for years and I was comfortable. It's a nice house, a homely house, but your new home, Alice' — he shook his head — 'oh, no.'

'Well, then' — she half smiled at him — 'that's that! But it's nice to know it could have been different. Now to get back to why

I'm here. I could have telephoned, I suppose, but I just couldn't speak on the phone about her taking the money. It was as if I was yelling it aloud for everyone to hear. What d'you think we should do?'

'Nothing at all. She's gone and, as she says, she would go again if she was brought back. So, wash your hands of her as I'm going to do. There's one thing I feel sure about, she wouldn't come back on her own were he to walk out on her again.'

'No; her spunk wouldn't let her.'

'What a life. What a life.'

Alice turned from him to walk down the room, and he followed her. There was no-one in the hall as he said to her, 'How did you come?'

'I have a cab outside. I had just about enough money to pay him.'

'Oh. Wait a minute.' He now hurried from her, down the corridor and into his office; and there, pulling open a drawer, he took out from a box a handful of sovereigns. And when he returned to her he thrust the money into her coat pocket, saying, 'That'll see you through for the time being. And look, about this personal matter, we'll work something out somehow. We can't leave it where it is.'

She said neither words of thanks nor anything in answer to his statement until, after seating her in the cab, he said quietly, 'I'll think of something some way. There must be a way out of this for both of us. I'll come round later.' Nodding at him, she said, 'All right. All right, Sam.'

As for Sam, back in the house, he almost ran up the stairs and made straight for Janet's room, and there he knocked on the door, calling, 'You in there, Janet?'

In answer to this the door was pulled open, and he said, 'I want a word with you,' and walked past her before turning and confronting her and saying, 'I have news. To me it's good news. I don't know what you'll think about it, but your mother and I want to get together again.'

'Oh.' She smiled widely now, saying, 'That is good news. I'm glad for you.'

'But there's a catch. She won't come back here.'

'Why?' Even as she said this she knew the reason; in fact there were two reasons: Maitland and herself.

After biting on his lip and looking to the side, Sam said, 'Well, you're one of the reasons, lass, you know: she thinks you never got on together.'

'That's true; but there's no reason why I should stay.'

'Oh, you're going to stay. This is your home.'

'Dad, I have plans of my own.'

'Well, at the present moment I don't want to hear them. I've enough to deal with.'

'I think this is just the time they should be voiced. And I think it would solve all your problems, too, because if Mam were to come back you wouldn't be alone any more. And I've only hung on as long as I have from coming into the open because I couldn't leave you alone.'

'Look!' He walked two steps back from her, flapping his hand towards her. 'I don't want any talk about coming into the open or what you're going to do. Just you listen to what I want you to do. I want you to go to your mother and tell her it'll be all right. If she comes back you'll do your best to get on together —'

'You know, Dad, at times I'm sorry for you because you know neither me nor my mother. All you are aware of and always have been is your own wants, what pleases you. Well, the time is past for that. You've lost a son and today you've also lost a daughter. Now you have a choice, you can lose me or you can keep me, but the only way you can do the latter is by letting me go. In any case, I'm going. And what's more, I'm coming into the open now.' Immediately she turned and ran from the room and down the stairs to the corridor, and there called out, not Maitland! Maitland! but 'Roger! Roger!'

When Maitland came hurrying from the passage into the hall, Samuel had reached the foot of the stairs and he watched his daughter put her arm through that of his butler and draw him towards the middle of the hall. And there they stood, and what she said now was, 'I'm going to marry this man, and as soon as possible.'

At this, Maitland's arm went around her shoulders and he pressed her tightly against himself as he said, 'I should have been the one to say that. I've wanted to for years. But now it's out. We mean to be married. We love each other and you can't do anything about it.'

'Take your hands off her!' The words were said slowly and deliberately.

'I have no intention of taking my hands off her, ever. I love her deeply, and I can say she loves me too.'

'Loves you! A superior skivvy? because that's all you are. That's all you've ever been, and always will be. You've been my servant, jumping to my word, keeping your place in this house only because I could use you.'

As Janet felt Maitland stiffen, she cried loudly, 'Don't take any heed of him. Yes, he's used you, for the simple reason he didn't know how to act in the house that he had bought and was so far above his station.'

'Yes. Yes. It might have been above my station but it's not above yours, miss. You've been brought up as a lady, and now you would lower yourself to link up with the likes of him, a man who's no better than Winter. And have you thought what he's after? You're a rich woman and, one thing I've learnt about him, he's no fool; he's a good actor. Nevertheless, he's what I said, he's a low-born servant. He's of that class. Now you, miss, move away, because I want to settle this in a way that he thinks he's good at.'

It was the sight of his daughter clinging closer to his butler that caused him to spring on her in an attempt to drag her away from the man he was hating at this moment with an almost insane rage.

When Janet screamed, Maitland's fist came out and knocked her father staggering back, and he managed to save himself from falling only by grabbing the high side of a heavy, black-oak hall chair.

And Maitland, knowing the onslaught that would be coming, cried to Janet, 'Get into the drawing-room! Go on, get away!'

Samuel came at him with arms flailing. He was a heavily built man and although he had only one good fist he had weight behind it. At first, Maitland did nothing but ward off the blows, but then his anger rose beyond control and he struck out, meaningly catching Samuel on the chin and sending him reeling back, to fetch up against the grandfather clock and send the chimes jangling. At this, like an enraged bull with head down, Samuel pushed at the man whom he had once looked upon as friend and guide through the troubled waters of middle-class society, but against whom at this moment, if he'd had a knife in his hand he would have repeated the action of his son. The force of his onslaught and flailing arms sent Maitland stumbling back to come up against the front door, then to be immediately startled by the doorbell ringing, which brought an interruption to the efforts of the combatants. The while, Janet and the two maids and Cook, who were crouched in front of the green baized door, paused where they were.

Shrugging his jacket straight around his

shoulders and running his fingers through his hair, Samuel stumbled back towards the foot of the stairs and from there, gasping, he now growled, 'Well, you're the butler-cum-footman-cum-local factotum, so open the door.' Then he turned to his female staff and cried, 'You, get yourselves away to your quarters.'

Maitland, who had also straightened his jacket, now walked to the middle of the hall and, staring at Samuel, he said, 'I am no longer in your service. Open the door yourself,' and made to walk towards Janet, still standing with her back pressed against the wall.

The bell rang again, and Maitland hesitated, but decided to disregard it. And it seemed that Samuel was making to renew his attack when the bell rang for the third time, causing him to pause before he staggered to the door and flung it wide.

He glared at the two men.

'Mr Fairbrother?'

'Yes, I'm Mr Fairbrother.'

'We would like a word with you.'

Samuel stared at them for a moment and the immediate thought he had was, Alicia; they've found her; she's done something silly. Yet, they weren't policemen. He continued to stare at them; then he said,

'What's your business?'

'May we come in? We'd like a word . . . in private.'

One of the men was tall and thin, all of six foot, his companion much shorter, but heavily built. Both were well dressed. Samuel looked from them back to where Maitland was standing with his arm around Janet's shoulders, and his teeth ground together for a moment before he backed a step and said, 'Make it short, I'm busy.'

The tall man looked around the hall, appreciatively it seemed, before he said, 'Well sir, I'm afraid it's to do with your late son.'

'What about him? You can't do anything more to him.'

'No; no, we're aware of that, sir. You see, it's a matter of a debt.'

'A debt? His debt?'

'Yes. He speculated, you see. We had allowed him credit time and time again over the past years, but I'm afraid, like most young men, he would not be warned and he became extravagant in what he laid on.'

'What he laid on?' Samuel looked from one to the other now. 'What are you? What d'you mean, laid on? Debts?'

'Yes, sir, debts, as you put it. We are bookmakers, licenced bookmakers. He owed us the sum of three hundred pounds.

474

He promised to pay by a certain date, but it wasn't forthcoming.'

'He paid you. He did!'

They all turned to gaze at Janet. She had moved from Maitland's hold and she cried at them, 'He paid it! I gave him the money. In fact, five hundred. He would have paid it.'

'I'm sorry, miss, but he didn't pay it. And you're quite welcome to come and see our books. We have our books audited, you know; we are above board. But three hundred pounds is three hundred pounds.'

'My son is dead and so is his debt.' They both turned swiftly at Samuel's words. 'You're a pair of sharks. If he had five hundred pounds he would have paid you those three.'

'He did not pay us those three.' The man's tone had changed. 'It was likely spent on his fancy woman. But you're a man of means and so I feel you should settle your son's debts.'

'Get out!'

Samuel's fist was raised again and now the man said, 'You had better not start any of that rough stuff, mister. You don't know what you're up against.'

'And neither d'you. I've told you to get out.'

'We want our money. If you don't pay it, we'll take it to court.'

'You can take it to hell, for all I care. And that's where you'll go if you don't get out of my house this minute.'

Samuel's fist hit the man's shoulder more in a push than a punch, but it had hardly reached its target when the man let blaze and Samuel found himself being battered in the face.

Maitland hesitated only a moment. But when he rushed to Samuel's assistance, his way was blocked by the small man, who now spoke for the first time: 'Keep out of it,' he said, 'unless you want a bashing an' all.'

Perhaps it was the biggest surprise of the little man's life when he found himself almost lifted from the floor by a blow under his chin that then brought him to his knees.

The tall man had Samuel so pinned against the panelling near the foot of the stairs that all he was able to do, and that weakly, was to try with his bent arm to ward off the blows to his face. His body was actually slumping when Maitland tore the man from him and levelled a blow at his stomach with a follow-up to his face; and he, in his turn, was so taken aback that for a moment all he too could do now was to ward off the blows.

The fray could have been brought to an end within the next few minutes likely by Maitland thrusting both men out of the door, except that Janet screamed when she saw the small man, who had been leaning against the side table, grab an eighteen-inch copper statue of an African warrior poised to throw a spear. And as she screamed she rushed forward; but was just too late: the figure came down on the side of Maitland's head, and he suddenly became still before slowly, as if taking his time, sinking to the floor.

For about five seconds there wasn't a sound in the room, and they all stood in their different places looking down on the prostrate form, the blood streaming over the side of his face.

'You've killed him! You've killed him!' Janet was kneeling by Maitland's side now, screaming, 'Roger! Roger!' As she put her hands on his face the blood ran over them and, looking up now, she cried at her father, 'Get a doctor! Get a doctor! And the police. Yes, the police.' She lifted one arm and pointed to the men, who were now stumbling towards the door.

Samuel stood looking dazedly down on the man he had wanted to murder; it looked as if someone else had done it for him. And

Janet screamed again at him, 'Get a doctor! Phone!' Then, 'Sarah! Florence!' And when the women ran into the room she cried at them, 'Get me sheets, towels, anything.'

Janet's mind seemed one enormous scream; it was screaming at everybody. She held the blood-soaked head and shoulders on her lap. The front door was open now and the two men had gone. Florence was kneeling by her side helping to swab up the blood. Her father was standing gripping the staircase post. And she turned her head now and screamed at him, 'You've killed him. That's what you wanted to do, wasn't it? kill him. He got this through saving you, and you're not worth it. D'you hear? You're not worth it. Get the doctor! Get the doctor!'

'He'll be coming, miss, he'll be coming,' said Sarah. 'Now don't worry, he'll be coming. Master will get on the phone.'

'Yes. Yes, he should be on the phone. He's happy now. He's finished him, so he's happy now. The only real friend he ever had, he's killed him.'

'No; no, he hasn't, miss, he hasn't. Mr Maitland's still breathing; he'll be all right.'

'All this blood. All this blood. Get an ambulance, phone an ambulance. He'll have to go to the hospital.'

'Yes. Yes, I'm sure he will, miss.' Sarah now looked to where her master was still standing gripping the top of the banister pillar and she said quietly, 'You'd better phone, master; it will be the hospital, I think.'

Without a word he moved from his support and went to the phone . . .

When Dr Campbell arrived he stood in the doorway for a moment and looked in amazement not only at the man who was covered with blood but also at the young girl. Quickly he divested himself of his jacket, then rolled up his sleeves and knelt down, saying, 'How did this happen?'

'They hit him on the head. They hit him on the head with the copper spearman.' She wagged her finger towards the statue, still lying where it had fallen near the panelling.

'Who hit him?'

'The bookmakers. The bookmakers.'

Dr Campbell paused in his examination and glanced from Janet to the two maids, then up at Samuel, all the while gently probing through the blood-soaked hair. Then taking a thick wad of linen, he pressed it tight against the back of the ear before winding a strip of sheeting tightly around the head, saying, 'He'll have to get to the hospital, and quick.'

It was Florence who said, 'Master rang for the ambulance.'

When the doctor got to his feet he looked at Samuel, saying, 'How long is it since you phoned?'

'What?'

'I said, how long is it since you phoned for the ambulance?'

'Oh, I don't know . . . just after I phoned you.'

'How did this happen?'

Samuel shook his head and muttered, 'Long story, long story.'

His voice low now, the doctor muttered, 'The maid said he s been hit with that.' He pointed to the figure, and in a still lower voice, he said, 'You didn't do it, did you?'

It was a moment before Samuel muttered. 'No. No, I didn't actually do it.'

'Actually? Did you make an attempt?'

'No; no, I didn't!' Samuel rasped out.

'All right, all right But it looks to my mind as if something, perhaps that spike, has pierced his head. It's no graze, of that I'm sure.'

'If he dies, I'll hate you,' cried Janet. 'D'you hear, I'll hate you. All my life . . . as long as I live. I will! I will!'

As Samuel turned away the doctor looked down on Janet with some concern, saying,

'Get up, dear. Get up. You can't do anything down there, and I would go and wash off that blood.'

'Wash? I'll never wash again. If he dies I'll never wash again.'

Gently now, the doctor took her arm and tried to raise her to her feet, but she would not get up, and remained there until the ambulance men arrived, when she pulled herself up, only to stand there swaying. But when the men lifted Maitland on to the stretcher and the doctor said, 'I'll ring the hospital and tell them I'll be along shortly,' she cried; 'I'm going with him. I'm going with him.'

Dr Campbell now motioned Sarah and Florence to him as he said to Janet, 'You can't do anything yet, dear. You must go and get cleaned up first. Then I'll want to see you.'

'I'm going with him! Get out of my way, I am going with him!'

As she made to move, her legs suddenly buckled, and again she was sitting on the floor, and the doctor, going to his bag, took out a bottle and, after shaking it vigorously, lifted a two-inch glass from his bag, and half-filled it; then going to Janet, he said, 'Drink this, dear.' But when her reaction was to shake her head, he suddenly gripped her nose, and as her mouth opened wide he almost threw the contents of the glass into the back of her throat. Gulping and coughing, she was forced to swallow it.

Addressing the girls, Dr Campbell said, 'Take her to her room and get her cleaned up; she'll be asleep in no time . . .'

The doctor then listened to a halting version from Samuel of what had happened as a result of the betting debt, without his mentioning what had taken place before the arrival of the two men.

'Well, now,' said the doctor, 'the police must be notified because, between you and me, if that spear or whatever it is in that statue has gone where I think it's gone, there's not much hope for your butler. If he doesn't die, then he could be left with brain damage. So, it's a police job, and I'd get on to them straightaway.' He bent to fasten his bag, and said, 'I'll let you know what's happening at the hospital; but the police will be here to question you.'

His hand on the door he turned to look at Samuel and he said quietly, 'You're going through a bad patch. But the one I think you should also worry about is your daughter. She seems very fond of Maitland; very fond.' He stared for a moment at Samuel before opening the door and departing.

Samuel remained standing in the middle of the hall, and staring at the rug on which Maitland had fallen. It had a blue background with a floral pattern here and there, and was somewhat faded but now there was a large dark stain on the edge of it.

Going through a bad patch, the doctor had said. What was happening to him? What was happening to all of them? Was he to blame for Howard, Alicia, Alice, now Janet, and . . . Maitland? He closed his eyes tight, and it was in the form of a prayer as he said, 'God, don't let the doctor be right, either one way or the other.' Then making for the phone he rang Alice, and what he said to her simply, was, 'Will you come over? I'm in trouble.'

14

Samuel walked out of the hospital, across the forecourt and to the car, where Mears was waiting. The man said, 'How did you find him, sir?' and in answer he only shook his head: he could not repeat what the sister had said, and then brusquely. It was she who had been on duty when his son had lain, under police supervision, at the end of her ward, and her look and manner had plainly said, You and your family again? Her words then had been curt: 'I can only tell you he's had his operation and he's on the danger list. If you will call again in the morning the doctor will give you all the particulars.'

From behind the wheel Arthur Mears said, 'Mike said he was a long time in the theatre, sir. They're both there still, Mike and Kate. They were great friends.'

He wished the man would shut up. He wanted to shut him up, but he couldn't: he felt ill and his throat was paining; he had thought his end had come under that fellow's hands. And it would have, he supposed, aye it would have, for the fellow had looked as mad as he himself had been. But why did it have to be Maitland who had saved him, and now could likely die as a result?

Something was clearly wrong with his life. There seemed no end to his problems. If Maitland died he'd have him on his conscience the rest of his life; if he didn't die his mind could be affected; in either case he himself would lose his daughter.

When he entered the house Alice was walking down the stairs. It was as if she had never left the place. She came up to him, saying, 'Well?'

He took off his coat as he said, 'I could get nothing out of them, except he's had the operation and he's on the danger list.'

As she turned away to walk towards the drawing-room he looked up the stairs and said, 'How is she?'

For answer, she said, 'The doctor was here again about half an hour ago. He left another draught for her; he said she should sleep for twenty-four hours. Jessie is with her.'

When they entered the drawing-room, Fanny, who was sitting by the fire looking at a comic paper moved uneasily on her chair. She gave her father a tentative smile before turning to her mother, saying, 'Are we going home now, Mam?'

'No; not tonight, dear. You're going to sleep in your old room tonight.'

'Will we go home tomorrow?'

Alice swallowed deeply before she said. 'Yes. Yes, we'll go home tomorrow,' whereon Samuel turned away, muttering, 'I need a drink. What about you?'

'No, thanks. I've just had a cup of tea.'

Instead of going into the dining-room for a drink, he went straight upstairs and into Janet's bedroom, where Jessie was sitting by the bed, and as if he were entering a sickroom he moved on tiptoe towards her, saying, 'She wakened at all?'

'Yes, once, a bit; but she seems to be having a bad dream.'

'Go on downstairs,' he said, 'and stay with your mother for a while. I'll sit here.'

After the door had closed on Jessie he lifted Janet's limp hand from the counterpane and stroked it, with the doctor's last words to him ringing in his ears: 'With this business, Maitland's mind mightn't be the only one to be affected; she's heading for a breakdown, if I'm any judge. She seems to have been under great stress lately. D'you know she came to me for something to make her sleep? and I told her a girl of her age should not need to be put to sleep; it should come natural. Now she's had to be put to sleep, for a time, at any rate.' And he had added, 'You've got a lot to think about.'

The man was nothing if not plain. But then you couldn't keep much back from him; he had attended them all for years. But why should he suggest that the blame for everything that happened lay at his door? All he had ever done was work, work for every one of them.

Oh, he felt rotten. He definitely needed a drink.

He went along to his own room and pulled the cord that was hanging near the bed-head, something that had caused much laughter when he had first come into this house.

When Sarah appeared, he said, 'Tell Mrs Fairbrother I've gone to lie down; and bring me a glass of whisky, please.'

He had just got into bed when Alice came into the room, paused at the door and looked towards him before slowly walking to the bed.

'My neck's sore,' he said.

'Yes. Yes, it would be; it looked red. In a way you're lucky it's just sore. Here's Sarah with the whisky. You'll feel better in the morning. I'll see to Janet.'

'You'll be staying, then?'

'Yes. Yes, I'm staying tonight. I'll be across the corridor.'

He nodded at her; then took the glass from the tray Sarah was holding out to him.

After swallowing the whisky in one gulp, he lay down; and Alice's hand hesitated a moment before it went out to arrange the eiderdown around his shoulders. Then, after turning the gas down low, she went out on to the landing and looked first one way and then the other, before shaking her head and making for Janet's room.

It was about four o'clock the following day when Janet came fully to her senses. However, she felt that she was still dreaming when she saw it was her sister who was standing at the bedside. 'Jessie?' she whispered.

'D'you feel better?'

'Better?' She pulled herself up on the pillows. She had been dreaming, dreadful, dreadful dreams. What was the matter with her? Her head still felt strange; it was daylight and she was in bed. She was about to ask, 'Why are you here?' when the thick, muzzy veil lifted and she clapped her hand over her mouth, muttering as she did so, 'Oh, God! Roger. Where . . . where is he?'

'Don't get excited, dear. Please, please.'

Janet now pushed Jessie away with the flat of her hand and stared at her, her lips moving soundlessly before she said, 'He's . . . he's dead, isn't he?'

'No; no.' Jessie shook her head. 'He's in hospital. He's had an operation. He's come through it.'

'What time is it? What day is it?'

'Saturday, dear, about . . . about four o'clock.'

'Saturday?' She twisted up her face. 'Let me get up.'

'The doctor says you've got to rest.'

Janet's answer to this was to throw back the bedclothes. But when she stood on her feet she swayed for a moment, blinked her eyes, then put out her hand and grabbed the head of the bed. And Jessie cried, 'You see, you're not fit to get up!'

Dropping down onto the side of the bed, she now looked at Jessie, saying quietly, 'Help me into my clothes dear.'

'No: I'd better get Mam.'

'Mam?'

'Yes. Yes, she's here. Dad asked her to come yesterday when you passed out, at least, the doctor put you out.' She smiled faintly. 'You were in a state.'

The picture was becoming more vivid in

Janet's mind. She bowed her head. She was again looking down into the face of her beloved and again her mind was smeared with the mass of blood, and she moaned, 'Oh, Jessie, Jessie. Is . . . is he really alive?'

'Yes.' Jessie's voice was firm. 'Dad was there last night; and I phoned twice today, and Mike and Kate have been at the hospital.'

'Mike and Kate?'

'Yes; yes, his friends.'

'Has Dad not been? Hasn't he been today?'

'He's in bed. He's all right, but the doctor said his neck was sore where that man gripped it, and all over he seems to be suffering from shock, like . . . like yourself.'

Janet was getting into her clothes now, and when she had donned her dress she said, 'Go down and order a cab, would you, please?'

'Mears is about, he'll take you in the car.'

'Yes, all right, all right.'

'But,' said Jessie firmly now, 'you can't go out anywhere before you have something to eat. You've been in bed since yesterday afternoon.'

'All I want is a drink, dear.'

'Well, I'll get you a drink; but you'll have

to eat something, too. I'll go down and tell Mam.'

Left alone, Janet again sat on the edge of the bed, and her body slumped as she thought: Mam back in the house. And she shook her head slightly, then muttered, 'What does it matter? I'll soon be gone. If only . . . Oh, Roger. Roger. I must see you.'

When Alice came hurrying into the room, saying, 'This is silly, you know. You shouldn't be up,' Janet got to her feet.

'I'm all right, Mam,' she said.

'You must have something to eat.'

'I just want a cup of tea.'

'D'you want Jessie to come with you?'

'No. No, I'll be all right.'

'The doctor won't be pleased. He said you should have forty-eight hours' rest.'

She made herself ask, 'How is Dad?'

'Oh,' said Alice lightly, 'he'll survive.'

Janet made herself walk steadily to the wardrobe and take out her coat and hat; but when she went to put on her coat her mother took it from her, saying, 'There'll be plenty of time to don that after you've had your tea. So come on downstairs.' And with that she went out, the coat over her arm, leaving Janet feeling that the years had slipped away and she was fourteen, fifteen or sixteen again, and her mother making statements or throwing off orders as she walked away . . .

An hour later she was standing in the hospital corridor facing the sister, who must have remembered her immediately, for she said, 'And how are you?'

'I'm all right. I would have been here sooner, but the doctor gave me a sleeping draught.'

'Well, from what I read in the papers today, you needed a sleeping draught after that fiasco. And there was a possibility that one of those fellows could have ended up like your brother. It's the luck of the gods that the gallows isn't waiting for him.'

Janet closed her eyes, then said softly, 'How is he, really?'

'As well as can be expected . . . Look, dear; come and sit down.' She suddenly grasped Janet's shoulders and drew her into her office. And after she had pushed her into a chair, she said, 'You're still feeling the effects of the draught I think. You shouldn't have come out. Now don't worry yourself: he's all right so far. He's your butler, isn't he?'

A new strength seemed to flow into her as she answered, 'No; he is not my butler, he is my future husband.'

The sister straightened her back, raised

her eyebrows and said, 'Oh. Oh, I see. Well then, I . . . I repeat, there's no immediate concern. He's a very lucky man. Well, what I mean by that is, with regards to the operation. His skull was cracked, but whatever went into his head — it was a model copper spear, I understand — missed a vital artery by a mere fraction. It was, as Doctor Crabtree said, a miracle in that it didn't penetrate the brain. But of course he lost a great deal of blood and altogether it will take him some time to recover. But then he seems a very healthy individual . . . for his age.' She had added this while looking hard into Janet's face. Then she said, 'I'll get the nurse to bring you a cup of tea and afterwards you may see him. He is barely conscious, and you must not excite him in any way. Try not to talk to him. You understand?'

Janet didn't answer, but merely inclined her head.

The cup of tea was strong and had little milk in it, and it was the third cup she had drunk in the last hour.

Maitland was lying in a bed in a side ward. It was a small room, yet it seemed to Janet that she had to walk a great distance from the door to reach the side of the bed. His head was swathed in bandages, with only his eyes, nose and mouth remaining visible. His eyes were open but there was a dazed expression in them; but as soon as he spotted her, this lifted somewhat.

She did not speak, but sat down by the side of the bed and, lifting his hand, she pressed it against her mouth for a time, before laying it back on the coverlet and still holding it.

For how long she sat like this, she wasn't aware. She spoke to him once and only two words: 'My love,' she said.

Then the Sister came in and whispered, 'I should go now; he's asleep. He will sleep for some time. Tomorrow he'll be better.'

She rose immediately from the chair, looked down again to what appeared the bloodless features of his face, then allowed the sister to lead her out.

In the corridor Sister said, 'Have you a conveyance?' and she nodded, saying, 'Yes. Mears is waiting with the car.'

The sister now called a nurse to whom she whispered, and the nurse took hold of Janet's arm as if she, too, were a patient, and led her along the corridors and out to where Mears was waiting.

In answer to some words the nurse had whispered to him he nodded, then helped Janet into the front seat and tucked a rug around her. Had she really been aware of the speed at which the car was driven back to the house, she would surely have objected.

He helped her out of the car and she muttered, 'Thank you. Thank you, Mears.' Then he hurried ahead of her to the front door and rang the bell. And when Sarah opened it he said, 'Miss is not very well.' . . .

'I told you you shouldn't go,' said Alice. 'You were still under that sedative. The doctor's been and he said it was madness.' Her voice dropped and she said gently, 'Come on; get to bed.'

She allowed her mother to take her upstairs and undress her; then she lay down and she slept naturally for twelve hours.

15

The event did not make the front page of the national Sunday newspapers, although details could be found on the inside pages. Of course it was doubtful if it would have even been mentioned there had it not taken place in the house of Mr Samuel Fairbrother, whose son had recently committed suicide while awaiting trial for murder. So it wasn't until the Monday that both James and Harry telephoned, James twice and Harry three times, each time to be answered by either Sarah or Florence, who told them that both the master and Miss Janet were out: Miss Janet, they knew, was at the hospital, and the master might be there, too. They weren't sure.

So it was at about nine o'clock, soon after Samuel and Janet had returned, when the phone rang again. Samuel picked it up and was greeted by a very irritated son who said, 'That you, Dad? This is James. Where on earth have you been? What's all this about? Has everybody gone mad at that end?'

'Well, James, this is your father. As to what all this is about, likely you've read the papers. That's why you sound so sympathetic. As to where I've been, I've been about my business most of the day and also visiting the hospital. As to, have we all gone mad? yes, I think we have. Good night.'

After he banged down the phone he said to Janet, 'That was your dear brother, James.' Then to Florence, who was standing nearby, he said, 'Something hot, Florence; on a tray will do. Soup or anything like that, tell Cook.'

'Yes, sir. The trays are all set; it'll be ready in a minute.' And as Florence scurried off across the hall Samuel put his hand out and took Janet's arm, saying, 'Come on and sit yourself down. I'll get you a glass of something.'

When she was seated in the drawing-room he stood over her for a moment, saying, 'You all right? Feeling faint?'

'No. No, I'm all right, but . . . but I'll be glad of a drink.'

When he hurried from the room she lay back on the couch. He had asked her if she felt faint. Yes, she did feel faint. She felt ill; and she supposed part of it was that she hadn't eaten since breakfast time, and then she'd had only toast. She had kept going during the day with innumerable cups of tea. They had been so kind to her in the hospital, allowing her to go in to Roger every now and again. How long had she sat in that waiting-room between times? It seemed, at the end, that she must have been there for days, because she knew every wooden block in the scrubbed parquet floor; she had read every word of the posters on the wall . . .

'Here, drink that up.'

She opened her eyes and reached out for the glass and, looking at it, she said, 'It isn't sherry.'

'No, you want something stronger than sherry tonight, by the look of you.'

'I don't like whisky.'

'Drink it up.'

She sipped at the glass, then lay back. And now he dropped into the big chair to the side of the fireplace, and after a moment he said, 'Did you make arrangements about having him transferred to a larger ward?'

'I asked about it, but they won't move him until . . . well, they said they couldn't move him at present; it was better that he stay where he is.'

'It's like a matchbox, that room.'

'Well, it's better than being in the ward.'

'Aye, I suppose so.'

She again sipped at the whisky, then asked herself: How was it that she could sit

here so calmly talking to a man about someone he himself would surely have maimed
if not killed, so patent had been his rage
and hate at the time? But it was as if a great
wave had washed over both him and her
mother.

And it was as if, too, he had picked up
her thoughts, for he said, 'Funny about your
mother and this house. I couldn't persuade
her to stay. As she said, she stayed as long
as she was needed, but now that we were
both all right she would get back home.
Funny to think she had never looked on this
house as home all the years she was in it.
But that's what she said.'

The door opened and Sarah asked, 'Will
I bring it in here, sir? It's on a trolley.'

'Yes. Yes, Sarah, bring it in here.'

The two women came in now with the
trolley and arranged a low table in front of
the couch and on it set the trays, each holding a bowl of steaming soup and a plate of
cold meats and salad; and Sarah, arranging
the napkins as she had seen Maitland do so
often, and placing the condiments to their
hand, said, 'There's a nice hot chocolate
pudding with sauce. I'll bring it in when
you ring, sir.'

'Very good, Sarah.'

The women left the room, and in the

kitchen Sarah made a remark to Cook, a very telling remark: 'It's odd,' she said, 'he's not yelling any more.'

Janet ate the soup, but when she made no attempt to eat the meat and salad he said to her, 'Now look, if you don't want to be in bed for another couple of days, you've got to eat. You may not feel like it, but get it down you.' And knowing he was right, she ate what she could.

After the meal they sat for some time without speaking; then he said quietly, 'This is the third full day. There should be a change soon. Did they say anything before you left tonight?'

'Just that he was holding his own.'

There followed a silence before he spoke again when, very quietly, he said, 'If he pulls through I . . . well, you'll get married, I suppose?'

'Yes. Yes, if he pulls through we will be married.'

'And . . . and you'll go and live at Sweet-banks?'

'Yes, Dad, we'll go and live at Sweet-banks.'

There was another silence before, still quietly, he said, 'What'll happen if . . . well, he doesn't pull round? Will . . . will you still go?'

'Yes, I'll still go and live at Sweetbanks.'

'Aye. Aye, well, I thought you might, so that's decided me.'

She now looked at him fully and he said, 'Well, you can't see me living in this place on me own, so I'll sell it. There'll be plenty who'll jump at it, because there's a lot of loose money flying around the town and people with big ideas, like I once had when I first saw this place. But the fact is, I can't live without company, and although Alice has agreed to come back to me, she won't come here, she says. Odd how she dislikes this place. Yet me, well, I've sort of grown to love it. But that wouldn't last if I was here on me own. No, it would drive me barmy. So, I'll look out for some place suitable because in no way am I going to live in her house. It was her choice when she left here but I never liked it. Anyway, it's in a street, and it's funny how your tastes can alter. I've got used to being surrounded by land. Won't you miss this place an' all? I used to think you liked this house.'

'Yes. Yes, I did, but I also like Sweetbanks.'

'Aye, so does your mother. But that's natural, I suppose. You know, you can't blame her for getting her back up at the way your gran left her. To my mind it wasn't a nice

501

thing to do. Oh aye, she had your welfare at heart, but there was a method in her madness where you were concerned and also a bit of spite against your mother because she had walked out on me. And that was damned silly when you think of it, because I was to blame. Ah, well, it's all over now, or nearly. I'm going to bed; and you, too? Come on.'

As he took her arm to help her up from the couch and continued to hold on to it as he walked her down the room, she could not help but wonder, if only this man could have brought his better self to the fore without her beloved having to pay such a price for it, she could this night have been the happiest of creatures.

16

The day, even the hour, when she was told he would survive would remain like a beacon in her mind. The sister had greeted her with a smile and two of the nurses who were generally on morning duty actually laughed when they met her, one saying, 'He's sensible. Well, I mean, he spoke rational.'

Both nurses, as did most of the staff, found this young woman of great interest; and to the younger one she appeared even romantic, for was she not a rich young woman who openly said she was going to marry her father's butler; and he so much older than her?

And Janet would always remember the look in his eyes. It was one of surprise, as if one or the other of them had been away for a long time and had suddenly reappeared. And of course, he *had* been away; and it was as the surgeon had said to her, 'He's the luckiest man I've met in a long time. He'll never have such a close call again. But mind, he's got some way still to go.'

That had been eight days ago. Now she

was sitting by his bedside in a different room. At the moment it was bright, not only with flowers but also with sunshine; and Maitland, who was sitting propped up in bed, had his eyes on the window as he said, 'It seems to be a beautiful day out there.'

'Yes, it is, dear, a beautiful day in more ways than one.'

'Oh, yes, in more ways than one.' His hand was holding hers. 'You haven't told me what made you late. Look, it's twenty past eleven. You're always here on the dot of eleven, and I get panicky if you're a minute over your time. But it was ten past when you came in this morning. Now, tell me, Miss Fairbrother, what held you up?'

She now held his hand between hers and quietly she said, 'I've been to see the Reverend Hatton, and he says that now I've got the licence he's at our service any time of the night or day.' She laughed as she said, 'Those were his exact words. He's such a nice man. So . . . Mr Maitland, what you must do is to obey orders, rest, and not talk so much, if you hope for this event to take place next week.'

'Oh, Janet, my dearest, my . . .'

She placed a hand on his lips, saying very quietly, 'If you get excited and your temperature goes up again, they'll turf me out.

Now listen to me, darling, everything's all arranged: we'll go straight to the Unitarian Chapel, and from there to Sweetbanks. I've already taken your belongings from your room. And I have it all planned out about the school.'

Smiling softly, he now said, 'D'you know something?' at which she bit on her lip and said, 'No; tell me, Maitland.'

'Well, Miss Janet, I think you are the most wonderful and beautiful woman in the world.' After a moment she responded, 'And d'you know something, Maitland? I know I am. I also know that you are silver-tongued and have a weakness for exaggeration.'

'You are quite wrong on both counts, Miss Fairbrother. But now,' and his tone changed as he said, 'I should be thinking that I'm going to marry a rich young woman, that I am going to live in her house, and that I am going to set up a business on her money, but I am not.' He now wagged his forefinger at her. 'In the forefront of my mind is that when I last saw my bank balance it stood at six hundred and twenty-seven pounds, and on that, for the next year or so, I shall be able to feed my wife and pay the maid's wages.'

'Just about, sir. Just about.'

Now he was holding her hand tightly between his own as he went on, 'But you know, I have no pride when it comes to depending on you. I know only that, given the opportunity, I will make that business pay; if not that one, the other idea of the old gentlemen' — he pulled a slight face at her now — 'by which time I myself will be doddering from one room to the other. Oh.' He patted her hand now, saying, 'That word "doddering". The policeman used it earlier on in a different context. He called to ask when did I think I might be able to "dodder" down to the court to give evidence of the attack. But, as I told him, I don't remember anything except exchanging blows with the tall fellow. After that it was oblivion. And don't you know, my dear, you'll be called upon as a witness?'

'Oh, yes, yes; but that doesn't worry me. The only thing is' — she now looked down towards the counterpane and their joined hands — 'd'you think there's any need to mention what happened before those men came in?'

'Of course not; none whatever.'

'I think Dad has been worrying about that. Although I said to him exactly what you've just said and that you wouldn't want that . . . you know, Roger, he's a changed man and I'm sad for him. I haven't heard him give a good yell in the past three weeks. And he seems so lost. You see, he wants to be with Mam again, but she won't come back to the house. And I can understand that because she was never happy there. He won't go and live in her house, because he doesn't like it; and so he's looking for another place.'

'Oh dear! dear! he'll miss the house, because you know, he loves it. And, somehow, I always saw it passing down the family; never to Howard, but to Eddie or one of the boys. It's a house that needs a family. Will you miss it?'

'No; because I'll be with you.'

The door opened abruptly now and the two smiling nurses appeared. The smaller had the louder voice and she said, 'This is the last day of your skiving, sir. It's on your pins for you this morning. And if miss will just leave you for five minutes we'll haul you out of there, because I for one want to see the last of you.'

'I don't. I don't.'

One nurse pushed the other now and the loud-voice one, looking at Janet, said, 'He's a flirt, miss, a heartbreaker. I knew it the minute I set eyes on him.'

Janet was now on her feet and, her face

straight, she nodded towards the nurse, saying, 'Yes, I know that; I've had a lot of trouble in that direction.'

The three of them now turned to the patient who was sitting with his eyes closed, one hand held to the side of his head that was still bound up; and when he said, 'Injustice! Injustice!' the loud voice came at him, 'Well, you're going to experience some more. So, if miss will leave us for a few minutes we'll help you to take the first step towards the hospital gates, and the sooner the better.'

Janet stood in the corridor amid the bustle of rattling trolleys and the to-ing and fro-ing of white-coated figures and nurses, and she repeated to herself as she smiled, 'Oh, yes, the sooner the better, the sooner the better.'

17

They had stood in the unadorned church before the Unitarian minister and he had read them the marriage service. Each 'I do' had been pronounced clearly and with fervour. Together, they had signed the register, as had their witnesses, Mike and Kate Talbot. No member of the bride's family was present.

Last night her father had said to her, 'I'd like to be there, lass, but . . . but I can't, because I can't get it out of me mind the feeling I had against him. And I would feel a hypocrite to go there and give you away to him, although I must tell you now that I feel you could go a lot further and fare worse. He's a good fellow, and he's of your turn of mind. Nevertheless, he was in my service for years.'

She had kissed him and told him she understood. And then he had told her that today he had somebody coming to look over the house and that he himself had been looking around, although he had not yet seen anything that he fancied. But it would come, and he hoped it would be soon, because he wanted to live with her mother again; and he was happy to know she felt the same way. And he had added, with the family off their backs, except for Fanny — because it was no good hanging on to Jessie, he knew that — they would have time to get to know each other as never before.

But at this moment they were thanking the Reverend and promising that they would attend his services: as she forthrightly put it, if not out of interest, then out of gratitude for his kindness. And he replied, 'Forget about the gratitude but work up the interest. That'll please me more.'

Some time later, when they were gathered in the sitting-room at Sweetbanks, it was agreed that the Reverend was a very fine gentleman and a man of wide sympathies.

Later, when they went into the dining-room and saw the spread surrounding the wedding cake Annie had laid for them, Janet turned and kissed the elderly woman on the cheek. And Annie, looking from Roger to Janet, said, 'You're not any happier than I am the day. And I'll look after you both, I will, I will.'

'We'll drink to that now, Annie,' Roger said.

And so, with Mike and Kate, they stood and clinked glasses . . .

After Mike and Kate had taken their leave and Annie had retired to the kitchen, Janet and Roger went into the sitting-room, where for the first time in their lives, they were alone together, really alone and without fear, and they were aware of it.

When he went to take her into his arms she slapped his hands saying, 'Come and sit down. You know they told you to rest for the next two or three weeks.'

Dutifully now he sat down on the couch and, pulling a wry face, he said, 'Dear — dear! What a beginning to a married life: not in the house five minutes and your wife throwing her weight about.'

When she dropped down beside him, their arms went about each other, and they kissed long and passionately before they sank to the back of the couch and lay looking at each other.

'I don't believe it. For years and years I've dreamed of it; well, thought of it at first as a kind of fantasy: I could see myself loving this young, intelligent girl, so full of life and ideas, so fearless in many ways, yet frightened in others; frightened that she would give her feelings away to this man who was so much older than herself; frightened of the wrath of her father, and who was not without the knowledge of what the revelations her feelings could evoke, and did evoke.' He stroked her cheek, then went on, 'Yet, my dear, it was all wishful thinking in the daytime and dreaming at night, until the day it was revealed to me how you felt. You were alone in the drawing-room and you said something and we laughed together. We were almost as close as we are now. Then your laughter ceased abruptly and you turned and almost ran from the room. D'you remember that day?'

'Yes. Yes, darling, I remember that day.'

'Well, from then I began to look forward. That was, until your grandmother died and you became a rich woman. That seemed to put, as Cook would say, the kibosh on it. And you know what people will say now, particularly those who see me as a man who has been a servant all his life? The nerve of him! they'll say. The cunning of him to prey upon the feelings of a young girl. And, of course, there's the money; and she has a house, too.'

'Oh, Roger! Roger; it doesn't matter what anyone in the wide world says, it has no effect on me. But, my dear, does it hurt you?'

'Strangely, no; because I know now if you had come into the house as a maid of any kind, I would have recognised in you the person I had been waiting for, the girl I had been waiting for, the woman I had been waiting for. No, my dear . . .' He bent forward now and kissed her again on the lips, and when she put her hand to his head and stroked the now bald patch that ran from his ear to the top of his spine and all of three inches wide, he put his hand on hers and said, 'Oh, I must do something about that. I think I'll tar it.'

'It's sprouting hair already. It's mostly covered at the back.'

'It isn't. You're lying. I looked at it this morning in a hand mirror.'

'All right, I'm lying —' She stopped at the sound of the telephone bell ringing from the hall and she said, 'That's our first phone call. I wonder who it is. Likely one of the boys.'

She sprang up and hurried from the room, and when she lifted the receiver and said, 'Hello,' a voice replied, 'Congratulations, Mrs Maitland.'

'Oh! Eddie. Oh! how lovely to hear from you.'

'How did it go?'

'The wedding? Wonderful, wonderful.'

'At the Registry Office?'

'No, at a Unitarian church, and a lovely minister took the service.'

513

'That's fine. That's fine. How is Maitland?'

'Very well; but he must take it easy for a time.'

'You know, Janet, I'm very pleased for you. I really am. As old Harry used to say, that fellow's got more brains than all of us put together. Anyway' — his tone now changed — 'I understand he nearly copped it, and all through trying to save Dad. And from what I heard from Harry, who had got it from the kitchen when he was through, the old fellow practically tried to murder him. Is that true?'

'Yes.'

'My, my! How is Dad, anyway?'

'Very subdued, I would say.'

'Was he at the wedding?'

'Oh no.'

'Well, anyway, dear, you give Maitland my best wishes. Tell him he's a lucky man.'

'By the way, where are you?'

'I'm in Scotland. We're only in for a few days and there's little shore leave. Everybody seems jittery at the moment. But I can't go into the whys and wherefores of that. Anyway, I've got to go now, but I just wanted to send you on your new way with a word from your favourite brother. Goodbye, Sis.'

'Goodbye, Eddie; and thank you.'

'Oh, by the way: if you ever have an argument don't try to throttle him like you did with me.'

She laughed as she heard the click of the receiver being put down, and her eyes were moist when she turned towards the sitting-room.

'It was Eddie. He's docked for a few days. He sends you his best wishes and he said that Harry used to say you had more brains than the lot of them put together. And, of course, he was right.' She was nodding down to him; then she added, 'But wasn't it nice of him!'

He held out a hand to her, saying, 'Come and sit down; I want you nearer to me, close by. We have to make up for the years that we had to stand politely at arm's length.'

It was about half an hour later when the phone rang again. This time it was James, and his greeting was different. 'I've just had a ring from Eddie. He tells me it's done, then. D'you think you've done the right thing?'

'Yes, James, I know I've done the right thing. I only wish I had done it sooner.'

'How's Dad taking it?'

'Well, since Roger nearly lost his life in saving him, how d'you think he's taking it?'

'Well, that's a small miracle, isn't it? because you were the apple of his eye. He had great hopes for you; but at least he expected you to keep him company for the rest of his life.'

'I'm well aware of that, James, but I always had different ideas.'

'Yes, of course. Anyway, I hope you'll be happy.'

'Thank you, James.'

'Oh, don't put on that stiff tone with me, Janet; after all, he was a servant in the house for nearly eleven years, and long before that too.'

'James.'

'Yes, Janet?'

'Next to Eddie, I've always held you in deep esteem. Now I'm going to tell you something. No matter how you succeed, no matter what you become in life, you'll never be half the man that Roger Maitland is: you haven't the brains, manner, or tact, that is natural to him. Nor will you ever know the happiness that he is experiencing at this moment.'

'Now, you look here!'

'No, James; you look here. Goodbye.'

She forced her features into a smile before rejoining Roger, and she made herself say straightaway, 'That was James. Eddie had phoned him. Now there's only Harry to get in touch. You know, I shouldn't be a bit surprised if he pops in the door; that would be Harry. Look, darling' — she bent over him — 'would you like to come along and see how I've planned out the rooms? There are ten good rooms, although previously we had never taken into account the two attics upstairs; they take up only half of the floor space, and the rest has been partitioned off. A little door leads into the area to enable a man to inspect the pipes. I went through the other day: panel off the pipes and you have another two rooms.'

He smiled up at her as he said, 'Will I ever get over the wonder of you?'

'Well, you can try,' she said, in a business-like tone. Then she held out her hands to him, saying more softly, 'Come and see now,' and they went from the room, their arms clasped around each other's waist.

And so passed the afternoon of the first day of their married life.

Annie served tea in the sitting-room at half-past four and they lingered over it, talking of this and that. And when Roger said, 'If I had been permitted I would have taken you to a theatre tonight. We would have had a box and then dinner after at Donald's. By the way he's promised me a canteen of cutlery for a wedding present. Isn't that kind of him?'

'You didn't tell him it was to be today?'

'No.'

'Why?'

He looked down on to his plate before he said, 'I was afraid; I felt I mustn't say I'm going to marry the woman I love, the woman I've always loved on such and such a date in case Fate should hear and step in with something extra. And now I want to shout it. Later on, I'll give him a ring.'

'Oh, Roger, I wouldn't have wanted to spend this evening at a theatre. If I was asked to choose this is the place I would have chosen to spend the evening of my wonderful day, relaxed and at peace, without fear of interruptions, and no small talk to cover up one's feelings. No; no theatre for me, Roger; just here, pouring out your tea.' She now took up the teapot. 'How d'you like your tea, sir?'

'Poured out, please.'

As they laughed together they heard the phone ring once more, and as Janet, saying, 'Oh, dear me!' made to get up he stayed her with a hand and said, 'I can hear Annie taking it; in fact, shouting into it,' and he laughed.

'She's slightly deaf. She doesn't like the phone.'

When the door opened with Annie saying in a loud whisper, 'It's Mr Samuel,' they both exchanged a glance before Janet said, 'Dad? Oh, don't say something else has happened.'

When she reached the phone, she said, 'Hello, Dad. Anything wrong?'

'No. No, lass, nothing wrong, but I suppose if I was a tactful man I'd leave this business until tomorrow, but somehow I . . . I can't. So, I wondered if I could come over and have a word with you and, of course . . . him an' all?'

'Is it important business?'

'Aye. Yes, it's important to us all, but . . . er . . . well, you've got to hear it first before you can start questioning it. The thing is, may I come over?'

'Of course. Of course.'

'Well, I'll be there in ten minutes.'

She kept her ear to the receiver for some seconds before she realised he had hung up. She then put it up on the wall stand. Then, walking slowly back into the drawing-room, she said, 'Dad wants to come over. He says he has something to say, to discuss.' She shook her head.

When Roger said nothing, she put her

hand on his shoulder and stood by his side for a moment, and he looked up at her, saying, 'Have you any idea? Is it trouble of some sort?'

'I didn't get that impression. But he seemed to imply that it concerns us.'

He forced a smile to his face as he said, 'Well, there's one thing certain; whatever it might be I couldn't stand up to him physically at the moment. So we'd better keep the matter to discussion, hadn't we? Don't look so worried, dear; it can't be anything really bad. It's just unfortunate though it had to be this evening. But still, we have all the other evenings.' Then raising his hands he brought her head down to his and, looking into her eyes and very softly, he added, 'And the night is long.'

For a moment she did not respond; but then she placed her lips lightly on his and repeated, 'Yes, the night is long.'

Annie let Samuel in. And when Janet heard their voices she made to go down the room, but before moving away she whispered, 'Don't get up. Stay where you are.' And he whispered back to her, 'I had no intention of getting up, dear.'

Janet opened the sitting-room door and saw her father handing his overcoat and hat to Annie. Then she watched him shrug his

jacket further onto his shoulders, which indicated to her that he was feeling nervous.
She said, 'Hello, Dad. Come in.'

He entered the room but kept his eyes on
her as he said, 'It's still a bit of a snifter
outside, but it's warm enough in here. This
room always held the heat, as I remember.'

She walked ahead of him and he followed
slowly up to the fireplace, and for the first
time since he had last looked down on his
butler as he lay unconscious in the hospital
bed, he was looking at him again, but looking at a different man: no longer a butler
getting to his feet when he himself entered
the room, and always at hand to help him
on with his coat, brush him down, hand
him his scarf, see that he had a clean handkerchief in his pocket, that he was wearing
the right cuff-links and collar stud to go
with a particular shirt; and the many other
services he had performed for him since
Alice had left the house. And he hated to
remind himself that over the past weeks he
had missed these services as he had never
imagined he would.

'How are you?' he asked.

'Quite well, thank you.'

No, 'sir' now; no getting to his feet.

When Janet said, 'He's not all right. It'll
be some weeks before he can say that with

truth,' Sam came back at her with a shadow of his old self, saying, 'Can you not let the man speak for himself? If he says he's all right, he's all right . . . Am I being asked to sit down?'

'That's up to you, if you wish to,' and there was the old tart tone still in Janet's voice, but Roger put in, 'Do sit down . . . please.' Then he went on, 'I understand you want to talk to us?'

'Aye, you understand right, so I'll get down to it and see what you think. You can only say no.'

He now turned to Janet and began, 'I've just come from your mother's. It was her idea really. You already know I'm selling the house. There's been two fellows after it, one I wouldn't sell to if he offered me three times what I paid for it, 'cos I don't like his nationality.' He did not say what the man's nationality was, but went on, 'The other seems decent enough, but a bit of a haggler. And, looking back, I remember that I didn't haggle when I took that place from her ladyship. I gave her what she asked and it was more than what she would have got elsewhere. But there you are: I wanted it and I got it. And by God, I've paid for it in more ways than one. Well, to get back to your mother. I don't want to leave there and I've told her that, but she won't live there. And, apparently, I've come to me senses in one way because I'm putting people before bricks and mortar, and I want to take up my life with her again.' He was now pointedly addressing Roger: 'But she's got her likes and dislikes and I've got mine, and I'll be damned if I'm going to live in her place. And I've been looking around and haven't yet found anything that suits me. Now, as I understand it, you're going into business, setting up a school, so I'm told, to train fellows like yourself and other members of a staff needed for the big houses, and that's what you intend to turn this into, a training ground. Well, as I see it meself, it's not the kind of place that would need a butler or a footman, or other flunkies in —'

'Dad!'

'Be quiet, will you? Let me have me say and don't try to stop me tongue.'

Looking at Roger again, he went on, 'My wife put it to me that the place for training such staff should be the big house and that, as her daughter, as she pointed out, was rotten with money now, why didn't she buy it just as it stood as I did, and sell me this one? Because,' his voice dropped now and he turned once more to Janet as he added, 'this is what she's hankered after. She was born here, you know; it was her home. She'll never be really happy anywhere else. So there it is, that's what I've come about. It's a kind of exchange. Not that I want it, mind; but if I don't want to live me life alone I've got to make allowances, and I'd rather see you back there' — he nodded towards Janet — 'than the fellow that's haggling with me, 'cos his idea is to turn it into a nursing home, mainly for elderly people, I understand.'

He stood now with his mouth slightly agape as Janet and Roger, exchanging glances, started to laugh.

'Well, I don't see anything funny in what I've said, but you tell me what there is and I'll laugh, too.'

It was Roger who answered him, saying, 'Some time ago, when I happened to mention what I intended to do when I retired, it was pointed out to me by a business friend that there is much more money in looking after old gentlemen, giving each his own suite of rooms and allowing him to bring his own furniture, which the proprietor would probably inherit on the man's decease. Only this afternoon we decided that if one scheme didn't work out within a year or two, then we could resort to the

524

old gentlemen: we could accommodate four or five comfortably. But it's strange, isn't it, that your client should wish to do the same?'

'Aye, it is. Yes, it is. Well, what d'you think?' Sam had turned to Janet. 'You're the one with the money.'

She closed her eyes for a moment. Her father may have softened in some ways, but the hard core was still in evidence. And so she answered, 'Roger has quite a bit of money of his own, more than enough to buy this house and refurnish it.'

'Well, that's good news. But only you have the cash to stump up for a house like that one.'

'What are you asking for it?'

The question coming from Roger surprised him. 'Sixteen thousand as it stands,' he said.

'You paid only eleven for it.'

'How d'you know what I . . . ? Oh aye, you were in their confidence, weren't you? Well, it was a damned sight too much. Seven thousand they charged me for the house and four for the contents. They would have been lucky if they had got five, had it gone to auction. As for the contents, well, I admit there was quite a bit of silver and furniture and stuff, but many of the carpets and curtains were faded, and still are!'

'There is a very large library of books which are worth a great deal of money, because some of the volumes are very old and would bring a good price at a book mart,' put in Janet.

'Oh, you've got it all worked out, but I happen to know the value of books. Moreover, whatever you get you would have to pay your agent quite a sum. So, if you're thinking of selling it privately, the cost of an agent should be taken into account.'

Roger turned to Janet now, saying, 'The price, dear, is beside the point. The question is, d'you want to go back there? Don't think about me: it doesn't matter where I am as long as I'm with you.'

Janet now looked at her father and she asked, 'Why won't you go and live in Mam's house?'

'Because I don't like it. It's stuck on a street; the traffic goes up and down. Anyway, we went through this the other night, didn't we? You know, in a way, I think you owe her this place. As I said before, you came to it through an old woman's whim, and it was a wrong whim. However, there it is. By the way, d'you happen to have a drink in the house?'

'Oh, yes; yes,' she said, and sprang up

and went out of the room, leaving Roger and Samuel together.

Sam turned and looked towards the fire, then presently he began to speak. His voice low, he said, 'I've something to thank you for. You nearly lost your life through saving mine. I won't forget that but for those two fellows coming in when they did, I might have committed murder meself, 'cos God! didn't I hate you at that moment! not only for taking my favourite daughter from me but for being the individual you are. You were always bigger than your boots, showing up my ignorance over the years. Oh, and for so many other things. People would speak highly of you while looking down their nose at me, and it all came out in that terrible, terrible urge, to put an end to you. And you know, I can't forgive you for being the reason why I felt like that, for being, in a way, the instigator of the murderous feeling in me.'

'I'm sorry,' said Roger, 'indeed I am, but everything you've said is imagination on your part. I am, at bottom, a very ordinary man. My manner was due to the training that was necessary to make a good butler, a good servant. I imagined I had achieved that. Never once did I aim to be superior; correct yes, because that is part of the duty of a man in my position, to give an example to those under him. But in no way to assume a superiority to those above him, for that would have been defeating the whole purpose and standing of the career, because butling is a career. And it is this principle that I want to instruct into others; particularly young men.' Roger paused, then went on, 'I can understand your feeling towards me because of my love for your daughter. In any case, it would appear to anyone to be utterly presumptuous. But about my attitude and feelings towards yourself, you are entirely wrong. Still, the past cannot be relived, and it seems odd to say now, but I'm glad that things happened as they did and that those two thugs appeared at an opportune moment, otherwise one of us would not have been sitting here at this moment, and the missing person would surely have been me, for in no way could I have imagined myself dealing you a fatal blow.'

'Huh! It's funny,' and now Samuel gave a rueful laugh, 'all that you've just said should make me feel better, but, you know' — he turned and looked fully at Roger now — 'it doesn't; it only goes to prove that at bottom you're a better man than I am, because I swear to God that I would have killed you that day if I could. Still, here we are: you're now my son-in-law. D'you find that strange?'

'I haven't thought about it in that way yet. I suppose I'll get used to it. But there is one thing I shall never do again and that is address you as "sir".'

'Oh, you won't? Huh! Well, I'll tell you something, you'll never get me using your Christian name. You've been Maitland to me all these years and you'll go on remaining Maitland whether you like it or not.'

'I don't like it,' said Roger now with a smile, 'but I'll put up with it.'

When Janet entered the room carrying a tray on which she had placed a decanter, a bottle and three glasses, she was surprised, in fact astonished, at the sight of these two men, not only smiling, but their smiles on the border of laughter.

As she poured out the two whiskies and a sherry she said to Samuel, 'I've been thinking.'

'Aye, well, let's have it.'

'Well, I think that if you get two thousand profit on the house and effects you'll be lucky. So I'll give you thirteen thousand for it and I want seven hundred and fifty for this.'

'Thirteen thousand! You've got a nerve.' He turned and looked at Roger now, saying,

'She's got a nerve. What d'you say?'

'I would say that after you have lived in the house for ten or more years, and had use of all its accoutrements, that in a way should be considered the interest on the money you put down. But seeing that that doesn't work these days, two thousand profit is very fair indeed.'

'Well, of course, you would say that, wouldn't you?'

'Yes, and may I remind you that you were talking of having to replace most of the carpets and drapes. They were all looking the worse for wear. The Persian rugs are practically threadbare; in many cases, there's only the pattern left. And the same applies to the Indian carpets. So I should imagine to replenish the carpets and the curtains, and that's not taking in the stair carpet and the runners on the gallery and landings, two thousand pounds would soon be eaten up.'

'Another thing . . .' They both turned to Janet now as she handed them the glasses of whisky, and said, 'I wouldn't want to pay that enormous sum at once, nor do I want to take out a mortgage, but I'd like to come to an agreement with you that it could be paid in four stages over the next four or five years and that at an interest, say of one per cent.'

Samuel almost spluttered into his glass; then he threw off half the whisky, put the glass down on the side table and said, 'Well, I'll be buggered! You know, if I'd had any sense I'd have taken you into the business when you were sixteen. You were lost in the library. You've got a nerve, you know.'

'Well, if you see it like that, Dad, I could take on a mortgage for ten or fifteen years. I know I would have to pay three per cent, but I would be holding on to my capital, and I could definitely get two and a half on that, perhaps even a little more if I shopped about.'

When Roger choked on his drink, followed by a fit of coughing, Samuel said, 'Aye, that's enough to choke anybody, that nerve. Ah, well . . .' He suddenly finished the remainder of his whisky, got to his feet and said, 'I suppose I've got what I came for, or what your mother wants, so I'll be on me way.' Then standing in front of Roger, he asked, 'What'll you feel like going back there now as master of the house?'

'No different from how I felt before.'

'Oh, because you felt you were master then?'

'Merely of my duties, as I pointed out to you. For you left no doubt in anyone's mind as to who was boss of that house, did you?'

'Huh!' Samuel turned away now and marched up the room, and after exchanging a quick glance with Roger, Janet followed him.

Sam was getting into his coat when very quietly, he said, 'There was something I meant to ask you. It's about that money you gave Howard. It was five hundred, wasn't it? Those fellows said he owed three, but it looks as if he didn't pay the three, doesn't it?'

'Yes. Yes, Dad, it not only looks like that, it is like that, he never paid the three. And I understand now that he was sorry for what he did, at least in that way, because he kept trying to tell me he was sorry about the money. At the time I thought it was that he had deceived me in saying he owed five hundred when it was only three. But what he was trying to tell me was he was sorry that he had not paid a penny. It likely all went on the woman. But I know that he was really sorry for what he had done and I forgave him, because, after all, it was only five hundred pounds and he paid for it with his life. Likely, if he hadn't kept that woman in money she would have had very little use for him and consequently he wouldn't have been in that room when the husband returned.'

He put his hand on to her shoulder and said, 'You're a good lass. I've always known it. That's why I didn't want to part with you. And now I'm off to tell your mother the news, and to say,' he turned his head to the side for a moment and paused before he finished, 'I'll stay the night with her there.' And looking at her again, he said, 'You see, lass, I couldn't bear to be on me own tonight. You understand?'

She understood, and her face, she knew, was flushed with her understanding. And then he said, 'Tomorrow it'll be different. Plain sailing from now, I hope. Anyway, I agree with your terms, and the quicker you can make the exchange the quicker I'll be able to settle down. When d'you think that'll be?'

She thought for a moment. 'Any time, Dad,' she said. 'I can leave this house as it is and as it always has been and go to what has been my home for so long, if you leave that as it is.'

'Oh, I'll leave it as it is, don't worry. I'll take nothing out except me personal belongings.' He bent towards her now and placed a hasty kiss somewhere to the side of her nose, then he was gone.

When she had closed the door on him she stood facing it and she leaned her brow against it and bit tightly down on her lip as the tears came into her eyes.

She next went to the cloakroom to give herself a breathing space before returning to the sitting-room.

There, Roger took her hand and drew her gently down beside him, and surprised her by saying, 'That man loves you nearly as much as I do. That isn't quite possible, but it's a lot.' Then he asked, 'D'you want to go back? D'you really want to go back there?'

'Yes; and for two reasons. The first is my mother will be able to come back into this house, and through time she might forgive me. The other is that it's a splendid place to start our business; we have everything there.'

'It's going to take a lot of money during the first few years until we get going.'

'Oh, I'm not worried about that, for we have enough to cover it, Mr Maitland. In fact, I'm not worrying about anything. Our future is set, darling. I still can't believe it.'

He was holding her close as he said, 'Nor can I. In fact, I don't think I'll ever believe it. I'll go into my dotage still doubting that I have you.'

Some time later they had said good night to Annie and were about to go upstairs when they were checked by the phone ringing once again. Janet answered it and a voice said, 'Hello, Janet. Have I to say congratulations?'

'Yes. Yes, Harry, you have.'

'I tried twice earlier, but I got the engaged signal. How are you?'

'Splendid.'

'Good. And Maitland?'

'He's splendid, too.'

'By the way, I've just been on to Mam. She tells me Dad is selling the house. That was a shock. I liked that house. Although I knew I wouldn't be seeing very much of it in the future, it was always nice to come back to.'

'Well, you can still come back to it, Harry.'

'What d'you mean?'

'Didn't she tell you the rest of it?'

'Is there a rest?'

'Yes. We are buying it.'

'You're buying the house, as it is?'

'Yes, just as it is. We are starting up a business there. And Mam and Dad are coming back here.'

'Ah, that's it, that's it. I felt she wasn't giving me the full story. So I can come back now and again, can I?'

'Consider it your home, Harry.'

'You're an amazing girl, you know, Janet.'

'So my husband tells me.'

'Well, all I can say is, good luck to you both. Tell him that, will you?'

'I will, Harry; and thank you very much.'

'Good night and God bless you.'

'And you, Harry, and you.'

She put the phone down and turned to Roger, saying, 'He told me to wish you good luck.'

'That was good of him. Harry is a nice fellow altogether. Come.' He held out his arm to put around her and together they went up the stairs.

He had watched the dawn break, had watched it spread over her face. She was lying on her back: her face looked pink and moist, she looked relaxed and she looked beautiful. She was beautiful, every part of her was young and beautiful, and she would never know how he felt for her, for there were no words as yet written that could express his feelings. He was forty-one years old. How many years of loving had he left in him? For how many years could he sustain passion, the passion of the night just gone? He would like to think it would go on for ever, or at least until he was fifty or sixty. But love changed: it had many facets, besides its physical, and that would merge into tenderness, understanding and friendship. Oh, they already had friendship and understanding, and tenderness; in fact, they had it all. And yet, he couldn't take it in. He couldn't quite believe it, not that he loved her passionately but that her love was equal to his own, as she had proved to him.

She stirred, turned on her side and opened her eyes, and her voice throaty, she said, 'You're awake?'

'I'm awake.'

'I love you.'

'I adore you.'

'You mustn't say that because Sister Monica said you must never use that word except when you are thinking of God.'

'Well, I had a talk with Him in the night and I asked Him if I could say I adore you. And He had no hesitation in giving me permission because you were the most worthy of all His creatures.'

'Oh, Roger, Roger. I'll love you till I die.'

'Oh, well, that's good enough for me, Mrs Maitland. And it's strange, because that's what He told me you would say when you woke up.'

Their arms right around each other, they rocked with their laughter. And when they lay still again she looked at him and, unsmiling, she said, 'I am looking forward to life. And this is the only morning I can recollect ever waking up and thinking that.'

The employees of Thorndike Press hope you have enjoyed this Large Print book. All our Large Print titles are designed for easy reading, and all our books are made to last. Other Thorndike Press Large Print books are available at your library, through selected bookstores, or directly from us.

For information about titles, please call:

(800) 257-5157

To share your comments, please write:

Publisher
Thorndike Press
P.O. Box 159
Thorndike, Maine 04986